"Remarkable power . . . *BUFFALO GIRLS* is first and foremost a work of resurrection. . . . What makes Mr. McMurtry's characters . . . so irresistible is that they are like children, captious, hilarious, unpredictable, irrepressible. They are never boring. . . . *BUFFALO GIRLS* gives the reader a sense of how eras ebb and flow, how the world and time itself are too huge for any one consciousness to embrace."

—*The New York Times Book Review*

"A marvelous, mythic crew of Westerners. Larry McMurtry, long sensitive to the nostalgic and fabulous aspects of the West, returns to its short history in *BUFFALO GIRLS,* with wonderful results. Not since *Lonesome Dove* has he written so movingly about the disappearance of the West and of the characters that its way of life sustained. And he does so with his trademark homespun narrative power. . . . The plot rewards lovers of the picaresque."

—*Houston Chronicle*

"*BUFFALO GIRLS* . . . shows one of our finest novelists at the height of his powers."

—*Minneapolis Star-Tribune*

"[McMurtry's] best trip to the Old West since *Lonesome Dove*. McMurtry uses language like a lariat, ensnaring the willing reader into a quirky corral with his flair for stirring up the mythical dust of the West."

—*Memphis Commercial Appeal*

"You have only yourself to blame if you don't read Larry McMurtry's *BUFFALO GIRLS*."

—"Larry King's People," *USA Today*

(more . . .)

Books by Larry McMurtry

POCKET BOOKS

New York   London   Toronto   Sydney   Tokyo   Singapore

For Diane

This book is a work of fiction. Names, characters, places and incidents are products of the author's imagination or are used fictitiously. Any resemblance to actual events or locales or persons, living or dead, is entire coincidental.

POCKET BOOKS, a division of Simon & Schuster Inc.
1230 Avenue of the Americas, New York, NY 10020

ISBN: 0-671-53615-X

First Pocket Books printing October 1991

15   14   13   12   11   10   9

POCKET and colophon are registered trademarks of Simon & Schuster Inc.

Cover art by H. Tom Hall
Cover photo by W. Cody/WainLight

Printed in the U.S.A.

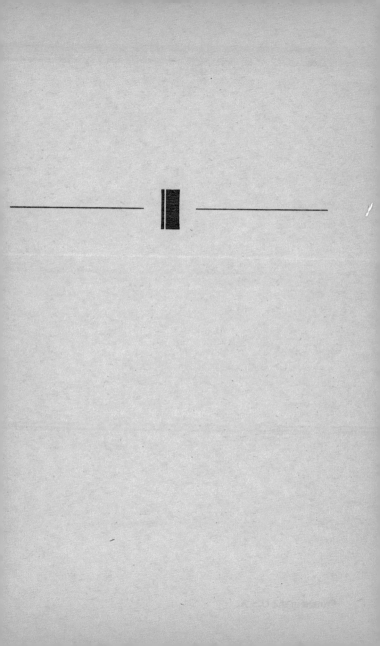

Darling Jane—

Here I sit, in the evening dews—you'll get some sopping big ones up here on the Yellowstone. I thought I'd write my hope a note before the light goes.

I call you my hope because you are, Janey. I will send your Daddy some money to get you a new dress for school—it's best to look nice, Janey, though I'm a sad one to say it. Last night I got drunk as a duck and rolled down the hill into a puddle—a pig couldn't have been muddier. If it had been later in the year I expect I'd have froze.

I dread the winters now although I've been all over these plains in the worst blizzards without a care. In my young days it would never have occurred to me to worry about such a little thing as the weather. "Powder River let 'er buck!" Blue used to say—I never did know what he meant by it but it sounded good at the time.

Blue showed up at Dora's, in Miles City, otherwise I might have escaped the puddle. Blue brings out the rowdy in me, he has since the day I met him down in

3

Abilene or maybe it was Dodge, those cow-town days seem long ago now, Janey.

Blue fell in love with Dora in Abilene, I expect he is still in love with her but why go into it? It ain't Dora he married. After Blue comes for a little visit—he's a great one for little visits—Dora will mope around and cry for two or three days. She'll hole up with Fred, that's her parrot, she says Fred's her only true friend but that's mush, Janey, I'm a true friend to Dora DuFran as she is to me.

I'd go to hell for Dora and she knows it, but she forgets about it when Blue rides off, I don't blame her, he is a reprobate. Ha, that's about as big a word as I would ever try to spell in a letter to my daughter, I fear it might upset you how poor your mother spells.

Well, Janey, the light's fading and I don't have much of a fire. I've gotten too lazy to gather much firewood, not that there is much on these plains. It never bothered me to sleep cold, though I will have to make better fires when winter strikes.

Tomorrow I'm heading down to Wyoming, I've heard my friends Ragg and Bone are living with the Shoshone. I wonder what they're living on, it couldn't be much, the Shoshone don't have much.

I miss Ragg and Bone, they've seen me through my life, Janey, them and Dora. I just have to go look for them when they wander off. It was Jim Ragg who finally introduced me to your father—I mean your real father, Wild Bill. I had to buy Jim twenty drinks before he would consent to introduce me, but I could get the drinks cheap and your father was the handsomest man in Dodge, still would be if he'd lived. I bought the drinks gladly but Ragg didn't introduce me gladly, I think he was scared. Ragg was a mountain man and liked to brag about all the massacres he'd seen, but saying hello to Wild Bill Hickok was another matter.

Wild Bill was known to be moody and if his mood turned cloudy he might just set down his drink and kill you. I had no worries, I knew Wild Bill wouldn't kill me, of course I admit that didn't mean he wouldn't have killed Jim Ragg.

Well, introduce is another big word, I think I got it correct though, I better stop this letter before my luck changes. Luck can change any time, it changed for Dora the day Blue met that half-breed daughter of Granville Stuart's—they say Mr. Stuart was a great man and had done great things but to me he's an old ruffian, he hung those men on the Musselshell and some of them was only boys. Maybe they did steal his damn cow ponies, I don't care, boys that young don't deserve no hanging. I weep every time I think about those boys' mothers, and how they feel.

You will be a mother someday, Janey, and have your sorrows too, who can outrun sorrow? Not me, Janey, and not Dora DuFran, not since Blue married Granville Stuart's pretty little half-breed daughter. I hope no man will do you so, Janey—I don't even want to think about it.

Dora tried yesterday to give me Fred, she says I need a friend and a parrot's better than nothing, but I wouldn't take him. He's not a bad parrot, though he can't say anything except "General Custer"—who taught it to him or why he wants to say it I don't know. You'd think living with Dora all these years Fred would have learned a more interesting stock of words, not that they'd be words I could put in a letter to you, Janey.

It's my pride that I can afford to send your Daddy money so you can be raised among decent people, not the riffraff and ruffians you'll find out here these days. There are people who would include your mother in such a description—in fact most people would.

But I didn't take Fred, I think Dora would miss him, she's the one who should be thinking a parrot's better than nothing, because Fred and nothing's about what she's got. I have Ragg and Bone, they are my true friends. Why they would think there might still be beaver down in the Shoshone country I don't know. It's a sign to me that the boys have drunk one too many rounds—if there were beaver along the old Wind River why wouldn't the Shoshone have eaten them, what else do they have?

What it's really a sign of, Janey, is that people can't give up hoping for what they once had, youth or you name it. When Jim and Bartle come west the west meant beaver—now they're old and the beaver have been gone for twenty-five years but the boys can't admit it, at least Jim can't. They still think there's a creek somewhere boiling with beaver that God saved for them. It's just how people are, Janey, they cling to foolish hopes.

But you will need to be studying your lessons and not wearing out your eyes reading my old gloomy words.

Don't worry about your mother, Janey, I have always got by. I'm hardy, I scarcely even coughed after sleeping in that mud puddle though I admit if it had been later in the year I wouldn't have been so lucky.

I've got my young horse Satan and my buffalo dog. Satan's a good horse and the dog Cody is a fine hunter, often he'll bring a rabbit and once he brought in a badger. I didn't know about eating badger, I took it to my friend Mrs. Elkshoulder and she cooked it in a hole in the ground, it tasted fine.

I call the dog Cody after Billy Cody—Buffalo Bill, I guess you've heard of him. There's a man with luck on his side if there ever was one, he'd have been dead years ago if it wasn't for luck. He ain't tough, there's hundreds of Indians who could kill him easily but he's still alive.

Billy's been writing lately, he's trying to get me to go with the Wild West show he started but I ain't that desperate I guess.

I *am* the Wild West, Janey, no show about it, I was one of the people that kept it wild, why would I want to make a spectacle of myself before a bunch of toots and dudes?

Not me, Janey, I'd rather sleep in a mud puddle every

night and rowdy it up with Blue and the other cow-pokes.

Goodnight, Janey, I'll stop I don't want to scribble on and wear out your pretty eyes.

Your mother,
Martha Jane

1

JIM RAGG WAS SKINNING A PRAIRIE DOG, WONDERING IF the fire would last until he got it skinned. A Wind River breeze—a gale, by most standards—surged down the gray canyons and sucked at the fire.

"Let's go somewhere else," Bartle Bone suggested.

"Right in the middle of supper?" Jim asked.

"No, I just meant eventually," Bartle said. "There's grit and then there's Wind River grit. I prefer the first kind."

"I think this prairie dog might have been sick," Jim said. "It moved kind of sluggish, like you do when you're sick."

"Well, if it was sick I'd prefer to go hungry," Bartle said. "I'm not up to digesting a diseased animal tonight."

Bartle was combing his fine beard. Among his few treasures was a fragment of comb he had snitched from a whore in Cheyenne. His beard was another treasure, at least in his view. Many western beards were filled with dirt, grease, and bits of debris, but he strove to keep his immaculate—no easy task in a rough, often waterless, land.

Bartle was determined, though. He also possessed a

fragment of mirror, which he had taken from a dead Sioux after the Custer battle. He and his friend Jim had been in the Sioux camp only the day before the battle, and soon heard of it; they had been among the first to observe the carnage. Bartle had taken nothing but the fragment of mirror, though the battlefield was strewn with the valuables of dead men.

All around them, as they stood stunned amid the bodies, Sioux and Cheyenne, Arapaho and Ree were carrying off their dead, singing as they lashed corpses to horses. Bartle had heard much Indian singing, but there was no precedent for the Custer battle, and the death songs that day were of a different timbre, one he had never heard before and would never hear again.

The singing mingled with the wind as the grass waved over the dead. One of the dead Sioux had a piece of mirror in his hand. Bartle saw the flash of sunlight on the shard of glass and, thinking it curious that an Indian had gone into battle holding a mirror, and then died holding it, had stopped and taken the glass. Then he went on walking among the twisted dead.

"I might be the only one who profited from the Custer fight," he said. "I got this mirror and look what a difference it made to my beard.

"Maybe the man who had it was responsible for flashing signals," he added. After much reflection, he had decided that best explained the mirror.

"That's just a guess," Jim said. "I don't see no reason to move just because you don't approve of Wyoming sand. Or are you telling me that you're ready to adopt the settled life?"

"I sure don't want to adopt it until we get someplace where there's something better to eat than sick prairie dogs," Bartle said, watching critically as his friend fixed the prairie dog to a spit.

Jim didn't answer. He squatted by the campfire and stared into space—the darkening, howling space of the Wind River valley.

Bartle put his comb and mirror away—barbering was a chancy affair, given the poor light and strong wind. The wind from the west howled around them. It whined, it keened, it sang, so strong at times that it was necessary to turn one's back to it in order to breathe satisfactorily.

"This country ain't so bad," Jim said. "The Shoshone like it."

"They may like the country but they don't like us," Bartle replied.

"Why, I never had a hostile word from a Shoshone," Jim said, somewhat startled by his friend's remark. "What makes you think they don't like us?"

"They're Indians," Bartle reminded him. "No Indians like us. The rich Indians don't and the poor Indians don't. The young Indians don't and the old Indians don't. The men Indians don't and the lady Indians don't."

"That's putting it pretty strong," Jim said.

"Even if the Shoshone liked us there would be no reason to stay," Bartle said. "There's no beaver in the river anyway. I doubt one has been here for a hundred years. It ain't the kind of river beavers like."

"There's creeks in those mountains though," Jim said, gesturing to the north. He sniffed at the prairie dog, which so far did not smell rotten. "If we do find beaver it'll be in the mountains, not out here on the flats."

Bartle said nothing. Lately, to Jim's distress, he had become more and more reluctant to talk about beaver.

"I mean to examine ever creek in the west before I give up on beaver," Jim said, as he had many times.

Bartle Bone, usually cheerful, felt a wearying sadness in his breast. The subject of beaver was a sore one, and had been for years. To Jim Ragg, it was a religion. Bartle had once felt the same, but his faith had long since been lost; now and again, though, he felt the sadness of the faithless.

As young men he and Jim had enjoyed three splendid years as beavermen, and several more that were passable, if not exactly splendid. But a quarter of a century had passed since those years. Other beavermen, friends of their youth, had long since died, been killed, or departed to safer lives. Few of the few who were left had any brains to speak of, any memory. Their talk, when they were sober enough to talk, was of the Custer battle, or else of Black Hills gold. Hardly a one could remember back twenty-five years to a time when millions of beaver still splashed in the cool streams of the west.

Jim Ragg was one of the few. He remembered every river, from the Oregon gorge to the headwaters of the Rio Grande. He remembered the cold ponds, the traps, the pelts. Of all the mountain men left, Jim Ragg was the only one—as far as Bartle knew—whose imagination hearkened only to beaver.

Gold didn't interest Jim, silver bored him, cattle disgusted him. Indian fighting gave him no pleasure, gambling made him restless, even his whoring was brief. Beaver meant more to Jim than women, cards, fortune, or anything else the Wild West had to offer.

But there were no beaver, as there were no buffalo, which meant for a true beaverman such as Jim Ragg that there was really no longer a West. In the flash of their own lives, a flash already dimming, it had been used up. It was a peculiar situation, and a sad one, Bartle felt. The snows still lay on the mountains, the grass still waved on the plains, the sky was still blue and deep as time; only a few details had actually changed—the beaver gone, the buffalo gone, the Indians whipped—and yet, when those things went the glory went also. The last time the two of them had straggled into Denver a bartender had shown them a poster of Billy Cody's Wild West show. Jim Ragg sneered—he had never had any use for Billy Cody—but Bartle had felt rather queer, and retired to a corner to drink a brandy. Halfway through the bottle he figured out what was queer.

"What Wild West?" he said, to a little blonde whore who stopped to tease him. "What Wild West? If Billy Cody can make a poster about it then there ain't no Wild West." At that point the whore skedaddled—she hadn't liked his mood.

Since then Bartle Bone had felt a little lonely, even in company of lifelong friends such as Jim Ragg or Calamity

Jane, the problem being that he nursed a truth he knew neither of his lifelong friends could stand to hear. There was no Wild West—that was the truth—but suggest as much to Jim Ragg and there'd be a fistfight; mention it to Calamity and a gun battle might ensue.

Not being able to discuss the matter with his true companions left Bartle feeling a little sad, but on the whole a little sadness was preferable to fistfights and gun battles, two sports he had lost his taste for.

"I wish you really liked to talk," he said to Jim. "I could improve your education considerable, if you really liked to talk."

"I don't mind talk," Jim said, though in fact an excess of talk did make him nervous.

"I didn't say you minded it, I just said I wished you liked it," Bartle replied. "But you don't, so I give up. Is that rodent cooked yet?"

"I'm doing the best I can," Jim said. "It's a small fire."

"I guess we oughta go look up Calamity," Bartle said. "She'll know the news. Calamity always knows the news."

"She might be too drunk to remember it, though," Jim said. "She needs to wean herself from all that drinking."

The prairie dog looked so unappetizing that he regretted he had even bothered to shoot it, much less cook it.

"There could be a passel of news," Bartle said. "We could be at war with China for all you know. The Chinamen could have captured San Francisco by now, or even Texas."

"I've never been to San Francisco, let 'em have it," Jim Ragg said. Texas was another matter, but it seemed unlikely to him that the Chinese had captured Texas. If there was war in Texas, half the old men of the west would have rushed to the fight.

"Even if there ain't no news I miss Calamity, and I have seen enough of the Wind River to last me awhile," Bartle said. "What's your mood?"

"Hungry, mainly," Jim said.

Darling Jane—

Didn't get far, Janey, I only come down the Tongue River a few miles. The older I get the harder it is to get started. Some days I just don't want to move—there are times when it's hard to see the point. You have your school and have to help your Daddy with the housework, I'm sure you are busy, Janey, people should be helpful, at your age especially.

Now that the smallpox has died down I don't guess I have any chores. Over in Deadwood when the smallpox hit they said I was the best nurse they had, the boys said they'd never forget me. Their shacks were miserable, some of them didn't even have shacks, just tents and not real tents either, rags would be a better description. Ha, I wasn't just the best nurse they had, I was the *only* nurse, nobody else would go near those dying boys— forty of them died anyway, I couldn't save them. I ain't a Doc, Janey all I could do was cook them soup and hold their hand—I hated to see those boys die, I have been gloomy ever since.

I may tear this up, why should you read it? I feel I should be writing you about cheerful things, the prairie flowers or maybe pretty sights I've seen. It's not wise to pass on painful memories, that smallpox up in Deadwood is painful to remember, nothing much worse has happened in my life. Wild Bill getting assassinated by the coward Jack McCall was worse and the Custer battle was worse, I lost many fine friends in the Custer battle. But that's just quick death, it happens—the sickness in Deadwood was slow, I guess that's why it seems worse.

I should just get my mind off it, Janey. I should remember what ripping fun Jim and Bartle and me used to have hauling freight to the forts—they thought they were degraded, mountain men ain't supposed to drive mules, but I loved driving them mules, I'd be driving them still if Custer hadn't took a dislike of me, Mrs. Custer had no better opinion I'm afraid. I thought Custer was a vain fool and look what he did—hundreds of men died because of him, not just soldiers either, newspapermen only

14

count the soldiers, but many Indians died too, you won't find finer-looking boys than some of those Cheyenne, I love to see them ride.

I was never able to get on the good side of a General, Janey—General Crook didn't care for me either but at least he was polite, Sheridan wasn't polite, he would have hung me right away if he could have found a regulation that allowed him to hang a woman for whooping and hollering.

Janey I like to yell at times, why not? The Indians like to yell too, maybe that's why I get along with Indians, who wants to just sit around and be quiet all the time?

I am not much closer to Ragg and Bone today, ten miles maybe. I can do sixty miles a day if I get up and get started. Satan can't figure out why we're traveling so slow, sixty miles to him is an easy trot. The horse ain't the problem, I'm the problem—if I'm feeling moody I'm hard to hurry. It used to drive Dora crazy, she's feisty, on the move every minute, but I sort of turn into mud, that's what I feel like, old thick mud. When Dora gets nervous Fred gets nervous, parrots are unusual that way —you wouldn't think a bird would care how a person was, but Fred's a bird with a nervous temperment. He used to sit on my arm pecking at a silver bracelet a Mexican gave me and saying "General Custer, General Custer." Fred you're going to say General Custer once too often and I'm going to strangle you, I told him once when I was in one of my mud moods. I guess he believed me, he went back to his perch.

Of course Dora would throw me out if I strangled her parrot—I might do it anyway, I'm hard to predict, Janey, I have done worse things than that. Your mother has not always been able to be good—it's hard if you have no one special to be good for.

Your father Wild Bill was special, they had to wrestle me down and stuff me in jail to keep me from killing Jack McCall after he murdered Wild Bill, I had a good bowie knife then and I was going to cut his liver out and hang it on a tree. An Indian would do that to his enemy and Jack McCall was my enemy, I wanted revenge. Jack McCall was later hung, he's lucky, he would have died harder if I'd been the one to kill him.

I guess such talk will shock you, Janey, I'm sorry, I have not had the advantage of living in a nice town like Springfield, thank God you're growing up in a civilized place. Out here the day never passes without someone threatening to cut out someone's liver and hang it on a tree—and it's not just all talk, people do it, not just Indians either. Jim Ragg has killed three men, all friends—he's terrible when he drinks, everyone with any sense leaves when Jim starts drinking. The three he killed were too drunk to think or they would have left too.

Bartle is the exception, Jim has never tried to kill Bartle that I remember, I hope Bartle is too smart to let Jim kill him—that would be a terrible thing.

This letter is not exactly about the prairie flowers, is it? I meant to be more cheerful, it was remembering the smallpox that set me on the downward path. I may just throw this letter away. Goodnight in any case.

Your mother,
Martha Jane

2

No Ears sat behind a large sage bush, watching seven cranes wade in the small creek. The cranes had arrived in the dark. Because he had no ears, the old man had felt, rather than heard, their arrival. Their great wings disturbed the air sufficiently to wake him from his light sleep.

The fact that it had been dark when the cranes arrived made No Ears suspicious. The cranes had shown bad manners, in his view. In the first place, they belonged in the Platte River, not a small creek in Wyoming. No Ears, an Ogalala, had lived by the Platte River most of his life; he had seen the cranes come in their thousands, year after year, to rest in the wide river.

No Ears had little patience with bad manners, whether in bird or beast. He liked things to behave as they should, and the caprice of the cranes annoyed him. Crazy Woman Creek was not the Platte. What did these cranes think they were doing, straying into such a creek? Even worse, they had arrived at night, a very unmannerly thing. In his more than eighty years, No Ears could not remember seeing birds behave so badly, and he considered marching down to the creek to inform them of his disapproval.

What kept him silent behind his sage bush was the suspicion that the cranes' arrival had something to do with him. It was well known that cranes were spirit messengers. All cranes were thought to have the ability to travel to the spirit place, and the seven cranes in Crazy Woman Creek were not ordinary cranes of the sort so common in the sandhills to the east. These were the great cranes that whooped—some considered that they spoke the language of souls, seducing tired spirits from people's bodies and taking them away through a hole in the sky.

The hole in the sky was said to be far to the south, near the shores of an ocean whose waters were always warm.

No Ears had never seen an ocean and had little interest in seeing one, but he had a keen interest in the hole in the sky—namely, an interest in seeing that his own soul didn't get snatched by a crane and carried away forever, through the hole.

No Ears thought well of the spirit world; he just wasn't ready to visit it, and it annoyed him that the seven cranes had come to tempt his soul. They were large birds—even the smallest of them could have stepped across the trickle of the creek in a single stride. Such birds could easily carry several souls, which were light things, as easily blown away as thistledown.

He wanted to stand up, march down to the creek, and tell the birds they had made a mistake. He wasn't through with his soul, wasn't ready to die. He had seen many men die—some had feared it, but many hadn't; many had died calmly, almost indifferently. From watching these many passings, No Ears had concluded that he just didn't want to die—calmly, indifferently, fearfully, or any other way.

He wanted to confront the cranes and make that fact known to them, but he knew it could be risky. He was old; his soul was very light. What if it floated out of his body for a moment? One of the cranes might snatch it as if it were a frog or a small water snake, and then carry it south through the hole in the sky. Even if he shot the crane his soul might still float away.

It was too large a risk, No Ears concluded. He had better just stay behind his bush. The arrival of the seven cranes was too suspicious. There was nothing worth their time in the immediate vicinity, except his soul. He might challenge them and scare them off, but there were seven of them. He felt outnumbered—so he sat, annoyed that birds would behave so badly, and galled that the soul's attachment to the body was such an undependable thing.

When No Ears was ten, his people were traveling on the Red River of the North and had gotten into a fight with some French traders. The traders, better armed, shot all the Indians and cut their ears off. No Ears was shot, but didn't die. He woke to discover that his people were dead and that he had no ears. An old blind woman was the only other person spared. The traders had hit her in the head and left it at that. No Ears led the old woman across the prairie, back to the Platte.

Lack of ears was a severe handicap to No Ears in his youth. Warriors laughed at him and refused to let him fight with them. Girls wouldn't have him. At fifteen he killed a wolf, took its ears, and persuaded a daughter of the old woman he had saved to sew the wolf's ears to his head. This effort earned him a certain respect, but in the end it failed. One night while he slept a dog tore one of the wolf's ears loose. Fleas by the hundreds collected in the other ear—finally, maddened by the fleas, he tore that ear off too. Part of his scalp came with it.

He never again attempted to acquire ears, though for many years he continued to miss them and for a time was haunted by stories of a Yaqui medicine man, somewhere in Mexico, who had medicines that could make missing body parts grow back. No Ears contemplated trying to find the Yaqui, but something always came up, and he never went.

After some fifty summers had passed, by which time No Ears had buried four wives, outlived all but a few of his own people, and survived many close brushes with death, he became comfortable with his handicap and even proud of it. He could hear, of course, but only in a whistly and erratic way; what he excelled at was smelling. Year by year, his capacity to smell had become more and more refined, finally becoming so keen that it brought him renown throughout the west. He could smell buffalo and he could smell rain. He could sniff a woman's belly and tell if she were fertile, and he could smell babies in the womb within a few days of their conception.

Above all, he could smell death. It was No Ears who walked into camp, a hundred miles from the Little Bighorn, and informed General Crook of the Custer massacre. Bodies rotted quickly in the hot June sun—the smell of hundreds of dead had reached him on the wind. General Crook believed him, too; few men doubted No Ears's nose.

Another thing that worried him about the cranes was that he couldn't smell them—they stood in the water on their long, stemlike legs, as neutral as air.

Also, it was No Ears's belief that death resided in the north. The hole in the sky was supposed to be in the south, but in his view that was only a trick to divert the victim's attention. The seven cranes had come from the north, a sure sign, to No Ears's way of thinking, that they had come on a spirit mission.

Carefully No Ears sniffed his hands. He had often wondered if he would be able to smell himself die, and the presence of the cranes made the question urgent. If his spirit had begun a quiet withdrawal, his flesh would soon begin to smell empty. He had often noticed an empty smell in the extremities of the dying, a sign that the blood was leaving with the spirit. No Ears sniffed his hands carefully and was relieved that they smelled fine. It indicated to him that his soul had no interest in leaving with the cranes.

Then a sound slapped the air. The startled cranes lifted their wings and began their slow, awkward climb into the air. Six struggled skyward and flapped off to the east, but one lay kicking in the stream.

Jim Ragg and Bartle Bone came walking up Crazy Woman Creek toward the dying bird.

20

"Whoopee, crane for breakfast," Bartle said. He had a bowie knife in his hand. When he came to the crane he stood astraddle of the small stream, grabbed the struggling bird's neck, and whacked its head off.

"This is a big bird," he remarked. "It takes a damn good knife to make that clean a cut on a bird this size."

Held up, the crane was almost as tall as Bartle, though not quite, Bartle being a shade over six feet tall. In his youth the older mountain men had called him Tall Boy and had assigned him the deeper beaver ponds. Jim Ragg, stumpy by contrast, could barely have kept his nose above water in some of the ponds where Bartle trapped.

Jim Ragg set down his gun and blanket and began to look for firewood. He had shot the crane in the head so as to spoil as little meat as possible, but Bartle whacked the bird's head off without commenting on the shot. Bartle could have shot at the crane for a week and not managed to hit it in the head; it was typical that he would compliment his own knife rather than the shot. Bartle liked to be the best at everything, but in fact was only an average shot. Brilliant shots made by others were always ignored.

Jim scanned the barren plain and didn't see much firewood, but both men saw No Ears squatting behind a sage bush fifty or sixty yards away.

"Would you be willing to join us for breakfast, or do you prefer just to sit out there and smell yourself?" Bartle yelled.

Of course No Ears expected to be asked to breakfast. He had known the mountain men since they were youths and had helped them on many occasions when they were less experienced and might not have survived. He had lingered behind the bush merely to enjoy a moment of relief at the departure of the cranes—the birds' behavior had shocked him badly.

He stood up and started toward the creek, but before he had taken three steps Bartle yelled at him again.

"Bring some of that bush with you," Bartle yelled. "There ain't much wood around here."

No Ears ignored this order, as he did most orders. This

was another instance of how a handicap could be useful. He could actually hear fairly well but was careful to leave the impression that his hearing was hopelessly damaged. Pretending not to hear always worked better with men than with women. When women gave an order they didn't care if you could hear it or not, they just wanted it obeyed.

"I wish you'd brought the bush," Bartle said, when No Ears walked up. "Cranes are tasty, but not if you're eating them raw."

"I saw some wood yesterday," No Ears remarked. "It is not too far from here. We could take the bird where the wood is and cook it there. I would have brought the wood with me but I didn't know anyone was in Wyoming."

"How far is the wood?" Jim asked. "How far and which direction? We ain't very interested in traveling south."

"That wood is north of here," No Ears said. "It would not take long to get there if we were riding horses."

"I don't notice any horses," Bartle said.

"No, I don't either," No Ears said. "I don't think there are any around in this part of the country. If there were we could smell them."

"How far's the wood if we walk?" Jim Ragg asked, anxious to know whether the wood was within a feasible distance. Once Bartle and No Ears got a conversation started, securing practical information became extremely hard.

No Ears began to have doubts about when he had actually seen the wood. It seemed to him that he had seen it the day before, but he knew that his mind had begun to jump around, like a frog or a grasshopper. Perhaps he had seen the wood ten years ago, or even twenty. The wood had been part of a wagon that had fallen to pieces, and it lay in a little gully not far from Crazy Woman Creek.

"If we walk we will be there before we piss the next time," No Ears said. "It is about that far, if it is there."

"Oh, if it's there," Bartle said. "I'm not walking two hours on the strength of an if."

"Me neither," Jim Ragg said, gutting the crane.

"Excuse me, I'll go cut off some of that bush," No Ears said

Darling Jane—

At this rate I'll be a year older before I get south of the Bighorns, Satan is disgusted. If he could he'd take up with somebody who covers ground a little faster.

What slowed me up today was three nervous soldiers, not one of them full-grown men. They didn't used to let boys that young soldier out here, but now that they think they've got the Indians whipped it's anything goes—I guess they'll be signing up little girls next, so watch out Janey, don't be tricked.

The three boys were hauling some goods over to the Crow agency, they had never been there before and were afraid they'd get lost. I told them they might miss the agency but it would be hard to miss the Crow, they're everywhere, they'll be helping you unload the wagon before you can even get stopped.

It's not getting lost these boys had on their minds, Janey, it's the Cheyenne. There's only a few Cheyenne now but they have a big reputation, they've earned it too. These boys don't know their Indians either, they seem to think old Crazy Horse might ride up and scalp them, I mentioned that he was a Sioux, but it did no good. I think some sergeant has been teasing them, telling them Crazy Horse is still alive. I don't know why grown men think it is such fun to scare boys.

The upshot was that I rode over to the Rosebud with them and pointed them on their way, they were sorry to see me go, they all miss their mothers I imagine. Since I had traveled that far out of my way I thought I might as well go visit my friend Mrs. Elkshoulders. She talked a

blue streak, mostly in Cheyenne, I didn't understand half
of it but she is a loyal friend. When Dora DuFran was all
but dead Mrs. Elkshoulders come all the way to Miles
City with her ointments and herbs and Dora pulled
through, without Mrs. Elk as I call her, Dora would be
gone.

The ointment smelled like grizzly grease to me, it was
rank, the only thing that smells worse than buffalo
hunters is grizzly grease. I have always been scared of
bears, anyone with good sense is, that don't include Blue,
one of the best stories about Blue is him roping the
grizzly. It was a young one, I guess Blue thought he could
handle it, there's no one as cocky as Blue, he thinks he
can handle anything but he couldn't handle that yearling
grizzly. The bear turned around and killed his horse—
Blue had to scamper out of there on foot or the bear
would have killed him too. Later Blue went back hoping
to find his saddle, he had had the saddle since his Texas
days and hated to lose it, but he lost it, the saddle was
never seen again. It taught Blue not to rope bears, it may
be the one thing he has ever learned in his life, Blue is
deadly stubborn.

But now the grizzlies have about left the plains, the
plains are too busy now, too many soldiers are running
around who like to think they're bear hunters, they're
fools, it's no sure thing hunting bear.

Last night I dreamed of you Janey, I often do. It's sad
that a mother only gets to see her little girl in dreams, but
as Dora would say it's better than nothing. You had won
a prize at school for doing your letters graceful. I hope
you will develop a good handwriting Janey, not a scrawl
like mine. I was proud while the dream lasted, it's a comfort to have a daughter who's good in school or can even
go to one, I never did. But then I woke up crying, I cried
all morning, it's another reason for the slow start.

Dora DuFran hates it when I cry, she says will you dry
up? She knows if I don't she'll start crying too and the
two of us will bawl like babies half the day, Dora about
her sorrows and me about mine. Hers are mostly the
result of being in love with Blue, I can't see that they

compare with mine—love a skunk and you're sure to get skunked. But that's my point of view, I'm sure Dora's is the opposite. The other day she told me she was thinking of moving to Deadwood, maybe she thinks Blue will let her alone if she's living in the hills. He won't—hill or plain means nothing to Blue, he'll want his little visits wherever Dora is. She asked me if I'd come with her— we'll always be a pair, she said.

Dora and I will always be a pair, I won't desert her, but life in Deadwood might be too painful, it's where Wild Bill is buried. He's in Mount Moriah cemetery, on Jerusalem Street. I have paid him many visits there—I visit him just as Blue visits Dora, except Blue's alive and Dora's alive—I guess they find some love amid their troubles. Blue being married elsewhere don't mean he's lost his passion for Dora.

But it's just a grave I'm visiting on Mount Moriah, Wild Bill's grave, he's been in it twelve years—you were already safe with your Daddy Jack when the coward McCall shot your father. I was not about to subject my precious daughter to these rough mining camps.

I think it's a mistake for Dora to move, the climate is healthier in Miles City, but Dora's restless—she's always restless, I expect she'll move anyway and take along Fred the parrot. Maybe Fred will learn some new words over in Deadwood, but what will I learn new? It's painful when your true love dies, that's all I'll learn in Deadwood, and I already know it.

They say Deadwood is civilized now and even has a mayor, I asked who and someone said Potato Creek Johnny, ha! I had to laugh. I knew Johnny down at Fort Fetterman when he was breaking horses for soldiers, no-body would have picked him for a mayor then. I wouldn't pick him for one now, though I count him a pal, he only found one nugget, finding one nugget don't mean he can be a mayor. The first thing he'll do is arrest me and Dora, or maybe he won't, we both know too much about him.

All this old stuff must bore you, Janey, I don't mean to write it, I started these letters thinking you might want to know a little about your mother's life—first thing you know it became a habit. I have no idea what you think about it—you are a bit young to be writing letters yourself. I want my little girl to be proud of her mother—I should have considered better, there's not that much to be proud of, at least it don't seem that way now. I am not a braggart Janey, I just try to be decent—some don't think I am, ladies don't, or women who call themselves ladies, there's a few in every town, how I despise them. I picked one of the old snoots up and threw her in the horse trough in Dodge City, it aroused a crowd and your father Wild Bill said I ought to vamoose for a while. It made me fighting mad that he told me that, what right did he have to tell me I had to leave Dodge or anyplace? No right, and I told him so, then I left anyway—I am too proud to stay where I'm not wanted, we were a long time making that up, but we did.

Well, this is another letter I might as well throw away, why would a sweet girl like you want to hear all this old stuff? I have wasted six sheets of paper on it.

> Good night Janey,
> Your mother, Martha Jane

3

DORA DUFRAN SAT BY HER BEDROOM WINDOW, warmed by a big cup of coffee and all the robes she could find to put on. Skeedle came up to bring her a little more coffee and laughed at the sight of Dora wrapped in three or four robes.

"Why didn't you put on a few more robes?" Skeedle asked.

"Buy me a few more and I'll put 'em on," Dora said. "This was all I could find in the closet."

"You could buy a buffalo robe from an Indian, I bet," Skeedle said. Skeedle was the premiere, and, in fact, the only blonde in Dora's establishment. She had been the premiere blonde for several years, and it was beginning to show. If a younger blonde ever showed up and wanted to work, Skeedle might have had trouble holding her position, but the danger of that happening was not great. With the mining towns still booming in Dakota the blonde population of Miles City was not likely to increase.

"Buffalo robes attract fleas," Dora pointed out. "I don't want to encourage fleas, the customers bring in enough as it is. Thanks for the coffee."

"You're welcome," Skeedle said, and left. She was

well aware that Dora liked to keep to herself in the mornings.

Dora heard the stairs creak as Skeedle descended to the first floor. Skeedle was not only the blondest whore in Miles City, she was also the largest whore, but that was fine, she brought in twice as much business as some of the prettier girls.

Fred was not particularly fond of Skeedle, being a rather jealous parrot. He kept his back turned while Skeedle was in the room, but as soon as she left he dropped off his perch and came waddling across the floor. Dora offered him her arm and he climbed up it and began to peck gently at the pearl buttons on one of Dora's robes. Fred liked all jewelry, but he was especially fond of pearl buttons. Dora set her coffee cup down and stroked the green feathers on the top of the parrot's head. When she did, Fred turned his beak and took hold of her ring, a cheap ring Blue had given her when they were still talking of marriage.

Out her window Dora could see the gleam of the Yellowstone. Far across it to the west there was a river called the Musselshell, where Blue had his ranch. Dora had never been that far west, had never seen Blue's ranch, but many a morning she had sat in sadness by her window, thinking about it, and about his house and his new wife, a sweet young half-breed woman. Dora had only Calamity's word for it that Blue's wife was sweet, but she was prepared to believe it. Calamity had been a guest in their house and had even gone to their wedding, a fact that had not sat well with Dora at the time.

"Blue invited me, what did you want me to do?" Calamity asked, when Dora challenged her on the point—as Dora, much hurt, promptly did.

"You're my friend, ain't you?" Dora said. "You could have mentioned me, at least. If you was in love with him and he suddenly slid past you and married somebody else, do you think I'd go to his damn wedding?"

"Well, it would be fair enough, if you did," Calamity said. She was a little drunk and had a hard time getting a grip on the complications such matters involved. She knew that Dora was upset because Blue had suddenly popped up married to Granville Stuart's daughter—that was understandable. But her own attendance at the wedding didn't seem to matter one way or the other. Blue wasn't marrying Dora, whoever went to the wedding, or didn't go.

"Blue's been my friend too, since Dodge or before," Calamity pointed out. "Don't you go to the weddings of your old friends?"

"I wouldn't if one of them was jilting my *best* friend!" Dora said. While it lasted, her anger was unrelenting.

"You shouldn't have never counted on Blue, that's the way I see it," Calamity said.

"The way I see it, you had to choose whose feelings to hurt and you chose mine," Dora said. "I'd hurt the man's, if it was me—not that many of them have really got feelings."

"Blue's got feelings, he just wanted a wife to help with the work," Calamity countered, trying to put the best face on it.

"Anyway, next time I get jilted I just hope you'll refrain from attending the wedding," Dora said, just before she burst into tears.

Later, when Dora's anger had drained away, she went looking for Calamity to apologize, but Calamity was in the Elk Belly saloon, well on her way to being vomiting drunk. It was a winter night, cold and sleety. Calamity was as likely to mount up and ride off at midnight as at noon—Dora's main worry was that she might pass out some night and freeze. Soberer specimens than Calamity had been known to pass out and freeze in the Montana winters.

Dora assigned a couple of town Indians to see that that didn't happen. Sure enough, Calamity rode off, fell off, and slept under her horse, but the Indians built a fire, covered her well, and brought her back to Dora the next morning, though in such a shaky state that she had to be carried into the house.

It was not the only quarrel the two of them had had about Blue, and in every instance, no matter how blatant his misbehavior, Calamity took Blue's side or found excuses for him. It infuriated Dora—she screamed Calamity out of the house many times, outraged because Calamity would never see, or at least would never admit. that she, not the man, was being wronged.

"He didn't mean it," Calamity would always stammer, when Blue stood accused. "You know he didn't mean it."

"I don't care if he meant it!" Dora yelled. "He did it. *He did it!"*

But in the end, when her anger died, Dora would begin to reproach herself, not for Blue, that laughing reprobate who usually knew exactly what he was doing, but for her treatment of Calamity, her sad old friend.

Calamity didn't understand men, or women, or love, or any of it, Dora always concluded, once her sympathies began to operate normally after some wild fit.

What awakened Dora's sympathies was the knowledge that Calamity's life was so peculiar, and so lonely. She dressed like a man, and had lived a life as near to a man's as she could get; it sometimes seemed to Dora that Calamity almost thought she *was* a man. Maybe it came from running with the boys too long. More often than not, she *looked* like a woman, though there was something indefinite in her look, a kind of in-between quality, that no one, man or woman, knew quite what to make of. At times Dora felt that Calamity had not quite made up her mind which sex to be. One day she'd be in a dress or even sport a fancy hat, and the next she'd be back in pants, cussing like a buffalo hunter and bragging about all the generals she'd scouted for, or the rides she had made for the Pony Express.

Blue, who had known her as long as anyone, maintained that Calamity's bragging was mostly just plain bragging, with little basis in fact.

"The drunker she gets, the more she lies," he put it, not unkindly—whatever his faults as a mate, Blue was a loyal friend to Calamity.

"No general would have let a woman scout for him," Blue pointed out. "He'd have been court-martialed, unless he was General Lee, and she sure didn't scout for General Lee. She didn't ride for the Pony Express, either —they shut down the Pony Express before I was even old enough to ride for it, and I'm older than Calamity.

"What she might have done," he added, in an effort to make their friend seem less of a braggart, "is tag along on a few scouts with Ragg and Bone. I think they took her with them sometimes, when it looked safe."

To Dora what he said just made the matter more sad; it made it seem that Calamity hadn't actually done much of anything except wander here and there on the plains, the little reputation she had the result of invention, or the indulgence of a few kind men; her stories and her story were mainly based on whiskey and emptiness.

Of course, the stories of half the people in Miles City, or perhaps in the west as a whole, were based on pretty much that, whiskey and emptiness; every night Dora's house filled up with braggarts who hadn't done half the things they said they had done. If every man who drank in the saloon had killed as many Indians as he claimed to have killed, there wouldn't have been an Indian left west of the Mississippi; if every miner had found as much gold as was claimed, palaces would stretch down the Missouri all the way to St. Louis.

But the men were just customers—Calamity was a friend. Dora didn't try to be much, but she did try to be truthful, and it made her nervous and a little uncomfortable always to have to suspect Calamity of lying.

"Oh, she just exaggerates," Blue said. "Everybody exaggerates, once in a while."

"You don't," Dora pointed out. Bragging was not among T. Blue's many failings; if anything he tended to understate his achievements as a cowboy.

"Well, you don't know that," Blue said. "I might exaggerate once in a while when you're not around."

"She's been talking about Wild Bill lately," Dora said. "I didn't know she even knew him, but now she acts like they were in love. Do you think he was ever in love with her?"

"No opinion," Blue said immediately.

"Why wouldn't you have an opinion?" Dora asked. "You told me yourself you knew him."

"Now you see, right there I'm caught in a fine exaggeration," Blue said. "I seen the man walk down the street a couple of times, and was once in a saloon where he was playing cards."

"That ain't what you said," Dora insisted. "You said you knew him well. Seems like if they were together you would have known."

"Myself, I was mostly with the herds," Blue said. "I didn't squander much time in Dodge City."

"Oh, hush, you liar," Dora said. "Calamity said you had at least twenty girlfriends in Dodge. How'd you get 'em unless you spent some time there?"

Blue looked amused—he rarely tried to deny that he was a sport.

"I'm cursed with a weak memory," he said. "I can't recall that I had a single pal in the town."

"You don't need to be such a devil," Dora said. "I wasn't even asking about you. I had a few loves myself before we met, what do I care if you had a thousand? I just wonder about Calamity and Wild Bill."

"He's dead, what does it matter?" Blue asked.

"He's dead, but Calamity ain't," Dora said. "I feel sorry for Calamity. I don't believe any man's ever loved her—plenty of women never get loved, you know. I get a sad feeling when she talks about Wild Bill, because it just don't sound true."

"That was years ago," Blue reminded her. "Maybe she forgot the true part. People do forget."

"Not the great love of their life, they don't," Dora said. "Do you think I'd forget you? Hell and everything else will freeze over before I forget you."

"I do doubt that Calamity ever had such a true love as ours," Blue said. His eyes grew misty and he kissed her —for all his brass he was a sentimental man at heart.

Now Blue, sentimental still, was married and living on the Musselshell. Many a day Dora sat wrapped in her robes all morning, watching the plains to the north, and if a dot of a rider appeared far away her heart quickened despite her; most times, of course, the rider wasn't Blue, and her hope turned to ache, to regret, to tears and listless misery. But every month or so the rider *would* be Blue, and a joy flooded her that she couldn't suppress, despite his betrayal.

"The Marquis de Mores gave me this robe with the pearl buttons," Dora mentioned to Fred, but the information was of no interest to the parrot. It wasn't of much interest to Dora, either, though it was a nice robe.

The Marquis de Mores had also been nice. He had once said something about taking her to Paris and getting her an apartment, but that was just the usual silly talk. After all, he had just moved to South Dakota to go into the cattle business. Then his tall, aloof wife arrived, and there was no more talk of Paris, and no more presents, either.

Still, the Marquis *had* liked her while it lasted. He wasn't T. Blue—no one was—but he had offered a decent affection. What Dora wondered was whether anyone had ever offered even that much to Calamity?

If they had, it didn't show—and true joys did show a little, Dora believed. Hers did, she knew—the miserable stretches didn't completely erase them. It was her sad suspicion that Calamity had had no joys, nothing for time to erase except her youth itself.

"What do you think, Fred? Loves me, loves me not?" Dora asked.

Fred looked up from the robe and cocked his head toward his mistress.

"General Custer," he said.

Darling Jane—

They call this dry old crack Powder River, it's easy to see why. Today for a change I made good time, otherwise I wouldn't be here, I'm a fair ways from where I started. I can't stand the rattle at Mrs. Elk's, she must have fifty grandkids and they all cry at the same time. Whoever said Indian babies don't cry ought to spend a night at Mrs. Elk's.

I no longer have the patience I once had, Janey, squalling babies make me want to grit my teeth, the little squirts hold no charms for me. However why complain? I owe them my early start.

Today I ran into a horse trader who had news of the boys, he says they're down on the Little Missouri traveling with old No Ears. At least they won't get lost, No Ears is the best scout left. General Crook tried to take him to Arizona to help catch Geronimo but No Ears wouldn't go, too hot he said. I doubt General Crook will catch Geronimo, he'll have to trick him if he does.

You'd think the boys would get tired of wandering, I do, Janey. I was around Miles City for two months and there's not much to do in Miles City. Fred the parrot is more intelligent than most people in Miles City and Fred only knows two words. You must think your mother is harsh to criticize people so, I should be kinder, I try, but then some old snoot with five or six corsets on will look down her nose at me and act like I have no right on the street with her, though the street might be just a mudhole anyway. It hurts—I know they're just old biddies, most people are friendly to me in Miles City, but somebody will always come along to treat me like dirt. Dora's tougher in some respects, she stares them down when they try to act uppity with her.

Dora has offered me a home, she says we're like sisters, I guess we are. I had no sisters, but Dora had three, they all died, I think Dora misses them. She offered to fix me a nice room with a feather mattress on the bed—she knows how partial I am to feather mattresses.

Sometimes I don't know what to think of myself Janey, my own behavior is a puzzle. I could be sleeping in comfort on a feather mattress, in the home of my best friend, too, but here I am, I'll be lucky to find a soft rock to use for a bed tonight, there are few soft ones along the Powder. I am lucky to have Dora DuFran for a friend, she has been loyal, someday I will tell her about you Janey.

Dora has no child herself, I fear she won't have one now that Blue has jilted her, she expected better of Blue.

I had better tell her about you though Janey and give her your address, I could always get called to the Great Roundup as Blue calls it, heaven is what people call it who haven't been raised in the cow country. Well, heaven if you're hopeful, I'm not particularly.

When Blue gets drunk he becomes sentimental about all his friends who have been called to the Great Roundup or who rode the long trail, he better watch it, he'll be riding it himself if he pushes Dora too far. I don't suppose Dora would really shoot Blue, though I have known women who shot at men, I shot at three myself but missed. I was so mad once I nearly shot a bartender instead of the card cheat I was aiming at, all three times it was over cards—I have never tried to kill anybody over love. Of course I might have shot Wild Bill I guess, he did marry another woman, just as Blue did. It never occurred to me to shoot him, I would have been the one shot if I had tried anything of the sort. Wild Bill had no mercy, I hope that ain't too harsh a thing to tell you about your father, it's the truth though, he just didn't, he would have shot me immediately if I'd shown up waving a gun.

Look at me, I never thought I had so much to say, I have used up nearly a whole tablet just since I started writing you Janey, it is something to do at night other than stare at the campfire. I am a little worried, I have not seen my dog Cody since around noon. He took after some antelope and I have not seen him since. I hope a bear didn't get him, he is a big dog but not big enough to handle a bear.

I feel a bond to Dora, Janey, I feel she needs me, maybe she is the only one who does. I think I will just ramble with the boys for a month or so if I can find them, then I might go back to Miles City and see how I feel about the feather mattress.

Old No Ears will be glad to see me, we are old friends. It was him that found me the time the horse threw me north of Fort Fetterman, he found me in a blizzard and led me in. I could not see six inches, he tied a rope to my belt, if he had let go the rope I'd have been riding in the Great Roundup ten years ago.

Goodnight Janey,
your mother Martha Jane

4

"I THINK YOU MISSED YOUR LAST CHANCE FOR GLORY when you decided not to go with Crook," Bartle said to No Ears.

"I'd have gone myself," Bartle added. "I consider Crook the best general left. I just didn't much feel like wandering around being shot at by Apaches."

"You'd have gone alone then," Jim Ragg said. "It's nothing against Crook. I just won't put up with that heat."

No Ears had decided to travel with the mountain men for a while. The cranes were less likely to settle where three men were camping together, which meant less temptation for his soul.

He had been thinking about his soul a lot since the encounter on Crazy Woman Creek. He wondered if perhaps his soul would grow feathers as it traveled with the birds. The business about Crook held no interest for him. He had heard of Geronimo and thought he would be a lot of trouble to catch. It would mean traveling with soldiers, something No Ears found inconvenient.

Even traveling with the mountain men had its inconveniences, the main one being that Bartle wanted to talk all the time. Jim Ragg also seemed to find this tendency of Bartle's annoying—he seldom said much himself and often refused to make any reply at all.

No Ears felt it was impolite not to reply; he would generally try to make some answer to Bartle's queries, but courtesy took energy, and No Ears would really rather they just all walked along quietly. That way he could apply more of his energy to thinking about his soul.

To everyone's disappointment the Morning Star Saloon stood abandoned when they arrived in Ten Sleep. Indeed, Ten Sleep itself—all three buildings of it—had been abandoned. The only resident was a black chicken that had apparently been left behind. The chicken lived behind the bar, and it squawked irritably when the three men arrived.

"I hate a black squawker," Bartle said. He wrung the chicken's neck and they ate it for supper. No Ears ate the gizzard and the neck, two chicken parts he had always had a craving for. In his youth he would run down prairie hens, mainly for the pleasure of eating their tasty gizzards.

"This was once a lively town," Jim Ragg said, depressed to find Ten Sleep abandoned. "It was more than ten years ago that we were through here, and it had three saloons. I hate to see a place dry up."

"I guess Ten Sleep just dwindled," Bartle commented. "I kind of like it abandoned. We could capture it without a fight and have it be our town. No Ears can be the mayor, I'll be the judge, and you can be the sheriff and arrest anybody that shows up if they displease you. We'll hold court once a week and charge big fines for trespassing or spitting in the street. Owning a town might beat beavering or gold mining, either, as a way to get rich."

It was a beautiful morning, not a cloud between them and Colorado. Bartle was still resting under his blanket, snug against the rear of the Morning Star, a little frame saloon that would probably fall down in another year or two, or else be knocked apart by travelers who might see the opportunity to snatch some free lumber. It was already quite drafty inside.

Bartle saw the abandonment of Ten Sleep as no great loss—it had flourished in the brief time that Texas cowboys were steadily pushing Texas cattle north to the Lodge Grass or farther. Those that didn't hit the town on their way north made up for the error on their way south. But that time was already dying—only a trickle of Texas cattle came up the trail now.

He liked the notion of owning a town, particularly a town with no population. He also liked to lie abed late, letting his mind toy with fancies of one kind and another, a habit in stark contrast to that of his two companions, both of whom had been up for hours. Jim Ragg exhibited distinct signs of restlessness; he was determined to find something to do, even though they were in a place where it was obvious that nothing needed doing. Mostly Jim was reduced to building fires and boiling stronger and stronger coffee.

No Ears was an easier companion in many ways. It was not clear to Bartle whether the old man ever slept, but at least he had no compulsion to invent early morning activities. Mainly, No Ears sat and stared into space, occasionally singing unintelligible melodies to his gods.

"What I like about Ten Sleep is that it's a town with elevation," Bartle said. "You can see a ways. I hate low country. That's another problem Crook's gonna have in Arizona. All that low country is apt to cause rheumatism and other diseases. Also, the rattlesnakes are more poisonous in Arizona."

"I don't know why you want to talk foolishness like that," Jim said. "Arizona ain't particularly low and the snakes ain't no worse than other snakes."

"Martha Jane is coming," No Ears said. "I see that big dog of hers."

Bartle sat up in his blankets and Jim stood up to look, but neither of them could see a dog.

"I thought I saw that dog yesterday," No Ears said. "It looks like it's lost."

"Well, consider its namesake," Bartle said, a little irritated at his inability to spot the dog. "Billy Cody's spent half his life lost but it ain't kept him from getting rich. Jim and me have never been lost but here we are, without a dime to split.''

Jim Ragg believed in being methodical. He inspected the horizon carefully, moving his gaze slowly from point to point. He concentrated as hard as he could, until finally his eyes began to water. The force of his concentration gave him a bit of a headache, but he could see no dog. It was no real surprise; No Ears's vision had often humbled him.

"I'm damned if I can see a dog," he said finally.

"He is pretty tired," No Ears said. "I think he has been chasing antelope all night. It may take Martha Jane a day or two to catch up with him."

No Ears was one of the few who still referred to Calamity by her given name. He thought it was a beautiful name, and was puzzled that people had decided to call her Calamity.

It seemed to him that it was unnecessary and even dangerous to change a person's name once the matter had been settled by the proper authorities. He himself had lived most of his life under the handicap of a nickname, but in his case it was understandable, since he had lost his ears so young. His real name was Two Toes Broken; not long after his birth a horse had stepped on his foot and broken two of his toes.

It saddened the old man to consider that he was probably the only person living who knew his true name. Perhaps there were one or two old women living somewhere along the Platte who would remember him as Two Toes Broken, but it was not likely he would ever see those old women, if even they still survived, and so would never meet a person who would greet him by his true name. It was a lonely fate, and he hoped his friend Martha Jane would avoid it.

It was a bit of a puzzle to No Ears why she had come to be called Calamity. His own nickname, by comparison, was perfectly simple, since anyone could take one look and see that he lacked ears. But the notion of calamity was a good deal more complicated—essentially it seemed to mean trouble; at least that was how Bartle had explained it to him.

Bartle might be right about what the word meant, but that didn't explain why so many people had chosen to attach it to Martha Jane. In No Ears's experience, Martha Jane was anything but a troublesome person. If he had been choosing a nickname he would have called her Helpful, because she had often gone out of her way to help him. Several times she had persuaded sheriffs to let him out of jail when the sheriffs had just been inclined to let him sit there without much to eat or smoke. She had also helped him nurse his last wife; the wife had died of smallpox anyway, but Martha Jane had done what she could to make her passing easier. No Ears knew of other instances when Martha Jane had been helpful enough to earn herself a kinder nickname such as Helpful. But he had never mentioned his view, even to Martha Jane herself. White people had a different way of naming, and also of nicknaming, it appeared. That was their way and there was no point in arguing with them about it. But he himself still thought it best to call a person by his true name unless special circumstances applied.

It sometimes occurred to No Ears that there might be a link between the fact that white people had weak eyes and the fact that they had little attachment to their true names. At the moment both mountain men were annoyed because they couldn't spot Martha's dog; if they couldn't see a dog merely because it had lain down to rest behind a bush a mile or two away, how would they see the truth in a person's name? No Ears had puzzled over white people's lack of insight for a good many years without reaching a firm conclusion about it. His suspicion was that white people simply had no serious interest in truth. What they managed to see was usually enough truth for them, even if it was only half of what was there to see.

The interesting thing was that both Bartle and Jim knew perfectly well that he could see better than they could. Both of them were annoyed, but neither of them tried to argue that the dog wasn't there. And when the dog had had its rest and came trotting into Ten Sleep, they expressed no surprise.

"Howdy, Cody—I hope you didn't wander off and leave Calamity lying out drunk," Bartle said, offering the dog their chicken bones.

Darling Jane—

I guess I could have been a book writer if I'd known what an easy habit scribbling is to get into, it is easy if you've got a good pencil. Bartle Bone wants to read whatever it is I'm writing, he would never dream it's a letter to my daughter. He thinks I'm writing about him no doubt—everybody knows Bartle is vain.

I told him I was writing a book called *The Wild West Adventures of Ragg and Bone, Mountain Men of the Old Days*. Bartle is already finding fault, he says the title is much too long. He would find a lot more fault if I gave him a glimpse of my spelling, he considers himself a fine speller though so far as I know he has not penned a line in thirty years. It don't make him modest though—Bartle supposes he can do anything anyone else can do, even spell.

I guess I won't listen to wandering horse traders again, that gent I met way back on the Powder gave me bad directions. I spent three days riding the Little Missouri, since he told me the boys were there. I saw no sign of the boys and no sign of Cody either, that is not surprising since the bunch of them were taking it easy in Ten Sleep all the while. You would have thought they would have scurried around and tried to find me once my dog showed up, they didn't though. Bartle is lazy and probably talked the other two out of making an effort. You can bet I gave them a tongue-lashing when I finally located them. Bartle just laughed. Not much fazes Bartle.

Jim Ragg don't look good to me, Janey—no color. I asked him if he was sick, of course he denied it. Mountain men will never admit to being sick, they pride themselves on being able to stand anything. I pointed out to Jim that quite a few mountain men have died as dead as other people, he had no answer for that—he could be rotting away and he would be unlikely to admit it.

We have been debating about where to go next, Janey —if we go anywhere. Bartle wants to take over Ten Sleep and build it up, he thinks it could be a fine town—ha, if it was a fine town none of us would want to spend five minutes in it. Jim Ragg is convinced there are beaver in the Owl Creek Mountains, he still has beaver on the brain. Bartle don't want to go, he's feeling lazy still. I think we might as well go, we don't have to stay long—if we don't go Jim Ragg will complain for years about all the beaver we made him miss.

No Ears calls me Martha Jane, of course it's my name but I've been Calamity so long it's odd to hear it. Dora still calls me Martha once in a while when she's feeling sweet. Blue don't, although he knew me when Martha was all I was ever called—so did Bartle and Jim. I don't know if I would ever have got west if not for Bartle and Jim, I was having a hard time finding my way out of St. Louis. I knew nothing then. I was hired to chop firewood, the man that hired me didn't realize I was a girl. Bartle and Jim were guiding ten wagons, I think they had only agreed to get them as far as the Arkansas, they took a liking to me and let me accompany the wagons. It surprised them that I could walk all day as good as a mountain man. Some of the ladies in the wagons didn't approve of my dress—I had hardly set foot in the west before ladies started not approving. I hope you will never meet with the kind of scorn I have met with, Janey, it leaves a bitter taste.

Now Bartle and Jim have nearly had a fight, it's a good thing we have no liquor here—if drunk, I fear they would have fought. Bartle's patience is about gone when it comes to beaver, he's finally ready to admit there ain't none to be found. He don't want to go to the Owl Creek Mountains or anywhere else in search of beaver. Bartle said he'd rather just stay in Ten Sleep and think for a few days—it upset Jim no end. Think about what? he asked. Bartle said nothing in particular, he would just enjoy the opportunity to do some general thinking. All right if you want to be lazy, Jim said, he has always considered Bartle to be somewhat on the lazy side. I ain't lazy but I've had about enough of walking up one hill and down the other looking for beaver with you, Bartle replied, he would have done better to keep that remark to himself, now Jim will sulk for days.

No Ears is worried that it might be getting time for him to die. He says some cranes showed up where they shouldn't have been the other night—he thinks they were waiting around hoping to make off with his soul. I will be sorry if he does die, I will have one less friend. But it ain't No Ears I'm worried about, it's Jim Ragg. If I knew where there were beaver I'd buy him a few, it's about the only thing that might cheer him up.

Now Bartle is trying to sing, he's singing Buffalo Girls, I am going to stop this letter, he might take it wrong if he saw me scribbling while he's trying to entertain us.

Goodnight Janey,
your mother Martha Jane

5

DORA'S HAIR WAS STILL FINE AND SOFT, WITH ONLY A sprinkle of gray in it. Some of the girls thought she ought to dye out the gray—"Old ladies don't belong in sporting establishments," Trix remarked—but Dora ignored them. For one thing, the Hotel Hope was *her* establishment; she had worked hard to get it and she made all the decisions, including the decision to let her own hair go gray if it wanted to.

Now that she was more or less retired, Dora rarely primped much, but she did devote some time to her hair, brushing it every afternoon for the better part of an hour. She had never considered herself particularly pretty; her soft, dark hair had always been her best feature. Sometimes in bitter moods she wished it would just go on and turn white; perhaps then she could get on with being an old lady and subdue the quick hopes she had had to contend with for so long—hopes it seemed would never be satisfied.

Even now, with Blue married, the hopes wouldn't leave her alone. In the afternoon, combing her hair, she found herself dreaming all the kinds of dreams she had always had: having a baby with Blue, living somewhere with him far from saloons and whores. Something in her didn't seem to want to consider that those dreams were hopeless; after all, she owned the Hotel Hope It behooved her to try to keep a hopeful attitude.

She was attending to her hair one afternoon, as a sunset that was looking more wintry every day colored the plains to the west, when Doosie came in, looking a little odd. Doosie, a black woman, was easily startled. It took very little to upset her. She loved routine and resented people who chanced to interrupt any of hers.

"I was given this card," she said, holding it out.

"My goodness, it's just a card, it won't bite you," Dora said. "Who gave it to you?"

"He's little and fat and he's wearing a yellow necktie with one of them stickpins in it," Doosie said. "I didn't like his behavior."

"My goodness, if everybody was as picky as you we'd go broke," Dora said, taking the card. "Did he make a suggestion? Is that why you're so nervous?"

"He called me a Nubian beauty," Doosie said. "What's a Nubian beauty?"

"I think it's in the Bible," Dora said. "You are a beauty, you mustn't get so nervous just because a gentleman pays you a compliment."

Engraved on the card, in elegant black letters, was a name that nearly caused Dora to drop her hairbrush: William F. Cody.

"Oh, gosh, Billy's here!" Dora said, excited. "He's got to be such a gentleman that he sends in his card. That fellow you took a dislike to was probably his servant. How do you like that?"

"He can watch what he calls me, that's all," Doosie said. "The less conversations I have with him the better."

"Well, is he still here—I mean the servant?" Dora asked.

"He may be, I ain't looked," Doosie said.

"Oh, go blow your nose," Dora said. "I'll find out for myself." She popped a couple of combs in her hair and hurried downstairs. It was mid-afternoon and a short plump man with a yellow necktie appeared to be the only customer. He stood at the bar, or rather slightly below it, imbibing a beer.

"Hello, I'm Miss DuFran," Dora said, wondering why Doosie was so spooky. The little plump man seemed harmless; he just had a bit of a twitch.

"Pleased—I'm Dr. Ramses, you may remember me from Medora, I took your picture once with the Marquis but I've since ceased to do much photography," the little man said, in a breath.

"Time has not stained your beauty, as the Bard said of Cleopatra," he added, twitching.

Dora tried to call him to mind from her Medora days, but failed. Her Medora days had been brief—it was hard enough now even to summon a clear memory of the Marquis de Mores, much less of this odd little man.

"Here's the picture, it might help you remember," Dr. Ramses said, smiling. He handed her a photograph. Sure enough it was her, looking such a girl, standing by the Marquis. Two of his greyhounds were also in the picture. The odd thing was that she was taller than the Marquis. She did not remember him as particularly tall, but it was a shock to realize he was *that* short.

"Were you with the medicine show?" Dora inquired— she had a vague memory of a medicine show. Cowboys had lined up to have their photographs taken, and evidently, so had she and the Marquis.

"Ma'am, I *was* the medicine show, in much the same way as you are the Hotel Hope," Dr. Ramses said, in a tone that touched her, she didn't know why. The little plump man with the big fake diamond in his stickpin had abruptly tugged her into the pool of memory; for a moment she felt like crying.

"There, it's just a snapshot, keep the photo, my name's on the back," he said. "Billy asked me to bring you his card. We arrived in town only an hour ago and you were his first thought."

"I'm glad somebody still gets to call him Billy," Dora

said, collecting herself. Doosie had not been entirely wrong to be nervous—Dr. Ramses took some resisting.

Dr. Ramses chuckled. "He told me you might think the card was overdoing it," he said. "Billy's still quite the democrat, as you'll see. I printed up the card at my print shop in St. Louis, same place where I made the photos. A card is useful if we need to see a governor, or even a mayor if we're in one of the larger cities."

"I'd be careful who I give them out to in Miles City," Dora said. "This ain't a greeting-card kind of a place. You've already spooked my maid."

"A handsome woman," Dr. Ramses said. "Sometimes my vocabulary runs away with me when I see a handsome woman."

"Since Billy's so formal now, perhaps he'd like to come to tea—you're welcome too," Dora said. "Come in half an hour but go light on the vocabulary when you're around my maid. I know it's hard for Billy to get his hair combed in half an hour, but tell him just to stick his hat on this time, I'm dying to see him."

Half an hour later, Billy Cody walked in, wearing the whitest buckskins Dora had ever seen, with a neat little beard and his hair combed to perfection. But his eyes were still soft as a boy's—Dora just had to hug him and kiss him. Besides, Billy would have been crushed if any woman resisted him for more than thirty seconds.

"My lord, who sews your buckskins, why didn't you bring me a set?" Dora asked. "I'd wear them in a parade, if the town ever has one."

Doosie stepped in the door, beaming, holding a set of buckskins just as white, with a touch of beadwork on the sleeves. There were other presents too: a hat with an egret feather, some elegant gloves from a store in St. Louis, a bracelet, and a necklace. Dora tried on the buckskins, and they fit as well as any clothes she had.

"How'd you know I'd still be my same size?" Dora asked, wondering why everyone felt so critical of Billy when he wasn't around. Even she felt critical of him when he wasn't around.

"Why, Dora, I knew I could trust you to keep your figure," Billy said. "If you was to lose your figure half the men in the west would give up and get married."

"Flatterer!" she said—but she liked it. "Who's that twitchy little drummer who's traveling with you?"

"Oh, Doc, I bought his medicine show," Billy said. "He's a character."

"Billy, did you really tote all this stuff from St. Louis for me?" Dora asked. He had always been a big one for presents, but this time he had outdone himself.

"I was only worried about mashing that egret feather," Billy admitted. "The hat wouldn't look like much without it." In fact, the feather had traveled safely in a gun case, and had only been stuck back on the hat at the last minute.

Dora looked at him thoughtfully. Billy tried to maintain a nonchalant manner, but it wasn't easy, considering what a soft spot he had always had for Dora DuFran. In the last year he had traveled the world and met many respectable beauties and even titled ladies, but in his eyes none of them excelled his Dora.

Of course, she had given him scant encouragement, and would probably have been indignant if he revealed that he thought of her as his sweetheart, and yet he did. The sadness of his life was that he had married Lulu, and not Dora. Amid the titled ladies and the respectable beauties, it was Dora he found himself thinking about, not Lulu, mother of his girls.

In his gloom he would sometimes imagine that Dora had married, that his chance for happiness was gone; as soon as he had boarded the Missouri steamer he had begun to inquire about her. No, not married that I know of, several people had said. The news made him feel as light as the clouds floating over the plains.

"Is Lulu well?" Dora asked, determined to be polite.

"Oh, Dora, why do you mention her?" Billy said. "You know that we're not happy. It was a mistake—it's always been you I love."

Dora just sat looking at him quietly. Her presents lay all around her, but it was himself her gaze fell upon.

"I thought you were silly to marry, Billy," she said finally. "I'm not sure it would suit you with anyone."

Billy felt he couldn't talk about it—all failure horrified him. He hurried to scoot the conversation as far from it as he could. "You know I'm an impresario now," he said.

"A what?" Dora asked. "Ain't that a person who sings in an opera?"

Billy chuckled—he couldn't bear to talk of his marriage, but felt his spirits rise the moment the conversation swung around to business.

"Nope, I have yet to earn a nickel singing," he said. "I doubt there's a choir that would have me. I just manage the show, me and Doc Ramses. We're out here right now recruiting talent."

"I'm more interested in you and Lulu," Dora said. "What's the matter?"

"Oh, I don't know . . . shucks," Billy said, his spirit sinking again. "I should have married you. I wish I could yet."

At that moment Doosie came in with the champagne— a dozen bottles had made the journey from St. Louis, safely packed in straw. Dora was glad of the interruption. Billy Cody's determination to marry her—which he had sustained now for over ten years—was a bit of an embarrassment. She had first said no to Billy in Abilene, Kansas, and here they were more than ten years later, sipping champagne in Miles City, and Billy was still yearning.

It made her wonder what men had for brains. Billy Cody couldn't be dumb. He had made people believe he had been a great scout, though no one of any experience in the west considered him much of one. More than that, he had worked up his Wild West show and made a fortune with it. So he couldn't be dumb, in the normal sense of the word. And yet he couldn't get it through his head that she had no interest in marrying him. Was he so vain as to think that a pretty buckskin suit would win her over? Or his little beard?

Over the years Dora had listened to a lot of men sneer at Billy Cody. Most of that she put down to envy—people would snipe at anyone with a reputation. She would not have claimed to be an expert on scouting or buffalo hunting or Indian fighting or much of anything, and yet it seemed clear to her that Billy's reputation was not as bogus as people wanted to think. He had worked for various generals—that took some ability. He had killed Yellow Hand—that took some brass. He had also killed lots of buffalo, and he had taken his Wild West show around the world, or at least around part of it. He might be a little silly, but he wasn't lazy, and most of the things he had accomplished took brains. Why did his brain stop working when it came to her?

"Billy, did you come all this way just to propose to me?" Dora asked.

"Well, it's one reason," he said. "I can't stay with Lulu forever. I figure if I keep asking you sooner or later you'll get tired of saying no."

"But what if I don't?" Dora asked pertly. "You'll divorce your wife and I'll still say no. Then what? You'll live a lonely life all because of one hardhearted girl."

"Aw, you ain't hardhearted," Billy said. "That line of talk won't sell."

"Well, it should, because I am," Dora said. "This is fine champagne."

"Doc Ramses picked it out," Billy admitted. "He's quite an expert on wines, and everything else too."

"I remember him now," Dora said. Her memories of the medicine show in Medora had begun to fill out. "He stuck something that was supposed to be a third eye in the middle of his forehead and claimed to be from Egypt or somewhere. Anybody could see that the third eye was just made of glass. But I guess it fooled some of the cowboys—the drunk ones at least. He pretended he could see the future and charged fifty cents for fortunes."

"Let's get him to tell ours," Billy said. "I bet he'd do it for free."

"No, I don't want to know mine, I fear it might be sad," Dora said.

"It won't be sad if you'll consent to marry me," Billy said. "Say, wait till you see Europe, Dora. It's splendid. In France it takes six hours just to eat supper, they have so many dishes."

"I thought you hoped I'd keep my figure, Billy," Dora said, grinning. "I doubt I'd keep it long if I spent six hours at every meal."

"Oh, you just take a dab from each dish," Billy said, feeling suddenly happy. Her light tone enchanted him. Just seeing her smile was worth all the slow miles up the river. Though nothing she had said sounded particularly encouraging, her look was, he decided. His mood lightened so that he felt he might float off the settee. It was his old confidence filling him as full as air fills a balloon. He had felt the same confidence when he'd once raced through the buffalo herds.

The buffalo had fallen, and Dora would fall too—but in a different way. When he had his confidence, nothing had ever been able to stop him, and he had it now. Dora was watching him closely, though; he knew he mustn't be tempted into an impatient act.

"Well, if you ain't ready to marry me yet, will you at least consent to a buggy ride?" he asked. "We could ride out tomorrow and picnic by the Yellowstone. I've had some grand adventures along the old Yellowstone."

"All right, Billy," Dora said. Why stick at a picnic?

"It'll be fine!" Billy said, wondering if he should risk one little kiss.

Darling Jane—

It's snowing tonight, Janey, it snowed all yesterday too. If this keeps up we'll be wintering in the Owl Creek

Mountains I guess. No Ears says we won't, he says it will stop tomorrow. No Ears is seldom wrong about the weather, I hope he ain't wrong this time. I would hate to winter in a place like this—also I would hate to winter anywhere with Jim and Bartle when they are out of sorts with one another.

Bartle was right, we should have stayed in Ten Sleep even if there was little to do, at least you can't get snow-bound in Ten Sleep. But Jim was determined to come look—we tramped around for three days, we saw a few muskrats but no beaver. In one pond we saw some sticks that Jim said had been a beaver house about twenty years ago. What did I tell you? The beaver sold out and left, Bartle said. Jim didn't like him putting it that way. I think myself Bartle is being too surly, he always is if he doesn't get his way.

Why are men so selfish Janey? Even the nice ones like Bartle are selfish and turn surly about the slightest thing. Your father was no different I'm afraid, he was Wild Bill, nobody could tell him anything and nobody better try. Perhaps that is the reason he quit me, I've got a mind of my own. I told him he'd get killed if he stayed in Dead-wood, that's why he quit me—suggesting that somebody might outwit him didn't sit right with Wild Bill. He came in with too much reputation, that's the way it always is, Janey. People will sulk around those with the big reputa-tions, hoping to bring them down. Sure enough a low coward like Jack McCall brought down the great Wild Bill, I have wished a thousand times he had listened to my warning.

So now I am snowed in in the Owl Creek Mountains with two mountain men and an old Indian. It serves me right—I had an opportunity to run a store once, Dora wanted to buy in with me, I've no doubt a few years of storekeeping would have done wonders for my reputa-tion, cleaned it up till it smelled like perfume.

Well there is little perfume to be had in the Owl Creeks. Fortunately Jim shot an elk about the time it started snowing, we are in no danger of running out of meat—or conversation either, Potato Creek Johnny showed up, he's as bad about gold as Jim is about beaver, he was down here prospecting. He couldn't believe his eyes when he looked up from his campfire and seen me and No Ears, the boys were elsewhere at the time, tracking the elk.

Johnny has been in Miles City, the news is that Billy Cody has showed up and is courting Dora again, that man has a hard head. He is taking her on picnics and wants to take her to Europe, I wish him luck, he'll need it, Dora won't go that far from Blue. She won't marry Billy either, even if he does get rid of Lulu—I guess Dora could change, though, people do. They get lonely—think how I would be without the boys.

I might do anything, even marry some old sot or run off with a stranger, who knows?

Jim and Bartle don't admire Billy Cody, they say he is all show. Jim says he couldn't find his way around a corner, I got mad listening to them talk. Billy's got plenty of show all right—he's a showman, why not? But he's been very decent to Dora, I think he has supported her when times were hard. Not many men will do that for a woman once she has turned them down. I told Jim and Bartle to stop running Billy down in my company, they both looked surprised—neither of them expected me to get so hot. Johnny didn't either—he may decide to go look for gold somewhere else, snow or no snow. My temper is uncertain, Janey, it has got loose from me a thousand times. If it gets loose while Johnny is here I might box his ears. He's a small man, I could whip him easily.

Johnny ain't all talk though. At least he did try to help me during that smallpox spring when a boy was dying every day. He brought me supplies and once helped me carry water, I should go easy with him if only because of that. No one else would go near those dying boys.

It's scary how quick sadness comes, Janey. Sometimes it falls on me in a minute, like hail from the sky—for here I am and what's next? I'm glad you don't have to live out here where it's so rough, this elk meat is so tough you have to chew it for an hour just to finish one bite. I'm surprised No Ears can get it down, he has few teeth. But you're in a decent place—it's a consolation. Study hard now and learn to write a graceful hand—then one day when I show up in Deadwood or Miles City I can read a letter from my darling girl.

Your mother,
Martha Jane

6

POTATO CREEK JOHNNY WAS DREAMING OF THE CREEK of gold—a dream that came to him two or three times a year, if he was lucky. He'd be wading in a creek whose water was so thick with gold dust that the flow itself seemed golden. In the dream, fortunately, he had been lucky enough to equip himself with several buckets. He filled the buckets as fast as he could with the golden water and then carried them to shore—all he would have to do was let the gold settle to the bottom of the buckets and he'd be rich. Soon both banks of the creek were lined with buckets, but the creek ran as golden as ever. When he filled his last bucket he waded back into the creek and walked downstream, in golden water up to his knees. Gradually the ground leveled out, and the creek slowed; the gold thickened until it was almost like mud, so stiff you could have spaded it out. Far away, where the stream meandered into a flat plain, all he could see was gold—a vast desert of gold.

For a man who liked gold—and Johnny was such a man—it was the best of all possible dreams; in this case it ended abruptly when the keening mountain wind shook the branch above his head, sending a shower of snow right in his face. For a second he was confused: a slanting ray of sun made the mist of snow above him look like gold dust too. But it didn't feel like gold dust—it felt like fine snow. Johnny sat up and shook as much of it as possible out of his hair.

"I guess it can't snow gold dust," he said to Jim Ragg, who was squatting by the fire. Jim Ragg ignored the comment, as he did whatever was said to him while he was making coffee.

No Ears considered it an interesting comment—it called up a dim memory of some story about the spirit time. It seemed to him that in the spirit time golden snow would not have been unusual, but he couldn't remember whether he was thinking of a story or a dream. It was interesting, though, that Johnny had mentioned it just after waking up, which indicated to No Ears that he had just dreamed it, so probably he himself had dreamed it. too. It was well known that men had dreams in common: his own people often shared their dreams, hoping to glean some information about the behavior of the spirits; but white people, in his experience, were less likely to share their dreams.

"Did you have a good dream?" he asked Johnny, just in case he felt like doing a little dream sharing.

"Better than good," Johnny said. "I dreamed I found the creek of gold."

"I have heard of that creek," No Ears said.

Both Johnny and Jim looked startled. Bartle and Calamity were still asleep, humps in the snow; snow had continued to fall for most of the night.

"Have you ever heard of a gold creek, Jim?" Johnny asked hopefully.

Jim Ragg shook his head—the notion was too silly to comment on. No Ears had probably just decided to have a little sport with Johnny.

Bartle Bone sat up suddenly, and as usual he woke up talking.

"If there was a gold creek there'd be a town bigger than San Francisco built on the banks of it," he said. "They'd build a canal clean across the country and let it all flow east so the Senators and bankers could swim in it.''

''I believe that creek is near the Bosque Redondo,'' No Ears said matter-of-factly. ''The Apaches know where it is.''

''Wake up, Calamity—let's go to New Mexico,'' Johnny said. He couldn't decide whether No Ears was joking or not; the old Indian sat by the fire, looking half dead. On the other hand, what if he knew something? The creek wouldn't have to be as rich as the one in his dream; he could be satisfied with a lot less gold than that.

''If there was any gold in New Mexico, Kit Carson probably stole it,'' Bartle remarked. ''He stole two dollars from me once.''

''Did he pick your pocket or what?'' Calamity asked without stirring.

''No, he just borrowed two dollars and never paid it back,'' Bartle said. ''That's theft, in my view.''

''I hate to think how much you've stolen from me then,'' Calamity said.

She sat up carefully, brushing snow off her buckskin shirt. If snow once got down her neck, she would go around feeling wet all day. She tried to bend her legs and found them reluctant to bend. Her knee joints seemed frozen, and her feet were too cold even to think about. She pivoted on her bottom, swinging her feet around toward Jim's fire. A little snow fell off one foot, causing the fire to sputter and Jim to look annoyed.

''I ain't gonna put out your dern fire,'' she said. ''You don't need to frown at me over a pinch of snow.''

Jim Ragg liked a small, economical fire, one you could crouch by without cooking yourself. Bartle's preference was for a fire that roared and spit and crackled. He piled on three or four logs and soon all were watching the fire warily from a safe distance. Now and then it spat a spark into Potato Creek Johnny's beard.

''Now I can't get close enough to thaw my feet out without setting myself on fire,'' Calamity said, annoyed. Jim underdid the fire, Bartle overdid it; the same went for everything else the two men attempted.

"This is a free country," Bartle said, well aware that his fire met with disapproval in some quarters. "Every one of you is free to build his own fire."

"You didn't build your own fire, you took mine," Jim pointed out.

"I wish I was still asleep," Johnny said. "I get nervous when people argue this early in the morning. Usually when I wake up there's nobody within thirty miles and I avoid the nervousness."

"Who's arguing? We ain't pulled our knives," Bartle said. "If you're so delicate, what are you doing out here with grizzlies like us?"

"I didn't know you was here till yesterday," Johnny explained. On the whole he was rather regretting his visits to the Owl Creek Mountains. Prospecting was better pursued alone.

Taken as individuals, he liked everyone in the group—but that was taking them individually: taken as a group, the matter was less simple. Jim and Bartle were known to be of uncertain temper; as for Calamity, few tempers in the west were as notoriously uncertain as hers. In a time of need there was no stauncher friend—it was in more relaxed times, when nothing particular was needed, that Calamity was apt to flare—and when she flared, the safety of the far horizon seemed a long way away.

Of the group around the fire, only No Ears was really easy to get along with. He said little, expected less, was a brilliant tracker, and a very decent weather prophet. Johnny fervently hoped that his prophecy of fair weather would come true, and that he could escape from the mountains before another blizzard struck. A winter with Jim, Bartle, and Calamity would put quite a weight on his nerves.

Calamity had felt sad in her sleep—every three or four nights, it seemed, she would awake to find herself crying. Some nights she had hardly wanted to doze off for fear of feeling sad in her sleep. Deep sleep wouldn't come, or a good dream either. Sometimes she felt so heavy inside that it was difficult even to roll over and seek a more comfortable position.

After such a night, the day was seldom any better: she woke without enthusiasm, or vigor, or purpose, unable to think of a thing to do that she hadn't done a hundred times, or might really enjoy doing.

"The dumps," she said aloud. "I guess I've just got the dumps."

No Ears didn't change expression—he seldom did—but the three white men all looked at her warily.

"Nobody's gonna appreciate it if you throw a fit, Calamity," Bartle said. "The snow's too deep—you'd catch us without a chase."

"Why would I want to catch you?" Calamity asked. "You can go stick your damn head in a hole for all I care."

There was a long, uneasy silence; then Cody came bounding into camp, a grouse in his mouth. He came to Calamity and, after she had petted him and talked to him a bit, gave her the grouse.

"This dog's a harder worker than any of us," Calamity said. "He's already brought in meat, and what have the rest of us done?"

She looked at Bartle, Jim, and Johnny, all three of whom still wore wary expressions; they looked melancholy and tired. No Ears, by far the oldest man there, was the only one of the group who looked cheerful—and he was an old Indian who had outlived his time and almost all of his people. Nevertheless he didn't look as though he slept sad at night. Even Bartle, who had more natural cheerfulness than the rest of them put together, didn't look as cheerful as he once had. Bartle looked gaunt and low.

It was the first time Calamity was brought up against the fact that Jim and Bartle were sad; she had always thought of them as happy out in the mountains, living the free life. But they didn't look happy this morning, and neither did Johnny, although on the whole she considered Johnny a lighter character—a few specks of gold dust in the bottom of a creek would keep him excited for weeks.

"It's like the snow soaking in," Calamity said, half to herself—she was thinking of her sad sleep. Young, she hadn't slept much; she let it rip most of the night with the cowpokes or the mountain men, the mule skinners and the soldiers; sad thoughts hadn't had much time to penetrate in the few hours she slept.

Now she slept longer, if worse; she didn't do much ripping, and the sorrows had time to seep through and settle on her heart and in her bones, soaking them finally. as the snow soaks through a shirt.

What was surprising was the way a little change in the drift of her thought made everything look different. She had known Bartle and Jim and Johnny when they were young, and in her thoughts they had never changed; years had passed, and then decades, and she still thought of them as young. Perhaps they thought the same about her, still saw her as the young woodchopper who wanted to go west, a girl who could walk all day beside the wagons and sit listening to their stories half the night.

What was obvious, though, looking at the three of them in a cold camp in the Owl Creek Mountains, was that none of them was young; without any of them thinking about it, or even noticing, they had grown old—not *so* old perhaps, in terms of calendar years, but then, what were calendar years to people who had never settled, or wished to settle? The calendar meant nothing; what meant something, in the reaches of the west, were energy, muscle, will—three qualities they had all once had in abundance, otherwise they would not have survived. The prairie ground covered thousands who hadn't survived: fresh boys, brave warriors, skilled men, hopeful and forthright women. Either they hadn't been tough or they hadn't been lucky—or were neither.

"This is silly," Calamity said. "I don't know why it took me so long to admit it. This is just plain silly."

"Are you criticizing my fire?" Bartle asked, puzzled by her tone.

"No, I'm criticizing your damn life," Calamity said. "And Jim's. And Johnny's. And mine. What the hell are we doing here?"

There was a long silence. Calamity rarely asked questions in the morning; she tended to sulk over her coffee;

she seldom became talkative much before the end of the day.

"Just trying to get breakfast, I guess," Bartle said—he had been about to cut himself off a piece of yesterday's elk haunch.

"What's got you so itchy?" he asked, wondering if maybe Calamity might be sick.

"Looking at you sourpusses, that's what," Calamity said. "All three of you look like you belong in a hospital, one that keeps an undertaker handy. Jim looks like he could die any day, and you're mainly skeleton yourself, Bartle. I know I'm no better. I expect I look as rough as sandpaper."

Jim Ragg was a little startled. He knew he hadn't been feeling too brisk lately, but he was a long way from death, in his view.

"That smart little Billy Cody figured all this out years ago," Calamity said. "He changed his direction and made more gold than Johnny's gonna find if he wades in creeks for the next twenty years. All this is silly. There ain't no gold, and there ain't no beaver. There's just four fools and an Indian, and the Indian's just in it for the company. I could be sleeping on a feather mattress in Miles City and not wake up every morning with my knees too froze to bend."

"There could be a vein of gold ten foot thick right here in these mountains," Johnny remarked.

"If there is you won't find it," Calamity retorted. "It's underground, and you ain't a mole."

"I admit Johnny ain't a mole, but what's the point?" Bartle said.

"Billy Cody made the point when he started his Wild West show," Calamity said. "The big adventure's over. It's over, and that's that. He's smart to make a show of it and sell it to the dudes. I think I'll go hire on with him, if he'll have me. It would be more enterprising than sitting around here watching us all get old and die.

"More comfortable, too," she added, holding out her cup.

No Ears poured her some coffee.

Darling Jane—

This bitter cold is something. I put the ink in the cof-
feepot to thaw it, it was froze solid. I am glad that No
Ears decided to come with me, there have been times
when I have trouble making a fire, and without a fire
tonight your mother would freeze for sure.

It's because I have no patience that I'm a bad fire-
maker. If it don't start I get mad, then I decide I'll just
freeze, I think, What's left anyway?

One reason I struggle to write these letters even in this
cold is so you'll know a little bit about me, for I could
someday get ate by a bear, or get my head knocked in by
some tough—these things can happen out in the west
Janey. I gave the boys a big lecture on how the west ain't
wild anymore, it upset their stomachs I guess. It ain't
wild like it once was when just the Indians and the animals had it, but it's still wild enough that someone who
runs loose like I do can get killed pretty quick.

No Ears felt he would like to come with me to Miles
City, I didn't insist but I am plenty glad he came, otherwise I'd worry all day about being able to make the fire.
I have made hundreds, you'd think I'd learn the skill, I
haven't. It even takes No Ears a while, and he is an
expert—finding dry wood is the first problem. Plenty of
men are no better at it than me, one reason Wild Bill
stuck to the saloons is because he couldn't have made a
fire in a week—he liked to stay around where there were
bartenders to pamper him, not to mention girls, there was
a thicket of them, too. As I say, he was handsome.

Well, Janey, my speech to the boys was a shocker,
they didn't like hearing me say Billy Cody was smarter
than them, they didn't want to be told that the fun is over,
either. I guess nobody does, but anyway it is. I think
Bartle is tired of the woods and the prairies, he would not
mind a little city life. He will have a time persuading Jim
though, Jim is stubborn—I have never seen a man with
less give in him than Jim Ragg.

It is deep cold tonight Janey. No Ears told me a story
—he says once on the plains he was about to freeze, there

was no wood and he had no shelter, all that saved him was a crippled buffalo cow he found. The cow was down but not dead, he opened her up and got in her belly. The cow lived till morning, it kept No Ears from freezing. Maybe that's too strong a story for your delicate ears Janey—it is just a story about what people will do to save themselves. I would not like to crawl into a cow buffalo's belly, but then I've got a good fire. Without it a buffalo's belly might look good.

I hope Billy Cody is still there when I get to Miles City, I expect he is unless Dora has chased him off, she will if he ain't careful. The man has always been perfectly nice to me. I should try to reform and not make fun of him like the rest do, after all it is no crime to start a Wild West show. I think Bartle wishes he had thought of it first. He got to the west a long time before Billy did, that don't make it his, though.

It's a wonder this tablet don't catch fire, I am sitting almost in the flames to keep the ink from freezing. Pardon the short letter, it's the fault of the conditions—brisk conditions, Jim calls them.

Your mother,
Martha Jane

7

"I SUPPOSE LIFE'S HARDER FOR WOMEN," BARTLE REflected.

"It's hard enough for me when it gets this cold," Jim Ragg said. It had only been in the last winter or so that he had begun to have difficulty staying warm. His feet pained him a good deal, and his ears got so cold that he occasionally found himself envying old No Ears. In windy weather he shivered most of the day and sometimes shivered at night, even with a good fire.

The difficulty with his feet bothered him most. Beaver meant wading—they didn't just walk out of the water and hand themselves over. In earlier days wading had never bothered him significantly; working in ice water wasn't pleasant, but the excitement of taking beaver made it easy to overlook the inconvenience.

What worried Jim was that his feet now troubled him all winter, and he had done no wading. If they did come upon beaver he wasn't sure he would be up to the work of getting them out.

The thought of standing up to his waist for three or four hours a day in water that was just one degree from ice was a worrying thought. What if he couldn't do it? He'd be the laughingstock of the west.

"It's rare for Calamity to complain," Bartle mentioned. "She's usually of a sunny disposition. I guess we should have left her in Ten Sleep."

As he talked, Jim Ragg glared at him from the other side of the fire. Of course, Jim Ragg rarely sat around smiling, but he often managed to look neutral, at least. This morning he looked hostile.

"Are you planning to murder me for my valuables?" Bartle asked. "You've got a murdering look in your eye."

"I ain't planning to go be in no Wild West show," Jim said. "I wasn't meant for the circus. But if you want to make a fool of yourself, head out. You ain't a woman and don't have Calamity's excuse, though."

"I've never been able to decide whether Calamity *is* a woman," Bartle said, mainly to change the subject. He was not in the mood for an argument about the future, not with Jim sitting there ready to charge. In that respect Jim was like Custer: get him in a tight and all he knew to do was charge. And if he didn't happen to be in a tight, Jim Ragg—like Custer—would charge just for the hell of it.

"I guess she's a woman and you oughta know," Jim said. "I recall you were sweethearts once."

"If we was, I was drunk and slept through it," Bartle said. "When was we ever sweethearts?"

"On that first wagon trip, the one that flooded out at the Arkansas," Jim said. "I seen the two of you sneaking off."

"Oh, that trip," Bartle said. "We did sneak off, but all Calamity wanted was for me to teach her how to throw a knife. She didn't own a gun at the time but she had a fairly good knife."

"Throw a knife?" Jim said, startled by the reply. 'Why would you ever throw a knife?"

"You wouldn't," Bartle said. "Not if you had good sense. Calamity claimed to have read some dime novel— a mountain man threw his knife at a grizzly and killed it.

Or maybe it was an Indian chief he threw it at. I never read the book myself.''

"I never accused you of reading," Jim said.

His mood seemed to be improving slightly, Bartle thought.

"So you thought Calamity and me was in love, is that it?" he asked. "Is that why you've been sullen the last twenty-five years?"

"No," Jim said. "I had no objection to you being her sweetheart, except that you stopped paying attention to business. If you'd paid a little more attention we might not have flooded out.''

Bartle snorted. "My god, Jim—I ain't Moses," he said. "I could have paid attention constantly and not stopped the Arkansas from flooding.''

"How *do* you throw a knife?" Jim asked mildly, realizing that his criticism had no validity. It had been an unusually rainy spring that year, and a rainy spring was clearly not Bartle's fault.

"I don't know," Bartle said. "I never threw one.''

"Then what'd you teach Calamity?"

"Tracking, mostly," Bartle said. "I taught her her tracks—what's a fresh track, and what ain't.''

"I did think you were sweethearts, though," Jim said. "Enough so you'd have no doubt that Calamity is a woman.''

"Nope," Bartle said. "She was quite standoffish, and still is. Once in a while she *does* dress like a woman now, but she didn't on that trip, if you'll remember. She wore pants the whole way.''

"Still, she must be a woman," Jim said. "Her name was Martha Jane. Nobody would name a boy Martha Jane.''

"That's a point," Bartle admitted. "She's still got that odd look, though.''

The sun had been out, but it disappeared; a snow squall was moving toward them from the Black Hills. Dark clouds hid the tops of the mountains.

"I've been thinking we ought to buy ourselves a couple of horses," Jim said.

Bartle felt gloomy, as he always did when the sun vanished. He didn't mind snow as much as he minded clouds.

"Horses to ride or horses to eat?" he asked, not particularly interested.

"To ride—I don't like to eat horse," Jim said.

"I don't like to ride 'em any better than you like to eat them," Bartle declared. "What's wrong with just moving around on our own two feet, like we always have?"

"My feet are getting tired, that's what," Jim said.

Bartle could hardly believe his ears. Jim Ragg, who had been ready to rush over and strangle him not ten minutes earlier, had just said his feet were tired. Bartle did his best to conceal his surprise.

"I ain't as tall as you," Jim reminded him. "This deep snow's troublesome to wade in."

"Yep, that's why snowshoes got invented," Bartle said. "I've always considered the horse a large dangerous animal. I'd about as soon own a bear."

"You *are* contrary," Jim said. "There's nothing wrong with horses."

"There was something wrong with that one that fell on me in Santa Fe," Bartle reminded him. "I guess you don't remember that—I was only busted up for six months."

Jim remembered it, of course. Bartle had been showing off with some cowboys, and a stout young bronc fell with him, rolled on him, and gave him a good kick, to boot.

"That came about from your showing off," Jim reminded him. "There's plenty of tame horses to be had."

"Aw, let's just live on a riverboat during the winter," Bartle suggested. "We could just drift along and watch it snow."

"You'd never agree to anything," Jim said. "You never have. I can't remember why I picked you for a *compañero*. Skinning beaver was the only thing you were ever good at, and you've probably forgotten how to do that."

The snow squall engulfed them; the plains vanished and the campfire began to spit, as swirling flakes fell into it.

"You wouldn't get weather like this in Arizona," Bartle said. "Maybe we ought to go help the old Gray Fox." That was the Indians' name for General Crook.

"You can—I ain't," Jim said. "Crook has been short with me once too often. If I had to vote for him or Geronimo for President I'd vote for Geronimo."

"You're full of surprises today," Bartle said. "I never heard you express an interest in who was President before. Have you ever voted?"

"No, but I'd vote if Crook were running," Bartle said. "I'd vote against him."

"Well, we could still go to Arizona," Bartle said. "We wouldn't have to work for Crook. We could work for Geronimo. Crook would hang us if he caught us, but if he can't catch an Apache I doubt he could catch us."

"I don't know how we'd fare in the heat," Jim said.

It was curious, but over the last several years he and Bartle had become more and more popular with the Indians and less and less popular with the soldiers. They had been at the great encampment on the Little Bighorn only the day before the battle, the guests of He Dog, the Ogalala chief. Gall himself had sat with them, and offered them meat; of course, with such sponsorship, none of the young braves dared lay a hand on them.

There were more Indians there that day than the two mountain men had ever imagined would gather anywhere; in their thirty years in the west they had probably not seen, in the aggregate, that many Indians. They themselves left the camp in a leisurely way, never imagining that the Seventh Cavalry, or any general in command of soldiers in the west, would be so suicidal as to attack such a camp.

Had they encountered Custer—or Reno, Terry, Gibbon, or any of the advancing soldiers—they would of course have pointed out that death awaited them on the Little Bighorn, and would have advised any and all to turn around and skedaddle. But they didn't see anyone, not even the Crow scouts, and gave little thought to conflict until they wandered back toward the encampment and heard the death songs.

The Indians were leaving then, such a mass of ponies and people in motion that it seemed the great plain itself was moving. Cheyenne, Shoshone, Arapaho, Blackfoot, Miniconjou, and the many divisions of the Sioux; Ogalala, Brulé, Teton, Yankton, Santee. Bartle and Jim sat on a low bluff and watched: the plains were covered all morning with the flow of the great exodus.

Watching the departure of the Indian peoples from the valley of the Little Bighorn that day was the most impressive and the most moving thing Bartle Bone had witnessed in thirty years in the west. Jim Ragg felt it, too. What they had stumbled on when they turned back that morning was the last act of a great drama. Jim had never seen a play above the level of a medicine show, but he knew that what he was watching was as great as any play.

"We'll never see nothing like this again," he said to Bartle. "Not in our lifetime."

"Nobody will," Bartle said. "It would be worth dying to see it."

But they hadn't died, and later, when they had gone on up the valley and walked through the chopped-up bodies of the veterans of the Seventh, the carnage had been anticlimactic. They had seen massacres before—smaller ones, admittedly, but the character of massacre varied little. What they had seen earlier—the Indian peoples making the plains move—was a rarer and a greater thing.

"Remember that leaving, Bartle?" Jim asked. Whatever they had been talking about—whether Calamity was really a woman, whether Crook would finally catch Geronimo—left his mind when he remembered the Little Bighorn.

Bartle Bone nodded. He would always remember that leaving.

"That was a glory, wasn't it?" he said.

No Ears woke Calamity out of the best sleep she had had in days. It seemed she always slept better when she was on her way to Dora's. Once she got to Dora's she could let down her guard, but letting down her guard was not wise out in the country.

"I don't want breakfast, leave me alone," she told No Ears.

"I think we better go on to town," No Ears said. "I think a white wind is coming."

That got Calamity's attention—by a white wind No Ears meant a particular kind of blizzard, one that brought with it billions of particles of dry snow. The wind might blow for three days, swirling the snow so densely that it became impossible to see. The white wind confused everything. The best scouts refused to move in a white wind. Cattle moved: they fell off cliffs, piled up in the bottoms of gullies or creeks. Even in town the white winds made life dangerous. Drunks got lost and froze in the street. A man might try to walk to a barn or outbuilding and not be seen again until the snows melted in the spring, when his body would be discovered.

Calamity and No Ears were out of food. They had

parted from the mountain men in a hurry and had forgotten to take their fair share of elk. No Ears scarcely ate, but Calamity had a healthy appetite. She often wished there were some prosperous Indians nearby, because prosperous Indians knew how to feast. She could remember feasts that went on all day in the rich villages of the Sioux.

But in this case there were no Indians nearby. The day before, Calamity had had an easy shot at an antelope but shot high. The antelope stood looking at her so steadily that it unnerved her. "Look off while I'm killing you!" she wanted to say, but then she missed by three feet.

"I should have let you take the shot," she said to No Ears later, feeling guilty. She felt she had let No Ears down, although he had not uttered a word of censure. She hated to shoot with a man looking, even if the man was a kind old Indian who wouldn't think of criticizing her. In earlier years she had argued for her right to take a shot, and, if the situation wasn't critical, Jim and Bartle would sometimes humor her; nine times out of ten she proceeded to miss, which was embarrassing. Her eyesight would waver, she'd lose the front sight of the rifle and finally grow nervous and shoot anyway, hoping to get lucky—which she rarely did.

"Well, you ain't no Annie Oakley," Bartle would sometimes say dryly as a deer or an antelope scampered away.

"I've seen you miss—you ain't no Annie Oakley neither!" Calamity reminded him, but she was embarrassed, anyway.

Annie Oakley was a prodigy. How many men *or* women did they think could shoot like Annie?

But the fact was, she and No Ears were meatless, and the prospect of spending three days meatless and also fireless—you didn't dare leave the camp to gather firewood—was enough to get her moving.

Even so, it was Satan who found the town. No Ears settled himself behind the saddle and held onto her and they raced, Cody running beside them, but they were still some distance from Miles City when the snow began to swirl up from under Satan's belly like steam. It rose higher, swirling so densely that she couldn't see Satan's head; she couldn't see the saddle horn, much less Cody or the road. It was terrifying—a white blindness so total that Calamity wanted to shut her eyes. She did shut them but immediately grew afraid. They had been racing beside the river. What if Satan accidently veered onto the ice and they went through? She felt she would prefer almost any death to a blind, icy drowning. She had seen corpses pulled from the ice, terror frozen on their faces.

Time and place were both lost in the white wind.

"Are you still there?" Calamity tried to ask, disturbed for a moment by the thought that No Ears might have fallen off. No Ears didn't answer, and she felt silly. How could a man without ears hear anything in such a situation? Reaching down, she felt his hands around her waist and was reassured.

Satan had been galloping; as the storm thickened he slowed to a trot, then to a walk. Calamity gave up thinking; she just rode. After a time it seemed to her that Satan was walking very slowly—perhaps he was on the ice. Then she realized he wasn't moving at all; he had stopped. With the snow blowing past them so constantly she had not noticed when he stopped.

She felt No Ears slide off the horse and had a moment of panic. Was the old man going to leave her? Where were they? Then she felt his hand on her leg—he was going to pull her off. For a moment Calamity didn't trust this—at least she was in the saddle, where she knew where she was. If she dismounted, in a second she could be lost, entirely lost.

No Ears tugged insistently and Calamity continued to grip the saddle horn in a death grip—it was her one point of location. But her reason struggled with the panic and fought it down. No Ears had saved her from a white wind once before. He had led her into Fort Fetterman at the end of a rope. He knew more than she did; she had better trust him. She swung off the horse and Satan vanished. Oh, no, we're lost, she thought, but No Ears clutched her coat. She took a step and her toe hit something that felt wooden. She kicked and felt it again. There seemed to be a shape in the snow. Suddenly a box of light opened just ahead of her. A shadow crossed the box; two hands grabbed her and pulled her into the tunnel of light.

"You beat all, out in this weather—nobody but you would be out in this weather!" a voice said, a little crossly. It took Calamity a moment to place the voice: her ears were too full of the sound of wind.

"Doosie?" she said.

It was Doosie; then Trix and Skeedle and the Ree boy they called Teat crowded around her. They got her out of the buffalo coat and sat her in a chair in the warm kitchen of the Hotel Hope. Calamity knew she was there, she could see she was there—No Ears, undisturbed but hungry, was already eating a bowl of Doosie's famous moose-shank soup. She herself didn't feel present enough to eat, though, or present enough to talk. It seemed she had left herself outside in the ghost-making wind. She felt so sure she was going into her ghost-life that a new panic took her: perhaps she had gone! Doosie and Trix and Skeedle didn't realize they were dealing with a ghost. They were all fussing over her, pulling her coat off, sweeping the snow off her coat with a broom, bringing her towels, talking, exclaiming, interfering, busy live people who didn't seem to notice or care that the body they were fussing over had been emptied out, blown out, left vacant. Calamity wished they would understand that.

Then there was Dora.

"Leave her be a minute, she's still scared," Dora said. She pulled up a chair and took Calamity's hand.

"Martha Jane, you're safe," Dora said.

Calamity began to weep. It was not true that she was a ghost. Dora DuFran, her friend, had arrived just in time to save her. Dora hugged her as she cried.

9

TEAT ONLY HAD TWO HOPES IN LIFE: TO MARRY TRIX, and to go with Mr. Cody and be in his Wild West show. Neither would be easy to achieve, he knew. Trix was the most popular whore at the Hotel Hope; though he had reason to believe that Trix was fond of him, it was rare that he got to spend much time with her.

Mr. Cody had been friendly on a number of occasions, and had even tipped him once for fetching his cigars from the buggy on a day when it was raining, but that was not the same as being asked to be in his show. Teat worried every day that Mr. Cody and Dr. Ramses would get up and ride out of Miles City without taking him with them, in which case he would be down to one hope.

In the meantime, while waiting for his hopes to come true, Teat had been assigned to Calamity, who had yet to recover her spirits after her desperate ride in the blizzard. She had become ill, and rarely got out of bed. Many times Teat saw her weep, though she seemed, from what he could see, to be undamaged. Some people got their feet frozen off in blizzards, or even their hands, but Calamity still had her hands and feet.

Hearing the lady weep made Teat want to go away. He

wished that Trix would immediately agree to marry him, and that Mr. Cody would take them both someplace they could be happy far from Montana.

It was clear to Teat that no one in Montana was able to be happy. The feeling the men brought with them into the Hotel Hope was a feeling of sadness, and that was also the feeling of most of the women who lived there; it was the feeling, as far as he could tell, of most of the people who lived in the town.

Miss Dora, the kindest person Teat knew, was herself unhappy unless Mr. Blue was visiting, and he wasn't visiting very often. Skeedle's children had died; she would cry whenever she thought of them. Doosie had long been parted from her family and was mainly in a low mood—so low, some days, that she would forget to cook. The thin whore named Ginny rarely felt well and almost never smiled.

Trix was much the most cheerful person at the hotel, which was one reason Teat had determined to marry her. He himself needed a lot of help staying happy, and Trix was the only one who tried to help him in his efforts.

"Teat, go outside and dig a hole or something," Trix would say, if she found him looking gloomy. "What does a cute boy like you have to be gloomy about?"

Teat took Trix's words to be command; he went outside and attempted to dig a hole in the icy ground, but Miss Dora looked out the window and saw him. In a minute she came to the back steps and informed him that Trix had only been teasing. "It's the wrong season for hole-digging," Dora said, amused by the boy's literalness.

Teat's family had been wiped out in a pointless skirmish around the time of the battle of the Rosebud. He showed up in town with a trader who claimed to have gotten him from the Crows. He was an appealing boy: Dora had liked his looks and persuaded the trader to leave him with her. He had been with her now for six years and was a good worker, though a little small for his age—he must have been at least fourteen. At some stage, too little food or too much misery had affected his physical development, though not his brain. He had learned to read English almost without help, and when there was nothing to do could always be found in the kitchen, reading stories to Doosie out of the magazines Dora took. Everyone liked the boy.

One of the biggest problems Teat had to contend with at the Hotel Hope was his name. Miss Dora had thought he ought to change it—she had suggested several names, but Teat was nervous about making such a change. He discussed the matter with No Ears, explaining that his name had nothing to do with bad morals, as some white people seemed to think. He had been a dark baby, as dark as a cow buffalo's teat, thus his name.

Privately No Ears thought the boy's parents had been in error to name him Teat—a name derived from some part of a he-buffalo would have been more appropriate, since the boy himself was a he. But he knew that naming was an imprecise affair; parents experiencing all the bother of a new baby often chose the first name that came into their minds. Witness his own name, Two Toes Broken. If the horse had not stepped on his tiny foot, he might have started life under an entirely different name.

No Ears didn't discuss his reservations with Teat. He was a nice boy with excellent manners, and if he wanted to keep the name, that was all right.

Morning was Teat's favorite time at the Hotel Hope. Dora kept the doors closed until two. Often the last customer didn't depart much before dawn, and after a busy night it took some time for the staff to make the place presentable again; time, too, for the girls to make *themselves* presentable. Usually they would begin to drift down in the late morning, to drink coffee and experiment with one another's hair.

In Teat's tribe, only warriors had taken as much trouble with their hair as Trix and Skeedle and Ginny. They were always examining Miss Dora's papers and magazines, looking for pictures that might suggest interesting new ways to fix their hair. Teat, who was busy at that hour emptying cuspidors and sweeping out debris, was often required to give his opinion on a particular experiment. Once he had been laughed out of the house for innocently suggesting that bear grease might improve the look of their hair. The women had laughed so hard that his feelings had been a little hurt. What was wrong with bear grease? In his tribe everyone had known that it was good for your hair—but the women in the Hotel Hope saw matters differently.

Trix knew Teat was in love with her; it was good news, as far as she was concerned. He was such a nice-looking boy, and so well mannered, that it would be a feather in any woman's cap to have him in love with her. "Teat's my real sweetheart," she was fond of saying, even in company—and in a way, she meant it.

The first time Dora heard her say it she immediately asked Trix to come to her room for a little chat. Trix was a child of the California gold fields; she had grown up in San Francisco, where attitudes about romance were somewhat more advanced than they were in Miles City. Dora had never been to San Francisco, but she assumed that such a great city would breed more advanced attitudes than one could expect to find in a frontier town on the plains.

"I wouldn't be calling Teat your sweetheart in front of the customers," Dora cautioned.

"Well, he is, why can't I say it?" Trix said, rather hotly—Trix was young and defiant. To Dora she looked Italian.

"It might get him hurt, that's why," Dora said. "A good many of the customers want to think you're *their* sweetheart. That's why they come—to have a sweetheart for a few minutes."

"I guess I can pick my own sweetheart," Trix complained, still hot. "My customers just come to slobber and squirt off. They're ugly. Who wants an ugly sweetheart?"

"Nobody, but plenty of people have one," Dora said. "Be in love with Teat—I don't care. Just don't mention it in front of customers. They don't like Indians in this town, and plenty of hard men show up here. If one of the hard ones decided he was in love with you, and then got jealous of Teat, what do you think would happen?"

"I don't know what would happen," Trix said, defiance replaced by a look of uneasiness. Her black eyes snapped when she was angry, but they weren't snapping now.

"What?" she asked timidly.

"They'd probably just shoot Teat down," Dora said. "Or else make up a party of drunks and take him out and hang him."

Trix left in tears at the thought that such a fate might befall Teat. Dora mentioned the matter to Calamity one morning, hoping to get her interested in something. Calamity was still low. She spent her days in bed, staring out the window at the snowy plains. Dora had seen her low before, but never for so long. Nothing interested her, nothing pleased her.

"You think I ought to send Teat away before something bad happens?" Dora asked.

"No. If they get after him just send him up here," Calamity said. "I'll shoot it out with 'em. I'd just as soon go out in a gunfight as to just get old and die."

"Don't you vex me—you will if you talk about dying," Dora said. "Here you've got a clean room to rest in, and Billy Cody sent you candy. Don't be talking about gunfights."

In fact, Billy had been the soul of courtesy. He had sent Calamity candy three times, visited her often, and offered her employment in his show. Calamity had scarcely responded, though the candy had disappeared little by little.

"I got no complaint about Billy," Calamity added— she felt a little guilty about having received him so listlessly. After all, she had risked her life coming to hire on; why couldn't she just say she'd hire on? Somehow the words stuck in her throat, along with all other words.

"Billy's perfect," she said, a little later. "If you had good sense you'd marry him."

"We won't talk about that," Dora said quickly. "I can't marry him, and anyway he *is* married."

"*Won't* marry him, you mean," Calamity said, stirring a little at the thought of Dora's stubbornness in refusing good-looking Billy Cody.

"Won't or can't—it's between me and Billy," Dora reminded her, feeling her temper rise. It almost always rose when she and Calamity got on the subject of matrimony. Calamity, who had never got within a mile of being married, nonetheless felt perfectly free to advise her on the matter.

"You won't even go to work for him, yet you expect me to marry him!" Dora said more loudly, her temper rising higher.

"Oh, shush down and bring me a rifle," Calamity said. "I want to be ready, in case I have to shoot."

Dora turned toward the window; when she turned back, Calamity saw tears on her cheeks—once again she had gone too far.

"Can't you get mad without crying?" Calamity said meekly.

"No—I can't and you know it!" Dora said.

"Don't bring me the rifle," Calamity said. "You might shoot me with it. I think I'll get up and get drunk."

It took another hour for her to actually get out of bed and into her clothes, but she did it. Then, while she was downstairs at the bar in the process of fulfilling her resolution, the door to the kitchen swung open and T. Blue walked in, his cheeks red from the chill, and his spurs jingling.

"Howdy, cowboy," Calamity said, feeling better already.

10

"STOP DRINKING THAT DAMN BEER AND DRINK WHISKEY with me," Calamity demanded, an hour later. She was glad to see Blue; he was one of those rare fellows who stayed so cheerful himself that his arrival could lift the spirits of a whole town, at least if it was a small town. For some reason, though, he was being irritatingly proper, sipping beer like a Missouri farmer and looking lofty as a deacon.

"Now, Martha, I'm reformed," Blue said. "I have been asked to stand for judge, and a judge can't be drinking too much whiskey. I might show up in court drunk and hang the wrong fellow."

"I consider that a joke," Calamity said. "A territory that would consider making you a judge has reached a bad pass. I'd probably be the first person you'd arrest, and I've known you all my life."

She did like cowboys, though, Calamity reflected. Blue seemed to be the only one in the room, and he shone like a flare. The miners, gamblers, mule skinners, and general drifters just didn't have the shine Blue had. He was looking over the room as he sipped beer, sizing up the card games and flattering the whores with an occasional casual glance. Of course, the glances he bestowed on Ginny and Skeedle and Trix had to be mighty casual, for Dora was likely to come down any minute. Word would soon get out that Blue was there—someone would holler his name, or Dora would just sense it.

"I suppose you heard I nearly got lost in a blizzard," Calamity said. She looked around for No Ears. In her mind the old man had saved her twice, for when she'd stepped off Satan in the blizzard she felt sure she would have stumbled off in the wrong direction and never seen the box of light if he hadn't kept a firm hold on her coat. Since then she liked to be reassured that No Ears was still around. If he wandered off and died—or if he just wandered off and left her—she knew she was going to be very afraid.

"It's the talk of the Territory," Blue said. "I prefer to stay in camp and trim my toenails on days when the snow's blowing. I got my directions mixed once in one of them blows and was in the middle of Canada before I noticed my mistake. I had a hell of a time getting the cattle back, too," he added.

"Yes, but you deserve trouble," Calamity said. "I don't."

Blue was far too nonchalant to bat an eye at her remark. Though his nonchalance was what made him so appealing, there were times when he overdid it. This was one of the times—she felt like kicking him in the kneecaps.

"Now what would tempt you to say a wild thing like that?" Blue asked. "Who's that dwarf over there?"

Doc Ramses had just walked through the swinging doors. If he had been a few inches shorter he could have walked under them. As usual he wore his yellow tie with the big stickpin in it.

Fred, who was perched at the head of the banister, had taken a fancy to Doc Ramses. He walked down the banister and squawked until the Doc came over and offered him an arm to perch on.

"He's a fortune-teller," Calamity said. "He works

with Billy Cody. They say he's even told the fortune of the Queen of England.''

''I bet he made up some pretty lies that time,'' Blue said. ''The Queen of England could chop your head off if you gave her a bad fortune.''

''Billy's been courting Dora,'' Calamity informed him. ''He brings her champagne once or twice a day. I bet he'd bring her bouquets, too, if he could find one in Miles City in the winter.''

''I seen that dwarf before,'' Blue said. ''I just can't think where. I expect he's a train robber or something.''

''You're going to be mighty annoyed when Dora marries Billy,'' Calamity said. ''You'll lope into town one day and find she's gone to China or somewhere.''

''Why, Dora wouldn't marry that rooster,'' Blue said.

''What makes you think she won't?'' Calamity asked.

''Well, what if she didn't like China?'' Blue said. ''She'd be stuck.''

''You're married—are you stuck?''

''I'm bogged, but I ain't quite stuck yet,'' Blue said with his winning grin. He looked up and saw Dora watching them from the head of the stairs.

''There she is now—she still looks like my girl,'' he said.

Dora had been watching them for some time, trying to fight down her feelings before descending to the saloon. She was not succeeding, though—it was like fighting down a flood. Struggling with the flood left her trembly in the legs, a feeling she hated. T. Blue looked as happy as ever; she wondered sometimes if he could imagine the heartache he caused her, coming and going. Sometimes she began to fear his going almost at the moment of his arrival. Where was the time for joy in such a life?

And yet, if he never came, would there ever be a time of joy? Or would it all just be the dumps, as Calamity called her low spells? Was it better to be up sometimes than down all the time?

There were other questions, no less difficult, that she had had to struggle with lately. Billy Cody had been awfully nice—he was dependable, amusing, unfailingly sweet; and he had convinced her that he meant to divorce his wife. Sometimes her heart ached a little for Billy, at the thought of how hard he was trying. It was sad that the one who tried should always fail, while the one who never tried always succeeded. Just the other day Billy had brought her a sled, and they sledded merrily downhill, once almost shooting onto the frozen Yellowstone. He didn't fail at making her have fun, at least. Sometimes she had the urge to try a little harder herself, to reward Billy for all his gay effort—she was tired of the flood inside her. Wouldn't peace be better, even if it meant damming the flood and keeping it dammed—a tricky task?

But damming the flood, if she could do it, might really not be kind to Billy, in the end. Billy was smart—discreet, but smart. He was not like most men, who had to have even simple things spelled out in capital letters several times before they could grasp them; Billy had surprised her recently by being ahead of her in his thinking, rather than behind, where she was accustomed to locating men. However thick the dam she built, Billy would soon figure out that the flood was still there, and that if it broke free again, as it always could, his nice love would be like chaff, like a straw.

Billy hadn't been able to change her much—not enough that she could be nice to him in the way she sometimes hoped to; but he *had* wedged his way into her life, sheer energy being the wedge. Where she had once had only one problem to contend with, she now had two, and one of them stood below her at the bar, drinking beer and teasing Calamity.

"Dora ain't hurrying on down this morning, is she?" Blue remarked. Now and then he stole a glance at her. She still stood in a darkness at the top of the stairs.

"Why should she? What would be to hurry for, unless it's to slap your face?" Calamity asked. "She's mad at me because I went to your dern wedding—you can figure out from that how mad she must be at you."

"Oh, damn!" Blue said. "That nonsense again. I would hardly subject my Dora to the raw ranch life—the first hard winter would kill her."

"I'd rather die of life than die of nothing," Calamity said.

"I'd know about the nothing," she added, sliding her glass across the bar. Teat, who was bartending at the time, poured her a little whiskey.

"I guess I've rode a long way in the slush to drink beer and be criticized," Blue said. He felt a little dip in his spirits. It was rare anymore that he got as simple a welcome as he felt capable of giving. The welcome was there, he had no doubt—it just took longer and longer to arrive at it.

Calamity was about to deliver a few more opinions when the saloon door swung open once more and Billy Cody stood in it, wearing a coat made of otter skins.

"There's Billy, this will be interesting," she said.

"Why, T., what a surprise," Billy said, though it wasn't, exactly. He offered his hand. Blue took it, a bit irked to discover that he was actually glad to see Billy. In his mind he had been ready to punch him but the minute Billy strode over and held out his hand the thought vanished. The man had an irritating likability as long as you were in his company; the minute he stepped out the door, though, the conviction that he was extremely irritating returned.

"Billy, you look prosperous," Blue said. "Do you find that the Chinese like cowboys?"

"Oh, we ain't tried China yet," Billy said. "I hope to get there eventually."

Then, as if remembering someone he had forgotten to speak to, Billy looked toward the head of the stairs. Blue looked, and Calamity looked also, but all they saw was an empty staircase. Dora DuFran was not there.

"So where's Dora—having a nap?" Billy asked.

"I expect she's having a nap," Calamity said.

Darling Jane—

Janey you'll have to forgive your mother, I have let months slip by without taking up a pen, I have no excuse. I just got low and lost the habit. Nearly dying in the blizzard was a setback, I could not get over it although I was not seriously ill, was only exposed to the blizzard a few hours and have been at Dora's ever since, my room is as cozy as yours is in Springfield I guess.

It was a long winter though—on the first spring day I thought I had better ride Satan before he forgets me, I had not rode him since he brought me to Dora's back door in the blizzard.

The snow had about melted off the prairies, it was muddy but a pretty day anyway, I thought I'd take a little ride to see if I'm game for adventure with the boys this summer. Not five miles out of town I jumped the grizzly. That old roaring bear scared Satan so bad he nearly threw me, I lost both stirrups, the saddle horn was all that saved me. If I had been thrown the grizzly would have had me for sure. I think the bear had just woke up—he didn't follow or he would have caught us for sure. I met No Ears before I got to town, he looked worried, I think he smelled the bear, he can smell things most men cannot smell, even Satan didn't smell this bear and horses usually do.

Blue wanted to get out of bed and go shoot the bear. Despite his bad experience the time he roped the bear he still thinks he is a bear-killer I guess. Of course Dora wouldn't have it, she had not nursed him for the broken leg and collarbone for him to go off and get ate by a bear. Few know the true story of Blue's injury, certainly his wife doesn't, Billy Cody doesn't either.

When he found Billy in town Blue pretended to ride off, he waited till night and then snuck back and tried to climb up Dora's drainpipe. He will try anything—it broke and he had a fall, the ground was frozen and no fun to fall on. The story Blue put out was that his horse pitched him into a woodpile, I guess a cowboy would feel better about being pitched into a woodpile than he would about falling off a drainpipe. Certainly it will sound better to Blue's wife. Who knows what she expects of Blue? I doubt she expects him to be climbing drainpipes in the winter, it's not common behavior.

The upshot was Dora got to have him for six weeks while he was mending. They were quite lovey-dovey. It was a rare opportunity for Dora, and Blue got nursed so well I imagine he'll come back and try to break something next winter, Dora's nursing has got to be an improvement over ranching in the blizzards up in the Musselshell.

Billy Cody finally went off. If he was discouraged by Blue's stroke of luck you couldn't tell it—Billy don't let much discourage him. He is getting together the biggest Wild West show of all, he has even got Sitting Bull to agree to be in it. I finally agreed to try it too, if old Sitting Bull thinks he can stand it I guess I can stand it also.

Janey, being scared by the blizzard and then by the bear has made me moody, it takes nothing to make me cry. Yesterday Doosie made me a pie and I cried, she thought I didn't like it and got upset. It don't take much more to upset Doosie than it does to upset me. I did like the pie, I made it up with Doosie later, we ate the whole thing ourselves except for a little piece Doosie gave Teat. There was none for Blue, he was outraged, Dora has spoiled him so now he thinks every sweet has to be for him.

In these low moods I will cry over anything, I cry because I miss you, Janey. I fear I will be old soon or even dead and never know my girl. Then I get to thinking of Wild Bill, if I could see him as I once saw him, if I could love him as I once loved him I would be the happiest woman in these territories. Well, Jack McCall spoiled that.

Lost is lost, why think of it? If the sun would shine more maybe I'd stop. Now Blue has gone back to his ranch and his wife, Dora is terribly down, she got used to Blue being here.

I told her it would happen and that it would take her six months to get over it when he got well and left. She got mad of course. What do you want me to do, send him off crippled? she said. I am sure Billy Cody saw through the woodpile story, he's a bulldog, I expect he thinks Dora will get tired of Blue sooner or later, she'll play out from all the coming and going.

Billy is younger than both of them, I guess he thinks he's got time on his side. Don't you listen to people who say bide your time, Janey, nobody knows if they've got time on their side or how much, younger people than Billy Cody have died in this country. Blizzards or bears or ruffians, there's plenty of things that can get you and get you quick.

I don't know why you would even want to read these letters, Janey. I mean to write cheerful things and then I write of dying. You are just a child and should not have to always be reading such things.

It takes a lot to amuse me when I am like this. Doc Ramses the fortune-teller was some help while he was here. He was a magician, he'll slap Teat on the cheek and pull a bear tooth out of his ear. Once he stuck a glass eye on his forehead and looked at me strangely, he said he knew a secret about me nobody else knew. I got annoyed, he knows nothing about me, he can't see much with a glass eye.

Still some of his tricks were funny and helped pass the time, but then Billy got restless to go round up Sitting Bull and all the other people in the Wild West show. They left a week before Blue left, now the town feels empty. Dora stays in her room all day and Skeedle is in vile spirits too, the other day we were all the three crying at the same time.

I said to both of them, we ought to hang ourselves if we can't do better than this, they agreed, but we won't do it, no energy.

I had word that Ragg and Bone are in Deadwood, it does not sound good, Jim is sick. I am going to head that way in a few days, No Ears said he would go. He is very interested in Doc Ramses's magic, he says it is better than most medicine men can do.

I am awfully scared of bears now, I'm almost too scared to ride to Deadwood and Deadwood ain't far. I had no fear once, I would just ride on by a grizzly if I saw one, none ever bothered me. No Ears says we will be safe, he doesn't smell any bears on the road to Deadwood. I think he is just bragging, nobody can smell every animal between Miles City and Deadwood.

Do you ever see the morning star in Springfield, Janey? I saw it today, the clouds broke, it shone so bright it made me sad and lonesome. I got up and knocked on Dora's door, she was just sitting there in her chair by the window. I felt silly for knocking, what was I going to say, Look at the star? But Dora wasn't mad, she invited me to come sit with her, I sat there with my thoughts, she sat there with hers.

I don't know what Dora was thinking about but that bright star called back old times for me—sad times, some of them. I remember when I went with Custer and his expedition into the Black Hills, it was the first big expedition to go there, it was a mistake. The Sioux didn't like it, and the land was theirs by treaty.

But Custer went in anyway and discovered gold, how I hated him, he looked at me as if I was no better than a cow, I can't describe his cold look. It was hard, Janey, all those soldiers and me. I tried to hire on to scout, at least I knew the main trails and the Indians didn't mind me, I didn't make a penny, Janey, they even begrudged me food. I finally offered to do laundry for the soldiers, otherwise I suppose they would have let me starve.

I hope you will never experience such hardship as your mother has, Janey, I was washing the soldiers' old filthy clothes in the same creek Custer discovered the gold in. All I got for that work was a little grub, I finally left camp alone, the Sioux were kinder to me. I guess they thought I was crazy, but they fed me and I wasn't asked to do no washing.

I knew then that war would come. What is a treaty when there is gold in the bottom of the creeks? It was that damn Custer that found it too, I hated him. He sat outside his tent feeding his pack of hounds while I washed clothes in the creek. Custer's dogs ate better than I did—you don't forget such things.

I shed no tears for Custer when he fell. I lost many friends in the battle—of course I regret they got massacred, it was all Custer's doings, he behaved as if he could do no wrong. I saw him quirt soldiers for the least little thing, he deserved what he got, good riddance.

You will read of all this in the histories, Janey, do not let them tell you Custer was a hero, he was cold and careless, listened to no one. If he had listened to his Crows he would have lived—of course the Crows knew what was waiting for him.

This will not interest you much, I am sorry to write at such length. The days drag sometimes. Ordinarily I'd just mount up and go, that's what people have always done out here—they mount up and go. But my nerve is not what it used to be—that's all there is to it.

Your mother,
Martha Jane

11

BARTLE HAD NEVER HAD SUCH A TIME WITH JIM RAGG. Jim did not appear to be very sick, not by the standards of the day—a phrase Bartle enjoyed using—but nothing Bartle could devise or invent had any effect on Jim's spirits, which descended rapidly once they arrived in the vicinity of Deadwood, and had so far refused to rise again.

"Your spirits are at worm level," Bartle remarked one day. "Camping with you is like camping with a worm. You wiggle once in a while, but you don't put out no conversation."

Jim was thoroughly tired of Bartle's efforts to cheer him up. He decided to prove Bartle's point by saying nothing. Maybe if he said nothing Bartle would shut up, though it wasn't likely.

At Jim's insistence they had camped about twenty miles from Deadwood, east toward the plains. Being in a settled community was more than Jim felt he could tolerate. Deadwood had its raw side, but it was still a settled community and Jim preferred to avoid it.

Many years before, not far from their present camp, Jim had killed the largest grizzly bear anyone had ever seen. Bartle had been in the camp at the time and not present at the kill, but when he walked out and saw the carcass he agreed that it was the largest bear *he* had ever seen.

Then three Sioux warriors came riding up—later they admitted that they had come with the intention of killing Jim and Bartle, but the sight of the great bear carcass distracted them from their purpose. They lost all thought of killing.

News quickly spread; before the sun set that day two hundred Indians or more had come to see the bear. As a gesture of courtesy, being conscious that they were guests in the Black Hills and not necessarily welcome guests, the mountain men gave the bear to the Sioux. The gift was accepted with dignity and the mountain men were invited to the feast that followed. The feast was a nervous occasion, though. Several important warriors— Black Moon, Pretty Bear, and Slow—were there; they were young men and had not yet acquired the fame that would attend them in later years, but it was not the young warriors who caused the feast to be such a nervous occasion.

The problem was a medicine man, an old Sioux whose eyesight was weak. As the feast was just commencing, the medicine man had a vision and announced that it had been a terrible mistake to kill the bear. He claimed that the beast had been the Grandmother Bear.

Indeed, the grizzly had been a she-bear. The medicine man felt the great skull of the she-bear and chanted and carried on for a long while. The Indians became fearful and somewhat agitated, the mountain men fearful and agitated, too. It was undoubtedly a giant she-bear, but did that mean it was the Grandmother Bear? The medicine man predicted that the end of the world might come as a result of the death.

Then, in the midst of the feast, a shower of falling stars was observed, which continued for half an hour. This alarmed the Indians still more; it seemed as if the medicine man's prophecy might come true almost immedi-

ately. A kind of panic resulted, during which Jim and
Bartle slipped away. They headed south, traveled only
by night, and didn't stop until they were two hundred
miles below the Platte. They counted themselves lucky
not to have been killed on the spot, and felt they would
have been, had they not been invited guests. But the
word would spread, and they knew they could expect a
violent welcome in the lodges of the Sioux for some time
to come.

They didn't return to the Dakotas for more than ten
years, by which time the old medicine man's prophecy
had proved to be invalid; the world had not ended, after
all, and the Sioux who were still alive and remembered
the great bear had decided it had merely been a very large
she-bear, and not the Grandmother Bear. In Sioux opinion the Grandmother Bear would never have delivered
herself up to the white man's bullet anyway.

"It wasn't a mile from here that I killed the big bear,"
Jim remarked. "I think that was probably the biggest
bear that was ever grown."

"You would think it, since you shot it," Bartle said.
"It was a large bear but not the biggest that was ever
grown—in Canada bears get twice that size."

"How would you know?" Jim asked. "You've never
been to Canada."

"I've never been to the moon, either," Bartle said.
"That don't mean I doubt it exists. Everybody knows
bears grow bigger in Canada."

"Name one person that knows it," Jim demanded.

"Lonesome Charley knows it," Bartle replied immediately—on the rare occasions when Jim could be
taunted into asking a question, he liked to have an answer
close at hand.

"Lonesome Charley is no judge of bears," Jim said.
"He's only got one eye. Of course a bear will look bigger
if you've only got one eye to look out of."

Bartle was making a stew as they talked. They stew
consisted of a squirrel and a few wild onions. The squirrel
had been so inept as to actually fall out of a tree. It had

landed right at his feet and he had brained it with his gun stock. Jim's rejoinder took him so completely by surprise that for a moment he was speechless. Why would anyone suppose that the loss of one eye doubled the size of what one looked at? And yet, that seemed to be what his friend had suggested.

"What you just said was so crazy I don't want to discuss bears anymore," Bartle said.

But Jim's memory had seized on the bear and the Sioux feast and the old medicine man's prophecy.

"Suppose it was the biggest bear ever grown," Jim said. "If it was, then that old blind Sioux was right. The world started ending about then. The biggest bear was dead—the west won't ever grow one that big again. That's a kind of ending."

"You're paddling with the wrong end of the paddle," Bartle said. "The world ain't ending and the old man was wrong. If you enjoyed town life we'd be eating better, too."

Bartle saw that Jim's gaze had frozen suddenly. He looked where Jim was looking and saw three riders watching them from a ridge to the north. It startled him so that he almost overturned the squirrel stew. Riders on a ridge had often made him jump—they could be hostile, and there could be a hundred more just beyond the ridge.

"What do you think?" Jim asked.

"That there ain't enough stew to go around," Bartle said. "It's just one squirrel."

"If they're killers it won't matter," Jim said. "Are they white or Indian? I can't tell."

Bartle couldn't tell either. All he could see were three dots on a ridge—now that he looked with more attention it seemed to him that he saw less. He would not even have sworn the figures on the ridge were mounted men. They might be men without horses, or horses without men, for that matter. They might be elk. It was unlikely they were buffalo, a thought he immediately voiced.

"I don't think they're buffalo," he said.

"Of course not—what a fool!" Jim said. "There's no buffalo now."

"I wish No Ears was here," Bartle said. "He could smell them and help us judge the danger. It's awful to be so weak-eyed you can't see your own murderers coming."

Jim kept his eyes on the ridge—he was pretty sure the dots were mounted men, approaching slowly.

"I am embarrassed," Bartle admitted. "Something must have happened to my eyes during the winter—and to yours, too."

The dots dipped from sight and didn't reappear for fifteen minutes, during which the mountain men ate the stew. Bartle ate more rapidly than usual.

"Are you gobbling that stew because you don't want to share it?" Jim asked. "Those was probably just elk we saw."

"I think those were Blackfoot we saw," Bartle conjectured. He knew it was a wild guess, but then why not guess wild?

"You ate that stew so fast it drowned your brain," Jim said. "The Blackfoot country is hundreds of miles away. What would Blackfoot be doing here?"

"Looking for old-timers to scalp," Bartle said. "There's fewer and fewer old-timers. They have to travel a good ways from home to find one worth scalping."

The dots emerged from a valley, no longer dots. They were very obviously three men on horseback, and they were not Blackfoot, either.

"It's Lumpy Neck, Billy Cody, and a short fellow," Jim said. "I expect Billy paid Lumpy Neck to track us."

Lumpy Neck was an old drifter they had known since their days on the Santa Fe trail. He had once been an indefatigable rider with a great reputation—he was said to have been the most daring rider ever to ride for the Pony Express. When that played out he had switched to stage driving and had driven stages over the high passes to California. Once the railroad put him out of business, he merely drifted, doing little insofar as anyone knew. Miles, Crook, Custer, and several other generals sought his services as a scout, but he refused to have any dealings with the military. He considered the whole west his home and could be encountered anywhere in it. He had an enormous goiter, thus his name, which some said had been given him by Crazy Horse. Jim and Bartle knew that to be a lie, for they had met the man in Albuquerque long ago, when Crazy Horse was no more than a boy. He had been called Lumpy Neck then—of course it was the kind of name an Indian would bestow. Of late he had mainly been seen in the company of an even older desert drifter named Tucson Jack, a desert rat whose beard was so long he could tuck it under his belt.

"I don't see Tucson Jack," Bartle observed, as the riders came closer. "I guess he died."

"He might have declined the company," Jim said.

"I'll be kind of glad to see Billy myself," Bartle remarked. "I'm interested to see if he's got any prettier."

Jim too felt a little perked up at the thought that Billy Cody was coming—for all his airs no one could deny that he was merry company, something in short supply in the environs of Deadwood these days. It was an odd thing the way attitudes toward Billy Cody varied. It was easy to criticize him and impossible not to be glad to see him.

"Who's that short fellow?" he asked. "What's that? He's riding a white mule."

"What would possess anyone to ride a white mule?" Bartle wondered, astonished.

"Hello, you beaver boys, we found you at last," Billy Cody said, jolly as could be. He jumped off his horse and shook hands warmly with both of them. He was still the dandy—his buckskins were clean and he wore a silk scarf at his throat.

The sudden rush of company tied Jim's tongue, but Bartle experienced no such problem.

"Howdy, Bill. There's nothing to eat, but tell your crew to dismount anyway," he said. "I admire the white mule. How are you, Lumpy? Did Tucson Jack pass away?"

"No, fell in love," Lumpy Neck said. "We may see

him before the night's over. I doubt this passion will last more than a few hours."

"Well, none of mine have, and some of them ain't lasted that long," Bartle said.

"I know you," he added, suddenly recognizing the short man on the white mule. "You're Pillsbury, who used to have the medicine show. We rescued you once when you were lost on the North Canadian, or am I mistaken?"

"No, that was myself," Doc Ramses admitted. "I found it hard to keep my bearings that day. It was around the Canadian somewhere that I left my name behind. I'm plain Doc Ramses now."

"Oh," Bartle said. Courtesy forbade him to inquire further into the name change.

Lumpy Neck was leading a pack mule loaded with food —sausage, cold hen, pickles, and cheese that had traveled all the way from St. Paul.

The mountain men felt a little embarrassed at having nothing to contribute other than a few shreds of elk jerky, which would have looked poor indeed in the company of such provender as the visitors brought.

Billy was disturbed by the condition of Ragg and Bone, two men who had encouraged him and helped him in his youth. Once, a four-hundred-mile stroll over the Rockies had been as nothing to them. Now they looked old, gaunt, and weary. Their tack was ragged, and they seemed almost starved.

"Boys, are you still beavering, or what?" he asked.

"Mostly just what," Bartle admitted. "There ain't no beaver, though Jim's reluctant to admit it."

Jim felt embarrassed—their quest for beaver must seem ridiculous to someone like Billy. More and more it seemed ridiculous to everyone, even to Bartle. But gold lay undiscovered in the ground for hundreds of years and no one criticized miners because they kept looking. Silver miners prospected for years without making a strike. Beaver were a lot easier to spot than silver or gold; it seemed wrong that a man could become a laughingstock for seeking beaver while miners were still considered serious men.

"Say, Bartle, are you kin to young Billy Bone, down in New Mexico—Billy the Kid?" Billy asked, feeling that the subject of beaver was not a comfortable one to have broached.

The new choice of subject proved a little prickly also.

"No kin," Bartle said bluntly. It had begun to irk him that everyone he met on the road asked him if he was kin to the New Mexico whiz.

"Well, I just wondered," Billy said, gacking up quickly.

"You men look gaunted out," Lumpy Neck observed. He had faded blue eyes and was anything but gaunt himself.

"We ain't of a stout build like you, Lumpy," Bartle replied, a little offended.

"Boys, I can't dawdle," Billy said. "You were kind to me earlier in life and now I'd like to return the favor. Come join my show and I'll make you prosperous."

"I'd go farther," Doc Ramses said. "I'd say we'll make you rich."

"Oh, don't excite them," Billy said. In fact, such talk excited *him*—he couldn't help it. The thought of how rich he would soon be was just too pleasant.

"Well, we've got some expositions coming up this year," Doc Ramses said. "Chicago is having one, and there's Queen Victoria's Diamond Jubilee."

Jim and Bartle exchanged glances.

"What are expositions?" Bartle asked finally.

"They're just fairs, really," Billy said modestly.

"I'd say they're considerably more than that," Doc Ramses said. "They're only held in the top cities, and countries around the world send their top heroes to them. There's a fortune to be made from expositions."

"Yeah, but how do you make it once you get to one?" Bartle wondered.

"We dress up and put on our show," Billy said. "I know the show might be thought a little silly, especially by old-timers and folks who came to the west early. But the crowds *love* to see our show—the riding and shooting and Indians and the rest."

"It might be too silly for me," Jim said, though in a friendly voice. He saw no reason to be critical of Billy, who, after all, had traveled a long way to find them—and had brought them a feast, to boot.

Billy Cody wasn't offended. It was the kind of statement he met with every day from old-timers such as Jim Ragg and Bartle Bone.

"Boys, you've got to look at it from the point of view of the younger generations," he insisted. "The whole eastern part of the country is civilized now, and the plains are filling up with towns. California is mostly settled, thanks to the gold rush. Colorado will be civilized soon—look at Denver! It won't be long before the only chance people have to see riding and shooting will be in a show."

There was a long silence. Lumpy Neck carefully sliced off a piece of St. Paul cheese. Doc Ramses was trimming his nails.

"I blame it on the Indians," Bartle said. "They gave up too soon. You're partly to blame, Billy. You're the one made a great name killing buffalo—next thing we knew they were all killed and the Indians were too starved to fight. If we had just kept the buffalo I believe the whole business would have lasted my lifetime," he added.

It was a theory he had been refining for years. What a monstrous mistake it had been to popularize buffalo hunting. Millions of them had roamed the plains—it still seemed hardly credible to men who had seen the great herds in their glory that so many animals could be killed in only three years. But it had occurred: it weakened the Indians, armies had marched, brave men had died, and now they were down to expositions.

"Yes, I regret that myself now," Billy said. "I've been buying them, you know—I buy every buffalo I see. I'm gonna try and bring them back. I have more than a hundred already, grazing on my ranch. I just sold ten to

Quanah Parker—he's going to try and get them started again on the south plains.''

"What was the most you ever killed in a day, Bill?'' Lumpy Neck asked. His curiosity was mildly perked.

"I confess it was four hundred,'' Billy said lamely. ''Of course I didn't often kill that many.''

"What's our part in the exposition?'' Jim Ragg asked. What Billy had just said about the buffalo interested him —he had never imagined that he would hear of anyone *buying* buffalo. But he had just heard it, and it gave him a sudden, mighty inspiration. If people could buy buffalo, why couldn't they also buy beaver?

Suddenly, rising clear as the moon, was the solution that had eluded him for years. Buy beaver! Spread them around in the creeks and ponds—let them breed! If Billy and Quanah could restore the buffalo, why couldn't he and Bartle do the same for the beaver?

Jim was glad it had grown dark. He felt he would have had a hard time concealing the excitement he felt. Of course, it would not do to reveal his plan to an astute businessman like Billy Cody—Billy would march off and beat him to it. After all, he had beaten everybody in the west to the notion of the Wild West show. He would surely be quick to see the profit in beaver farming, if that was what it ought to be called.

"What part would we take in the exposition?'' Jim repeated, startling Bartle considerably. It had not occurred to him that Jim Ragg would even consider being in a Wild West show, much less an exposition.

"Well, you're mountain men, almost the last,'' Billy said. "What we plan for the Queen is to do the whole west, from start to finish.''

"We may take it all the way back to Coronado,'' Doc Ramses said. The entrance of a few *conquistadores* seemed to him the perfect way to start the pageant. He had history on his side too; but it sometimes took more than history to sway William F. Cody.

"Now, I don't know about Coronado,'' Billy snapped, a little annoyed that Doc was so quick with his ideas.

"He was Spanish and I don't know that we ought to bother with the Spanish part—it ain't what people want to see."

Doc Ramses let it pass—clearly, now was not the time to advance his argument for starting with Coronado. He was not giving up, though. It might be possible to insert the idea into Billy's head in such a way as to make him think it had been his to begin with. If he decided it had been his to begin with, then the *conquistadores* might still lead the parade.

"I see you two as Lewis and Clark," Billy said to the mountain men. "After all, that's when the west started—with their expedition. And you men are perfect to play them. You'll be my stars, boys!"

Jim's mind was still on the wonderful prospect of buying beaver—perhaps some could be purchased in Canada. Working for a bit in Billy's exposition would no doubt be the easiest way to make enough money to get things going.

"I'll do it," Jim said. The Lewis and Clark part hardly mattered; getting money to buy beaver with was what mattered.

"How about you, Bartle?" Billy asked. "Here's your chance to outshine your young cousin in New Mexico."

"I told you he wasn't no kin," Bartle said, more than a little put out with his old partner, Jim Ragg. For years, ever since the Custer battle, he had been trying to get Jim to consider a new line of work; now Billy Cody had ridden up and seduced him with a hunk of cheese and the promise of a lead role in what was, after all, just a glorified medicine show.

Calamity Jane would have fainted had she been there to witness such a disgusting turn of events.

"Lewis and Clark are no heroes of mine," Bartle said stiffly. "Anyone can walk to Oregon."

"Don't you be stubborn," Jim said. "Lewis and Clark will do. Who do you want to play—Custer?"

Bartle was astonished. Now Jim was reprimanding him for *his* reluctance to be in a medicine show.

"Boys, don't quarrel, just say you'll do it," Billy said.

"It's easy work and you'll get to see the sights. You'll come back so rich you can buy a white mule like Doc's, to carry your equipment around."

Bartle looked at Jim, who fixed him with the murderous glare he commanded when out of sorts.

"Oh, well, was we quarreling?" he asked mildly. "I don't care if we go. It might do the Queen a passel of good to meet a fresh fellow like me."

12

IN THE MIDDLE OF A WET, COLD MAY, THE YOUNG
woman named Ginny died. Dora would have judged her
to be not more than twenty-two. She had been poorly all
winter—indeed, had been poorly most of the two years
she had worked at the Hotel Hope—and before anyone
could do much about it she took a cough and succumbed.
They buried her on the first really warm day of the year,
a beautiful sunlit day, the prairies looking glorious and
the sky vast and blue. The boy Teat dug the grave, weeping; he had a soft heart, and had developed a quiet fondness for Ginny.

"If she had only seen this pretty day," Dora remarked
sadly to Calamity. "A few sunny days like this one might
have pulled her up."

Calamity had had no luck making conversation with
Ginny—the girl spoke so low you had to strain to hear
her—and watched her burial with no great grief. Dora
had the great grief, and getting *her* pulled up would be
the first task.

"Dora, maybe it's better," she said. "She was not a
happy girl, and it wasn't because she hadn't seen the sun

103

shine. If life just don't suit you maybe it's best just to cough and fade out, like she did.''

Dora's heart was wrenched; the death of the young had never been a thing she could bear. She trembled and held Calamity for support.

"She wouldn't have had to be a whore forever," she said. "She might have met a cowboy."

Calamity hugged her friend, as Dora cried. Ginny had already met quite a few cowboys—and still she was dead. This death, added to Dora's troubles with Blue, was a bad development. Dora had never been the healthiest woman in the world herself. She had abundant spirit but less than abundant energies; she had never been robust that Calamity could recall.

Calamity had to help her into the buggy, while Teat and No Ears filled in the grave. Trix and Skeedle, who knew Ginny better, had not been up to coming to the graveyard; Doosie was back at the hotel, cooking everything she could find to cook. Cooking was Doosie's response to death.

No Ears had been fond of Ginny, too. She had had a light appetite, and she often gave him the remains of her meals. In his view her light appetite was the clue to her early demise. It meant that her soul, too, was light, and not well weighted in her body. He himself was not a large man, but he took care to finish his meals.

After a wait, they had buried Ginny without a ceremony—the preacher had been too drunk to find his Bible. Dora had bravely sung a hymn, all alone, and that was it. Calamity was shy about singing unless drunk.

"I'm not having no luck here in Montana, Martha," Dora said on the ride back along the river. "Now Ginny's died. Maybe I ought to sell out and move on."

The thought made her weary, though; she liked the little hotel—her bedroom window offered a fine view of the plains. Of course, almost every window on the plains offered a fine view of the plains, but she liked hers better than any she had seen. Soon the prairie flowers would bloom and fill the horizon from end to end.

"Move where?" Calamity asked. "You've been moving around this old west ever since I've known you. Where is there left to move?''

"Lots of places, you know that!" Dora said. Calamity loved to contradict her. Even after a funeral she was contrary.

"Where is there that's any different, I meant," Calamity said. "You should have gone with Billy if you wanted to move—that man's a constant mover.''

"I might just move to Deadwood," Dora said. Thoughts of Billy Cody made her all the more sad—though she didn't want to marry him she missed him keenly. He had come every day and cheered her up; he could talk about anything, and he kept her laughing. Now he was gone, and the laughter too.

The customers, few of whom had cared much for Ginny, got the benefit of Doosie's cooking anyway; there was a modest wake, Calamity got quite drunk, and Dora retired early to cry all night. She could think of little to look forward to; and, from a business point of view, she was down to two girls and might have to go spruce up and go back to work herself unless someone younger and prettier could be found.

Looking at herself in the mirror the next morning, it seemed to Dora it should not be hard to find someone younger and prettier. She was forty, an age she hadn't reached without struggle, often a hard struggle. Her face was beginning to carry time's tracery, and it seemed to her she was getting too thin. Doosie thought so too, and often scolded her about it. "Fat lasts longer than skinny," Doosie commented.

"I may look skinny to you, but I'm fat compared to what I used to be," Dora insisted, remembering her starved childhood on the Kansas prairies. Her father and mother had scratched away their lives trying to raise food for the children. There had been little at any time and less once the war came. Every time they would get a pig, a calf, a few chickens, the first troop of soldiers that came by would take them. Her father finally dug a hole in the creek bank to conceal potatoes in; it worked for potatoes, but you couldn't hide a pig or a calf in a hole in the creek bank. For two years it seemed they had nothing but corn —hard corn at that, and not much of it. Her mother died, her sisters died, her brothers left; Dora stayed with her tiring father, helping him scratch at the resistant ground. When her last sister died, Dora was almost too tired to care—looking at her sister in her bare coffin, she had an almost overwhelming desire to change dresses with her; the dress that was being lost in the burial was far better than the rag she wore.

When her father died, Dora took his shoes—otherwise she would have had to walk into Abilene barefooted. At the door of the first house where she stopped to look for work they mistook her for a starving Indian, so dark was she burned from having worked in the sun. They treated her like an Indian, too—Dora felt she might have died from loneliness if the cowboys hadn't come that summer.

Once the cowboys came, life in Abilene flowered, and, little by little, Dora flowered too—she filled out, lost her burnt look, became for a time a local beauty. It was that summer that she met Blue; their love began with an act of hasty commerce in a room above the Old Glory saloon. Far from being led reluctantly into the sporting life, Dora jumped into it. The last year with her silent father in the cold cabin on the plains, the rest of the family dead, the prospects hopeless, hunger the one certainty, seared away what those who could afford them called morals. The cowboys up from Texas who loped into Abilene and winked at her didn't have to wink twice. For a time, Dora couldn't stand to be alone; she would go with anyone— when she was solitary even for a few hours, memories of loneliness and misery overwhelmed her. Better to drink and sing and hoorah with the cowboys, the steady stream of youths who for twenty years filled the plains with their laughter and their need. Dora loved the laughter and was touched by the need, so different from the constant hunger for food that had been her childhood. Even after she was comfortable, living in places where there was food all around, the strength of her fear of hunger surprised her sometimes, attacking her so in her sleep that she would have to leave the bed of some snoring cowpoke—

Blue, often enough—and go find a piece of cold beefsteak and eat it, to put the memory down.

Doosie came in not long after dawn to find Dora sitting with her mirror in her lap and Fred on her arm, a tired, puffy look on her face. She offered Dora her coffee.

"How was the wake?" Dora asked.

"Martha's asleep on the floor right now," Doosie remarked. She considered Fred an ugly chicken and glared at him.

"She's slept on worse than my floors," Dora said. Then she thought of Ginny and began to weep again; deaths affected her more each year, particularly the deaths of young people. She herself had struggled on through good times and bad, but at least there had been *some* good times—Ginny's thin face had never once lit up with joy that she could remember.

"Maybe it's time to give up on Miles City," Dora said. "Maybe it's time we tried another town."

"Another town might be worse," Doosie said.

"Oh, why do you think so dark all the time?" Dora asked. "This is the Hotel Hope. Why can't you ever be hopeful?"

Blue had forgotten one of his gloves in his eagerness to escape after his convalescence. Dora kept it on her table, although it was foolish to do so—it carried his smell and his feel, and made her miss him.

She picked up the glove and popped it on her knee a couple of times, feeling restless.

Doosie made no reply. She saw that Dora was feeling better after her cry. With Dora feeling better, things might get back to normal, and Doosie did like it when things stayed normal.

"Want an egg?" she asked.

"Please. I want two," Dora said, "and don't fry them hard as rocks. You *could* help me be hopeful, if you weren't so stubborn. I get tired of having to supply all the hope around here."

"It's your hotel," Doosie said. "It ain't mine—and I didn't name it."

Darling Jane—

You'll never guess who showed up from Deadwood last night, Ragg and Bone. They traveled over from Deadwood to find me and try to talk me into going with the Wild West show. It's good they came. Yesterday morning I woke up on the floor—Blue leaving and Ginny dying is a bad combination, Dora can't take much more of this leaving and dying.

I worry about Dora, Janey—sometime I am going to tell her about you, I have not done so yet for fear of making her sad. Dora had a baby boy in Abilene, she had a baby girl in Medora, in the Dakotas, they both died. She has lost several too through miscarriages, Dora is not really strong. If she knew I had a sweet girl it would make her miss her babies, I know that.

Dora looks too thin to me, I am her only friend—her only old friend, I mean. I have known Dora since the beginning. The first time I saw her she was thin, just pencils for legs—people now don't realize how hard it was during the war. I was lucky because of Jim and Bartle, they let me come with them. They were good hunters, at least Jim was, and there was always meat. Dora wasn't so lucky, she told me she could only remember having meat a few times when young.

I was jealous of Dora in the old days, once the cowboys came and Dora began to eat better she soon got some meat on her bones, she was the prettiest girl in Abilene, the prettiest girl in any of the cow towns for that matter. All the cowboys left her presents, ribbons and bows and pretty trinkets, most of the cowboys between Texas and Dakota were in love with Dora at one time.

It was her own fault she didn't marry, I told her so often. Plenty of cowboys asked her—Blue claims he asked her two hundred times in one year, he exaggerates and lies but I heard him ask her more than once myself. About the time Dora finally got in the mood Blue found his Indian maiden—half Indian I mean. That's the way things happen in this old world Janey, people just miss, they're contrary and won't yield or give in even when they want to.

Nobody ever bought me a ribbon or bow in my life, no man, that is—I didn't want them. In those days I had no use for girls. I wanted to run with the dashing cowboys or the wild mountain men, you name it. I was gawky, also I despised women's dress. I suppose ten years passed without me wearing anything other than pants, I owned no dresses, not even one to go to funerals in.

Dora was one of the few women I could tolerate in those days, although she was the opposite of me. Dora liked ribbons and bows, she liked being the sweetheart of all those cowboys. I didn't care, I loved her the minute I saw her, she took to me just as quick and didn't mind that I chewed tobacco and smoked and cussed. Dora saw the girl in me when I couldn't even see it myself. We're buffalo girls, we'll always be friends, she said. Many a time we danced together, I'd pretend to be a cowboy in those dances.

It's sad that Dora lost Blue. Of course, there's lost and lost—the man was here just last week, he's not dead like some of my best pals, Lonesome Charley, Wind River Bill, and others that have fallen. I asked Dora why she didn't marry Blue right off, when he proposed those two hundred times. The truth is I feared to starve, she told me once. I knew he would be gone with the herds and leave me for weeks on some old ranch. I can't go back to that, I get too scared of starving. But Blue wouldn't leave you to starve, I said—he'd pack a smokehouse with beef. Blue would never allow you to starve—is that really your reason?

I guess it was her reason, Janey—she got a scared look in her eye. You don't know how close I came to starving, she said. I'll never be left on some old ranch where I might starve, not for him or anybody, I'll stay with the towns from now on.

That conversation put a different slant on things, Janey. It made me see that I had been lucky. Of course on our first trip to Santa Fe there were days when provisions were skimpy but it was not like what Dora went through, she must have been through hell to give up her great love. I told Blue about it, I thought he ought to know. Later he told me he would leave her a cook and twenty beeves whenever he left. At the time he barely owned a saddle, that was thanks to gambling, Blue would gamble away a month's wages in a few minutes. He couldn't afford Dora or anybody else because of his recklessness with cards, I've see him bet all on weak hands many times.

I started to write a letter about Ragg and Bone, the next thing I know I've filled half my tablet with scribbles about Dora and Blue. I feel like Dora is my sister and Blue my brother, I have known them so long, to write of their troubles is not so strange, I suppose. What other family do I have except you, Janey?

Jim and Bartle are like my brothers too, sometimes I wish we had all died together in the Indian wars, I would not like to have to get by without them. Wherever they wander I know they will always show up someday, looking for me.

The reason they have decided to go with the Wild West show is because of a grand idea of Jim's to buy hundreds of beavers and turn them loose in the west again. They got the idea from Billy Cody, who has been buying buffalo. It shows you how times change—when I come west the plains were covered with millions of buffalo, you couldn't have sold one for a penny. They wiped them out and made them valuable, Billy helped too, now he's the one buying them. Jim has no interest in buffalo, he wants to buy beaver and is willing to go all the way to England and perform for the Queen in order to get wages to buy some.

I told them I might go if they behave. Of course they won't behave. It's exciting though—can you imagine your mother meeting the Queen of England? You can bet I will stay sober on the day I meet the Queen. She has been Queen for fifty years, I have only been alive for thirty-eight, I think it is thirty-eight, she was already Queen when I was born. I have seen pictures of her, she is about as fat as Doosie, what does it matter if you're the Queen? Maybe if not for slavery Doosie would have been a queen in Africa herself.

Dora ought to come with us, I am trying to persuade her, she should sell this hotel and travel, undoubtedly there's plenty to eat in England or they wouldn't have such a fat little Queen. We will be gone six months, there are going to be shows in Washington D.C. too. If the President came that would be grand, I would meet a President and a Queen on one trip.

I think it would be good for Dora to come—let Blue cool his heels. He can ride and rope to his heart's content, when we get back he might behave a little better though probably not.

I fear when you grow up you will have men lie to you Janey, the truth isn't in the male, not that I can tell. Bartle Bone has made up thousands of lies in my hearing, it's all he does all day unless he's traveling. He is downstairs right now telling lies to Trix, the next thing you know he'll be proposing to her. The fact is, Bartle's getting old, a girl as spritely as Trix would be a fool to take him seriously or take him at all for that matter, I don't suppose he has a cent. Jim will have a fit if Bartle falls in love just as he is ready to leave for England, Bartle has caused Jim too many delays already—Jim will froth at the mouth if Bartle dares to fall in love now.

I don't know who I am to play in the show, myself I hope, Janey. I sure ain't an actress. I hope I will be allowed to take my horse Satan—I don't trust strange horses. My dog Cody I am going to leave here in Miles City, Doosie will look after him. No Ears is coming with us, they always need extra Indians, Billy says. Once he thought he had forty Indians to be in a show in Richmond. All but two wandered off and he had to paint up some cowboys and make them pretend to be Indians. The cowboys didn't like it—they considered themselves too grand.

These letters get away from me, Janey. They run on like antelope. I only mean to write a line or two to let my little girl know her mother loves her, the next thing I know the pages are flying by. If I had known earlier it was so easy to scribble I would have hired on with a paper. I have no great respect for the men who write for papers. They know little and confuse everything, I suppose the people who read papers know even less. I knew Kellogg, he liked me, he said he was going to write a book about my exploits. Then he went off with the Seventh, to write up Custer's great victory, that was the end of Mr. Kellogg. I will stop and go now Janey—I had better go see what is going on with Bartle and Trix.

Your mother,
Martha Jane

13

No Ears had begun to worry about the ocean. When he had first agreed to go with Martha Jane to see the Queen of England he had supposed they would go horseback, perhaps taking several pack animals loaded with presents and provisions. It would undoubtedly be rude to visit a great queen without bringing presents, though when he mentioned this to Bartle, Bartle waved the notion away.

"The Queen's got the whole British Empire to pick from—let her give us presents," Bartle said.

No Ears was not quite certain where England was, but he had formed the impression that it was on the other side of Canada. The reports he heard indicated that it rained a lot in England—he thought it might be wise to purchase a slicker before he started out. He himself liked slickers because they were light. Buffalo robes eventually grew sodden in rainy weather and were cumbersome to drag around.

One afternoon Jim Ragg came riding into Miles City with most of an elk packed on a mule. He had been scouting south in the Bighorns, hoping to locate a sufficient number of ponds in which to deposit the beavers he hoped to acquire on their travels. The elk had walked in front of him and he had been considerate enough to shoot it and pack the most edible parts of it onto his mule, Missouri. He had bought the mule on credit in Miles City.

"I've carried my own grub around these parts long enough," he informed Bartle, who had declined to accompany him on the scouting trip.

"You're getting spoiled in a hurry, ain't you?" Bartle remarked. "Next you'll be wanting a buggy."

Doosie took charge of the elk and soon had a roast cooking. The smell pervaded the whole of the Hotel Hope—a crowd soon gathered in the kitchen, waiting for the roast to be ready. The crowd consisted of Bartle, Trix, Skeedle, Calamity, Dora, Teat, No Ears, and Doosie, who went about her business doing her best to ignore the seven superfluous persons who had settled themselves in her way. Teat made himself useful, carrying water and keeping wood in the stove.

Jim Ragg had declined to wait for his own elk to be ready to eat—he kept a haunch and walked off with his mule toward the Bull Mountains, on the same quest he had just returned from. Again, Bartle had declined to accompany him.

"Jim's had about enough of you sitting around town," Calamity informed him.

"A sightseeing trip don't interest me right now," Bartle commented. "I'm resting up for my visit to the Queen."

"I wish I could go to England," Trix said. She had no objection to Bartle, though he was old and rather smelly. Far worse men had been sweet on her, though, and she saw no harm in encouraging Bartle, up to a point. The winter had been long and chilly; she had already made up her mind not to let another one catch her in Miles City. Ginny's sudden demise had made a big impression on her. She herself wanted out while she had her health.

Calamity sat at the table wearing her odd, distracted, lost look. No one Dora knew could look so lost—and Calamity was a big woman. When she looked that way it was a lot of lostness to cope with.

"Why should a Wild West show just have cowboys and Indians?" Bartle asked. "What would the west have been without saloons? Why not have a saloon in the show for the cowboys to whoop and holler in?"

"It would be too much trouble to haul a saloon to England," Calamity said. "Billy says it will be trouble enough just getting the animals across the ocean."

That was when No Ears learned that traveling to England meant crossing an ocean. It worried him slightly, for he knew that the hole in the sky where souls went was somewhere near an ocean.

Later, full of elk, the party dispersed. Calamity got drunk and fell asleep on the back porch in the warm sun. Bartle and Trix went upstairs. Teat helped Doosie clean up. Skeedle was engaged by a party of five surveyors—she was skilled at dealing with parties—and Dora went into the bar and played the piano for a while. An Italian musician who had been court-martialed out of the army for striking an officer had given her a few piano lessons years ago in Nebraska. She could play "Annie Laurie" and "Drink to Me Only with Thine Eyes," and, when the mood struck her, she could provide a fair rendition of most of the popular ditties of the day.

Today she chose "Believe Me, if All Those Endearing Young Charms." Two of the surveyors, finished with their play in Skeedle's chambers, sat in the bar and wept. Soon Skeedle came down and listened, too. Dora was glad to see her; Skeedle was a woman of considerable poise. It was usually calming to have her near, especially if several morose surveyors were getting drunk and sobbing together as they sat listening to Dora play the piano. No doubt it reminded them of close times with their mothers and sisters. Everything except what occurred in the bedrooms seemed to remind them of close times with their mothers and sisters.

Watching the surveyors weep over a few bars of sentimental music had the effect of making Dora feel stony. She had had a mother and sisters, too, but her close times with them had consisted of watching them die, one by one, on the Kansas plains, and then burying them. Her memories didn't make her weep; they just made her feel hard.

No Ears enjoyed listening to the music. When Dora struck a note particularly hard it seemed to him the note traveled directly into his head. Of course, in the saloon there was no wind—on the prairie the wind often snatched away sounds that might otherwise have made it into his head.

That night No Ears had the first of several dreams about the ocean. He knew he was in a dream when he saw the face of a friend of his called Sits On The Water, a Yankton Sioux he had hunted with frequently some thirty years before. Sits On The Water was fond of canoes; he also liked steamboats, flatboats, keel boats, and rafts. Anything that floated interested Sits On The Water. thus his name. Once he had killed a bear from a boat. The bear had happened to swim by, and Sits On The Water had killed it with a lance.

Sits On The Water had sometimes convinced No Ears to come into a boat with him, but No Ears had never liked sitting on the water and never enjoyed those boat rides. He didn't feel he could smell well while in a boat. Of course, near the shore, he could smell frogs, mud, mussels, rotting fish, muskrats, ducks, cranes, certain snakes, and other shore-hugging creatures; but in the middle of the great Missouri he could smell only whatever happened to be in the boat. He thought there might be a giant fish under the boat and it troubled him that he wouldn't be able to smell it if the fish grew angry and attacked. He imagined that the giant fish had the temperament of a hungry bear, and was consequently unable to enjoy boat rides after that.

His friend Sits On The Water had enjoyed one too many boat rides, finally. His canoe turned over one spring day right in the middle of the great Missouri when it was in flood. Sits On The Water had wanted to ride the flood, but the flood took him. His canoe was found many miles downstream, but his body was never found. It was No Ears's view that the great bear-fish had swallowed

Sits On The Water—in a way it served him right for spending too much time in boats.

Yet in No Ears's dream, Sits On The Water reappeared after an absence of many years and tried to persuade No Ears to come and ride in a boat on a river that was so wide No Ears could not see the far bank. No Ears was reluctant, but suddenly he was in the boat, and in it alone. Sits On The Water had vanished from the dream. No Ears was drifting in the boat and the river had become wider still—for now he could see neither shore. All he could see was a great plain of water as endless as the sky. The water and the sky became harder to tell apart, and finally impossible. Thinking he was breathing air, No Ears suddenly took a big breath of the river and began to drown. As he was breathing the river he saw a huge brown shape swimming toward him. He tried to swim away from the bear-fish, but though he wanted to swim fast, he seemed to swim more and more slowly.

When he woke up he spent the rest of the night thinking about his dream. It was the most ominous dream he had had for many years. The night before the Custer battle he had had a very bad dream also, but since then his dreams had been mostly good. He dismissed the bear-fish as being merely a spirit fish—if bear-fish had existed in the Missouri, some of the old people in his tribe would have known about it. Though they lived on the Platte, they often hunted on the Missouri and would have heard of such a dangerous fish.

The part of the dream he could not dismiss was the part about confusing the ocean and the sky; if the ocean was indeed as large as the sky, it seemed to No Ears that such a thing might happen, with very dangerous consequences for those who traveled on the ocean. They might begin to breathe the ocean, thinking it was the sky.

The next morning, when Calamity woke, he asked her how long it would be necessary to be on the ocean.

"Well, I hear it's a big ocean," Calamity said. "I've never seen it myself."

Bartle was sitting nearby, trying to sew up one of his moccasins. He had stepped on a knife someone had lost

117

or discarded and had gashed the moccasin. As needle-work was not his speciality, he was making a poor job of sewing it up.

"I have read somewhere that it's three thousand miles across the ocean," he said. "It might be a little less, I guess."

"How far does a boat go in a day?" No Ears inquired.

"You've seen steamboats," Bartle said. "The Missouri's thick with them. Why don't you go clock one?"

"Why don't you ask Trix to sew up that moccasin, if you like her so much," Calamity said. "Or else ask a squaw."

"I'm afraid of squaws," Bartle admitted.

"For what reason?" Calamity asked.

"For the same reason that I'm afraid of you," Bartle said. "You're unreasonable, and so are the majority of squaws. They may kiss you, but if they don't they're just as likely to cut out your gizzard. I'd rather have a hole in my shoe than lose my gizzard."

No Ears felt a little peevish. It was hard to get precise information from Calamity, or Bartle, or white people in general. Even those whose lives had been in danger many times were content to be vague about vital matters on which one's life could depend.

In fairness, he had to admit that many of his own people were also often vague about important facts, such as how far a gun would shoot or how quickly a man could drown if the banks of a river were too far away to swim to. It was because they failed to collect precise information about life-threatening matters that so many people, white and red, were no longer alive.

No Ears prided himself on finding out well in advance what he needed to know. It was because he was so diligent in gathering information that he was still alive. Almost all the people he had known in his youth, Indian or white, had been less diligent, and were dead.

He was very curious about the ocean—if the ocean was anywhere near three thousand miles wide, then it was a force to be reckoned with, a force as powerful as the sky, or the moon, or the storm. He wanted to know more about the ocean so as to be prepared, but Miles City proved to be a poor place in which to acquire precise information. Not shy, No Ears went up and down the street asking anyone he met if he knew anything about the ocean, but for most of the day he drew a blank.

Potato Creek Johnny, who had wandered into town a day or two previously, exhausted, half-starved, and lacking in either gold or silver, made a typical response when No Ears asked him.

"No, I ain't seen an ocean and I ain't interested either," Johnny replied. "If there was gold in one you'd have to drown to get it, and that's an unwelcome prospect."

Johnny devoted what little energy he had left to attempts to talk Skeedle into doing him favors on credit.

"It would take a whole gold mine for you to catch up with what you owe me already," Skeedle remarked. She liked Johnny well enough but was skeptical of his ability to locate gold. Besides, the survey team was still in town and her leisure was limited.

No Ears found out so little about the ocean that he was considering making a preliminary trip to it for purposes of inspection, when he happened to inquire of a blacksmith named Maggs. Mr. Maggs had grown up in Galveston and knew more about oceans than the rest of the population of Miles City put together. He had sailed the seven seas, and was on his way from San Francisco to the Great Lakes to run a steamer when his ambition deserted him. Since then he had lived in Miles City, being a blacksmith. He missed his old calling, though, and promptly told No Ears a great many things about the sea.

"I would allow three weeks to get to England," Mr. Maggs said. "It's good swimming water, but you can't drink it."

That startled No Ears, and his astonishment grew when the blacksmith informed him that all the oceans were salt. No Ears repeated this amazing news to several people, all of whom agreed with the blacksmith. The one thing the local humans seemed to know about the ocean was that the water was salt, and not drinkable.

This news caused No Ears so much concern that he began to regret having promised to go on the trip. First there was the danger of confusing the water with the sky; then there was the equally troubling danger of not being able to secure good drinking water.

A boat was only so big, and Cody seemed to be planning to take many animals. If the planning was not done well, it could mean a thirsty trip. It might be necessary to kill the animals for their blood—on badly planned trips in his youth, No Ears had had to drink the blood of animals to keep from dying of thirst. Though it had saved him, it had been unpleasant, a thing he would rather not do again. Seeing the Queen might be interesting, but if she was only a small queen seeing her might not make up for the hazards of the trip.

Another unfortunate fact he discovered about the trip was that Sitting Bull would be along. Sitting Bull was not a pleasant man. Once he had surprised No Ears when he was drunk and tried to blow smoke into his head through his open ear holes, a very rude thing to do. Also, Sitting Bull was crazy about women and had the advantage of fame; if there were any young women in England, Sitting Bull would soon marry them all.

But the irritation of having to put up with Sitting Bull was minor compared to his concerns about the dangers of the ocean—dangers everyone but himself seemed to be taking much too lightly.

One night he had an idea. Jim Ragg had returned in the night from his scouting trip in the Bull Mountains. As neither Bartle nor Calamity was up, he presented his ideas to Jim.

"I believe we should ride around the ocean," he told Jim. "If we start soon we should be able to ride around it in plenty of time. We could ride a train if you want to. They are much faster than boats."

"You can't ride around the ocean," Jim informed him. "It goes to the top of the world." He was not quite certain of that information, but it seemed to him he had heard it.

"There's oceans in both directions," he added. "The

Pacific is on one side of the country, and the Atlantic is on the other. We're using the Atlantic—England's just on the other side of it, I believe.''

Jim realized that he did not know a great deal about oceans and did not much blame No Ears for looking dissatisfied with the sparse information he had given him. But getting the group to England was Bill Cody's job—it was *his* Wild West show.

No Ears walked off into the prairies and sat in the grass all day, thinking about the information he had just received. The knowledge that there were oceans to east and west was troubling news. In his experience great bodies of water had a tendency to run over and cause floods. The floods he had witnessed interrupted many lives, including the life of his friend Sits On The Water. Perhaps being on a big boat was not such a bad idea after all. It might be that there they would have the best chance of not having their lives interrupted.

That night No Ears dreamed of the ocean again, but this time it was a better dream because he remembered only to breathe the sky.

14

"GENERAL CUSTER, GENERAL CUSTER!" THE PARROT said.

T. Blue felt like wringing the parrot's neck—a bird that could only say one name deserved to be cooked and served up with dumplings, as far as he was concerned. The novelty of hearing a bird say "General Custer" had worn off several years previously.

But Fred sat on the arm of Dora DuFran, nibbling on an old iron key she had given him. If he wanted to stop nibbling the key and say his two words, there was not much Blue could do about it.

In truth, he was not so much angry at Fred as shocked by Dora, who had just informed him that she intended to leave Miles City and settle in Belle Fourche. From Blue's point of view it was a most inconvenient plan, since it would mean a considerably longer trip every time he went to see her.

Dora was looking at him with a mixture of hurt and defiance, a look he was quite familiar with. She had always had a tendency toward defiance but had only begun to look hurt since his marriage. Before that he had usually been the one to look hurt, and indeed, he felt rather hurt at the moment.

"Now why the devil would you want to go way off to Belle Fourche?" he asked. "Just as things were getting settled, too."

"I wouldn't say they're settled," Dora said. "Do I look settled to you? If I do, then you might as well go outside and talk to your horse."

"I meant settled in terms of a good location for business," Blue said, aware that they hadn't been talking about business.

"No, you mean convenient for you," Dora said. "I'm just the right distance off so I won't be upsetting your wife—I doubt she even dreams that I exist."

"But a wife is one thing and a love is another," Blue said. "I wish I had a dollar for every time I've explained that to you. If I did I could afford to abandon the cattle business."

"I'm sure you're right," Dora said, scratching the soft feathers on her parrot's head.

"If I'm right, then what's the matter?" Blue asked, feeling that they must have had that exact conversation, word for word, before. He had no wish to repeat himself, but when Dora looked the way she was looking it was better to talk than to stand there hoping for peace.

"The problem is I might have wanted to try being the wife for a change," Dora said.

"You was offered a hundred chances, and you didn't care to risk it," Blue reminded her, feeling huffy.

"No, but I might have this time," Dora said. "I may have turned you down, but I never said I wanted you marrying someone else. So far as I'm concerned you can go fall off the drainpipe and break your other leg—only when you do, look for another nurse. Calamity and the boys are heading for England and I'm moving to Belle Fourche."

"Hell, why not go to England yourself, if all you want to do is get farther from me?" Blue said. "Go on—be a regular Lillie Langtry."

"I have to support myself," Dora reminded him. "I can't just be taking fancy trips to see the Queen."

"Billy would buy you a railroad car if you'd go, and you know it," T. said, feeling even more huffy.

"Let him buy his wife a railroad car," Dora said. "You're the one who should be going to England with the show—you're as good a rider as Texas Jack or any of them other cowboys. The Queen might give you a diamond."

"I imagine she'd put me in jail," Blue said. "I'd miss you so much I'd get drunk and sleep in the street. They're strict about things in England, I hear."

Dora knew she was being somewhat unfair—after all, T. had pestered her to marry for years; she had turned him down because she couldn't face the ranch life. He liked the wide-open spaces and she liked towns; it didn't seem they'd be a very good fit, none of which reduced the hurt she felt when he told her he had married someone else.

Now it seemed he was always around again. He had shown up twice since his convalescence, and his convalescence had ended only the month before. It annoyed her that he just assumed he could show up whenever he wanted to and get a kiss or a bedfellow for a week, or hot meals in the kitchen, or whatever else he might want.

"If I had a diamond I'd give it to you right now, and maybe you'd be sweet," Blue said. "Why is Calamity joining the show? She can't ride and she can't shoot—about all she does is drink and tell lies. Why should the Queen want to hear a bunch of Calamity's lies?"

"I thought you liked Martha," Dora said. "She's an old friend of Billy's—I guess he just thinks it would be decent to give her a job. She's expected to drive the stagecoach and she does have experience at that."

"She don't that I know of," Blue said. "She might have driven a freight wagon a few times. If Calamity tries to drive a stagecoach she'll probably turn it over and spill all the passengers out.

"It might give the Queen a laugh, I guess," he added,

feeling that Dora was at last getting in a slightly better humor.

Dora was mainly feeling that it would be a lonely fall with Calamity gone, Blue in and out; moving to Belle Fourche would at least give her something to occupy her mind—she always enjoyed setting up house, choosing curtains and rugs. There might be more miners and fewer cowboys down that way, but that didn't discourage her. Cowboys were appealing, but poorly paid—exactly like the one standing in front of her looking hangdog. The girls fell in love with them, ran off with them, neglected to charge them, and provoked fights by encouraging two or three at the same time. The girls behaved better with miners, most of whom were older—it was uncommon to find young men who wanted to spend their days in the mines.

At the same time, she felt sad at the thought of the move. She felt she'd lost something in Miles City; perhaps it had been a way of hoping, a way of thinking about the remains of her life. Blue wouldn't marry just to unmarry. If he seemed more ardent, more lovestruck than ever, it was probably only because he was restless about settling down. Once he settled, though, and children came, there'd be a turning; he wouldn't come so often, or care so much. His young wife might not engage his attention, but the situation would—he'd grow up and start wanting to make his mark, and she herself would not get to be involved in it, much less help him make it.

"Dora, won't you change your mind?" he asked. "Can't you stay here? Can't we just be as we've always been?"

Dora didn't answer, though she finally let him take her hand.

But when T. Blue rode west the next morning toward the Musselshell, he could not get his spirits up. They hovered down near his stirrups, though the morning was bright and the plains in their summer fullness, the yellow grass waving. When he first rode west toward the Musselshell, he had had to worry about keeping his cattle, his horses, and his scalp. Now those worries were diminished. Unless he stumbled onto a mad renegade, his scalp was probably safe.

Still, he felt lower in mood than when such a ride had meant danger. There were dangers and dangers, it seemed. The old kind, the kind involving renegades and breakneck races over uncertain country kept one awake and alert, keen to the business of living. Relax and you might be gone, unless you possessed abundant luck.

T. felt he did possess abundant luck: he had swum rivers in which other men drowned, survived stampedes in which other men died, escaped bullets that had gone on to cut other men down. No defeat or contretemps depressed him for long; his energies would bob up and he'd be off at a rapid clip for new sights and fresh pursuits.

The shift in Dora, though, wasn't to be survived as easily as bullets, rivers, stampedes. He had assumed from her many refusals that she wouldn't mind if he married, so he had married; it was done, and he had no complaint about his wife, who was young, pretty, competent, devoted. Indeed, he loved her too.

He just hadn't imagined that securing a helpmate would affect Dora so. When he got annoyed at Billy Cody, tried to climb the drainpipe, and busted himself good, Dora had taken him in, nursed him, and been as sweet as ever. She didn't exactly send Billy packing, but it was clear who she preferred. Yet in that time something shifted. Dora evidently thought the fact that he stayed with her to get well meant that he was going to stay with her forever. He hadn't said it, but Dora believed it—the day he pronounced himself well and proposed to go back to his ranch, she turned to ice. He expected anger, he got an icicle—and since then, though he had returned twice, riding the long distance across the plains, Dora had not really melted. He had to strain and joke merely to be tolerated—and yet Dora and he had been sweethearts for twenty years, moving, more or less in step, all the way up the plains from Kansas to Montana.

Was all they had shared just to be memories now, because he had married? It seemed so. Getting saddled up to go home, he stopped and hugged her and asked once again that she not go, not move farther from the Musselshell.

"I'm moving, T.—let's don't talk about it," Dora said, offering her cheek when he bent from his horse to kiss her goodbye.

He had not gone five miles west, and his mood had not lifted a stirrup's width, when he saw a strange party right in his path. It was Calamity, trying to mount her horse. No Ears held a stirrup steady for her, but Calamity was having a hard time getting her foot in it. Twice she heaved a foot up and both times missed the stirrup and fell down. Her big shaggy dog barked furiously when this happened. The dog seemed to think it was all the horse's fault.

As Blue approached, No Ears led the horse over by a low stump. He helped Calamity balance on the stump and then positioned the stirrup, but Calamity wobbled at the last second, jumped, missed the stirrup, and kicked the horse in the flank. This spooked the horse; it jerked No Ears down and dragged him for twenty or thirty yards before the old man got him stopped.

The dog barked even more furiously; he seemed on the point of attacking the horse.

"I can't believe you're too damn drunk even to get on your horse," Blue said when he got there. "It's barely sunup—what are you doing drunk at this hour?"

"Oh, Blue, don't scold me," Calamity said. "Don't you remember all the times we drunk all night?" She was near tears from embarrassment. No Ears had walked all the way from town to find her once he noticed that Satan wasn't in the livery stable; she had ridden out to watch the sunrise with a cowpoke, whose name she couldn't remember. But the cowpoke didn't seem to be anywhere in sight; maybe he had changed his mind in the livery stable and gone back to the saloon—she couldn't remember that part very clearly. Now she felt trembly and confused and was fearful that she might get sick any minute if she didn't manage to get mounted and back to town.

T. Blue in one of his temperance moods was the last thing she needed.

"You goddamn preacher!" she said. "Help me get up. You've toasted the sunrise as often as any man I know, don't you scold me today. I've got to go off to England this afternoon, and it's upset me."

Blue was amused—Calamity had him on that one; he was no man to be lecturing ladies on the evils of drink, even ladies who were too drunk to find their stirrup.

"I've toasted the dawn, I admit, but I've never been too drunk to get on my horse," he said, more for argument's sake than anything. In fact, he had spent more than a few nights asleep under his mount, too drunk to remember that he even owned a horse.

But he got down and helped No Ears steady the stirrup —the horse was getting more and more disturbed and might soon bolt if Calamity kicked him in the flank a few more times. Even with his help, Calamity couldn't hit it, so Blue cupped his hands and got her to put her foot in them; once she managed that, it was no trouble to heave her up. She was sopping drunk all right; her breath smelled like she'd been drinking kerosene, and she had no sooner taken the reins than she dropped both. No Ears patiently retrieved them.

"It's a good thing No Ears has adopted you," Blue remarked. "You've reached the age where you need a guardian, Martha."

Now that she was up, Calamity felt like resting for a bit until her stomach felt a little more settled. Satan had already put up with a good deal—he might not appreciate being vomited on.

"You'll be old yourself someday, and then you won't be so goddamn fresh," she remarked, although in fact T. Blue looked rather subdued—for him.

"You better comb your hair a little better before you curtsy to the Queen," Blue said. "If you ride up looking like you do this morning she might mistake you for Sitting Bull."

"I intend to buy a wig, for your information," Calamity said. His manner irritated her so much at times that if she had been armed she might have taken a shot at him —she *had* taken two or three over the years, all wild.

"Oh, one of them artificial scalps," Blue said. "Get a red one while you're at it. We need more redheads in this country. Have a smoke."

He offered tobacco to Calamity and No Ears, and they all had a smoke and watched the tall grass wave for a few minutes. The buffalo dog wandered off to chase three deer.

Calamity's stomach settled a little, and she began to notice what a grand day it was. In the afternoon they were to start east to catch the steamboat on the Missouri. The thought made her feel sad. Why had she agreed to leave the plains? What did it matter what the Queen of England looked like? The plains were her home, the ground of her life. What if she never got back? What if she got rowdy in England and got sent to jail? Of course that had happened even on the plains, but they seldom kept her too long in the little prairie jails. The deputies soon tired of feeding her or listening to her rattle on.

In England it might be different. And what if the big boat sank? Even No Ears was apprehensive about the ocean, and No Ears had lived a long life, through pretty chancy times. Only two nights before, in Dora's saloon, the fat blacksmith Maggs had been talking about how whales could sink boats. He explained to No Ears that a whale was as big as the house they were drinking in— some of them were bigger. Maggs claimed to have seen a whale that would cover the whole parade ground at Fort Kearney. No Ears had been alarmed to hear of a fish that large and had peppered the blacksmith with questions, so many that Calamity had passed out while he was still peppering.

She was soaked from sleeping in the dewy grass; her hands were shaky, and she felt queer. Getting presentable enough to meet the Queen seemed an immense effort in itself—not to mention the thousands of miles of travel that had to be accomplished first.

"I don't want to go, Blue," she said. "I wish people

would just leave me alone. I just want to stay here with my friends and be buried near Bill Hickok when I die."

Blue, of course, immediately changed his tack. He was looking a little more like his frisky self, and when he was frisky he would argue with a stump; whichever side of an argument the stump took, Blue would take the other.

"Now, Martha, I was just joking," he said. "You oughta go on—at least it'll be a ride."

"Why do I need to cross an ocean just for a ride?" she asked. "I could start right now here and ride a thousand miles in any direction, if I just wanted a ride."

"Well, no," Blue said—he enjoyed splitting hairs when she was least in the mood to have a hair split. "You could clock off a thousand miles south with no trouble, or a thousand miles east, but if you went a thousand miles north you'd need to learn to talk Eskimo, and a thousand miles west would put you about a hundred miles off shore, in the Pacific. I doubt if that black horse could swim a hundred miles, either."

"Go piss in your ear, Blue," Calamity said. "I didn't request a map. I'm glad Dora's moving. It's about time she cut you loose and let you wander."

"Thank you for the smoke," No Ears said, setting off for town. He had neglected to buy the slicker and decided he had better go do it while Blue and Martha Jane were having their conversation. He had experienced their conversations before and knew they were apt to be lengthy. Though he had little to pack, he did want to take some care in selecting the slicker. He wanted, if possible, to find one whose collar would protect his earholes. Also, some slickers had collars that collected rain like a cup when they were raised. If England was as rainy as had been reported, a little time spent selecting an excellent slicker would be time well spent.

The dog Cody had returned from his chase. He barked at No Ears as No Ears walked away, but the old man kept going and was soon out of sight in the waving grass.

"Cody don't like the party to be split up," Calamity observed.

"I don't neither," Blue said. "I think we've all stuck

together this long, we ought to stick together till the matter's finished. But I can't get Dora to see it that way—she is just determined to move."

"If you call being married on the Musselshell sticking together, then hoorah, let her buck!" Calamity said. "I don't think Miss Dora DuFran looks at it quite that way."

"No, she takes a stubborn attitude, as usual," Blue said. "I'm sure you'll defend her, stubborn or not—you would never be inclined to help *me* in a matter like this, I'm sure. You'd rather ride off and visit the Queen."

"I guess it does beat riding around the west listening to you and Dora complain about one another," Calamity observed. "You two started complaining about one another in Kansas, and here we are in Montana years later and you're still complaining. I stopped paying it any attention back down the road several years, if you want the truth. I think you two ought to just shoot it out, and whichever one turns out to be the widow will have nobody to blame but yourself.

"If Dora loses, I'll adopt Fred," she added. "If you lose, I hope you'll will me your six-shooter—I gave it to you to begin with, if you remember."

"We ain't gonna shoot no duel, and you can have this gun back any time you want it," Blue said, though he didn't offer to unbuckle his holster and give it to her. It was a sturdy Colt revolver—Calamity had won it in a poker game somewhere. She had a gun she liked at the time and had given this one to him for his birthday.

"Blue, let's don't argue anymore, I'll start to cry," Calamity said, feeling that she might cry anyway.

"Oh, don't cry—I hadn't meant to be arguing," Blue said. "It's just that I've got a long ride and I'm chattering in order to put it off a little while. I'm half a mind to go back to town with you—Dora might be in a better mood by then."

"Or a worse mood," Calamity reminded him. "Her moods don't usually float too high on the day that you leave, even if she is mad at you."

They sat and had another smoke.

"Remember that time you and me and Billy and Jack Omohundro raced all the way from Fort Leavenworth to Fort Kearney?" Calamity asked. "Those were the free days. We didn't have a bit of business in Fort Kearney either. We just did it to do it."

Blue did remember. It had been a lark—the four of them just wanted to ride their horses fast. He himself had just served a three-day jail sentence for roping a banker (he hadn't known the man was a banker and had dragged him only ten yards; three days seemed excessive, but the banker had influence); Cody started bragging on his horse; then Texas Jack Omohundro started bragging on *his* horse; Calamity never had a horse worth bragging about, but she was always ready for a lark, and the next thing you knew the four of them were racing across the prairies and didn't stop until they noticed Fort Kearney off to the north.

"Yes, I recall it was a glorious ride," Blue said. "I hadn't got respectable yet. I suppose Texas Jack is accompanying you to the palace, ain't he? He always acted like he belonged in a palace, even when the scoundrel didn't have a dime."

"He may go along, I can't say," Calamity said. "He and Billy are too pretty to make good partners—they'd both want to hog the mirror."

"Now, Jack's a humbler sort than Billy," Blue said. "Every man I know's a humbler sort than Billy."

"I'd say you're just mad because Dora's softening up toward Billy," Calamity said. "You might as well go and have a bunch of kids, Blue—Dora's checked you off. I expect Belle Fourche will suit her fine."

Blue denied it vehemently, but it was an old business, he and Dora, and they both knew it. They bantered for a while longer—Blue's mood improved a little, but Calamity's continued to waver.

"I used to love leaving, now I hate it," she said. "I get to wondering if I'll ever see my pals of the prairie again."

"Sure you will, Martha—all of them but me will be in England, riding prancing horses," Blue said. He rode over and shook hands with her—it was an old joke he and Martha Jane liked, shaking hands upon departure, as if they were both just cowboys. In fact, there were plenty of cowboys who didn't have the grip she had, even when her stomach was not well settled.

Her grip was about all that was still strong enough—the rest of her looked in rough shape, and Blue had to wonder, as he rode west across the sighing plains, if Martha Jane would make it back from her long journey. Her face was bloodshot—she had begun to pick up a touch of age, it seemed; her pals of the prairie might soon be missing *her*. It worried him and saddened him—Martha Jane had been part of the western life ever since he had known the western life; as he rode on and thought about the possibility of her passing he remembered what she had said about being buried by the side of Wild Bill Hickok, a cold killer who would not likely have deigned to spit on her while he was alive. That was an odd note—he had meant to ask her about it but it had slipped by in the conversation. Now he would just have to save it until she returned from her visit to the Queen.

15

TEAT SAT ON THE TOP STEP OF DORA'S BACK PORCH AND watched the party prepare to depart. Trix was there, sighing and pouting. Right up until the last minute she hung onto Bartle, half hoping he would decide to take her along. Wouldn't it be fun to see England? On the other hand, wouldn't it be sad to leave Dora and Skeedle, Doosie and Teat? She felt mixed, cried one minute and laughed the next. Dora and Skeedle both had wet eyes, and Calamity was so upset that it took both mountain men to hoist her onto her horse; she had been drinking all day and was not in control of her legs, or any other faculties.

Teat didn't really want to go—no journey and no Queen could tempt him to leave Trix's side, and yet, with all the women crying and the men looking somber, he began to feel sad himself. There was no doubt in his mind that life involved too many leave-takings, too much going on.

When he was a small boy his people had moved often, but they moved together and made camp together; no one left for long, unless on a hunt or on some important spirit quest.

But then the soldiers came and killed his family and most of his tribe; the Crows had taken him in, and then Dora had taken him in, and he soon observed that in the villages of the whites, no one stayed long. Men appeared in the saloon, were there for a few weeks, and then never appeared again. Girls came for a while and then vanished. All the talk in the kitchen the last few days had been of moving. Trix talked of going to Texas, Skeedle favored California, Calamity and the mountain men spoke of a place called England. No Ears talked of the ocean, where great fish might live. Dora assured him that he was welcome to come when she moved the saloon to Belle Fourche, but inside, Teat felt worried; it seemed that people did not stay together anymore for very long. In his tribe the old men and women had told stories from long-ago times and Teat had felt good, sitting in the shadows and listening. The tribe had always been together; hearing the stories made him feel they always would be. But then, within an hour, the tribe ceased to be—the few who survived, like himself, were widely scattered. He would never have the tribe again, never be with his people, or any people who felt it was important to stay together. Someday Trix might leave with some party much like the one that was leaving that day. She might have gone with the old white man if he had asked her.

Teat felt that one reason he so often felt sad was that he didn't understand enough. The old people of his tribe had understood the pattern of life and knew how to follow it and live correctly—it was his misfortune they had been killed before they could explain the pattern to him and show him the correct way to live. Now no one was left who knew the pattern, who could describe the correct way; now people simply wandered at will, as the whites did. No Ears was old, and could have been helpful, but he was preoccupied with other things, such as getting a good slicker to shed the rain, or attempting to keep his soul from leaving before it was ready.

As the party got nearer to departure, Teat felt more sad. He remembered something his grandmother had said to his mother the night before the soldiers attacked. His grandmother was one who could see ahead.

"Tomorrow we will both go home, by a road we do not know," his grandmother had said. Teat had recalled her words many times and had even heard her repeating them in his dreams.

His grandmother had been right—now No Ears and the others were going to take a road they did not know. No soldiers might come to kill them, but other things could—a great fish could, or a great storm could. It seemed foolish. Try as he might, Teat could not gain an understanding of it. He sat on the top step saying nothing.

Jim Ragg said nothing either, and carried nothing but his rifle and effects. He had no interest in the journey, the Wild West show, or England. The job ahead didn't involve him; it was just a task that had to be done before he could get back to beavering. Only the week before, a cowboy who had drifted down from western Canada told him there were still plenty of beaver to be seen there—you just had to go north a way, past the settlements. Jim was prepared to go north; England was just a detour.

Skeedle, who had always been secretly fond of Jim, hugged him and tried to get him to show some of the usual sentiments of departure, but Jim was a poor subject. He had no objection to Skeedle and, in fact, liked her, but in his mind he had already left and the weeping and hugging just seemed tiresome.

"The thing to do is go," he said several times, but no one heard him.

Dora felt timid with Jim—always had—and skipped over him in the round of hugging. The company of women made no impression on Jim—at least her company didn't.

Bartle Bone, on the other hand, gloried in leave-taking. He cheerfully accepted kisses and hugs all around, several from Dora, several more from Skeedle, and many from Trix—much of his time in Miles City had been spent accepting leave-taking favors from Trix. Bartle even kissed Doosie, more than once. It fit his notion of male destiny for women to weep when men left. The one thing that attracted him to soldiering was the sight of all the wives and whores around an army camp lined up sobbing as the cavalry clattered away, or the foot soldiers marched. A few such scenes made up for all the cardplaying, burial details, and lice-collecting that constituted normal army life. Better to march off with Custer and die on the Greasy Grass than to do laundry forever in Fort Leavenworth.

"You didn't die with him, though," Calamity pointed out, as he was explaining his theory of leave-taking the night before.

"No, I haven't died with any general yet," Bartle cheerfully admitted. "I haven't found one smart enough to throw in with."

He managed to prolong the leave-taking until Jim Ragg was grinding his teeth—a crowd had gathered, for it was not every day that a party left Miles City to go perform for the Queen. Potato Creek Johnny planned to accompany them to the steamer, if not farther; several drunks became confused, thinking they were expected to go too. They stumbled around uncertainly, getting in everybody's way.

No Ears wore the splendid bright-yellow slicker he had finally selected, although it was a clear, breezy day.

Calamity had to be tied to her horse; she was so drunk and unhappy it was feared she might flop off any minute and hurt herself.

"I wish you'd change your mind and come, Dora," she said several times. "I don't like to travel so far from you, or be gone so long."

"Well, don't, then, who's pushing you?" Dora said in a shaky voice.

She stood by Calamity's horse, holding her hand—every time Calamity bent down to kiss her her tears showered Dora's face. Calamity cried so much and showered her so many times that Dora felt she ought to be wearing No Ears's new slicker. She felt trembly and more than a little unsettled herself. For a time she had been happy in Miles City. Blue's little accident had been a boon; they had had some of their sweetest times in the past winter. Not since the early years in Kansas had she felt so close to Blue, and it seemed he had felt it too. It seemed for a few weeks that they had come at last to the place they had supposed they would get in their first few months of love, when he was a brash young cowboy and she a pretty buffalo girl. It was what they had talked of in Kansas; finally, in Montana, it happened, or seemed to. But then he had begun to feel like cowboying again, and had ridden off one morning as if their time together had been nothing—as if it were common.

Dora's heart took such a drop that morning that she didn't know if she would ever fully recover her feeling for Blue; now Martha Jane, the other pal of her youth and companion in the adventure of life, was going far away. Martha Jane was sober more and more rarely; what if she died of drink and never returned? They would both be gone, Martha Jane and Blue—what could she do then but get old and be alone?

Doosie was irritated—Bartle kept forgetting things. He trooped back through her kitchen, allowing drunks to follow him. She wanted the party to go—she had cooking to do and didn't welcome such interruptions.

Trix soon wore out her emotion. Now that it was settled that she wasn't going, she felt a good deal relieved. Old Bartle had too many bad habits, such as wearing his moccasins in bed or dribbling tobacco juice on the sheets. She much preferred Teat—he was respectful of her—and had begun to look forward to life in Belle Fourche. There might be some dandy fellows in Belle Fourche.

Skeedle walked off before the party was quite gone. She had made plans to get her fortune told that day by an old Spanish woman who lived in a little hut with her goose. The old woman usually gave her a good fortune—she saw riches in Skeedle's life, and the thought of riches was so pleasant that Skeedle could keep happy for a week or two just thinking about the old woman's predictions.

Finally everyone got tired of leave-taking. The drunks wandered off; a few fell down unconscious. Dora was overcome by her feelings and hurried upstairs to cry in private. Trix went inside to see if any dandy fellows were in the bar. Three cowboys came racing by—one of them saw a goat and took down his rope and roped it. He then proceeded to drag it around. By the time Jim and Bartle, Potato Creek Johnny and No Ears finally walked out of town leading Calamity's horse—she had passed out and was sound asleep in the saddle—everyone had lost interest in the departure except the boy Teat, who sat alone on Dora's back porch and watched them leave. The five people were soon out of town, ever-diminishing ripples in the rippling prairie grass. They seemed to Teat like a little tribe. It made him feel lonely to see them disappear.

1

No Ears didn't like the great plain of water that they called the Atlantic Ocean. At first he had been pleased with the boat they were to make the passage on. He had not imagined that so large a boat could be found; he could not help thinking how much his friend Sits On The Water would have enjoyed a trip in such a great vessel.

Anchored at rest in the harbor in New York—a smoky town No Ears had no interest in—the boat seemed more than adequate to transport several villages to England or anywhere else touched by the great ocean. It was like a floating town, with many houses in it and a kind of small enclosed prairie below, where the animals could be kept and given hay. At first the animals were restive—No Ears supposed that to them entering the ship was too much like entering the stomach of a great fish—but once in their small prairie, with straw for grass, they soon settled down.

It was only after leaving the harbor and setting off across the restless, moving plain of water that No Ears came to see the sharp inadequacies of the boat. Once in the middle of the plain of water, the boat seemed tinier to him, in relation to the ocean, than wagons were in relation to the plains of grass. Also, though he knew that water moved and was powerful—after all, a flood had taken that experienced waterman Sits On The Water— he had not imagined the immense power of the great ocean. The plains of grass seemed to move only when herds of horses, cattle, buffalo stampeded across them; but the plains of water moved always, with a strength greater than any strength he had ever imagined. He felt the movement even in his sleep in his little room. Men tired, animals tired, even the great winds tired and left the earth calm, but the ocean was stronger than men, animals, and wind put together; No Ears could not tell that the ocean ever tired, or ever rested.

He had certainly not expected to encounter such a force in the last years of his life; he spent all the daylight hours and several starlit nights sitting silently on deck, studying the mysterious waters. He knew that he could not learn much; he was too old to acquire the kinds of knowledge of the plains of water that he had had about the plains of grass. Still, he hoped to learn a little. Watching the birds was interesting; even when they had been on the ocean several days, the birds still flew around the boat, and when the cook threw scraps in the water the birds came in white swarms to catch the scraps before they could sink into the depths where the fish lived. Several times, just beneath the surface of the water, No Ears had observed a great many fish swimming together in immense herds. Cody told him that the fish traveled in schools—to No Ears it was just another word for herd.

It was a startling thing to see so many fish coursing through the great plain of water. No Ears had always supposed that the earth was mainly prairie, and that nowhere were there beasts as numerous as the great herds of buffalo that had traveled the prairies in his youth, indeed, for most of his life—until the whites had suddenly killed them all not long after the war they made with one another.

Unfortunately the whites had survived the war with one another, and had turned their need to kill upon the buffalo and upon his own people. It was a shock to his people and even to the whites themselves that all the buffalo had been killed in so short a time; but traveling on the ocean made No Ears realize that the world was far larger than he had supposed and that the destruction of the buffalo, and even of his people, was a smaller thing than it seemed to those who only knew the plains.

Small children and even some grownups in his own tribe believed that the prairies had no end. He himself had believed at one time that the world was all prairie. But he had once gone west with some Blackfeet and come to the end of the prairie in that direction; and on this very trip, he had ridden off the prairies on a train and entered the region of trees, a closed-up region that he didn't like very much. It might be that the prairies were endless if one went north and south, but he had seen them end to the west and to the east, and was forced to conclude that the prairies did not make up quite as much of the world as his people thought.

After many days on the ocean, he was forced to think once again about the size of the world. Clearly it was far larger than anyone in his tribe realized; they reckoned in ignorance, which was not good. He decided that as soon as he got back from England he would journey to the Platte and try to visit as many people in the tribe as he could so as to inform them that they were mistaken about the prairies comprising the main part of the world. It now seemed as if most of the world was ocean—water that you could not drink. The sailors brought up bucketsful of seawater and used it to wash the deck. No Ears tasted a little and found it indeed very salty. Obviously the whole bottom of the ocean must be salt to make the water so salty. And yet it didn't bother the herds of fish, which meant that fish had powers he never suspected. Several times they ate fish that came out of the salty waters, and the meat of the fish did not taste salty, a very curious thing, for the flesh of even the largest deer would give some clues as to what the deer had been eating.

No Ears slept lightly during the trip. He did not dare risk sinking too deeply into sleep—if he did, the powerful ocean might suck out his soul as quickly as one sucked marrow out of a bone. Also, he was excited and nervous, and he wanted to spend as much time on deck as he could; he might not get another opportunity to study the ocean, and he wanted to secure as much correct information as possible.

He had stopped worrying about the great fish that could swallow houses, when he saw the whale. The size of the boat had lulled him, for it was hardly credible that any fish could be large enough to threaten such a boat. Also, none of the herds of fish that swam around the boat contained individual fish of any size. A few were the length of his leg, but most were just fish, no different from those that swam in the Missouri or the Platte. He decided that the great fish was just a dream fish—the dream spirits sometimes like to frighten people with dream beasts of one kind and another.

It was dawn when he saw the whale, a gray sunless dawn when water and sky were the same color and hard to tell apart. No Ears had spent the night on deck and was a little sleepy when the dawn finally came. He had lost his fear of breathing the ocean and was resting calmly. At first, because he was a little tired, he did not see the whale. A sailor saw it and began to yell. The yelling meant nothing to No Ears, although he was afraid for a moment that the boat might be on fire. The sailor kept yelling, and soon people began to run out of their rooms. Then, in the haze, he saw the top of the water moving in a strange way—the water moved as if a giant mole were working just beneath it. The water kept moving, in the way the dirt moved when a mole was tunneling a few inches below the surface of the ground.

No Ears watched without alarm as the water moved in that curious way—he was still in his sleepy mood. But then the great whale broke the surface and he instantly ceased to be sleepy at all. He forgot for a moment that he was on the water; he felt that he was seeing the birth of a mountain. A group of little fish that had been swimming above the whale came up, too, and began to flop down his shiny sides. The seabirds got a few of them.

The great fish was so large that No Ears had to turn his head to see it all. Its tail stuck past the end of the ship, large as a large tepee. To No Ears's shock, the immense fish, almost the color of the dawn, suddenly blew a great spume of water out of the top of its head. The water rose like the puzzling geysers that blew water into the air in the Shoshone country—fireholes, some called them. The firehole water was hot—No Ears could not tell whether the whale's water was also hot, but he immediately wondered if there could be a connection between the whale and the fireholes. Soon many of the people on the boat had run up on deck; they began to shoot guns at the whale. Calamity stood at the rail and shot at it with her Colt pistol. Cody and Texas Jack arrived but did not shoot. The mountain men came up with their rifles but were too amazed to shoot. Many sailors were shooting. The great fish paid no attention to any of it. Some of the bullets went wild and slapped the water; a few pecked at the whale, but the whale swam on.

No Ears was irritated by all the shooting—it was obvious that only a cannon could affect such a fish, and no one had a cannon. He felt that the shooting was likely only to anger the whale, in which case it might smash up the boat and swallow them all. It was silly, the urge people had always to be shooting. It should be obvious that such a great fish must be allowed to swim in peace.

Foolish members of his own tribe sometimes shot arrows at bears that should have been left alone, and were eaten as a consequence. He himself felt that shooting was very much the wrong approach to this whale. The best thing to do might be to throw a few cattle overboard, or even a horse, if they could spare one. The whale might take the animals and leave them alone.

Fortunately the whale left them alone anyway. Once he calmed sufficiently to react sensibly, No Ears realized that the whale was actually a good distance from the boat —it was only its immense size that made it look close. It needn't worry about the pecking bullets, and it didn't. It merely swam away. When it was several miles away, No Ears saw its great tail flash as it dived.

"If a fish that big tried to come up the Missouri, there would be no Missouri, I guess," Bartle said. "It'd splash all the water out."

"I wish these idiots would stop shooting," Jim Ragg said. "What do they think they're shooting at? The whale's probably five miles under water by now."

Calamity was still firing her pistol in the direction of the whale, but once she took her last shot she came over to them and sat down.

"Well, that was excitement," she said.

Jim Ragg glowered at the sailors, several of whom were resolutely firing in the direction of the vanished whale.

"What do they think they're shooting at, the ocean?" he asked.

"They're just boys, Jim," Calamity said. "They just like to shoot their guns."

"If they'd kept quiet we might have got a better look at it," Jim said. "I despise wasteful gunplay."

"Despise them if you want," Bartle said. "I expect they'll shoot until they run out of ammunition."

Calamity sat by No Ears and reloaded her pistol. "I hope I can shoot as good as Annie by the time we get to England, otherwise I'll get fired," she said.

Every day Annie Oakley stood on deck and had her servant throw clay pigeons out over the water. She shot them with a shotgun; at times the weather had been rough, but no one had seen Annie miss. The sailors and many of the cowboys and Indians who were expected to perform stood around and watched, hoping to see Annie miss—but Annie didn't miss.

"They might be trick clay pigeons," Bartle suggested. "Maybe they're just built to fall apart when you throw them."

Annie had been cool to him—in fact, she was cool to everybody—which made Bartle reluctant to admit that she could shoot so brilliantly. She was a neat, pretty woman who soon collected a boatload of admirers, but did not appear to be interested in any of them. All she was interested in was shooting. Such single-mindedness annoyed Bartle; and some of her more stylish admirers, such as Texas Jack Omohundro, found it irksome too. Texas Jack owned an interest in the show and regularly tried to outdress Billy Cody, though he rarely succeeded.

"I think that was a very old fish," No Ears remarked. Seeing the whale seemed to him to be the most extraordinary event of his long life, and he deeply regretted having so few of his own people along to discuss it with— the white people were too shallow even to appreciate what an extraordinary event they had just witnessed. Of course there were around a hundred Indians on board the boat, but most of them were too young to be serious about things of real importance. Red Shirt, for example, had shown no better sense than the sailors; he, too, had emptied his Winchester at the whale.

As for Sitting Bull, he was so indifferent to everything except his own fame that he rarely even came on deck, preferring to sit in the boat's saloon and squeeze white women when they asked for autographs. Most of the white women on the boat had already been squeezed several times, and had more Sitting Bull autographs than they could use.

"I wonder if that was the First Fish," No Ears said. It was so large and looked so old that it could well be the First Fish—it might even be the first beast of any kind. Whether a fish could be considered a beast was a question too subtle for him to discuss with white people; he resolved that if he got anywhere near his home again he would try to find some old people from his tribe and discuss the whale with them. The thought that he might have seen the First Fish was so exciting that he began to wish the trip was over so he could carry the information to where it was needed, that is, to his people. Old people were always interested in information that bore upon the great question of when the world began, and what means the spirits used to create it. It seemed to No Ears that the great fish he had just seen might be as old as the world itself; it might have been only a minnow when the world began. If the whale was indeed the oldest fish, all the fish in the ocean or in the world might be his children. It was thought by some old people he had talked to on his trip with the Blackfoot that the first beasts were both male and female and each could make its own young. Perhaps the great whale fish he had just seen was the grandfather of all the fish in the world.

To No Ears that was a tremendously exciting thought, far too exciting in its implications to be shared with white people—they had quickly lost interest in the whale, once it went under the water. Soon Martha Jane and the mountain men went off to eat breakfast, after which they would sit inside all day and play cards. No Ears was glad when they left. He did not want to be bothered with white people's conversation when he was trying to think about such complex matters as the nature of the First Fish, or the beginning of the world. It occurred to him that perhaps souls didn't go into a hole in the sky, after all; perhaps they went into the sea, to the depths where the great fish lived.

While he was thinking about that, Red Shirt came over and wanted to be admired and flattered. Cody had had some fine white leggings made for all the Indians and had also bought Red Shirt a splendid bandanna in St. Louis; now Red Shirt required constant attention of a sort No Ears was in no mood to give. There would be no living with Red Shirt's vanity if the white photographers took his picture many more times.

No Ears brusquely sent Red Shirt away, only to see Sitting Bull coming on deck wrapped in his messy blankets. Sitting Bull stood at the rail a long time, staring at the water. He looked annoyed—probably he had expected the whale to wait for his arrival. He frowned at the water, trying to make the whale hurry on back so he could have a look at it. Sitting Bull had always frowned at the world that way, trying to bend the world to his will. For that reason No Ears had always considered Sitting Bull slightly ridiculous. The great whale was not some dog of Sitting Bull's, a creature who could be summoned with a frown. A man as intelligent and powerful as Sitting Bull ought to have learned such things, but Sitting Bull still frowned if things didn't behave exactly as he wished them to.

After frowning at the water for a while, Sitting Bull came over to No Ears. No Ears tried to make it obvious by his demeanor that he was thinking and would rather not be interrupted, but Sitting Bull interrupted him anyway.

"Where is the big fish?" he asked. "I thought it was here, but I don't see it."

"It was the great whale," No Ears informed him. "He went back to his home."

Sitting Bull knew No Ears didn't like him but he didn't care. He only wanted women to like him. "If I thought he'd like to eat an old man like you I'd throw you in the sea," Sitting Bull said. "Then when he came back to eat you I'd get a good look at him."

"You should have come upstairs a little sooner," No Ears said. "The whale visited us but people shot at him and he decided he would rather go home."

He ignored Sitting Bull's insult. Sitting Bull always sprinkled his conversations with insults; if you responded to them he might go on talking for several hours, bragging on himself.

"Give me your slicker and I will trade you these blankets," Sitting Bull said. He had been admiring No Ears's slicker and had decided he wanted it for himself.

No Ears didn't answer. His slicker was one of his proudest possessions, and also one of his most useful. Spray from great waves often splashed over the deck but his slicker kept him perfectly dry. Only his face sometimes got a little wet. It was only another of Sitting Bull's insults—Sitting Bull knew he would not be such a fool as to trade a fine slicker for his smelly blankets. It was easy enough to buy blankets in any town.

Sitting Bull's eyes flashed angrily when it became apparent that No Ears had no intention of handing over his slicker. That was no surprise—he was given to terrible angers when he didn't get his way. But many sailors were around, getting ready to wash the decks. Sitting Bull was not likely to kill him with a lot of sailors looking, although of course he might—the man had no interest at all in what white people thought.

"I think that whale was the First Fish," No Ears said, hoping to change the subject. Sometimes it was wiser to talk to Sitting Bull than just to sit while he grew more and more angry. A little speculation about the beginning of the world might calm him down.

"You can ask him next time he comes," Sitting Bull said. "Then I am going to throw you over and let him eat you. I think I'll take that nice slicker first, unless you want to wear it while the big fish eats you."

Sitting Bull seemed to be getting angrier; No Ears was becoming a little worried, but fortunately Cody came on deck just at that moment. Sitting Bull immediately stopped making threats and went over to shake hands with Cody and borrow some tobacco.

No Ears was glad Cody had distracted Sitting Bull. He pulled his slicker high up around his head, for the seas were growing rougher, the waves splashing high. That was fine—in rough weather people would have to look out for themselves and would leave him alone. He wanted to watch the ocean for a while and think about the beginning of the world. Also, he wanted to think about the magnificence of the great whale.

Darling Jane—

I am afraid this will be a desperate letter, I feel desperate if that's the word. Your mother was not meant for travel, not for long travels like this one to a country across the sea. I have my pals Ragg and Bone it's true, but I miss Dora, I have been crying for her almost every night since we left America and we left it a good many nights back. It seems like the miles are too many, it's not like a ride on horseback down to the Wind River or somewhere, the Wind River is in the west and all the west is my home, Dora's home too. She don't wander like I do but she has done her share of moving around in our old west.

I expect she is in Belle Fourche now, she was determined to go. Probably she found a dandy house to make into a saloon, I bet it is pretty and cozy, I do wish I was in it. Dora promised to keep a room for me, I know she will.

I was a fool to come with this show, I don't know why Billy asked me, he has been nice enough, and he advanced me money several times. Billy is quite polite but I don't think he is interested in having me do much in the show, maybe I will ride in a race or something, they have an act called the Assault on the Deadwood Stage or maybe it's Attack, I get the acts mixed up. There's also an Attack on a Settler's Cabin, I believe. It comes to the same thing, Indians and whites pretending to be fighting, shooting at one another with blank shells and holding up wigs that are supposed to be scalps. They say thousands of people will pay to see it—they say they are coming from France and other lands, I can't see why, and neither can the cowboys or the Indians Billy brought along. Texas Jack is going to run a racehorse with some English rider, maybe Billy will, too, it will be at the Queen's racetrack, I think.

But I don't know if I will be driving the Deadwood Stage. I don't know what I will be doing. If they think I am going to put on a corset and sing a concert they can think again, I don't like to sing in public. I refuse to throw targets for Annie Oakley either. She has been rather stiff with me, she is stiff with everybody, it will be hard to find someone who wants to throw targets for her. Bartle hates her, he hates any woman who gives him any talk of the sort he don't want to hear. We all kid him about it—we remind him that she is the best shot in the world, she stands on deck all day and shoots clay pigeons, you will never see her miss, she could easily shoot Bartle even if she was at one end of the boat and him at the other.

I was sick four days because of the boat, it rolled around constantly, even Bartle got sick. He and Jim are not getting along—Jim is not relaxed a minute, he wants to do the show and get his money and come home. You can't hurry a boat across an ocean—he might as well quiet down.

Bartle and me have taught Red Shirt and Sitting Bull to play cards, they both love cardplaying now. They ain't very good though, Bartle has won both their wages for the rest of their lives, I think. Red Shirt is a handsome Indian, I think Billy is a little jealous of him, some of the women think Red Shirt is better looking than Billy, of course Billy don't like that, he was having enough competition from Jack Omohundro, he and Billy are old rivals but neither of them expected to be out-handsomed by an Indian.

I don't trust old Sitting Bull, he is a cunning old Sioux, if he knew how to run a boat it wouldn't surprise me if he organized the Indians and killed us all. He could take the boat to China or somewhere, they'd never catch him.

Sitting Bull is familiar with women, too familiar, but he don't bother me, perhaps he doesn't regard me as a woman. Whatever the reason I am glad.

I am going to enclose some photographs, Janey—they are the ones we sell at the exposition. Little Doc Ramses took them—he brought along some movable scenery in the ship, a scene might be the Rocky Mountains or a gold mine, some scenic view, he will pose you in front of it for hours and make photographs to sell. There is even an old tame longhorn they brought along, we have all had to pose in front of it. I suspect it is an ox, longhorns were seldom tame.

Doc Ramses wanted me to sit on the old steer, I said no, the other pictures were silly enough. I would be the laughingstock of the west if Blue or some other cowpokes saw a photo of me sitting on an ox. I said I would drive it in the parade though if they can borrow a cart to hitch it to. I once drove an oxcart in the gold fields, they were bigger oxen than this old steer.

I have got to reform, Janey—get my spirit up and have some fun. I have been in difficult conditions before, lonely conditions, but I have never let it get me down for long. While I am healthy I am going to locate the fun if there is any handy. Jim Ragg has been glum all his life, I am glad I ain't like Jim. He feels sorry for himself because the beaver got used up—and it was him and Bartle that helped use them up! You'll find plenty of cowboys like that, they'll cuss and complain because the country's all settled up when it was them that settled it! Then they claim women are crazy and don't make sense. Montana was just Indians when they started bringing in cattle, now look at it. The cowboys ruined it, now they're mad because it's ruined.

It's hard to have fun on a ship, there's only one saloon, there were plenty in St. Louis, plenty more in Baltimore and New York. Me and the boys hit them all. I hope this don't shock you Janey to know that your mother is a carouser, but you have known a more settled life, not like the life we have out west. Buffalo gals won't you come out tonight? That has been the way I've lived, Dora too, neither of us have wasted too many nights. Maybe you will get educated and have a nice family—put your time to better use.

They say we will make England today, I'm glad, it's hard to keep a lively spirit when the boat rolls day and night and there's nothing to look at but this old gray ocean. I had no notion there was so much water in the world, Janey—it's monotonous, more monotonous than Kansas, I felt Kansas was monotonous enough.

I don't know what to make of little Doc Ramses, it is almost as if he is courting me. He says he will take me to an opium den when we reach London, then he gave me a yellow necktie, he says it will look good in the show. Doc is polite to a fault but he is wasting his time if he is courting me, I'm through with it—I'll tell him so if he pesters me much more.

Well, Janey, this letter is gloomy, the next will be better I promise. I will hold off writing until I have seen the Queen, won't that be grand?

Your mother,
Martha Jane

2

Doc Ramses was beginning to regret the decision to bring Sitting Bull to England—the management difficulties with the irascible old Sioux were constant.

At the customhouse, before they had been off the boat an hour, there had nearly been a killing. A stolid young customs officer, in the course of doing a methodical job, made a little too free with Sitting Bull's possessions, causing Sitting Bull to conclude that the man was about to make off with his pocket watch, a handsome silver timepiece only recently presented to him by the mayor of St. Louis. Sitting Bull had come within an ace of cutting the man down with his Winchester; seeing the commotion, Red Shirt had drawn his knife and several other Indians looked to their weapons. Fortunately Jack Omohundro had snatched the watch out of the young man's hand before he could be murdered.

That night, all safely camped in a park near Earl's Court, Doc had called a conference of the show's top management—that is, himself, Cody, and Texas Jack Omohundro.

"What I think is we've got to take away the real ammunition and put blanks in everybody's guns," Doc argued. "The Queen's not going to come see us if four or five of her subjects get shot—and if the Queen don't come we could lose money on this whole enterprise."

"Shucks, the Prince of Wales is coming," Billy said. "I guess we could do without the Queen if we had to."

Sometimes Doc irritated him with his constant worrying. The man was a good organizer, but had little grasp of the subtleties of publicity. If actual fatalities could be avoided, a shooting or two wouldn't hurt—after all, they weren't the Tame West show. Why did people go to circuses, if not in hopes that someday the lions would consume the lion tamer, or at least maul him good?

"Who was you thinking of disarming, Doc?" Texas Jack asked. "Just the Indians?"

"Well, cowboys can shoot Englishmen too," Doc said, realizing he was on thin ice at the moment.

Texas Jack Omohundro was reputedly the best card-player in the west. No one could remember seeing him change expression; certainly Doc Ramses had never seen him change expression. Texas Jack was watching him now, cool as ever, his eyes ice-blue. He was not quite as fastidious as Cody—he didn't spend as much time selecting his bandannas or cravats—but he did devote some attention to his mustache, which bent sharply at each end, framing his mouth in brown.

"My boys ain't going to take kindly to being asked to walk around with unloaded guns," Jack remarked. "Sitting Bull hasn't stayed a chief all his life by being dumb. What if he figures out about the blank ammunition and puts some real bullets back in his gun? He'd be loaded to kill, and my cowboys would be loaded with blanks."

Billy could hardly repress his irritation at the grating way Jack kept referring to the cowboys as "his." More than once he had slipped up in conversation and referred to the whole show as "his," when in fact he had only a minority interest and could not possibly have made the whole thing pay were it not for Cody himself. The posters said "Buffalo Bill's Wild West Show"—Buffalo Bill was the name every single person in America associated with Wild West adventures; the fame of Texas Jack was merely local by comparison. It was all he could do to keep from reprimanding Jack for his promiscuous talk, but he polished his engraved Winchester and held his tongue.

Doc Ramses felt it had been a mistake to encourage Billy to take Texas Jack as a partner; it meant handling two volatile spirits rather than one. Good manners rarely failed Bill Cody, and when they did, little more resulted than a brief storm. So far, good manners had not failed Texas Jack either, but Doc had some trepidation about what might occur when they did. The measure of his temper had not been taken—not yet.

"Now, Jack, the Indian wars are over," Billy said mildly. "Sitting Bull and the young braves are on the payroll, just like the cowboys. What's fair for one is fair for all."

Texas Jack let the comment settle a bit before he replied.

"Just because you made peace don't mean Sitting Bull has," he said. "Just because you pay him a wage don't mean he won't lift your liver, either. I'm for keeping everybody armed—it's safer that way, don't you see? Sitting Bull knows I'm a faster shot than he is—he won't shoot me if he knows I'll be firing at him even as I fall."

"Let's talk about the horse race," Billy said. "That's more important."

"You won't think so if somebody mows down six or eight Englishmen," Doc Ramses said, annoyed that his sensible point was being ignored.

"Why, Doc, what's come over you?" Texas Jack asked. "I would not think that a fellow who rode at Sand Creek would squirm so over a few Englishmen. There's plenty of Englishmen, I guess, and Bill's got a point. We ain't the Tame West—at least I ain't."

"I was just a bugler then, I didn't order the massacre," Doc Ramses protested. It seemed he would be bloodied forever by the carnage at Sand Creek, although he himself had not fired a gun and had even kept two Indian children from being brained by Chivington's frothing Coloradans.

"Jack, leave Doc alone, we can't undo Sand Creek or the rest of it," Billy said. "Let's plan the horse race. You and me ought to try and finish in a dead heat, providing we can both beat the English pony. We have to beat that English horse, though—if I fall back you take him and if you flounder I'll take him. Think of the tickets it'll sell if we beat the Derby winner."

Of course, there was no danger of them losing—the English were so sure of their superiority that they had made no objection to having the race run over a mere quarter mile, though few thoroughbreds could even get untracked in that distance. With him and Jack on their swiftest cow ponies they could race to victory—the fine point was to avoid victory over each other in this first race. A dead heat would make the headlines—they might get in another race, attract another crowd, before they left. It meant more money.

"Billy, I'll try not to beat you, but don't cuss if I can't restrain my horse," Jack said, putting on his hat.

"I think I'll go look up Calamity," he said. "Speaking of shooting, why don't we disarm her? She's already shot up three music halls. You know how wild she gets when she's drunk. I'm more nervous about Calamity than I am about Sitting Bull."

"I was against bringing her," Doc Ramses reminded Billy. "I was for parking her in St. Louis—they know her type in St. Louis."

"Oh, now, where's your notion of showmanship?" Billy asked. "Let her shoot up the music halls—she's Calamity Jane! Do you want her to sew napkins? I say, let 'er buck! It'll just sell tickets."

With no further comment, Texas Jack departed.

Darling Jane—

Whooee, Janey, I swore I'd improve and I have. Yesterday was the big horse race and did we all have fun! It was held at a place called Ascot, the Queen didn't come but the Prince did, he's a pretty fat prince. Billy and Jack and Annie and Sitting Bull got to meet him, I think Red Shirt met him too. I didn't—most of us were kind of roped up under a tent until after the race.

Of course Billy and Jack ran off and left the English horse, the latter was just getting in stride when the race was over, Billy had kept the race short for that reason. The English horse would have caught them eventually but not in a quarter of a mile. I thought the crowd was going to swarm down and lynch the poor jockey, I felt sorry for him, he didn't have a chance in the race, then people cursed him and said he'd let the Empire down. If I were him I'd leave the country, they might catch him and lynch him yet.

After the race we all mounted up and ran our horses up and down in front of the lords and ladies, we were all stiff from the voyage and it felt good to be on horseback. The Indians did some war whoops and the cowboys some cowboy yells. It was plain the people watching had never seen such a spectacle, they quieted down and watched. Annie did a little trick riding, she is a regular acrobat, some people are born with gifts, Annie Oakley was. She has got plenty of ability—even Bartle admits that.

I believe Prince Eddie has an eye for the ladies, he had several in his box. Bartle became jealous, as he always will if he thinks someone has more girlfriends than he does. It is just luck that he's a prince, Bartle said—he wouldn't last long in the Rocky Mountains. I'd like to see what he'd do with a grizzly.

I'd like to see what *you'd* do with one, Jim said, he thinks Bartle is slipping and could not handle a grizzly in his present condition, he may be right. They are all confused about Lewis and Clark, I don't think they will really have to act much. I think Doc Ramses just means for them to lead the parade and fire off muskets a few times.

The grand thing about England is the music halls—Bartle and I go every night while Jim sulks. Nothing can improve Jim's mood but the music halls have improved mine. They are a lot like saloons but far grander than any saloons we have out west, unless there are some grand ones in Denver. I rarely get to Denver—Bartle claims the saloons there are nothing special.

In these music halls you get singing and clowns and a regular show, Bartle and I laughed so much at the clowns we almost got sick. We are determined to get Jim in a music hall eventually, if these clowns can't make him laugh, then Bartle and I are going to give up on him, we'll let him miss the fun if he wants to.

The first time I got rowdy and shot off my pistol in a music hall it scared everybody badly. They don't wear guns in England. I even got in the papers, I am saving all the stories so you can read them someday. Now me shooting off my pistol has become a regular thing, they'd throw me out if I didn't. Doc Ramses thinks they'll be offering me a job pretty soon. He thinks I could make a pretty penny just firing in the air once in a while.

Doc still looks at me funny, I will be minding my own business and look around and catch him looking. He has some strange habits himself, one of them is talking to dead people, Janey. He has found some gypsies and goes to see them often. They travel in little wagons—I suppose it reminds him of his days in the medicine show. I went with Doc once to meet some, I was a little frightened, they look rough. They even had a little bear with a collar around its neck—it was a small bear, not a grizzly.

Now Doc wants me to go with him to a seance, that is a party where you talk to the dead, at least that is how he explained it to me. He said I could even talk to your father, Wild Bill. There is an old woman who runs the seance, she knows how to call the dead, or so Doc Ramses claims.

Oh, Janey, of course I want to talk to your father—it has been so many years. But I am scared. What if he has forgotten me? What a big disappointment that would be. If I do it I am going to ask Bartle to come, I would feel safer.

I asked Bartle if he wanted to converse with any dead

people, he said yes, General Custer, he wanted to ask why he had been such a fool as to fight five thousand Indians with two hundred men. If I was Bartle I'd try to think of someone friendlier than General Custer to talk to —I reminded him that most of the dead people we know are friendlier than Custer. We could ask Wind River Bill what caused him to disappear. When last seen he was perfectly healthy, camping on the Tongue River, there has been no sign of him since, I guess it has been ten years.

You could not call England a sunny country, unless you wanted to lie. The sunshine is scarce here, it drizzles like it used to back in Missouri when I was a girl. The Jubilee starts in three days, I believe there is going to be a mighty grand celebration, yesterday the bagpipers arrived. The sound scared the horses to death, it also alarmed the Indians and some of the cowboys, you should have seen them grab their guns.

But it was just bagpipers from Scotland. Some Africans arrived too. They are half-naked and carry spears. There are other wild-looking groups from all the parts of the world the Queen rules over. Virtually all of them are armed, this camp is filling up with violent groups. There are even a few elephants. No Ears has spent a good deal of time studying the elephants, he thinks they are important beasts but not in the class with the whale. No Ears was very impressed with that whale, he thinks no creature can compare with it. I was a little tipsy when the whale showed up, to me it was just a big fish.

We better get this Jubilee started, Janey, if all of us wild ones from the Queen's dominions sit around here armed to the teeth war is likely to break out, she'll have a massacre to celebrate instead of a Jubilee. Some of the Africans look like competent fighters. Even Sitting Bull thinks so—he has been introduced to several great chiefs, Zulus I think, I could be wrong. Sitting Bull behaves himself with these Africans. Old Sitting Bull does not want to get stomped by an elephant, I don't blame him.

I am still thinking about the seance, Janey, I don't

know if I want to talk to the dead. I will be dead soon enough—not anytime soon Janey, don't be alarmed. It's just that we'll all be dead soon enough. I might save my conversation until then.

Your mother,
Martha Jane

AT FIRST JIM SUPPOSED THAT HE WAS BEING MADE THE butt of a joke—or at least that Bartle was trying to trick him when he came running up claiming to have found beaver in London. Jim had been watching some skinny men with turbans feeding the elephants when Bartle jumped out of a buggy and came running across the park.

Naturally Jim was startled—it had been several years since he'd seen Bartle look so excited. For a moment he feared there might have been a killing. Everyone's nerves were on edge, waiting for the Jubilee to start—it would not be surprising if a killing resulted. Calamity was in an erratic state, up one day and down the next; she might well have shot someone in a saloon.

So when Bartle came out with his news, Jim didn't believe it.

"It's true," Bartle insisted. "They've got at least twenty beaver, maybe more."

"In the middle of a city?" Jim said. "Have you been to the opium den, or are you just drunk?"

"No, they're beaver from Canada, just like the ones you want to catch," Bartle said. "They've got them in a big pond. There's some muskrats, too."

"Well, I don't doubt the muskrats," Jim said. "You'll see muskrats anywhere."

"I guess you'd sneer at Moses!" Bartle said, exasperated with Jim's skepticism. "They call the place a zoo. It's as if old Noah unloaded his ark right there—there's every kind of creature you've ever heard of and plenty that you haven't."

No Ears was standing nearby; he found the information interesting.

"Where do the beaver live?" he asked.

"In a beaver house, just as if they were in the Tetons or anyplace," Bartle said.

Jim didn't really believe it, and No Ears had his doubts, but Bartle certainly believed it, and Bartle should know a beaver when he saw one. Jim decided he might as well see for himself. He asked No Ears to come with them. If they got lost, as was certainly possible in a confusing city such as London, three heads might be better than two, even if one of the heads was earless.

Jim felt dull, as he had for most of the trip. Certainly London was an unusual place, and he was being treated well—still, he felt dull. Bartle scampered about, seeing the city, but Jim mostly stayed with the show, reminiscing with the cowboys or some of the older Indians, particularly Two Hawks, a Brulé Sioux almost as old as No Ears. Two Hawks knew more particulars about the Custer battle than anyone Jim had yet encountered. It was an odd thing to admit, but after nearly forty years of hiding from Indians or living in fear of Indians, Indians were turning out to be the only people left he could trust.

He didn't really believe there were any beaver in London—it was just another of Bartle's jokes. Bartle was drunk most of the time, and was incapable of the truth even when he was sober. It was so foggy when they got to the big park that at first Jim merely concentrated on keeping his bearings. They had scarcely stepped out of the bus when a man on a large bicycle nearly ran into them; he had a little horn on his bicycle that squawked rather like a goose, and he squawked it at them impatiently, as if they had no right to be there.

"Dern, this fog's solid," Bartle said. "I have never seen such a place for fog—one minute you can see where you're going, and the next minute you can't."

The damp, cottony fog hovered near the ground. No Ears couldn't see much, but he could smell a great deal, and what he smelled startled him. He had long since developed a kind of index of animal smells, keen enough to alert him in case he was approached by an unfriendly animal, such as a bear, on a dark night. What startled him was that the smells coming to him through the cottony fog were not contained in his index at all. Clearly there were animals around, but they were not animals he was familiar with.

No Ears felt rather alarmed—for one thing, he smelled large birds, and ever since the great cranes had come and lurked around him waiting to snatch his soul, he had not been comfortable around large birds. The fact that he could not see the birds made the matter more chancy.

Jim Ragg felt a little disgusted with himself for having let Bartle lead him astray so easily. As far as he was concerned, the fog explained everything. Everyone knew what an encouragement fog was to people with too much imagination. If you stared into a fog too long you would see whatever you wanted to see, or more commonly, whatever you *didn't* want to see. Even experienced frontiersmen had been known to empty their guns into a fog, convinced that they saw Indians sneaking up. Once, on the Red River of the North, he and Bartle had seen a heavy river fog produce complete panic in a crew of keelboaters, who, of all people, should have understood the distracting properties of fog. One keelboater looked into the fog too hard, thought he saw an Indian; soon every man in the boat was firing wildly. When the fog cleared, all that was there was the waving grass.

Bartle, no doubt drunk, had seen a muskrat slide into a ditch and had proceeded to conjure up beaver. But now they were there, trapped in the fog, and there was nothing for it but to try and find their way back to the encampment.

The three men inched along, taking care to stay together. For several minutes they saw nothing. No Ears felt particularly unhappy with the fog; it was so dense that his soul might well leave without his even noticing it. The mountain men, only a yard away, might not notice either.

Then they all heard a snuffle, a little to their left. Bartle put out his hand and felt a fence. The snuffle had sounded somewhat cowlike; on the other hand it had not sounded like a normal cow.

"Don't worry, boys," Bartle said. "There's a fence between us and it."

"It has a powerful smell," No Ears said. "It smells worse than dead muskrats."

"Well, it's just that musk-ox," Bartle said. "I seen it yesterday. They've got it in with another smelly creature."

No Ears noticed that the fog was rising. He could see the mountain men's legs—then, farther along the path, he could see several pairs of hurrying legs, belonging, he supposed, to English people who were so accustomed to the fog that they knew how to walk through it without harm. A stream of sunlight slanted down, making a white band in the smoky fog. He could vaguely see two beasts standing very close to them. The beast that stood closest and smelled the worst seemed to be composed almost entirely of hair. It had two thick, curving horns, but otherwise was entirely covered with thick, smelly hair—it did not even seem to have eyes. It merely lived inside its hair. Beside it stood a smaller beast, also very hairy. To No Ears's astonishment, a boy appeared beside the two beasts; the boy began to pull hay out of a cart. He dumped the hay in front of the two beasts, who ignored it. The boy scratched the smaller beast's back, but the beast paid no attention.

"Hey, what sort of buffalo are these?" Bartle asked the boy. "And which way to the beaver, may I ask?"

The boy was so surprised at the sight of them that he almost ran away. He had not expected to see two mountain men and an old Indian without ears staring at him while he did his work.

"This is our musk-ox and our yak," he said nervously, once he had recovered from his surprise.

Jim Ragg studied the musk-ox closely. He thought it would be a task to kill it; both the horns and the hair looked capable of stopping a bullet. The other animal looked about as dumb as a buffalo, if more heavily padded.

"What about the beaver?" Bartle asked again. "My *compañero* here ain't convinced you've got any beaver."

"Oh, we've got 'em, but I wish we didn't," the boy said. "I don't like to get near 'em, because of those big teeth. They bite right through wood—I don't want one of them biting through me."

Jim was startled. The boy knew what a beaver looked like, obviously. Maybe there *were* beaver in the park—but what an odd place to find them, with the streets of London just a few strides away.

No Ears had a scare. Across the path from where they stood, he saw a large pink bird standing on one leg. The bird was almost as large as the great cranes, but the great cranes were gray and this bird was pink. While he watched, the bird put down his other leg and walked into what remained of the fog. No Ears was glad the bird had chosen to leave; still, a large pink bird was a disquieting thing to encounter. He began to wish he had stayed in camp and watched the elephants.

"Keep going, them beaver are to the left, you kind of curve around once you pass the hippo," the boy said.

Jim picked up the pace immediately—the fog was breaking and there was no longer much danger of getting lost. No Ears stopped dead when he saw the hippo. At first it looked like a beast made of mud—very ugly. The English seemed to have made an effort to collect ugly beasts—the musk-ox and the yak had been fairly ugly, though not as ugly as the muddy hippo, which he took to be a kind of mud pig.

Bartle enjoyed the hippo and stopped with No Ears to

watch it for a bit. Jim Ragg hurried on. The path curved, as the boy said it would; even before he saw the beaver he heard a sound he had not heard in many years: the slap of a beaver's tail on water. A little fog still drifted across the surface of the pond when he heard the beaver slap the water; it was a sound he had first heard on the Platte as a boy of sixteen; it was the sound that had called him on, deeper and deeper into the west, to the Missouri and then the Yellowstone, all the way to the dangerous Bitterroot; then it became a sound he heard less and less often as the beaver vanished from the Bitterroot and the Tongue, from the golden Madison valley, from Wyoming, from Colorado; the last time he had heard the beaver's slap was high in the Medicine Bow forest more than ten years before. He had listened for it in vain ever since—but here it was, at last!

As he walked down to the pond a fat, shiny beaver, floating on its back, looked up at him, unafraid; through the lifting fog he saw a large beaver house as impressive as any on the Platte or any other stream.

"Beaver," he said aloud, startling a woman who walked past under an umbrella.

When Bartle and No Ears tired of the hippopotamus and walked on along the path, they saw Jim Ragg sitting on the grass by the pool, watching the prime Canadian beaver swim around. Occasionally, just for the sport of it, one would slap the water with its tail.

Bartle stopped a discreet distance away—his old *compañero* would probably just feel embarrassed if they approached him at such a time. After all, a long search had ended—best just to leave the man alone.

No Ears was happy to leave him alone, and the beaver, too—he wanted to see what other ugly animals the English had put in their pasture.

"I guess we'll know where to find old Jim for the next few days," Bartle said, as they watched a small herd of striped goats climb on some rocks. "He'll be a while getting enough of the beaver."

"I wonder where that pink bird went," No Ears said,

but he had scarcely spoken before he looked around and received a worse shock still. A bird far larger than any he had seen in his life came trotting along the path they were on, pulling a small buggy with two children and a woman in it. Looking more closely, No Ears found that he could not be sure that the approaching creature was even a bird. Its legs were scaly like a bird's, and longer than the legs of some horses; its body was the size of a small pig's, and covered with feathers, yet the creature did not seem to have wings and showed no interest in flying. It trotted along as rapidly as a pony; it had a long neck and a bald head, and it looked at them angrily—yet it had consented to pull the buggy with two boys and a rather fat woman in it. The little boys wore neckties and caps. No Ears had seen many angry birds in his lifetime, including several very angry eagles and some bad roosters, but he had never seen a bird that looked as fierce and unfriendly as the large creature pulling the buggy. The same boy who had been feeding the musk-ox sat on the seat of the small buggy, guiding the huge bird by means of a little bridle.

Bartle and No Ears stepped aside and the creature passed without attempting to do them harm.

"They call that an ostrich," Bartle volunteered. "They sell rides in that buggy—I took one yesterday. It'll pull you all around the zoo."

"If it is a bird I would like to see its egg," No Ears said.

"It's a bird," Bartle assured him. "I don't know if it's a cock or a hen."

"Do you think it could fly away with that buggy?" No Ears asked. It seemed to him that people were very foolish to risk themselves in a buggy pulled by such a bird. Of course, the bird did not seem to have wings, but then it was a very strange bird and might have some means of flight that didn't involve wings. Its legs seemed very powerful; perhaps it could merely jump into the air and float for a while. He had often seen birds floating on the air, but this was not an ability people had. The little boys in their neat caps would undoubtedly fall out of the buggy and die if the bird suddenly leaped into the sky.

"It's a heavy bird," Bartle said. "I doubt it can fly. I've seen grouse so fat they couldn't fly."

No Ears felt that the issue of whether the great bird could fly was only one of many issues that he would need to consider before he could feel at ease in the English people's collection of strange and ugly animals. Though he disliked Sitting Bull, he thought he might invite Sitting Bull and one or two of the more mature Indians to visit the park and observe the ugly animals. At least he would then have someone to confer with who understood animals. No whites that he had met really understood animals, though they could be quite skilled at killing them. He had only been in the zoo place a few minutes and already had seen more unfamiliar animals than he had encountered in a lifetime on the plains.

"I think we should go back to the camp," he said to Bartle. "I don't want to be pulled in a buggy by that large bird."

What he needed was time in which to think about the animals he had already seen. None of them would take as much thought as the great whale fish, but that didn't mean it would be wise to ignore them. That was the mistake all white people, and even some red people, made: ignoring animals. Animals had far too much power just to ignore.

No Ears didn't want to see any more unusual creatures until he could collect his thoughts regarding the ones he had already seen—but he and Bartle were in the middle of the zoo place, and before they could make their way to the street he saw a number of sights that added considerably to all that he needed to think about. He passed a huge cage that contained what appeared to be a tribe of tiny, hairy men who jumped around and chattered in their own language and climbed trees. Bartle said the furry men were called monkeys.

Then they passed a very large furry man, sitting in a cage doing nothing, and several cages containing huge, sleeping cats, some striped and some with manes like buffaloes. No Ears was glad the large cats were asleep.

He tried to hurry Bartle along and paid no attention when Bartle tried to tell him the names of the many creatures. He had too much to think about as it was without worrying himself immediately with the names of every beast. They were almost out of the park—he could hear the clatter of horses in the street—when they passed a little pen containing another creature so strange that it simply could not be ignored. This one walked slowly, like a porcupine, and had a long snout like a tube. No Ears thought it might be a tiny elephant of some kind, but Bartle told him it was an anteater. He claimed the beast used its long snout to reach down into anthills and suck up ants. It was a good-sized beast and would probably need to suck in a great many ants in order to keep itself fed. No Ears wondered if the boy whose job it was to give hay to the hairbeasts and to drive the buggy behind the great fierce bird also had to find ants in sufficient supply to sustain the large anteater. If so, he would have to do some hard looking because the ground in England seemed too wet to contain very many ants. If the boy did find them, how did he collect them and take them to the anteater without being badly stung? No place he had ever been raised as many questions as the English zoo place.

"I hope that pink bird left," he remarked when he and Bartle were safely in one of the bus-buggies on their way back to the encampment.

"Oh, it just walked off, I guess," Bartle said. "There's a little lake or two that I didn't show you. Jim was too eager to get on to the beavers."

Soon they were back in the camp. Bartle went off to look for Calamity to see if she was in the mood for cards, or perhaps would rather pay a visit to the music halls. No Ears was glad to be left in peace. He settled down by one of the big baggage wagons to smoke and begin to sort through the problems posed by the existence of so many strange animals.

On the bank of a pond in the zoo, Jim sat happily all day watching the beavers slap their tails, and float, and dive, and rise. He stayed until darkness hid the pond, and even then sat for a while listening to the sound of beaver.

Darling Jane—

I done the seance, Janey. It was in a part of London where the houses are all black from coal, the children look like they're starving and are all black as soot. The beggars are everywhere, London swarms with them. I didn't care for the trip, I don't like to see people that poor. They make the Shoshone look like millionaires.

The little woman who ran the seance was twisted, her back had been broken. Doc Ramses said she fell off a train, certainly she was unusual. She reminded me of the old Mexican woman in Miles City who tells fortunes. The Mexican woman had a goose, this one had a pig, it was a well-behaved pig I must say. The old woman fed it orange peels while we were waiting for the dead people to speak.

It was just me and Doc Ramses and No Ears who went. Jim won't leave the beavers now, and Bartle was going to take Annie Oakley a bouquet or some present. He is still wooing her, it will do no good—Annie Oakley don't care for Bartle. She is the best shot in the world, and Bartle is just an old mountain man with a nice beard. I am a little unfair to Bartle, he has been a good friend to me—there's no doubt he's vain about his beard though.

Doc Ramses keeps looking at me funny, he thinks he knows my secret—he don't, Janey, nobody knows my secret. When you are older I will attempt to tell you, you will understand then that when I got the nickname Calamity in some ways it ain't far wrong. Little Doc Ramses may be able to see the future but he can't see my secret, Janey, no one can. If he expects to put me in a freak show he has chosen the wrong person and I will tell him so if he becomes too bold.

It was a dark little house, just lit with candles. I was nervous about the pig at first. There was another person there when we came in, I suspect he was a banker, he was very well dressed. He wanted to contact his wife who had drowned herself—he was telling her that he missed her, that the children cried all day—it is terrible that a mother of children would do that, Janey, drown nerself, yet people do it, they get too sad and can imagine no other way out. This banker was a broken man, pleading with his wife to come back from heaven, of course she can't, she's gone.

I was awake all night, trying to think of what to say to your father if the seance worked—it only worked for No Ears, he soon began to talk in the old Sioux language. Later I asked him if he was talking to his wives or his children, he said no he was only talking to the old woman he saved the day the traders cut off his ears. He had not meant to speak to the old woman, he really wanted a few words with Black Kettle, the old chief Custer killed on the Washita. No Ears said Black Kettle was an old friend but instead of Black Kettle the old woman started talking, she said the spirit place was no happier than earth. Hearing that has made No Ears determined to stick it out another few years.

I didn't try to contact your father, Janey, I got shy, I felt he might not want to be bothered—why would the dead want to be bothered, they're at peace—at least they're dead, it would be a strain for them to have to hold a conversation with someone they hadn't thought of in years.

I thought though I would try to have a parlay with Wind River Bill, the curtains blew and I heard a sound like the wind coming, but I didn't hear Wind River Bill, not a word. I told the old woman I wanted my money back, I gave her some English money. She got on a high horse and refused—she said the man I wanted to speak to wasn't even dead, of course he didn't answer. If it turns out she's right and Wind River Bill ain't dead he's going to get a slap from me next time I see him. He hasn't been around in ten years, what kind of friend is that? Of course he could be in Texas.

I let the old woman keep the money, she can buy oranges and peel them for her pig, having a twisted back must be very painful.

The Jubilee opens tomorrow Janey, there will be a grand parade and your mother will be in it. They say there will be a crowd such as never has been gathered on earth. Chiefs have come from everywhere, a few too many chiefs, maybe, war nearly broke out between our Indians and some that came over from Canada. Sitting Bull wanted to start the war, he lived in Canada for a while when he was on the run after the Greasy Grass. He claims the Canada Indians didn't give him enough help, what that probably means is they didn't give him enough presents, he is annoyed because the horse they gave him died. Sitting Bull expects too much, of course all horses die, this one just died immediately, I guess—that would be enough to make him hate the Canada Indians forever.

On Saturday we are going to do our show for the Queen. I am riding shotgun on the Deadwood stage, it shouldn't be too hard, all I have to do is shoot off blanks when the Indians come up whooping and hollering to assault us. Texas Jack is going to drive the stage, and Bartle and Jim will be passengers—if you ask me that's ridiculous, they were supposed to be Lewis and Clark and the Deadwood stage wasn't running when Lewis and Clark passed through. I may be wrong about that Janey—I know little history but I think Lewis and Clark had to walk all the way to the ocean and back—of course they might have ridden in a boat part of the way.

A man named Buntline showed up, a writer, I met him once, years ago. He has bought me two meals already, he says he wants to write up my adventures when we get home. He says he has already written more than a dozen adventures about Billy Cody—they are big sellers, he says. Stanley was here also—I am confused about Stanley, I thought he was just a newspaper man but Bartle says he is a big explorer. He was telling Bartle stories about Africa, now Bartle wants to stop there on our way home.

I miss Dora so much Janey—I have had no news of Dakota at all, Montana either—sometimes my heart beats fast at night if I have a bad dream. I wake up thinking what if Dora's dead when I get home, what would I do? Of course she was perfectly well when I left, I have no reason to be fearful, still I am Janey. Dora is not very strong, Blue is right not to subject her to the hard ranch life, she might not last.

Buntline and Doc Ramses don't get along—Doc claims Buntline cheated Billy on some of the adventure books. He had better not cheat me, I will set him back on his heels if he does, or maybe flat on his back. Buntline is persistent he says he will make me richer than I have ever been. Ha, it would not take much to make me richer than I have ever been, Janey. I pointed out to him that I have never been exactly well-to-do, not in the class of Lillie Langtry or some other great actress, right now I only have two dollars and I borrowed those from Bartle. Annie Oakley is the one who is rich.

The big news is that Jim Ragg finally found beaver, they're in a zoo. I have been there twice to see them, everyone has to go to please Jim. Everyone but Texas Jack that is, he says he has no desire ever to see another beaver. That annoyed Jim. It was not mannerly of Jack to say that, but then Jack has never stooped over very far to please anyone, he is like your father in that regard. Wild Bill would have said something in the same vein, he was never known to say excuse me or anything polite in his life. Sometimes I think Jack Omohundro is trying to imitate your father, Janey. He's grown a mustache just like Bill Hickok's. Jack claims they were friends but I never heard your father mention Jack Omohundro.

I hope Buntline does write up my adventures, at least I would have a little more money to contribute to your schooling, also I could help Dora—I could pay my rent for a change. When this Wild West show ends I will just be adrift again, Jim and Bartle too. We're all getting old, Janey, Jim looks like an old man and Bartle is not much better, none of us are feeling well, we are not used to this English damp. The only one thriving is Billy Cody, I don't know where Billy gets his pep, but he's got plenty. He's the toast of London, he goes out every night—they all want to hear how he scalped Yellow Hand. Jack don't get invited nearly as much, naturally he is jealous. Billy even met Lillie Langtry. He brought her to camp one day, my, she was elegant—I got shy and didn't meet her, I looked too rough. I hid behind a wagon but I got a good look at her as Billy was helping her into her buggy, she has servants to attend her just like the Queen.

Wish me luck in the show Janey, I don't know why I ask, of course the show will long be over before you read this. Still it is comforting to think my daughter would wish me luck. I just hope the stage don't turn over, I have always been nervous when riding in stagecoaches.

Your mother,
Martha Jane

4

LORD WINDHOUVEREN, ATTENDED BY SEVERAL GUN-
handlers, several journalists, his footman, his valet, and
six boys from the kitchen—the boys were to set up a
splendid picnic lunch for himself, the Prince of Wales,
and anyone noble who might show up—waited in perfect
confidence for the arrival of the American team, if a single girl and a few rough attendants could be called a team.
There was a rather stiff breeze from the south, but Lord
Windhouveren—generally acknowledged to be the best
shot in England—expected no difficulty. Let the Oakley
girl worry about the breeze.

A shooting match was scheduled, each gun to shoot at
one thousand thrown targets. At his club the night before,
there had been some discussion of the number. Several
experienced guns were there, men who had hunted in
every corner of the Empire, and all doubted that the number would ever be reached. Seldenham, himself a notable
shot, felt sure the young lady would have enough before
they had even thrown two hundred pigeons. All the
gentlemen were perfectly polite and none had any wish
to insult Miss Oakley; she had comported herself far better than the other Americans who came with the Wild

West show—possibly excepting Buffalo Bill himself. He was clearly a presentable fellow, though the lamentable horse race at Ascot in which the English jockey was disgraced had lodged resentments in many breasts.

Lord Windhouveren felt a modest pride in having been chosen to avenge the silly horse race—he had always felt that horseflesh was unpredictable, nothing the nation should place its confidence in. Once a horse had stepped hard on his foot; three of his toenails eventually had to be removed, and the aggravation had caused him to look askance at horses ever since. Guns were another matter. Point a gun correctly and it would do its work; of no horse, so far as he knew, could the same be said.

Now, as he watched the American party approach in several buggies, followed by their own team of pressmen, he had no doubt whatever that his marksmanship would prevail, and he felt a distinct impatience to get on with the event. He *did* hope the Prince of Wales would arrive promptly, but he had known Prince Edward for many years and knew that, while he might hope for a prompt arrival, it would be foolish to expect it. Prince Edward was known throughout the world for his princely unpunctuality.

Annie Oakley had forbidden old Bartle to speak to her on the way to the match; Jack Omohundro was also warned to let her be, and Billy Cody had been consigned to another carriage, since there was no hope of keeping him quiet. Annie detested chatter before a match, and didn't welcome it after. Men might fall in love with her as much as they liked; she had no objection to bouquets and sweets and would even accept a muff or a pretty fan now and then, but she always made sure it was clearly understood that they all had to stand back and stow their sweetheart talk when she was preparing to shoot. She was, after all, a married woman, and happily married, too. She didn't want silly words pouring in her ears—she wanted to concentrate. When she concentrated she saw sharp mental pictures of herself making perfect shots. There would be the sky, then a target would fly across it, a gun barrel would quickly catch up with the flying target, and the target would break to bits. Her mental pictures were soundless, and her shooting was as soundless as she could make it by fitting cotton plugs of her own devising into her ears. Once her eyes found the target the gun would swing precisely and the target would explode.

Bartle thought Annie Oakley was as pretty a woman as a man could want—of course there was Lillie Langtry, but Lillie Langtry might as well be an angel for all the chance he had with her. Annie was not in heaven, she was right there in the buggy, pretty and pert, if rather steely in her demeanor. Of course, she had her match to think of, whereas he could take a more relaxed approach and mostly think of her.

By the time they had the guns unpacked, the ammunition laid out, and small barrels of water to cool the gun barrels rolled into place, quite a crowd had gathered. Stanley was there, and Buntline, and Russell of the *Times*. Stanley shadowed Bill Cody—his interest was, in the main, stars—but Russell of the *Times* preferred to interrogate the mountain men. He was an unkempt fellow in a shabby brown coat, himself not much different in appearance from a mountain man. Texas Jack regarded him with distaste and walked off upwind so as not to be required to smell him.

"Men, do you think Miss Oakley has a chance?" Russell asked.

Bartle considered the question impertinent. "What sort of gent are you?" he asked.

Jim Ragg was loading Annie's gun. He ignored the palaver.

"I am no gent, I'm a reporter," Russell replied. "If Lord Windhouveren loses, he will have to leave the country—the disgrace will finish him. Is Miss Oakley up to it?"

Annie herself was pulling on her shooting gloves. She had nodded politely to Lord Windhouveren and then stepped away from the crowd. She wanted to keep her mental pictures sharp. She put the cotton plugs in her ears, arranging them carefully so they wouldn't give her an earache. Texas Jack had positioned himself near the trap containing the clay pigeons. By focusing just to his left she would see the targets the moment they left the trap. She didn't need to hear anyone say "Pull!" She only needed to see the targets promptly. Texas Jack wore a black shirt, which would contrast well with the white clay targets. Annie felt quite relaxed, as she always did when it came time to shoot. The mountain men might look old and dirty, but they knew guns. They knew when to cool a barrel. All she had to do was take the guns and break the targets.

Bartle felt that Russell of the *Times* must be exaggerating with his talk of the English gent having to leave home if he lost—though it was true that the crowd at Ascot had jeered the poor jockey brutally when he lost the race. He was just a poor jockey, though, not a great gent like Lord Windhouveren.

"Annie's up to it," Bartle said. "I hope the gentleman has got a nice place picked out to move to, if he's that set on moving."

"Lord Windhouveren once killed nine hundred grouse in a day," Russell remarked.

"Oh, well, Billy Cody killed six hundred buffalo in less time than that," Bartle said, exaggerating considerably out of national pride. "And Annie Oakley can outshoot Billy Cody blindfolded, or folded any other way you want to fold her."

"*I* can outshoot Billy Cody," Jim Ragg said, annoyed by Bartle's tendency to always brag on Billy. "And I'm just a tolerable shot."

Fifty birds had been thrown when Prince Edward and his retinue drove up. Prince Edward felt sleepy and a little dyspeptic; still, he was determined to witness Windhouveren's triumph. The man had often had him to Scotland to shoot, and the arrangements had been excellent. Miss Oakley, of course, was not unappealing; at moments the Prince found her *quite* appealing, but that was another matter. She could hardly expect to triumph over Windhouveren, a man who had brought down nine hundred grouse in a day. It gave the Prince a bit of a start to have it whispered to him that at fifty pigeons Windhouveren had missed three times, while Miss Oakley had yet to miss.

"Perhaps he had a late night," Prince Edward said to his companion, Daisy, Countess of Warwick. "I'm sure he'll brace up presently."

Lord Windhouveren did brace up. He broke forty-eight targets in a row before missing twice more. Unfortunately, Miss Oakley had yet to miss. She *did* miss the hundredth shot, but that still left him four behind.

"She handles her gun admirably," he said to his handlers. "I expect I'll catch her this hundred."

Still, he didn't feel quite right. His Purdeys refused to swing quite as smoothly as they always had. Changing guns seemed to make no difference. There was something about the small figure of Annie Oakley that he had begun to find vastly irritating. She never looked at him—she never looked at anyone. She seemed oblivious to the fact that the Prince of Wales had arrived with the Countess of Warwick. She seemed to have no sense of the importance of the occasion, or to have taken into consideration that he was the best shot in the nation, perhaps the best shot in the Empire. Her lowbred practicality was beginning to annoy him—to annoy him quite considerably. She said nothing, never smiled, never looked around, had not even bowed to the Prince; she just took her gun and broke target after target.

They had agreed to a short rest after each two hundred and fifty targets. When the count was reached, Lord Windhouveren had missed ten targets; Annie Oakley had only missed three.

Out of deference to his sovereign, Lord Windhouveren walked over to the Prince's tent and accepted a glass of champagne. The Prince looked stiff and displeased. The usually ebullient Countess, chief flirt of her age, showed no signs of ebullience. She was thinking how difficult it would be to get Eddie in a good mood again if Windhouveren, a pompous braggart, actually allowed himself to be beaten by a snippet from America.

"Brace up, Windhouveren!" Prince Edward said. "No nonsense now! Break your bird."

Lord Windhouveren went back to the line feeling distinctly uneasy. The Prince of Wales rarely rose so early, even for a sporting event; it was plain that he would not look kindly upon defeat. Windhouveren glanced at Annie Oakley to see if he could detect signs of fatigue; he saw none. She had not bothered to sit down, had only taken a little tea. Still, he considered that she might tire. A gun that felt light at the beginning began to feel deucedly heavy after seven or eight hundred swings. Let her keep her lead for now; he would take her in the last two hundred.

Never in his long life of shooting had Lord Windhouveren concentrated as hard as he did on the second two hundred and fifty targets. He concentrated as if his life depended on it—as if he were firing at advancing Zulus or shrieking disciples of the Mahdi. Yet a sense of injustice rose in him in proportion to the intensity of his concentration. Instead of shooting better, he shot rather appallingly worse.

When the five-hundredth target had been thrown, Lord Windhouveren had missed twenty-nine targets. Annie Oakley had missed eight. The shocking thought that he might actually lose could not be forced out of his mind. He wanted to strangle the girl. Why wouldn't she miss? He had never supposed for a second in his life that any woman could outshoot him; now one was doing it, and doing it quite casually. The filthy old men in their smelly buckskins loaded her guns and handed them to her as if it were the simplest business in the world—she might have been shooting sparrows, not being matched against the finest shot in the kingdom. An appalling calamity was occurring, and the deuced thing was, Lord Windhouveren had no idea how to stop it.

In the circumstances he thought it best not to approach his sovereign during the halfway break.

The thought that Windhouveren might lose had occurred to others, too. Stanley had stopped pestering Buffalo Bill and stood in amazement, watching the girl shoot. Russell of the *Times* sat with his back against the wheel of a buggy and scribbled on a pad. Before the match began, Buffalo Bill and Texas Jack had ambled among the gentry, smiling and accepting large wagers at long odds. The gentry had unanimously bet on Lord Windhouveren; now a number of the men were scowling. What did the man think he was doing? His shooting was an appalling embarrassment. A number of pale ladies, jolly only hours before, foresaw a difficult evening—none more so than Daisy, Countess of Warwick.

"I was never fond of Windhouveren," she gently pointed out. "I've told you so, Eddie."

Prince Edward was at a loss for words, though far from at a loss for indignation. With every Windhouveren miss he flinched; it didn't help his dyspepsia at all. It was inconsiderate—indeed, impertinent—for the man to go on missing. Windhouveren had ample estates, too; he usually produced excellent arrangements. It was a very great nuisance that he continued to miss.

"I am not a man to overlook a nuisance," he remarked darkly to Daisy. He was not telling the Countess anything she didn't know.

"She's a nice shot, ain't she?" Bartle remarked to Russell of the *Times*. Champagne flowed liberally among the observers; despite his attention to the guns, some had flowed into him.

"She's better than that," Russell said. "I'd choose her for my regiment any day, if I had a regiment. Windhouveren's finished—that's how I judge it."

"I admire your beard, sir," Bartle said—he was picking up a little English style.

At the end of seven hundred and fifty targets, silence prevailed on the field. Only the quick pop of the guns and the occasional stamp of a buggy horse broke the silence. Even the breeze seemed to seize the sound of the guns. Lord Windhouveren had missed forty-seven targets, Annie Oakley only ten.

Russell of the *Times* scribbled, Stanley walked around with his hands in his pockets, Buffalo Bill and Texas Jack held their peace; no use rubbing it in.

Windhouveren took a draught of beer; as he was drinking it he noticed the Prince's carriage leaving. The sad thought occurred to him that he might never see Prince Edward again.

The gentry stayed to the bitter—exceedingly bitter—end. Lord Windhouveren missed sixty-five targets, Annie Oakley only sixteen.

Though she had won, Annie was not overly pleased. Nine hundred eighty-four out of a thousand seemed to her only fair shooting. She had never expected much of the Englishman; he was clearly no shot. She felt she had been lax in her adjustment to the wind. The news that Billy and Jack had won over two thousand pounds in bets didn't interest her. She felt she had better come back to the field tomorrow and get in several hours of practice. Perhaps if she paid Bartle and Jim, they would come load for her.

The boys from Lord Windhouveren's kitchen were instructed not to unpack the picnic baskets. The twenty pheasants, the goose, and the leg of mutton would not be eaten—at least not then. "Splendid shooting, ma'am—quite the best I've seen," Lord Windhouveren said to Annie Oakley; as a gentleman, as well as a sporting man, he meant it, but Annie Oakley hardly seemed to notice. He said as much again to Russell of the *Times*, who thanked him politely. Buffalo Bill, too, was very polite; he said it was Annie's practice on shipboard that helped her adjust to the breeze.

"Where shall we go now?" his Lordship's aged valet asked—he was disturbed by the gray look on his master's face.

"I expect it will have to be India, and now that damned Curzon's there!" Lord Windhouveren said.

5

At Cody's urging, Ned Buntline tried his hand at a Lewis and Clark skit—in fact, he produced six versions in the course of a morning. Speed had ever been his forte —but Ned was a cool judge of his own productions and knew that in regard to Lewis and Clark, his work lacked spark.

Of course, Lewis and Clark were among the great names of history, but what had they done that you could make into a drama? For drama you needed death or, at the very least, battle. There was no doubt in Ned's mind that death had its part to play in every successful story.

His own highly successful career had only served to reinforce this view. Crockett dying at the Alamo, Custer massacred on the Little Bighorn, Billy the Kid shot down young in New Mexico—his vivid accounts of those famous deaths had produced huge sales. He had even done fairly well with Bigfoot Wallace and the black beans; although Bigfoot had actually drawn a white bean and lived, nineteen of his Texas bravos had drawn the fatal black beans and been stood before a firing squad in the city of Mexico.

Death had been there, as it had been when Billy Cody

killed Yellow Hand—whereas Lewis and Clark had made it back. True, they had opened the west, but where was the climax?

"Sacajawea," Billy Cody insisted. "It was a story of jealousy—two brave explorers and only one Indian maiden. At least we could have them flare up and shoot off their long rifles at one another."

"What long rifles?" Bartle asked. "Jim and me just brought plain Winchesters."

Billy almost wished he hadn't brought the two old-timers. He had tracked them across the Dakotas and then brought them across the ocean only to have them disagree with him about firearms.

It sometimes seemed to him that he was the only one in the whole troupe who could see the greatness of the pageant they were part of: the Pages of Passing History, they called it in the show. It seemed that he alone could feel the wonder of the past they had all lived, as it came alive in recreated scenes. The rest of them thought it was just silly, or wanted to argue endlessly about details.

Sometimes, contemplating the gap between himself and the troupe, he felt a considerable sadness, so sharp that once or twice it came near to overcoming him. These people he had gone to such trouble to hire, riding from agency to agency to persuade Indians to come, collecting a cowboy here and a Pony Express rider there, didn't see the glory of their own lives. They just saw trivial detail.

Jim and Bartle had been the first white men to trap the dangerous Bitterroot. They were *true* mountain men, the spiritual sons of Lewis and Clark, of Fremont and Pike; they had known all the great Indians too: Red Cloud, Spotted Tail, Crazy Horse, Gall, Dull Knife, Touches the Sky, and many others. They had been there almost at the beginning of the great western adventure, and had walked the very paths followed by Lewis and Clark, the men he wanted them to play. As he saw it, their lives were part of the fabric of a great time: they should realize it.

If *they* didn't, Buntline certainly should; he was a writer and could be expected to display a little imagination—and yet, no one seemed to realize it except himself and maybe poor Calamity, who, at the moment, was sleeping under the Deadwood stage, dead drunk. Dead drunk now, and dead drunk most of the trip—and yet she alone, with the possible exception of No Ears and one or two other Indians, understood what it was that made their Wild West show a spectacle that held the attention of people everywhere: lords and ladies, queens and earls, down to the poorest street urchin.

Calamity and he knew what they all should have known: that the story of the west was a great story. You had a wilderness won, red race against white race, nature red in tooth and claw, death to the loser, glory to the victor: what could ever make a nobler show? It seemed to him that it was finer than Dickens, and Calamity—who hadn't read Dickens—thought so too.

Yet now he couldn't even get the celebrated novelist Ned Buntline to write in Lewis and Clark, the men who got it all started.

"I told you Coronado would work better," Doc Ramses said. Doc was always one to insist that his ideas were better than anyone's.

"Oh, what did Coronado do, except get lost and wander all over Kansas?" Billy asked.

"Well, he found the Brazos River," Texas Jack said. "I was born not two miles from the Brazos River. If he hadn't found it, where would that leave me?"

"Don't you suppose the Comanches knew where the Brazos River was long before Coronado?" Billy exclaimed, exasperated by the ridiculous arguments he was hearing.

"If they did, it's not common knowledge," Texas Jack remarked. Of course, now that Billy had called his attention to it, it was rather likely that not only the Comanches but Kiowas, Kickapoos, and various other tribes might have stumbled on the Brazos in their travels.

"Coronado was Mexican and you don't even speak the language!" Billy snapped, still annoyed at Jack.

"Why, Bill, I may not speak it, but I can court in it, and I have," Texas Jack said, amused at how hot Billy got when things didn't go his way in regard to the show.

"We could rent some suits of armor," Doc Ramses mentioned. "There's plenty of suits of armor here in England."

"No, Coronado ain't part of the *American* story," Billy insisted. "We ain't doing the whole history of the world—if we were I guess we'd have to get Calamity to play Eve."

That notion brought the company up short: Calamity had been unusually quarrelsome of late.

"If Calamity had been Eve I doubt the whole business would have gone much further," Bartle said. "Her tongue's getting rougher, and it never was smooth. If she was Eve, Adam might as well have let the rattlesnake bite him."

"Oh, now, be fair," Billy said. "She might just dislike the climate here."

He felt obliged to take up for Calamity, though she had recently been nothing but trouble. He had had to get her out of jail three times; she could often be seen drunk outside some bar. Then she had given them all a dreadful scare by falling off the Deadwood stage while it was in full flight from Red Shirt and his boys—and on the very day the Queen was there too. If hands less cool than Texas Jack Omohundro's had been driving the team, she would likely have been run over and killed. As it was, people assumed it was just a stunt, that she was just pretending to be shot; Red Shirt had the presence of mind to jump off his horse and pretend to scalp her—all the Indians carried wigs in their belts, in case a sudden scalping opportunity arose. The Queen thought Calamity's fall was the most thrilling part of the show, too—or so her man, Mr. Ponsonby, had said.

Unfortunately Calamity had taken to cursing anyone who interfered with her behavior in the slightest, and this the London constabulary was not willing to tolerate.

Billy couldn't find it in his heart to be severe with her, though—she was too bound up with his memories of Dora, and he did miss Dora terribly. If only she hadn't had such a troublesome fondness for T. Blue, he believed he could have persuaded her to come.

He decided, thinking about it, to dispatch Dora a few souvenirs of the show—programs and such—to show her how grand it was. Perhaps next year, when they did the big exposition in Paris, Dora could be persuaded to come too.

But he could not help feeling irked with Doc and Ned, Jack and the mountain men, as well as many of the cowboys and Indians. They were all living legends, in the main thanks to himself, and yet they didn't seem to appreciate the legend part. They just wanted to go on living, as lazily as possible. Sitting Bull was the exception. He might be a scoundrel and a braggart, demanding endless attention, but at least he cared about his own legend. He was Sitting Bull—he had said so to Queen Victoria herself, and the Queen had been properly impressed. She had even given him an engraved saber, which he displayed proudly and might yet use to slice off a few heads if people weren't careful.

Jim Ragg got up and left the discussion. He didn't object to being either Lewis *or* Clark—let Billy and/or Ned decide. After all, Billy was handling the expenses; let him order up what skits he wanted.

He put a buffalo robe over the sleeping Calamity and went striding off through London to see his beavers. He had long since learned the route and rarely bothered with the buses—he frightened the passengers too much, and in any case he preferred to walk.

Jim felt light and calm—it was wonderful what having a few beaver to watch had done for his disposition. Everyone commented on it, particularly Bartle. After years of daily argument, Bartle suddenly found Jim a hard man to raise an argument with. The restlessness that had driven him for twenty years had vanished. Every day he spent his mornings with the beavers, returning to do his bit in the parade, or perhaps work as a stage passenger; then he went back to the zoo, often sitting by the pond far into the night.

There were eighteen beaver, and he had named them all, mostly after mountain men he and Bartle had gone up the Missouri with. His favorite he named Hugh Glass, after the mountain man who had been clawed almost to death by a grizzly and had then made his famous two-hundred-mile crawl to safety. Hugh the beaver was a big fat specimen who would swim right over to where Jim sat and look at him impertinently. Sometimes Jim brought the beavers a few stalks pulled from the bank of the Thames, but more often he merely sat and watched them, happy that they were there. He was calmed by the knowledge that the world had not been emptied of beaver, as had seemed to be the case for so many years.

The boy—his name was Oliver—who fed the musk-ox and drove the ostrich cart passed Jim so often that he outgrew his shyness, stopped to talk, and became a kind of friend.

Intrigued by Jim's concentration on beaver—in Oliver's view the zoo held far rarer and more interesting beasts—he often tried to get Jim to explain why he fancied beaver, and only beaver.

"Why not otters?" Oliver asked. "Why not seals?"

Jim liked the boy. Sometimes he walked with him on his rounds and watched him feed the various creatures under his care. Some of them were fierce—the huge old warthog, in particular, worried Jim—but Oliver was careful and never got into trouble.

Jim would have liked to explain to Oliver why he devoted himself to beaver, but the longer he looked at the beaver and at the freckled English boy, the more he felt at a loss to explain. It meant looking too far back in his memory, reviewing too many years and too many hopes.

"Well, you see . . . ." he said more than once, and more than once Oliver waited patiently for the old man to finish the sentence. But Jim never could. How could he explain his attachment to beaver to a youth who had never seen the upper reaches of the Missouri or any of the western lands in their prime? To explain it would be to explain his life, a task Jim didn't feel up to.

"I've just always fancied them," he said finally, aware that the answer was inadequate. "You'd have to have seen them as I saw them in the old days, when you found beaver in every pond."

"What I like is the mongoose," Oliver said. "You ought to see it fight a snake—now and then we give it one."

"Why, I expect it's a dandy," Jim said—he did like the boy. Even so, he was glad when Oliver left, so he could sit alone with the beaver again.

Darling Jane—

I'm afraid you won't be proud of your mother today Janey, I'm ashamed even to write about what happened, but it may get in the papers, I had better tell it. I fell right off the Deadwood stage with the Queen watching. We were all nervous having the Queen there, I guess I was more nervous than most, I started to shoot my gun and I just tipped off. Texas Jack did marvelous to keep the stage from running over me. Red Shirt had the good sense to jump off and daub some red paint on my head and pretend to scalp me. The Queen thought it was all part of the show. Billy Cody was white as a sheet though, he knew it wasn't part of the show. I guess if I had been killed with the Queen watching they would have had to close down.

I did not meet the Queen, Janey, only Billy and Jack and Annie and a few chiefs met her, Sitting Bull I think and Red Shirt. They say she took a fancy to Red Shirt, I guess she likes handsome men. Red Shirt is as handsome as any, Billy and Jack are both jealous of him, he gets so much attention.

I saw the Queen only from a distance, I was disappointed. She is short-built and seemed fat, she reminded me of Mandan women, they are mostly short. I am not suited for royalty though, they are too dressed up and stiff, I get nervous just seeing them from a distance. I have not spent my life among royalty, I don't know how to behave. Anyway they only want to talk to Billy and Annie, they have got the style down better than the rest of us. The Prince said it was a pity there weren't more women like Annie—I wonder what his wife thought about that?

Lately Annie has been nicer to me, that's because her husband Frank finally got here—he came on a later boat. It is a surprise to me that Frank and Annie get along so well, he was once the big star and fancy shot, not her. The first time they matched up she beat him by one shot. Few men would like that but I guess Frank Butler liked it, he gave up the business and married Annie. I'd like to see Bartle marry somebody who beat him at shooting or anything else, Blue either. I have beat men at their own games many times in my life, Janey—none of them have asked me to marry them though.

Sometimes when I see Annie and Frank holding hands I get sad—I will never have that, Janey, it's sad to live a life and have nothing to show. Billy just keeps me in the show for kindness, he won't trust me on the Deadwood stage again.

Speaking of the stage, a few days after the Queen came the Prince showed up with four kings, they all took a ride in the stage. I don't remember what the kings were kings of, Janey—Denmark was one, I think. I have no idea where Denmark is. I don't think Jack Omohundro cares much for kings, I think he would just as soon give them a spill. I have never seen him race around the arena so fast —the horses were in a froth and the kings plenty scared, I bet. Billy was in a rage that Jack took such liberties with the Prince and the kings. Now Jack is threatening to take his money and leave—Jack is independent, he would as soon leave as not. Also he is jealous of all the attention Billy gets.

Billy's name is in the papers every day—why don't they just make him king? Bartle says. Bartle is not enjoying himself much. Jim spends all day with the beavers, and now Frank Butler is here and Bartle can't court Annie anymore. Mostly, Bartle stays drunk—he likes the music halls. Billy likes the attention, though—he would keep us here all summer if he had his way.

I am ready to go, Janey. I have seen enough of merry

England, I still don't know what's merry about it. I have been put in jail three times just for cussing—of course I know I oughtn't to cuss, my little girl would not approve, but they shove so in these music halls I forget and let her rip.

Bartle is testy also, he says he has never felt as crowded as he feels in London. He says he might run amok if he don't get back to the western spaces before long. If Bartle runs amok in London there will be hell to pay—they have far stricter laws here than we have out west. I have been many places in the west where there was no law at all and none on the horizon either.

Jim is the only one happy, the man is beaver crazy. He has even talked of living his life in London so he can go to the zoo every day and watch beaver. That startled Bartle—I ain't living mine here, he said. Well, yours is yours and mine is mine, Jim replied. Bartle almost ran amok at that point, he was so mad. I have spent thirty-five years with you and by God you had rather have the company of a beaver, I guess, Bartle said. Jim refused to argue further.

Billy and Ned have devised a good routine for the show, it is called Pages of Passing History, it starts with just the Indians worshiping the old spirits, then come the beavermen, the cowboys, the settlers, the Pony Express, buffalo hunters, all the things that happened in the west right up till the outbreak of the Indian wars. Then you get the wars and there's lots of whooping and scalping and it ends with Custer. After that it is just trick shooting, and Antonio Esquivel does some roping. He is a champion roper, the cowboys are jealous of his skills.

They say forty thousand people came to see us one night, I didn't count them but a passel comes every night, I'm surprised anyone could count them correctly. It's never less than twenty thousand, they say. I doubt there are twenty thousand people in the whole west, Indians and all. Ain't that strange, my dear? More people stacked up around our arena than there are in the whole west?

The person who is most impressed with the crowds is Sitting Bull. He and I have taken to getting drunk together, we are both so rough no one else wants to get drunk with either of us. Sitting Bull is in love with Annie Oakley, he calls her his little sure shot. She had her picture made with him, he is very proud of it and shows it to anyone who will look. Of course Annie Oakley has had her picture taken with all the kings and hundreds of swells, she is everybody's little sure shot I guess. Sometimes it seems she is even more famous than Billy. She blows kisses to the crowds, and has learned how to curtsy. I don't say it to criticize her—Annie has lent me money. I am just surprised that a country girl like Annie has learned to do the royalty stuff so well. How did she learn? She is never nervous, if she is she doesn't show it.

Sitting Bull told me he had no idea there were so many whites—he is amazed. If he had suspected it he says he would have left for Canada and a good deal sooner, killing Custer was just a waste of time, as he sees it now. He says every Indian in the west could kill a white person with every step they take and the whites would not be missed. That may be an exaggeration Janey—Indians take a lot of steps. I suppose it was just his way of saying he didn't realize how outnumbered he was. I didn't realize it either—it sure didn't feel that way when me and Jim and Bartle used to roam around surrounded by thousands of Sioux, we didn't know we had all that help available over in England.

I hope next time I write it will be from the American shore, I don't wish to stay here any longer than I have to.

Your mother,
Martha Jane

Bartle Bone had his criticisms to make of England—the dampness was a nuisance, and it was rare that he could even glimpse anything that could be called a sky. Sky was just something English people had to get along without. Also the smoky air was offensive. But most vexing of all was being in a town where there were such substantial numbers of policemen. St. Louis boasted several policemen, and New York contained at least a score, but London fairly swarmed with them. It made him anxious to get back west of St. Louis, where one could traipse a long way without encountering one.

The one factor that redeemed England, in Bartle's mind, was the women. Jim Ragg might choose his beaver, Annie and Billy cotton to royalty, Jack Omohundro flaunt his passion for gambling dens, the Indians indulge in plentiful tobacco, the cowboys dote on being stared at, Calamity enjoy her gin palaces: what he liked were the girls.

Bartle had observed that women were like game: scarce in some places, plentiful in others. He had always particularly enjoyed redheads; it had been his despair that so few could be encountered west of Kansas. In Montana and Wyoming there were almost none. Redheads were to him what beaver had been to Jim Ragg: just not there.

But then, here's London. Before they had even made camp he had spotted at least twenty redheaded women. Bartle was thrilled. Let Jim waste his time at the zoo. Bartle devoted his own leisure to the hunt for redheads, ending up with a different one almost every night. They were as abundant as buffalo had been in the old days. In certain streets, at certain times of the evening, they almost ran in herds.

At first the girls were a little afraid of Bartle. Not many Londoners walked around in buckskins, and Bartle's were not the freshest. New outfits were available, of course—Billy had brought over a whole wagonful of costumes, including plenty of fresh buckskins, but Bartle was particular and couldn't find anything to his liking except a nice pair of Shoshone leggings, which he took.

In time, though, as cowboys and ropers and the other vagabonds who had come over with the troupe drifted into the streets, the girls grew less fearful, and consequently, richer. Bartle soon began to feel the expense severely. In the west he had seldom had to scrape up cash for a woman more than four or five times a year; in London he found himself scraping it up four or five times a week. He had never expected pleasure to be cheap, but had not imagined he would ever be in a place where its costs could mount up so quickly.

It wasn't only redheads that walked the streets and crowded the music halls, either; there were sizable numbers of blondes, too, and brunettes of every shade. Bartle once even fell in with an Egyptian; the haggle over price was strenuous, but otherwise he liked her fine.

The abundance of women of all shades seemed to him a very good thing; it prevented or at least reduced the likelihood of the kind of situation he had experienced in Montana with the delightful Trix. In a place like Miles City, with fewer than five women to choose from, attachments of a worrisome nature were apt to develop; along with the attachments came expectations which had either to be satisfied or disappointed.

Bartle hated disappointing expectant women, but he had the feeling that he might hate satisfying them even worse.

Jim Ragg had little interest in women; it was one of the frustrations of their friendship that Bartle could never get Jim interested enough even for the purposes of fruitful conversation. That left Calamity as his main source of dialogue on such matters; Calamity was not entirely satisfactory either, since, as far as Bartle could tell, she had never had much in the way of attachments.

Lately, somewhat to everyone's surprise, Calamity had begun to talk about a great romance she had had with Wild Bill Hickok. No one who knew Hickok could remember him having said two words to Calamity—Jim Ragg shook his head at the notion—and some were of the opinion that the two had never met, or if they had, it would only have been in Deadwood, a week or two before Hickok was killed.

Despite this confusion, Bartle did find that he could talk about love and whatnot with Calamity more freely than he could with most people. Once they had been drinking gin in a saloon that smelled of fish, probably because it was next to a fish market, not far from the Thames, and Bartle expressed the view that he might possibly marry in his old age if he could find anyone suitable.

Calamity looked half drunk and half awake, but the remark hit her the wrong way and her black eyes snapped.

"What, desert Jim?" she asked.

"Oh, no, he could have his room," Bartle assured her.

"Jim Ragg won't hang around if you marry," Calamity said. "That man's a wanderer."

"You're a wanderer, but you'll have to stop sometime," Bartle said. "If you don't settle somewhere you'll likely come to grief."

"What's that mean?" Calamity asked.

"Oh, you'll ride off in a gully, or a bear will get you, or you'll freeze in a blizzard, or some young warrior who don't realize the fight is over will shoot you down," Bartle said.

"You're just talking about dying," Calamity said. "I've already come to worse grief than that. I guess you've lived so carefree you know nothing about grief."

Bartle briefly reviewed his life and decided she was probably right. He had used the word carelessly, but then he had been thinking of Calamity's future, not his own past. He could recall some capital hardships, but no significant grief, unless it was the death of Lonesome Charley Reynolds, a man both he and Jim had liked enormously.

Calamity proceeded to explain how lucky he had been.

"You've had no wife to die," she said. "You've had no child to die. Look at Dora—she's borne two children, and they're both dead. She may not have another, and that'll be another sort of grief, I guess—dying with no one to follow you."

"I wish I hadn't brought it up," Bartle said. "A whole lot of the populace engages in marriage, though. I'm a member of the populace so I guess I could, too. I just sometimes wonder what it's like."

"I ain't engaged in it myself, so why pick me to ask?" Calamity said. "Why can't we just sit here and get drunk? Ask Blue about marriage next time you see him. He's probably an expert by now."

Then she seemed to lose her energy—she had a large face and when it fell into a sad expression there was a lot of sadness at the table.

"You're pesky, Bartle," she said. "You'd do anything to satisfy your curiosity, wouldn't you?"

Bartle shrugged. He felt rather at fault, without quite understanding where his guilt lay. Calamity cried a few tears, snuffled back the rest, got drunk, and went to sleep. Bartle decided he would pass marriage by as a subject the next time they had a talk.

The great unsettled question, as far as he was concerned, was what to do about suddenly rising expectations of the sort women were prone to. Stop too long with some winsome woman and the next thing you knew you'd be plowing or tending store, or something else very near the opposite of the life of a free mountain man.

The fact was, there were some very decent women in the world—now and then he would encounter one so decent that she made the thought of taking up the plow look good. It had happened to him often, but something would always finally come up to break the spell. Jim Ragg would get a hankering for the far yonder, or Calamity would, or *he* would; the pangs of longing might travel with him for a while but in time they would subside, lingering only as an occasional mist in his eye.

The troupe was only ten days from departure when Bartle went out for a little hunt in the streets one night and met Pansy. She was not even a redhead; she was a blonde, and so small he could almost have put her in his pocket. Indeed, he had been on the point of passing Pansy by, thinking she was merely a schoolgirl who had lost her way—though there was nothing beseeching in her manner, as there might have been with a lost school-girl.

Bartle looked twice, and then again; on the third look he fell in love.

"If you please, I'll be very nice, sir," Pansy said. Her blue eyes were the biggest thing about Pansy—Bartle could tell that even in the poorly lit street.

Her polite manner touched him; too many women had tongues like sandpaper; very few had ever called him sir. She was neither bragging nor wheedling; she was just politely direct. Someone who would be very nice was exactly what he was wandering around looking for.

"Well, where's your room?" Bartle asked, a bit embarrassed to be discussing such things with someone who looked so young and prim.

"I've no room, sir, I'm poor," Pansy said. "I wish I had a room but I ain't, yet."

Bartle was a little shocked; he had yet to encounter a girl who lacked a room, though most were rather poor.

"Where do you sleep, then?" he asked.

"In a doorway, sir, if no one will be kind," Pansy said. Something in the girl's manner touched Bartle; she seemed so decent. The whole business made him feel so awkward that for a moment he felt he should just walk away.

"Are you an orphan?" he asked, not sure what prompted him to ask the question. The west was full of orphans; he had been one himself when he went west—his parents had died within a month of each other. Jim Ragg, too, had lost his mother and had no idea where his father might be. Calamity talked of a sister somewhere, but seemed quite vague even on the subject of her sister's name, sometimes calling her Belle, at other times Jane.

If a thinly peopled place like the west was so full of orphans, a great city such as London must have thousands—it was very likely that Pansy was one of the thousands.

"No, sir, I'm from Birmingham," Pansy said.

"If you ain't an orphan, why ain't you home?" Bartle inquired. "You seem a very nice little miss."

"I left home because there were so many on the pallet," Pansy said. "I've been gone awhile now."

"Oh, well then . . ." Bartle said, uncertain as to what he should do with this information.

There were several lodging houses in the neighborhood; Bartle had been in some of them and knew that most were grimy and bare. After strolling along with Pansy for a while, he decided he didn't want to take her to a lodging house.

"I'm with the Wild West show," he said, thinking the news might reassure the girl. "Have you seen a performance yet?"

"Goodness, I guess not," Pansy said, looking startled. "I have only seen the posters. I am in no position to afford shows."

They walked awhile, Bartle occasionally stealing glances at her. Of course, she wasn't wealthy, but she seemed very neat. He was accustomed to far more ragged girls. However, she was barefoot, which troubled him—it was chill.

"I hope you're kind, sir," Pansy said. They had

strolled quite a distance and she was beginning to feel worried.

"Look here, you've sirred me enough," Bartle said. "Just call me by my name—it's Bartle. If you care to sleep in a tent, come with me to the campground. We've only five shows yet to do, but you can see all five—you'll be my guest."

"It's a good sound tent," he added, thinking she might have worries on that score.

Pansy Clowes had no worries on that score; the old man seemed nice, on the whole. Old men were usually nicer than young men in her experience.

When they reached the campground the smell of all the animals was rather strong, but the tent was far nicer than she expected. It was nicer, in fact, than the hovel she had left in Birmingham; and the old man was such a kindly sort that he fixed her a bunk of her own.

When Jim Ragg came in from a late-night visit with the beavers, he found a young barefooted English girl asleep on his bunk. Bartle Bone sat watching her, as a father might a child.

"Here, take my bunk tonight," Bartle whispered. "Little Pansy's all worn out."

"Why, let the child sleep," Jim said mildly. "If I'd realized you'd got married I'd have slept in the zoo anyway."

He took a blanket and went outside, meaning to bed down in a wagon, but Bartle followed him out.

"Her name's Pansy Clowes," Bartle said, not sure Jim had heard him the first time.

"Oh, that's fine," Jim said. "You can introduce us tomorrow."

"I'm feeling peculiar about this," Bartle admitted.

Jim Ragg was amused. Bartle seemed more than peculiar; he seemed completely rattled.

"I always expected you to marry," Jim informed him. "I just didn't expect you to marry at such an early age. I thought you'd wait till you were about No Ears's age."

"I don't expect it's *that* serious," Bartle said. "I just met the little miss an hour ago."

Since they were leaving London soon, Jim decided to go spend a night with the beaver. He walked back to the zoo through the foggy streets, rather amused by the turn things had taken for his old friend. Along with the amusement, he felt a little relieved. Keeping Bartle on the move had become more and more of a strain. Bartle's heart had not been in the search, not for many a year; also, it seemed to Jim that he was showing his age more. Perhaps a settled life with Miss Pansy Clowes would be the best thing for Bartle, after all. He himself could go to Canada and locate beaver; once he got a bunch established in Montana, perhaps Bartle could be some help.

Within a few days everyone in the troupe was remarking on what a good influence the young Birmingham maiden had had on the old mountain man.

"Look at him, he's like a fresh puppy," Calamity said. "She's just a girl he met in the street at night. She captured him without a struggle."

No Ears observed the change in Bartle with no surprise. Aging men and young girls were an old story. He had married two young wives himself; although they had soon died he considered it had been an excellent arrangement. After all, anyone was likely to die.

Bartle himself could scarcely believe his good fortune. Even Annie Oakley, known to be stiff with females, liked Pansy and hired her to sew rips in her costumes and keep them neat. Jim Ragg liked her to the extent that he had no objection to her; only Calamity remained skeptical—at times Bartle thought Calamity must be jealous, unlikely as that seemed.

As for relations between Pansy Clowes and Bartle himself, they could not have been better—not in his opinion, at least. She still slipped up and called him sir once in a while, but that was a small error. He discovered that she was not quite so girlish, not quite such of a slip as she had seemed when he first glimpsed her on the street; Pansy had seen a bit of life. But on the whole her decent manners touched Bartle so much that he began to worry about his own deportment a good deal—and his appearance as well. What if she suddenly left him? He felt he would carry the pang forever if that happened.

The thought worried him so much that he not only changed his buckskins for some that were newer and fresher; he also found a barber and squandered a few days' wages getting properly trimmed.

"What's that smell on you?" Pansy asked pertly, her eyes brightening, when he came rather timidly into the tent after his visit to the barber. Bartle was so taken with the spirited way she said it that he asked her to marry him on the spot.

The wedding took place the day before they sailed for home. Billy Cody took time to come, and so did Sitting Bull, who had taken a liking to Pansy and gave her his autograph several times. Jim Ragg unbent and kissed the bride. Jack Omohundro danced a Texas fandango with her, and the great vaquero Antonio Esquivel twirled his lariat in a tight loop around bride and groom to ensure that they would remain together forever.

The only cloud on the horizon was the absence of Calamity, who was eventually found in jail. She had gotten quite drunk and cussed a sailor; the sailor blackened her eye; Calamity thus fired her pistol at him several times, frightening him badly but otherwise doing him no harm. Later she was found asleep in an alley and taken to jail.

Bartle himself delayed his wedding night long enough to get Calamity out. When he tried to express his disappointment that she had missed the ceremony, Calamity, who looked frightful with her swollen eye, first shook her fist at him, and then began to cry.

"I've retired from going to weddings, I guess," she said, when she felt better.

7

NO EARS FINALLY PERSUADED SITTING BULL AND SEVeral of the older Indians to go to the zoo with him so they could take information about some of the unusual animals back to their tribes. No Ears felt strongly that as many tribes as possible should know about such beasts as the great mudpig, the anteater, and the ostrich; also the large cats and the even larger white bear. Even if the people in the tribes never saw a mudpig or the great white bear, the information might still be important. The animals might appear to them in dreams; it was simply good policy to learn as much as possible about such animals and pass the information on.

Sitting Bull became very angry while walking around the zoo. He was very much annoyed that the whites had collected such ugly animals—and not merely ugly— many of the animals were clearly quite dangerous; only people as stupid as the whites could collect such animals and pasture them near their homes.

Sitting Bull took a particular dislike to the warthog— not only was it extremely ugly, it was also quite clearly ferocious. Sitting Bull wanted to go back to camp, get his rifle, and come back and shoot the warthog before it broke loose and began to kill people.

By the time they actually returned to camp, Sitting Bull's anger had increased. He immediately began to try to persuade the young braves to steal some real ammunition from Cody's wagon and come back to the zoo with him. They would have a fine hunt and rid the world of many dangerous and obnoxious animals. The young braves, who were rather tired of shooting off false bullets in the Wild West show, were perfectly willing to accompany the old chief on a hunt.

No Ears and Two Hawks, a sensible Brulé Sioux, tried their best to put a stop to the notion of a hunt in the London zoo. The whites would be very disturbed—it was necessary to point out how outnumbered the Indians were, should war result. Also, there was the ocean to get back across—even if they fought their way out of London, they still didn't know how to run a boat.

Sitting Bull was not convinced. He wanted to go back and shoot the warthog before he started to have bad dreams about it—the great white bear was also worrisome. It was just the kind of animal likely to cause troublesome dreams; he thought they ought to get on their horses, ride through the zoo, and wipe out as many of the bad animals as they could. As for the ocean, it was only a big lake. If they followed its shoreline they would eventually get around it and make their way home.

Sitting Bull's opinion about the ocean was popular with quite a few of the Indians, none of whom was looking forward to getting back on the great boat. Most considered that they had been very lucky to make it across the ocean the first time. Two Hawks himself had been very uncomfortable on the ocean; he had spent much of the voyage singing his death song. He reminded everyone of the great whale fish. What if a herd of whale fish tried to attack? The thought of a herd of whale fish did not improve Sitting Bull's mood—or anyone else's mood, either.

Fortunately Cody appeared in time to keep everyone's mood from getting any worse. Cody wanted Sitting Bull and a few chiefs to go with him to something he called a wax museum. It seemed to be a place where they kept wax carvings of great chiefs of various tribes. Cody told Sitting Bull and Red Shirt and one or two others that the Queen particularly hoped they would let the carvers of the wax museum make statues of them; that way the Queen could visit the museum once in a while and be reminded of the visit they had all made to her country.

No Ears decided to go along. He thought he might enjoy seeing a few carvings. Even if the carvings were ugly, he might enjoy seeing the buildings along the way. It was a puzzle why whites felt they had to put their buildings so close together.

As they clumped along the river, he saw that there were even little tribes of people who lived in boats. Cody was doing his best to keep Sitting Bull in a good mood, telling him several times what a great honor it was that the Queen wanted him to have his statue carved so she could remember his visit. Despite Cody's efforts, Sitting Bull remained in a surly temper. As a guest, he felt it was incumbent on him to do what the Queen requested, but what he really wanted to do was go back and shoot the warthog.

The first thing they saw when they got to the museum was a statue of Cody, and another of Annie Oakley—they had only been finished the day before. Sitting Bull was very taken with the statue of his little sure shot and began to ask if he could buy it. He was told he couldn't, which didn't improve his mood. He grew annoyed when the man who was going to make his statue began to measure him, but Cody finally got him to behave.

No Ears was not particularly interested in the statues; he felt it might be more interesting to go back and study the tribes who lived on boats. Of course it was odd that the whites had filled a whole building with statues of dead chiefs or their women, but he didn't take much interest in the proceedings until he happened to see one of the men who worked in the museum sticking a pair of ears on the head of a tiny statue.

Jack Omohundro, who stood beside No Ears, saw the

point immediately. He looked at No Ears, he looked at the statue that was having its ears fixed, and he walked over to the workman and got right down to business.

"Is that a statue of a midget?" he asked.

"Yes, Tom Thumb," the man said irritably; he seemed to be in the kind of mood Sitting Bull was in.

"A nasty little brat pulled his ears off," he added. "It's happened before and it will happen again."

The man had a sizable goiter on his neck, but he knew his business; he quickly worked the ears back onto the statue.

"The point is I've got a friend here who needs a pair of ears," Jack said. "How much to make him a pair?"

The workman had quite a start when he looked around and saw that No Ears indeed lacked ears.

"Lord Gad!" he said. "Who pulled this old fellow's off?"

Once his professional curiosity was aroused he quickly became more friendly; he came over and gave No Ears's head a close inspection.

"Whoever sawed 'em off should have sharpened his saw," the man remarked. "They done a rough job. Let's go down and see what we can find."

They went down some stairs until they were quite a distance under the earth; to No Ears's astonishment they were taken into a large room filled with parts of people. One whole shelf, the length of the room, contained heads —but the heads had no features. There was a shelf of hands, and a shelf of feet—even a shelf of torsos. Smaller shelves were covered with ears and noses. The workman studied the shelf of ears for a while and then held up two that seemed about right for No Ears. He rummaged in a drawer and found a mirror so No Ears could look at himself and take part in the selection.

No Ears began to get the shakes. He had seen whites go in stores and try on hats and other garments, but he had never supposed that the hour would come when he would be trying on ears. The workman had become very friendly; he seemed ready to spend all day seeing that No Ears got exactly the ears he desired.

The selection wasn't easy, either. No Ears had the shakes so badly he could hardly keep the various ears shoved up against his head long enough to consider which looked best. He changed his mind several times; he felt upset and could not remember to talk in English. He began to express his opinions in Sioux. Jack knew a little Sioux but not enough to follow No Ears's discussion, which was rather particular; he ran upstairs to get an Indian who could help, and soon, to the workman's amazement, the whole party was down in his workroom, helping No Ears pick out ears.

When so many eyes fixed upon him, No Ears grew even more shaky—he began to despair of making up his mind. One set of ears would seem correct for a few seconds; then he would see another that seemed better. Everyone else had an opinion, too—one would argue for one pair, someone else for another. A young brave named Plenty Horses, who seemed to dislike his own ears, wanted someone to cut them off for him so he could have a new pair. Several people wanted to buy a spare set of hands or feet in case they lost theirs in battle.

Fortunately Cody finally showed up and solved the problem by buying No Ears a dozen pairs of ears.

"They're wax, they might wear out," Cody told him. "Let's get a supply while we're here."

The workman with the goiter, who turned out to be a patient fellow, gave No Ears some special glue to help him fix the ears to his head; he carefully explained how the glue was to be put on and taken off.

"Now these won't do for every day," the man cautioned. "If a brat grabs one, it'll spoil it. If I was you I'd just save them for weddings or maybe funerals—they'll do fine for special occasions."

He gave No Ears a nice wooden box to keep his ears in. Of course, when they got back to camp everyone wanted to see them; two or three pair were badly smudged before curiosity diminished. Fortunately the workman at the museum had given the party a sackful of wax limbs, arms and legs mostly, that had been broken off statues and were no longer deemed useful. These kept most of the crew amused.

For the first few days No Ears did nothing but guard his ears from all comers. Sitting Bull was jealous because he had not been given any ears; he demanded that No Ears present him with a set. No Ears resisted and fortunately his understanding friend Cody came to his aid. Cody gave him a fine box, lined in velvet, to keep the ears in. The box even had a lock and key so that No Ears could lock up his ears whenever he wanted to.

The box with the lock and key reassured him for a while, but not for long—it was all too obvious that virtually everyone in the troupe envied him his wax ears. Sitting Bull was far from being the only one who coveted them—even his old friend Two Hawks, who had two perfectly good ears of his own, pestered No Ears for a look and even asked if he could borrow a pair for a few days.

No Ears soon came to feel quite resentful of the fact that everyone coveted his new ears. All the people who envied him had real ears of their own and had had real ears their whole lives, whereas he had spent nearly seventy years without ears of any kind. It annoyed him that people couldn't simply have the good manners to let him enjoy his ears in his own way.

No Ears told Calamity of his disappointment in the manners of his friends while the two of them stood at the rear of the great boat as it sailed away from England. No Ears felt a little sad; he had not liked England, yet it had to be admitted that the English were ingenious. No Sioux had ever ever thought of making him wax ears; no American had, either.

Calamity did not look well. She had taken to drinking and fighting with sailors almost every night. The police had taken her pistol away; without her pistol she could not scare the sailors, and thus got regularly pummeled. She looked so battered that she refused to have her picture taken with the troupe before departure. Cody, after one look at her face, had not insisted.

"It's good riddance to England," she said, as she and No Ears watched the gray shore fade into the gray sea.

She was in such a warlike mood that No Ears was rather fearful about what might happen once they returned to America. What if she didn't want him to travel with her anymore? Where would he go?

"I can't wait to see Dora," Calamity said. "Do you reckon we'll be there in a month?"

"I'm afraid someone will steal my new ears while we're on this boat," No Ears said. It had become his darkest fear.

"I'll keep 'em for you," Calamity suggested. "They'll be safe with me. Nobody wants to get near me now. I've even got too rough for Sitting Bull."

No Ears adopted this suggestion. He hid his box of ears under Calamity's bunk; he visited her cabin several times a day to make sure they were still there.

On the sixth day out from England No Ears saw something as impressive as the whale fish; he saw a great mountain of ice floating in the sea. The ice mountain was so large that it took the ship all day to leave it behind. No Ears watched it as long as he could see it. A sailor informed him that there were thousands of ice mountains in the northern seas.

Before No Ears could think too much about the ice mountain, a storm struck the ship. The storm continued for three days, and long before the third day everyone on board was sick. The one exception was Annie Oakley, who was unaffected by the storm, though she did have to interrupt her shooting practice. Most of the Indians began to sing their death songs again, but No Ears felt too sick even to do that. Calamity decided she should sing a death song too, and she sang "Buffalo Girls." Her voice was too weak for the singing to be heard over the crash of the storm.

"I'm never leaving the shore again if I get out of this," she said after each spell of vomiting.

Sitting Bull got so sick that he wanted to shoot the captain of the ship, a man he had never liked. One of the elk got loose somehow and rushed around the deck frantically before jumping into the sea. No Ears watched it happen. The great sea immediately swallowed the foolish elk.

In the agony of the storm and the long fatigue that followed it, the box of ears was gradually forgotten. No Ears unlocked the box and looked at the ears only when no one was around. He fixed them to his head when he was alone. After some reflection he decided it was far too late to present himself in public as a man with ears. For seventy years he had been No Ears; everyone in the west knew him by that name. If he were to suddenly appear wearing ears, it would only confuse everyone. Some of his friends might think he had become a bad spirit and refuse to speak to him.

In private, though, when everyone was asleep, No Ears often opened his box and quietly fixed a pair of ears to his head for an hour or two. With ears on, he could sit and smoke and peacefully dream his way through a different life. He dreamed himself as he would have been as a young man like others—that is, with ears. He saw himself taking many more wives and becoming much more prosperous than he had been. He saw himself as a leader in battle, helped by his keen ears; he saw himself as a chief of his people, though in truth he had been something of an outcast.

Most pleasing of all to No Ears was an ability he acquired, thanks to his fine ears, to dream back the conversations he had missed in life due to the whistly and uncertain nature of his hearing. The voices of old-time people began to float back to him in his dreams. He heard again his lively young wife Pretty Moons; he heard his friend Sits On The Water describing the best tactic for catching angry turtles; he even dreamed back a conversation he had once had with Crazy Horse, an abrupt man who didn't have too many conversations. Crazy Horse had been in the mood to kill some soldiers that day, but whether he had done it had never been clear to No Ears. In the dream memory, though, he saw Crazy Horse coming back with three scalps, indicating that he had followed his mood.

All the way across the great ocean, No Ears attached his ears in private and listened to voices from the old times. It occurred to him that the sea must be very old; he had been taught to believe that the sky was the First Place and the Last Place, but as he sat and looked at the endless sea he began to wonder if perhaps the belief was wrong. Perhaps the ocean was the First Place; perhaps it was also the Last Place. Perhaps it was to the sea that souls went; the story about the hole in the sky could well be wrong. The very fact that he could hear so clearly the voices of people long dead made him wonder if perhaps the sea was not the Last Place; its great depths might contain all the dead and all their memories, too.

Sometimes Jim Ragg came on deck while No Ears was dreaming back voices. Occasionally they would sit and share a smoke. No Ears knew there was no need to hide his ears from Jim—Jim had no interest in ears. He knew that Jim had long been an angry man—it seemed that he was angry with his own people for having killed all the beaver. In London, though, he had discovered that all the beaver were not gone; they just lived in zoos now, where their life was easier, since no one was allowed to trap them. The discovery had changed Jim a lot. He didn't seem angry anymore. Even the fact that Bartle had taken a young wife didn't bother him.

Most people found Jim a more pleasant companion now that his anger was gone; No Ears had to admit that he was more pleasant, and yet he found Jim disquieting to be with for some reason. No Ears thought the matter over for several days without being able to decide what bothered him about Jim. The mountain man was perfectly friendly, and once or twice had even helped him adjust his ears when he hadn't got them fitted on quite right. And yet, something was troubling about the man.

While he was dreaming back the brief conversation with Crazy Horse, Jim Ragg walked by, and No Ears suddenly realized what was bothering him: Jim Ragg wasn't really there anymore. His spirit had been an angry spirit, like Crazy Horse's. Now it had gone. The realization made No Ears shiver a little. If Jim's spirit had gone, his body was not going to last too long. That was why conversations with him were rather disturbing: his voice came from the Last Place, just as Crazy Horse's had.

This realization shocked him so much that he confided it to Calamity next time she came on deck. Calamity's stomach had been slow to settle down after the passing of the storm. She spent a good deal of time at the rail, vomiting; No Ears watched her closely at such times. People who were ill often did foolish things; he didn't want Calamity to make the same kind of mistake the elk had made when it became so sick with fear that it jumped into the sea.

When Calamity recovered enough to sit down with him and accept a smoke, No Ears told her of his conviction that Jim Ragg's spirit had left him.

"I think he's gone where Crazy Horse is," No Ears said. "He is on a road he doesn't see."

"Sometimes I think you must get drunk in secret," Calamity said. "Then you stick on your new ears and think you know things you don't really know."

No Ears didn't press the point. It was obvious that Calamity was not feeling well; she had not been feeling well for most of the trip. It was hard enough to talk to whites about the spirit world when they were healthy; if they happened to be unhealthy, as Calamity was, the effort was a waste of time.

"What do you hear when you sit there with your ears on?" she asked.

"I hear some old-time people," No Ears said.

"You're doing better than me then," Calamity said. "I don't hear nothing but this old howling wind."

No Ears said nothing; he didn't want to argue about his dream conversations.

"Well, say hello to Wild Bill for me, if you happen to be speaking to him," Calamity said, as she got up to make her unsteady way downstairs.

Darling Jane,

This will be the saddest letter I have written you yet,
Jim Ragg is dead. It happened in Chicago by the lake, so
sudden neither Bartle nor me even saw it, Pansy didn't
either though we were all not ten feet away. We had gone
there to do one last show, they were having a big fair by
the lake. Billy had been so nice we felt we couldn't refuse
—he allowed us ample money to get home. I am sure he
can afford it but many that can afford it wouldn't do it.

I know that will strike you as odd, here I am writing
about Billy Cody's fortunes, the truth is I would rather
write about anything other than the death of Jim Ragg. I
didn't expect it, none of us did. Well, No Ears did, I
should have listened to him, but what good would it have
done?

A man they call an anarchist stabbed Jim in the ribs,
the knife was so small no one saw it, Jim didn't, he just
thought the man bumped into him. He sat down on a
bench and died before he even realized he was stabbed.
He bled to death inside, at least he didn't suffer. He just
said he was a little tired and we decided to sit and eat
some spun candy, while we were eating it Bartle said he
thought Jim didn't look right, of course he didn't, he was
dead.

I have never heard of an anarchist Janey, they say
there are many of them in Chicago and also London, I
didn't see any in England though. We saw the little man
that stabbed Jim, he was a very small man, I think he was
loco or crazy, he thought Jim was the Emperor of Austria
that's why he stabbed him. You would have to be crazy
to mistake Jim Ragg for the emperor of anywhere, Jim
bore no resemblance to an emperor. The man was raving
and screaming by the time they drug him away. I have
never seen Bartle so stunned—of course it is hard to
believe that a man could just walk up and stab Jim and
Jim not even know he was stabbed. Bartle blames it on
crowds, he says in a crowd it's so crowded you don't
even notice your own death, he's right, too, Jim Ragg
didn't, and he has witnessed hundreds of deaths.

Later Bartle wanted to go to the jail to make sure the killer would be hung promptly. At the police station they told us he is too insane to hang. Bartle was disgusted—out west no one is too insane to hang.

Billy Cody was nice as usual, he too was shocked at Jim's death, but not as shocked as Bartle. Billy made all the arrangements for Jim to be buried but at the last minute Bartle balked, he said Jim ought to be buried in the west. Now they are going to put his body on a steamer with us at Dubuque, he will be buried as soon as we reach the Missouri—anywhere along the Missouri would suit Jim fine, Bartle thought.

Of course we are all grieved, but Bartle is the most grieved. He partnered with Jim more than thirty years. Bartle has seen sudden death before, we all have, still, Bartle is having trouble adjusting to the fact that Jim is gone. It is a good thing Bartle has Pansy for a wife. I don't like her much but Bartle does—she cannot make up for Jim Ragg, nobody can, I will miss the man too. I was thinking of Jim last night—what I wish is he had been more of a talker. If I scratch my memory I can remember many things that Bartle said over the years, also things Dora said or even Blue—Blue's are easy to remember because they're mostly too raw to repeat—but it is hard now for me to remember one thing that Jim Ragg said, he has only been dead a week too. Perhaps it is my fault, Jim only liked to talk about beaver, they never interested me, they're just animals with big teeth.

The question is, what will Bartle do? He has never done anything really, he just followed Jim around the west. Jim did most of the work, Bartle provided the conversation. At one time they guided wagon trains, later on they scouted for the soldiers—neither of them liked that, but they did it. In those days, knowing the country, knowing where the water holes were, and where you could get across rivers was a skill you could sell. Even I sold it, and I never knew the west half as well as Bartle and Jim. Half the people out there in those days earned a living showing newcomers around, wagon trains, or whoever wanted help getting somewhere.

Now there's no need for scouts—the steamers or the railroads will get you close enough. I don't know what old scouts like Bartle and me will do, I guess we could work for Billy but the show only tours part of the year and he probably wouldn't want to hire me again anyway —all I did was fall off the stagecoach and embarrass him in front of the Queen. If I could shoot like Annie I'd have a job forever, but I can't—nobody else can either, she beat the English gun by forty-nine birds.

I thought I might get some money out of Buntline, but Buntline is hard to pin down—he might do this, he might do that. About the best I could get out of him is that he is planning to take a look at Montana pretty soon. When he does he will stop by and write down a few of my tales. Billy Cody laughed when I told him that, he says Buntline never writes down anything, he just makes up tales. He thinks Buntline will write me up in dime novels and make me an outlaw worse than Belle Starr. If he does he's in for trouble, your mother has never been an outlaw, Janey. It's true I took food for the miners during the smallpox horrors—I paid for it later, though, it was not much food anyway. Even people who don't like me, there are plenty that don't, will admit that I'm honest— if I don't leave you anything else Janey at least I will leave you a good name.

Your mother,
Martha Jane

8

Jim Ragg was buried near the village of Dubuque; the best Bartle could do for him was to get him buried on the west bank of the Mississippi. The captain of the boat they had planned to take down to the Missouri refused to have a body on his vessel, and that was that.

"I will not do it, sir, not for you and not for the President," the man said. "I have never carried a corpse on my boat, and I don't plan to start now."

"Well, you'll start now if I shoot you," Calamity said. She had been in a dark mood for weeks, and Jim's death had done nothing to brighten it.

"Madam, if you talk like that I'll put you off," the captain said. He was a gruff fellow from Boston; he had been on the river fifteen years and did not tolerate complaints.

"You won't if I shoot you," Calamity said, but it was an idle threat—she had not yet purchased a weapon, thanks to being broke. Bartle might have loaned her his rifle so she could shoot the captain, but then again he might not have. Bartle had grown a good deal less free-spirited since his marriage; now and then he would get drunk and whoop and holler, but mostly he kept still. His

218

little wife, Pansy, had a bluff in on him, in Calamity's view. Or maybe it wasn't a bluff.

"I favor rapid burial," Pansy said, after they had buried Jim with the help of a slothful gravedigger who had to be urged twice to keep digging; the grave wasn't deep enough.

"It's more hygenic," she added.

"He wasn't religious, though, if that's what you mean," Calamity said. Since reaching America, Pansy had become rather interfering, Calamity felt. Pansy had sided with Cody's plan to bury Jim in Chicago, although she had scarcely known Jim a month. So far Calamity had held her tongue, though. Bartle was crushed as it was —a quarrel between herself and his new wife wouldn't help matters. Besides, dragging Jim around really served no point, since he was dead. Listening to Cody and Bartle arguing about burial, and what kind of coffin to get, and how Jim should be dressed, made her feel the whole business of being buried was completely ridiculous.

"I'm telling you now, just leave me where I fall," Calamity said. "If I happen to fall in Deadwood, drag me up the hill and bury me by Billy Hickok, but if I'm elsewhere just leave me where I fall."

"Well, all right," Bartle said uneasily. Concluding burial arrangements for Jim had been difficult; he hoped he wouldn't have to do the same for Calamity, too. His own simple conviction that Jim ought to be buried in the west had caused endless trouble. Billy Cody thought it was absurd to take a dead man from Chicago to Dubuque, much less up the Missouri, but he did help arrange for Jim to be put on a train. At almost every stop somebody tried to have the coffin removed, though Jim was making far less trouble than many of the living passengers. Long before they got to Dubuque the whole thing had come to seem silly. He would have been glad to bury Jim anywhere, but no sooner had he resolved to do it than the railroad officials gave up and stopped trying to remove the coffin.

The graveyard was not far from the bluffs of the Mississippi, which was fortunate: the gruff Boston captain was about to cast off when they got back to the boat. It was a pretty day; skeins of geese flew over them as the boat slipped through the sunlit water. Calamity was drinking, No Ears was smoking, Pansy was sewing. Bartle couldn't think of any activity worth doing. It was mighty queer, traveling without Jim. More than that, it was novel; he had never done it. They had met the day after he left his home in Illinois, and had been together ever since; now he was traveling on, with Pansy and Calamity, and Jim Ragg was staying forever in a graveyard near Dubuque.

"It'll be a lonesome trip up the Missouri this time,' Bartle said to No Ears. "I guess I'll have to try and be a better shot now. Jim mostly furnished the grub.''

No Ears didn't have his ears on; he could see, though. that Bartle was not quite himself. No Ears liked Bartle: he looked at him closely. Bartle stood at the rail looking sadly back toward the distant bluff where his oldest friend was buried. No Ears felt that Bartle's spirit, too. was almost gone. Probably it had been linked too closely to Jim's, and Jim's had always been the stronger spirit; even Calamity agreed with that. When Jim's spirit left to return to the Last Place, it had begun to pull Bartle's with it. Bartle's spirit was light as a rabbit pelt—Jim's departure might pull it away as easily as one skinned a rabbit.

While he was considering whether to speak to Bartle, to give him at least a chance to detach his spirit from the dead man's, No Ears looked toward the sinking sun and received a terrible shock. Six great cranes were flapping slowly westward; they crossed the face of the red sun in their journey west.

No Ears knew then what had happened: he had made a mistake that morning when he had hidden behind the sage bush near Crazy Woman Creek. He had assumed that the cranes had come for *his* soul; it had been a silly error, one he should have known better than to make. He thought the cranes were after him because he was old. Of course, that was nonsense. Spirit messengers cared nothing for age; often they took the souls of babies who had only just been born, or of young men or young women in the prime of life; his wife Pretty Moons had barely been of an age to marry when the spirits took her.

The cranes on Crazy Woman Creek had not been after him at all, No Ears realized: they had been after the mountain men. The mountain men had shot one of them, and then fooled them by slipping away to England, but their traveling had only meant a brief delay. The cranes had returned and taken Jim Ragg—when they wanted, they would take Bartle, too. His light spirit would be easy to carry away; to the cranes it would probably be no heavier than a minnow or a little water snake.

No Ears watched the cranes go, six flying shadows against the burnt light of sunset. He felt very uneasy; he did not like to travel with people who were going to die. It was for that reason that he had made no name for himself in battle. He did not mind the fighting itself, but he did not enjoy the company of people who would soon die.

The next day he sat on deck, watching Bartle with his young wife. Bartle tried to fish a little, but he was not good at it; he only caught a large turtle. That was not a good sign. Thinking back over his many visits with the mountain men, No Ears realized that Bartle had never been a good hunter; he rarely brought in game. He was also weak when it came to making fires. He seemed to be one of those men who were interested only in women. It was a failing No Ears could sympathize with because he had once been the same way. Getting wives had interested him more than war.

He knew, though, that getting wives was even more dangerous than war; he suspected that Bartle's marriage to the English girl might prove more dangerous than war. The English girl reminded him too much of his last wife, whose name was Sun-in-Your-Face. She had first been called Quick Ferret, but had been renamed once it was obvious that she was of such beauty that to look at her made one blind in the mind.

Certainly Sun-in-Your-Face's beauty had made him blind in his mind. He had wanted her so much that he didn't notice that she intended to kill him. He never knew why the beautiful Sun-in-Your-Face wanted to kill him, but there was no doubt that she did. She once took the spleen of a sick dog and mixed it with his food in order to kill him. No Ears soon became very sick; it was while he was near death that he realized it was his wife's doing. He saw her sharpening a knife and realized she meant to finish him with it—she was impatient that he was not already dead. Fortunately he had his gun handy and had just enough strength left to shoot her. Sun-in-Your-Face looked at him with a terrible hatred when she realized she had taken too long to sharpen her knife. He didn't know why she wanted to kill him; he had been good to her, he thought; he had bought her several very pretty and well-tanned robes, and his tent was a fine one. Perhaps she only wanted to have the fine tent to herself. After her death everyone congratulated him for having outsmarted Sun-in-Your-Face; it seemed to be common knowledge that she had wanted to kill him, though no one had mentioned it.

But then, his people understood such things; they usually knew when a woman planned to kill a man, or vice versa. It was not so with the whites on the river steamer. No Ears could see that Bartle had no idea that his young English wife didn't like him; perhaps it was mainly that she did not desire him. No Ears's nose had not lost its keenness, and if there was one thing above others that he excelled at smelling, it was desire. He could smell it immediately in both women and men. Even in its early stages, desire had such a strong smell that it was hard to miss. No Ears knew that the rude captain had a great amount of desire for Bartle's wife; the captain smelled goatish. But the girl named Pansy had no desire for Bartle; No Ears slept not far from them and would have known it if she fancied their mating. Such was not the case.

These thoughts made No Ears very uneasy. Jim was dead and Bartle—unless he was lucky and his wife fell overboard or was taken by the captain—probably did not have long to live. Calamity was drunk a great deal and would not be much help if there was serious trouble.

No Ears studied the matter all day; he began to have the feeling that it was time to leave the whites to their own lives and deaths and go back to his home. He had better get off the boat and walk over to the Platte River —the weather was good and it would be a pretty walk. Perhaps he would be able to find a few of his people and tell them about the great whale fish and the other interesting things he had seen.

He did not like to leave Calamity, but he felt he had better do it while he felt like walking home. Later he could go up to Montana on the steamer if he wished, or perhaps catch a ride on a train. He did not think it wise to stay with the white people when they were being so careless with their lives. The six cranes could return at any time; if there was too much trouble he might not be able to keep one of them from snatching his soul.

The next morning he told Calamity what he was planning. Calamity looked disappointed but did not try to talk him out of it.

"Go if you feel like it, while the weather's pretty," she said. "I'm aiming to go back and find Dora. Come for the winter, if you can make it. You oughtn't to be wintering hard, at your age."

"I hope your horse is well and that no one has eaten your dog," No Ears said. Calamity had left her black horse at Fort Leavenworth and her dog with Dora in Miles City.

"I don't expect they've eaten my dog," Calamity said. "They'll be chewing all day, if they do. That dog is tough."

Bartle Bone was slightly disquieted by the news that No Ears planned to depart. Of course, there was no reason the old man shouldn't go. There was no reason to stop him, or to encourage him, or to do much of anything, that Bartle could see. He felt rather dazed; now he had a wife to support and had had no practice at such a task. Pansy had become noticeably more brisk since they struck America—she had been sharp with him several times and would doubtless be even sharper if he flagged in any significant way, such as by failing to support her.

She seemed to expect to live in a house, though Bartle had never owned one and had no idea how to go about getting one. He was a poor carpenter and would not be able to build a decent house before winter. Perhaps Dora would allow them a room. If she didn't, he had no idea what they would do. He had married hastily, without planning anything—of course he had assumed when he married that he would always have Jim and Calamity around to help him. Jim Ragg had always been competent at whatever he took up—no doubt he could even have built a house that would satisfy Pansy, if it had come to that.

But it hadn't. Now Jim was dead and Calamity almost never sober; No Ears, a sensible old man who could frequently be counted on for reliable advice, was leaving to walk to the Platte River.

To Bartle it seemed a poor homecoming. Pansy had never been to the west: what if she took a dislike to it? Most of the English he knew *had* liked the west, but then they had all been men, and what they liked was the game. He had been trying to teach Pansy to shoot; she was erratic with a pistol, tolerable with a rifle; still, he could not imagine that she would take to the west because of the game.

For the first time, the notion that he was now responsible for Pansy's support crossed his mind. It was an upsetting thought, too. With the show going on, there had always been plenty to eat; Billy Cody doled out pocket money; most of the troupers gambled most of the money away, but could still usually afford to get barbered or go on a toot and pursue other expensive frolics. With money and grub so plentiful, Bartle had never really thought about having to support a wife.

Except for a little scouting, and now and then a little freight hauling or a spot of stage driving, Bartle had never had a job. He had just traveled the country, living off Jim's skill with the rifle. If absolutely required to shoot, he shot, but mostly he left it to his old friend, a superior marksman. If he tried to travel the country with Pansy he would have to shoot—of course, that was silly. He couldn't travel the country with Pansy. She was an English miss, not a mountain man.

The steamer stopped at a little dock on the Nebraska shore. No Ears took a blanket and his box of ears, shook hands with everyone, and got off.

"If I had my horse I'd go with you," Calamity said. Seeing No Ears preparing to leave made her suddenly panic-stricken. She had not been separated from him since the day he had saved her from the blizzard. He was a small man and very old. Seeing him with his blanket and his ears stabbed at her heart. He had the plains to cross—a long walk. Would she ever see No Ears again? And if she didn't, who would advise her? Dora was fine for town advice, but Dora knew nothing of country dangers.

"I wish I had my horse," Calamity said. "I'm too fat now to walk to the Platte with you."

No Ears left without delay. To Calamity, watching him from the boat, he looked as old and dried up as the weeds along the river's shore.

"Maybe I should have just married him," she said to Bartle. She still felt disturbed.

"Marry No Ears?" he asked, astonished. "The man is twice your age. What would be the point?"

Calamity felt like punching him; she felt like punching somebody, and nobody else was handy.

"You're twice your wife's age," she reminded him. "More than that—you're three times her age, at least. What do you reckon the point is for her?"

Lately Bartle had begun to worry about that very point himself. He usually had a quick retort to anything anyone might say, but this time he had none. He was aware that Calamity didn't like Pansy; Jim hadn't liked her much, either, though he had unbent and kissed her at the wedding. Suddenly life, which had always been a lively, sporty thing, seemed to be nothing but heartache and confusion.

He wished Calamity could break her tiresome habit of asking unanswerable questions—speaking words that called up worry was a bad trait. The notion that Calamity might marry No Ears seemed ridiculous; they weren't even sweethearts, at least not so far as he had observed. Now he was forced to consider that in some people's eyes it was ridiculous that Pansy had married him, a broken-down old mountain man with no income. When forced to consider the matter, he realized he had no idea what the point might be for Pansy. He scarcely knew his own mind anymore, and could not pretend to know hers as well. Pansy was quick with opinions, but among her opinions, he could not recall that she had mentioned what she considered the point of their marriage to be.

More and more, Bartle found himself wishing that the crazed anarchist in Chicago hadn't picked Jim Ragg to stab. There had been hundreds of people walking by the lake that day—why, with so many possibilities, had he picked Jim Ragg to stab?

9

PANSY KNEW THE BOSTON CAPTAIN WANTED HER. SHE
had begun her life in the London streets at the age of
eleven; she had now reached the age of sixteen and considered herself an expert on the desires of men. She read
them as quickly as educated people read newspapers.
The captain wanted her, but that was common—it was
not the important fact.

The important fact was that he was taking his boat in
the direction she wanted to go: south, to where it was
warm.

All her years in London, Pansy had been cold. She had
spent nearly six years shivering; some girls got used to it,
but Pansy never had. She hated the chill. The best thing
about the Wild West show had been the warm tents and
the heaps of buffalo robes. For the first time in years she
slept warm; it was worth marrying an old man for a while
to sleep in a warm tent rather than a chill stone doorway.

On the voyage over, Pansy had heard several people
talk about the western winters. Evidently they were long
and severe. That news was enough to convince Pansy
that her marriage to old Bartle had served its purpose:
she was in America, and the southern parts of America

were said to be quite warm. Old Bartle was not bad to her, but he was of no interest. The elegant Mr. Cody had been of considerable interest, but Mr. Cody was full of himself and scarcely looked at her. He did mention how warm the south was, though. He and Annie Oakley had done an exhibition in New Orleans, a city he claimed was always warm.

Knowing no more than that, Pansy decided New Orleans would be her destination. She would have been pleased to attract the interest of Mr. Cody but he was evidently not a man who sought women very strenuously. He even seemed to think she loved old Bartle, when she had merely chosen him as her road to warmth. It was a pity Mr. Cody had no more need for women than he seemed to, but Pansy felt she had neither the time nor the opportunity to change him.

The American summer, or the little that she had got to see of it, had been all she had hoped for. It was warm in New York, and even warmer in Chicago. But on the train west to Dubuque she had felt the breath of the prairie autumn. It was a sharp enough breath to convince her she ought to get on to New Orleans as soon as possible.

The fact that the captain wanted her was lucky—the one problem she had to consider was what to do with old Bartle. Again, the fact that they were on a boat and not a train was lucky. Jim Ragg had wanted to take the train west; Pansy had argued for a boat from the beginning, but if it had not been for the splendid luck of having old Jim killed, she might well not have prevailed. Bartle was far too willing to side with his friend. If the train had been chosen she would have had no option but to sneak off to Chicago and stay lost until they left; no doubt she would have had to work awhile, in order to get a passage to New Orleans.

But by good fortune, Jim had been killed; by even better fortune, the old Indian was gone, too. Pansy hated the old Indian—he had been far too watchful. He was always on deck, smoking; often she caught him watching her. It would have been hard to do much, either with the captain or Bartle, without old No Ears knowing what she was about. He even stayed on deck most of the night, playing with his ears. Calamity sometimes sat with him, but she was usually dead drunk, and consequently less of a problem.

The dilemma Pansy had to wrestle with, as the boat steamed down the Mississippi, was whether to kill Bartle or merely announce that matters were quits between them, and then leave with the captain.

Her older brother, Ben Clowes, who had brought her to the streets of London and put her to work, had been a firm believer in killing as the most certain means of really terminating involvements of all kinds.

"The dead won't be turning up to make trouble for you," Ben had put it—advice Pansy always remembered, though she had never acted on it.

Ben had been a robber who aspired to be a murderer. He planned to make a specialty of sneaking into the houses of very old people of some means and snuffing them out, if possible by strangulation. It seemed a good plan, but unfortunately Ben had come to ruin due to the unexpected tenacity of his first victim-to-be, a very old lady. He managed to enter her house; she had looked frail, but when Ben grabbed her by the neck she proved to be too strong for him. She broke free and slammed him twice with a poker; she yelled for her servants, who slammed him several more times and called the police. Because of the age of the intended victim, Ben was hanged.

Ben's unfortunate failure at strangulation made Pansy cautious. It taught her that in killing the essential thing was to make sure of your victim; the question that now faced her was whether there was a means by which she could make absolutely sure of finishing old Bartle, if murder proved to be her choice. Bartle was often drunk but he was not really frail. He was set on teaching her to shoot—a project which held some hope. She could shoot him and pretend an accident. But it was chancy; she was new to shooting, and might miss the vital spot even from a close distance. Perhaps if he was drunk enough, she could whop him good with the gun some night and push him overboard; the difficulty there was that there was no guarantee he would drown. If an eighty-five-year-old lady wouldn't be strangled, Bartle might well not drown. Worse still, he might manage to cry out and be heard.

Ben's remark about the finality of killing someone who posed a problem was no doubt valid, but it seemed to Pansy it might require an expertise she simply did not have. Ben had been a cold planner, but he had failed. Bartle, accustomed to danger, might prove to be more than she could finish; still, she would have enjoyed finishing him: the old brute was smelly, careless with his tobacco, and far too amorous.

After a day's reflection, Pansy told herself she had to be practical. She had always attempted to be practical; there was no sense taking chances in a new country.

Consequently she began to smile at the captain, who was not slow to notice that he was being smiled at. He soon began to beam in response. Pansy watched his movements and knew when he went off duty. On the second night after No Ear's departure she made herself as prim as possible, even tying her hair with the white ribbon Bartle had given her for their wedding. Then she met the captain outside his cabin door.

"I will be nice, sir, if you like," Pansy said. She felt quite confident—she had always considered that she enjoyed an advantage over men. After all, she had what they wanted—they could have it, but only if they helped.

"Eh, ma'am?" the captain said. He had observed the young woman watching him; indeed, he was not unaccustomed to such attentions from his female passengers. The authority he wielded as captain gave him a definite advantage with the female sex. Still, in the case of this particular female, he had not expected such a sudden move.

Pansy decided the man was tiresome; few of his sex weren't. Even in the plainest and most obvious situations, they frequently required some leading.

"Nice, sir," Pansy said, trying not to mock him. "I said I would be nice."

"Bully, then!" the captain said.

10

BARTLE CAME ON DECK, HOPING THAT THE COLD BREEZE would sober him enough to enable him to deal with the startling situation he suddenly found himself facing. Oppressed by the sad homecoming, grieving still for his lost friend, Bartle had adopted Calamity's method for aborting dismal thoughts. He had begun to split her bottles with her.

Now, with a dull headache, and a cold wind bringing autumn down the Missouri, he had just been told that his wife meant to leave him. Her notion was to journey downriver to New Orleans accompanied by the Boston captain.

"We just got married—it's only two months now," Bartle pointed out.

Neither Pansy nor the captain said anything. What seemed cruel to Bartle wasn't that Pansy had decided to leave—drunk or not, he was sharp enough to realize that he had begun to bore her—but that the two of them had decided to leave him at a time when his head felt as if a carpenter had hammered it for a while. His tongue, usually agile, felt thick and slow.

"Well, Pansy, I guess I am surprised that you want to leave," Bartle said. "Do you have a reason?"

He felt silly even saying it; why ask a woman if she had a reason, when the reason, gruff as ever, stood beside her in his blue coat?

"I've come to love my dear Johnny," Pansy said crisply, with a modest glance at the captain.

Calamity, propped against a pile of ropes, observed the proceedings without surprise. The little English whore was tired of Bartle; probably she had had no interest in him to begin with other than securing her passage. She felt a little relieved that matters had come to a head so soon. She had not looked forward to traveling upriver with the aloof young girl.

Despite her relief, she hoped for his sake that Bartle would make a stiff response. Since Jim's death, Bartle had gone slack. He rarely looked lively, and Bartle had always been the lively one, a man with enough spark to lift everyone's spirits at times when spirits were leaden.

Bartle knew he ought to shoot the brazen couple, or at least fight the captain, but he did neither—his gun wasn't handy, and neither was his anger. Facing them, he only felt a kind of wistfulness.

Part of it was that he knew he would miss his Pansy; having such a soft girl to warm his nights had been a rare treat. The other part of it was that he had begun to miss himself—the wild mountain man the Buntline types celebrated, half horse and half grizzly, the kind of character who would grab the Boston captain by the neck and shake him like a rat before pitching the little flirt who stood beside him into the river.

Bartle had done such things, but he didn't feel like doing them that morning. Seeing his friend die on a bench in Chicago had convinced him that it was foolish to go out of one's way to seek revenge. Life would deal out revenge enough for whatever wrongs people did. Life would settle with the Boston captain, sooner or later; it would settle, at some point, with pretty Pansy Clowes.

He had ignored the normal codes of behavior all his life—the freedom of the mountains was mostly a freedom

232

to ignore codes of behavior—and he didn't feel like pretending they interested him now. Jim Ragg had been the one who was code-bound. If Jim had been married to Pansy and she had proposed to depart with the Boston captain, Jim would have immediately shot the captain, and probably Pansy, too. Bartle had often tried to tease Jim about his strict behavior; there was something of the preacher in Jim—his sermon just happened to be beaver.

"If that's your wish, then I guess I'll just tip my hat," Bartle said. "Me and Calamity have got to catch our steamer."

Pansy Clowes was slightly affronted. She had married the old brute, after all—a stiffer argument than that would have been in order. Occasionally, in London, there had been contests for her favors; men had become violent over her and flailed at one another with their fists. Pansy enjoyed such occasions; she never felt surer of her power than in those hot moments when men fought over her. It would have been a good test for Johnny, too, to see if he could draw blood from old Bartle.

Though disappointed that Bartle had behaved so coolly, Pansy reminded herself of her resolution to be practical. She was in America, not England. Exciting as it might be to watch Bartle and Johnny battle for her, there was a distinct chance it would end the wrong way. Bartle might be the one to draw blood, and he might draw it in fatal amounts, in which case, since they seemed to be in a naked wilderness, she might have a deuce of a time getting down to New Orleans before the cold set in.

"We'll set you ashore, sir," the captain said. He had been a bit uneasy about the prospect of conflict himself. He had heard that Bartle Bone was an old Indian fighter —such men were the devil to predict. One had bitten the nose off a friend of his from Providence. His friend had lived to describe the savage attack. A doctor had attempted to sew the nose back in place, but the sutures had become infected and his friend had had to make do without his nose, lack of which was a big disadvantage in New England. He had finally emigrated to Australia, where mutilation was said to be more common.

With that memory fresh in mind, the captain had resolved to protect his nose at all cost. He was relieved that the old trapper was so agreeable about the matter.

Calamity considered raising a ruckus on Bartle's behalf —she had a desire to stir him up, to see if she could get him to behave like himself again. On the other hand, she felt queasy, and was very glad that Pansy was leaving. Much more of Pansy would not have been tolerable. Another reason for restraint was that girls of Pansy's sort were unpredictable. If Calamity roused herself and tore into the captain and knocked one of his ears off with a rifle butt or otherwise bloodied him, the girl might decide her new beau was a coward and choose to stay with Bartle.

"You didn't say much this morning," Bartle observed, once he and Calamity had settled themselves on the steamer *Yellowstone* and were looking at the muddy Missouri. Pansy and Captain John were by then enjoying a beefsteak in St. Louis, gone forever. Bartle still felt wistful—when would there be another such lithesome girl to warm his bed?

"She was your wife," Calamity said. "If you didn't care to stop her or stomp that sailor, I didn't consider it my place to interfere."

Night fell; the plains lay around them. They sat together on the deck of the little steamer, splitting another bottle. Both knew what a long river they had to ride; it edged northward, up the country and across the plains; more than any river it bound their youth to their age. Ghosts of lost enemies and lost companions dwelt by its banks: ghosts of a breed and ghosts of a race. Bartle had never imagined that he would be riding up the Missouri without Jim Ragg. As the prairie moon rose, Calamity mostly thought of Dora.

1

DORA MET OGDEN IN THE MIDDLE OF A MUDDY STREET in Belle Fourche. She had crossed to the hardware store to buy some tacks and curtain rods. Since Teat left to go work for Blue on his ranch, she had had no one to run such errands for her. The morning mist had become a driving rain; the few planks that had served her as a bridge on the trip over were soon pressed deep into the mud by passing wagons. Dora waited a bit, hoping the rain would let up; she had a touch of the weak feeling that had been plaguing her more and more lately, and sat down on a keg of nails to wait.

Instead of diminishing, the rain increased; though the hardware man, Mr. David, was kindly, and would have let her sit all day, Dora decided she had best get back. She might as well go and take her soaking.

She was not without experience in crossing streets that were little more than swamps; the streets in some of the cow towns would swallow a calf in certain seasons; in bolder days she would take off her shoes and stockings and plow through barelegged. But her bolder days were behind her. She was new in Belle Fourche; she didn't intend to affront the local ladies unnecessarily, even if an inconvenient emphasis on propriety meant getting herself a scolding from Doosie, who hated cleaning up muddy shoes.

Dora set out with her umbrella and had not got even to the middle of the street when the mud, violent as an animal, sucked off one of her shoes despite the fact that it was tightly buttoned. Dora balanced on the other foot, trying to keep her umbrella overhead and not drop her tacks and curtain rods. She tried to reach the shoe without dipping her skirt into the mud and couldn't quite. The shoe had all but disappeared; the top was slippery with mud and she could only reach it with her fingernails, unable to get a grip on it. Her other foot was sinking deeper; the street seemed to have no bottom. No doubt that shoe would come off, too, when she attempted her next step.

Dora began to feel a little desperate; there seemed no hope of getting her shoe, and she could not stand poised on one leg in the middle of the muddy street forever. Already her leg was cramping; she would be lucky not to fall into the mud. If she had to go home with her dress ruined, Doosie would not get over it for days.

At that point she saw a team of large horses splashing toward her. Her heart sank—there went the dress!—but then she heard the driver yell "Whoa!" The team stopped well out of splattering range and a huge young man jumped down.

"You are in a fix, aren't you, miss?" he said. Without being asked, he pulled her lost shoe out of the gummy mud and then to Dora's astonishment simply picked her up and carried her to his wagon.

"Where did you want to go, miss?" he asked, when she was safely on the wagon seat.

Dora felt embarrassed to admit that her house was scarcely thirty yards away. The boy and his team had just passed it. She didn't like to ask a man to turn his team to deposit her thirty yards from where she sat.

"I'm just there," she admitted, pointing at her house. The youth watched her with large, unblinking blue eyes. Though just a boy, really, he was one of the largest men she had ever seen; he seemed to be built like a tree.

"I thought I could make it home, but I didn't step light enough," Dora said. "You mustn't trouble yourself. I can just take off my other shoe and wade it."

"I guess you won't, though," Ogden said. Now that she was on his wagon seat, he could not believe that he had actually had the boldness to pick up such a pretty lady. Although she had clearly been in a predicament, with one shoe lost eight inches deep in the mud, it was still unlike him just to go pick up a lady. He had never been forward with women; indeed, he had never been anything with women. He had just happened to notice Dora and didn't want his horses to splatter her dress. He had jumped out of the wagon meaning to offer her a hand, and then just picked her up without thinking. Now that he saw how lovely she was, he began to feel his shyness coming; it felt as if it was coming in a rush. On occasion, usually at picnics, when some girl had spoken to him or accidentally touched him, his shyness had come in such a rush that he would almost faint. The lovely woman on his wagon seat obviously didn't wish to scare him; but she was female, and that in itself was scary.

He looked at her solemnly for a moment. He had a big face, big eyes. Dora felt she had never before been exposed to quite such a large solemnity. Why are you so solemn, mister? she wanted to ask—but of course that would be a ridiculous thing to ask someone who had just rescued her from a muddy fate.

Ogden considered turning the team, but the house was just a few steps away. Unusual as it was for him to carry a woman twice in one day—except for his sisters, he had not carried one in all his previous life—it was clearly the quick solution to getting her safely home.

"Carrying you's the quickest," he said, turning his eyes aside. He got down and held out his arms, hoping the woman would just arrive in them somehow. If she did, he would promptly carry her home.

The sight of the young man with his arms held out and his gaze turned away was so comical that Dora laughed. Without realizing it, he had backed two or three steps from the wagon. Dora realized she would have had to make a skillful leap to land in his waiting arms.

"What's your name, mister?" she asked. She decided she liked this young giant.

"Ogden Prideaux," he said, astonished at the question. He looked, and realized there was a gap between him and the wagon; he stepped closer, and Dora, who felt she wanted to be carried, put a hand on his shoulder to steady herself. At that point, Ogden's shyness struck with full force; he felt his legs tremble as he carried Dora through the rain to the front door of her house. Then he knocked loudly on the door but forgot to set the lady down.

A black woman opened the door and looked at the two of them in silent astonishment.

"Did she break her leg?" Doosie asked. It was the only explanation she could come up with for why Dora might be resting in the arms of such a very large man—resting happily, too, from what Doosie could see.

"Goodness, no, I just lost a shoe," Dora said. "Ogden, would you care to set me down?"

Ogden just managed to. He set her down and awaited orders. He had momentarily forgotten that he had a wagon and a team of horses waiting in the street. Other wagons were having to squish around them. Two or three drivers were annoyed that someone had left a wagon smack in the middle of the street in order to go whore— it was only mid-morning.

Ogden was oblivious. Dora sat down on her own front step and took off her other shoe. The buttons were slick with mud; getting the shoe off took a while.

Doosie still stood in the doorway. She didn't know what to make of the man, or of Dora. The one certainty was that Dora should not have tried to cross the street while it was raining. Usually if a man showed up too early, or if it was someone they didn't want in the house, Doosie had only to block the door and glare and the culprit would slink away. But this young man was so large and his appearance so unexpected that Doosie didn't feel up to glaring at him. Anyway, he wasn't trying to come into the house. He just showed no sign of trying to leave.

"You've helped a lot, Ogden," Dora said—she felt she could use his first name. "If you care to come in I'll offer you tea. Are you fond of tea?"

The last thing Ogden would have expected was an invitation to take tea with a lady. He was not accustomed to expecting anything, but if he had been more used to expecting, he still doubted that he would have expected to be asked to tea. He would have liked to accept, but his tongue felt stuck; for a moment he didn't say anything.

Dora noticed that the young man had blushed a deep red; so deep was his blush that he seemed incapable of speech. Doosie, too, was incapable of speech, so shocked was she that the large boy had been invited in.

Dora was a little surprised to find herself developing a frisky feeling. In recent years she more and more rarely developed her frisky feeling, the very feeling that had driven Blue and not a few others mad with love. She had supposed her frisky feeling was gone forever; even Blue didn't provoke it often anymore; she was too disappointed in Blue. But for some reason, looking up at Ogden looming like a tree on her porch, she felt distinctly frisky. It might be fun to lure this big specimen of a male indoors and see if she could manage to untie his tongue.

However, there was the problem of the wagon. It was right in the middle of the street and was beginning to cause commotion.

"Maybe you ought to hitch your wagon first," she suggested. "I fear it's in people's way."

Ogden remembered the wagon—there it was, and yet it felt like something he had owned long ago, in another life. Still, if the lady wanted him to hitch it, obviously he had to go hitch it. He started heavily down the steps. When he had descended far enough that his head was about level with the lady's, he turned and found her grinning at him. But what had he done that was funny?

"We've not been formally introduced—let's just do it western style," Dora said, offering him a small hand to shake. "I'm Miss Dora DuFran and I would be pleased if you'd join me for tea. Once you hitch your wagon, of course.''

"Ma'am, I intend to come right back," Ogden said, though getting his tongue unstuck took quite an effort.

"Who's going to clean them boots of his?" Doosie asked, once he had gone clomping off through the rain. "He can't come in in his boots—they're big boots!"

"Oh, blow your nose," Dora said. "Nobody asked you to do anything about his boots."

"I'm responsible for the floor," Doosie reminded her —Dora's precipitous decisions often annoyed her, and this one annoyed her a good deal. "I ain't having no five pounds of mud on the floor this early," she emphasized. "It's too early! We ain't even open."

Dora was watching Ogden. The driver of a wagon stopped behind his jumped off his seat as if he intended to fight, but when he saw how big Ogden was he changed his mind rapidly and pretended he had only got down to mend his reins.

Ogden didn't notice—he popped his horses, and pulled his wagon to the side of the street.

"It's early, we ain't even open!" Doosie insisted. "Look how big he is."

"Well, you may not be open, but I am," Dora said, picking up her muddy shoes. "I guess it won't kill anybody if I ask a gentleman for tea."

"Look at how big he is," Doosie said, still annoyed. "We'll have to make the tea in a gallon bucket."

"Then go find the bucket," Dora said with a laugh.

2

LATER, ONCE THEY HAD MARRIED, DORA FELT ALMOST guilty for the speed with which she had captured Ogden. She had made some rapid conquests in her day, but none so rapid or so complete as Ogden. Sitting awkward and frightened in her parlor that morning, drinking what turned out to be almost a gallon bucket's worth of tea, Ogden became hers. Perhaps it hadn't even taken that long. Perhaps he had become hers when she looked at him beneath the dripping umbrella on his wagon seat. Making him hers was so easy that it felt a little unseemly; but she had no impulse to spare him or even to slow her conquest. Ogden was awkward, even wooden, but at least he was all of a piece, and simple in a way that few men were. Blue was the love of her life, but Blue was too complicated; once, the complications had excited her, engaged her; now they just wearied her—of course, she would always love Blue, she couldn't help it, but she felt too sad and too tired to go on with it. Blue loved being complicated; he thought he would beguile her forever with his devilish and reckless ways. Well, that he might, at some level; but at the level of day-to-day life she no longer felt lightened by his devilish and reckless ways.

She needed someone she could be at rest with, someone large and simple. Ogden was both, in an endearing way. He wasn't large outside and small inside, as so many men were. His dimensions were of a piece. It would not occur to him to be ungenerous; what he had, he gave. It didn't even occur to him to question her—to Ogden, Dora was an oracle of truth, to be listened to and loved and obeyed. It startled him to find out that she was almost the age of his mother, but once that shock subsided he quite forgot that she was almost the age of his mother. Dora scaled down and then closed the whorehouse before Ogden quite grasped the fact that his wife had been running a whorehouse. When he did realize it he behaved exactly as he had when he found out her age; he was surprised, and then he quite forgot it. He himself had been too scared of women to visit whorehouses but attached no blame to Dora for having run one. Once Dora took him to her bed it became obvious to him why whorehouses made money.

Only twenty-two, Ogden had experienced powerful yearnings, but had not really understood what the yearnings tended toward. He knew that people mated—after all, he had four strapping sisters—but no one had ever informed him that the act was pleasant. But Dora persuaded him otherwise, and the pleasure that resulted left him tongue-tied with surprise. Before that, his best pleasures had been swimming, or fishing, or maybe just running for a mile or two over the prairie. Sometimes Ogden felt so full of energy that he just burst off and ran. Because of his tendency suddenly to run, he had been considered rather strange back home in Wisconsin. His mother, worried by his odd behavior, had tried to curb his running, but Ogden couldn't control it—there were times when he felt he just must run, or else pop from all the energy inside him.

Once Dora led him into the mating act, Ogden seldom felt that imperative need to run. Now and then he still might lope a mile or two, but the frenzied speed that had once characterized his running diminished a lot.

Without meaning to, Ogden more or less ruined Dora's

business. The Hotel Hope, so recently moved from Miles City to Belle Fourche, began to lose most of the customers it had just begun to acquire. Skeedle, so actively sought in Miles City that she scarcely had had time to think, had so little to do in Belle Fourche that she took up fortune-telling as a sideline. Trix, sprightly as ever, had two or three devoted customers, but could rarely find anyone to dance with; then a cowboy bound for San Antonio passed through on his way south, fell in love with Trix, and in two days Trix was gone, bound for a ranch on the Frio. Opinion was divided as to whether Trix would tolerate the cowboy all the way to Texas; Skeedle felt that her departure had more to do with ambition than love.

"I predict she'll leave him in Denver," Skeedle said. "Trix always said she wanted to see Denver."

"That boy was sweet, though," Dora pointed out. Marriage to a sweet cowboy was the dream of many a buffalo girl—it had been her dream, too, and yet, for fear of the country, plus a silly determination not to give in to Blue, she had let the dream slip by. For years she had cried about it, cried about it, cried about it. She had even cried about it the morning she met Ogden—she had had to hold cold rags to her eyes for an hour before she felt presentable enough to cross to the hardware store. How odd it was that she had recovered herself, crossed when she did, waited just the right amount of time on the keg of nails, and then set out for home again, only to lose her shoe just as Ogden was coming. What if she had decided she felt too grim to leave the store? What if she had held out a few minutes longer, stayed put on the keg of nails until Ogden had passed? She would have missed him. Now that she had him, the thought that a change in timing of even a minute could have meant missing him forever was disturbing. Dora, who had so often sat looking out her window wishing Blue would come, but knowing it would be difficult even if he did, now looked out her window in a state of amazement—amazement at her luck.

The business life was over, though. Skeedle was more

interested in telling fortunes, for one thing. Trix was gone, for another. But the principal reason business was over was Ogden himself: though perfectly friendly, and not the least judgmental about whoring—it was obvious to Ogden that if such great pleasure could be bought there would be men willing to buy it—his large presence frightened away many potential customers. Dora found this amusing; Ogden was one of the most peaceful males she had ever encountered, and yet most of the men that came in to the bar were afraid of him. He was just so large. Experienced whorers knew that most whores had a special fellow, a customer who loved them and might become fiercely jealous despite full knowledge of the requirements of the trade. The new customers at the Hotel Hope assumed Ogden was just such a fellow; they might be feeling rowdy, but fewer and fewer of them seemed to feel rowdy enough to risk an encounter with a jealous Ogden.

Once Trix left, Dora didn't bother looking for another girl. The bar did fair business—she would just get by with the bar. Once in a while, usually when Ogden was off hauling for the mines, a party would arrive and engage Skeedle for an evening. Or a new girl might show up and work for a few days before drifting on to Miles City or Helena or somewhere.

Two weeks after she met him, Dora asked Ogden if he wanted to marry her. She knew it would never occur to him to ask her because it would never occur to him that she might accept, or even consider it.

The question caught Ogden unaware and caused him to blush so deeply that he couldn't speak. He had cherished the deep hope that he could stay with Dora forever, but he feared that such a thing was impossible and he tried not to let the hope swell. Marriage was beyond his imagining. He wasn't even sure what you had to do in order to be allowed to marry. His shyness was so deep that he supposed that alone meant marriage was out of the question. And then, with no warning, sitting on the bed with him, wrapped in her housecoat, Dora brought it into the question.

"Married like Ma and Pa?" Ogden asked.

"Well, I don't know your Ma and Pa," Dora said. "I guess they're probably pretty well matched, from the size of you. Do you want to marry me or not?"

She felt a slight pang of embarrassment at her forwardness—of course, this big boy wasn't going to refuse her.

"Would we do it today, or when?" Ogden asked, his thoughts in a riot. He had come to the west meaning to farm; he had read a pamphlet describing the wonderful farming opportunities that abounded in the Dakotas, and here he was. But so far he was just a freight hauler; he didn't have a farm, and Dora had confessed to him that she didn't like farms much. How to manage the future seemed quite a puzzle. Ogden didn't understand the steps involved in marriage; on the other hand he felt a frenzy not unlike the frenzy that had once caused him to run. In this case his frenzy was to get the marrying done immediately, before Dora changed her mind.

"We could—or tomorrow," Dora said. She was surprised at her own impatience, which was so sharp she felt capable of being quite ruthless about getting her way. For more than twenty years she had danced away from every opportunity for marriage; now she not only wanted to marry Ogden, she wanted to marry him immediately. She suddenly felt that everything depended on quickness, though there was no real reason to think it did. But she felt it anyway—she wanted it concluded, and concluded now!

They located a preacher and got married the next day, with Skeedle, Doosie, and Potato Creek Johnny in attendance. Johnny just happened to be in town—he had been in love with Dora for years and always dropped by when he was in her vicinity. She had never been sweet on him, but she was friendly to a fault—and there was always hope.

Watching the wedding—Dora had bought Ogden a new coat to be married in; it was handsome but rather tight in the shoulders—Johnny concluded that he might just as well quit hoping. It seemed to him that a pretty tight knot was being tied. Later he got drunk and cut the cards with

Skeedle, the prize being her favor. Johnny won the cut and spent a happy night.

"Calamity will be surprised when she comes back and finds you married," he told the happy bride the next morning. The groom was sleeping late.

"She won't be the surprisest, though," Doosie said. She wore a long face and spoke in a dark tone, although she liked Potato Creek Johnny—he always complimented her cooking extravagantly.

"Well, who knows when Calamity will get back?" Dora said. She felt happy and was determined to ignore any line of commentary that might spoil her mood.

Potato Creek Johnny didn't intend to be a mood spoiler. He was merely imagining Calamity's amazement when she returned and discovered that Dora had married this huge youth. He thought Dora DuFran had become more beautiful than ever as a result of her union and wished her nothing but the best. Dora finally getting to be happy made the whole world look better.

Johnny assembled his gear and set off—it might be the day he would find the creek of gold, although that was unlikely. He had long since waded all the creeks within a day's walk of Belle Fourche, and though one or two might carry an occasional gold fleck, none was the creek of gold. Only in wide-spaced dreams did he encounter the golden creek.

Despite Dora's cheerfulness and Ogden's big-boy courtesy—Doosie had to admit that he was a mighty polite boy; not once had he tramped in with muddy boots—Doosie continued to wear a long face and speak in dark tones. The marriage shocked her, and she did not bother to hide her shock. Dora, who ought to know how things went between young boys and older women, had acted hastily and foolishly, in Doosie's view, and foolishly not merely in terms of youth and age; foolishly in terms of where her heart lay.

Dora couldn't put up with it any longer; no matter how patient she was, or how nicely Ogden behaved, Doosie remained stiff, mighty stiff.

"Why do you look that way?" she asked Doosie finally —Ogden was out shoeing one of his draft horses.

Doosie made no reply; but she continued to look that way.

"You are the hardest person to get along with I've ever met, I guess," Dora said. "All I did was get married. Don't I have a right to get married?"

"Yes, but that don't make it smart," Doosie replied.

"What was so smart about what I had, I'd like to know?" Dora asked. "I'm forty-one years old, and what did I have?"

Again, Doosie sulled. She didn't enjoy long conversations. In her opinion people talked far too much; what was talk? What did it solve, if people were just going to go on and do anything they wanted to? Talking couldn't undo anything that had been done, and it rarely stopped people from making the most obvious mistakes.

"I don't know what to say," Dora said. "You won't talk, you won't smile, you won't look at me. Is it Ogden you don't like?"

"I like Ogden but I don't know Ogden," Doosie pointed out. "You ask me what you had—what you had was freedom. And you had a warm house, too."

"I've *still* got a warm house—my goodness!" Dora said, exasperated.

"You ain't got freedom, though," Doosie said. "You'll never be seeing freedom again. He's got you now and he'll keep you."

"You make him sound like a jailor," Dora said. "Freedom isn't something everybody needs for their whole lives. About all I did with my freedom was cry. You think crying's better than being the wife of a nice young man?"

"Yep," Doosie said.

"You're a hard one then," Dora said. "Ogden's never given me orders. He wouldn't think of it. I give *him* orders. I told him he better go shoe that horse. He wouldn't think of telling me to do something."

"You just been married a month," Doosie said. "Give him time. He may decide that men are supposed to give the orders."

Ogden soon came in, and Dora gave up, but Doosie's attitude didn't improve. She did her work as precisely as ever, but she still wore a long face. Dora didn't like to scold her—Doosie had been with her for years—but she found her long face increasingly hard to live with. Besides, Skeedle suddenly left to try her hand at telling fortunes in Fargo; this left Dora with no one much to talk to. Ogden was too young, Calamity not yet back. Dora needed talk, too. She wasn't meant to live in silence, with just her thoughts. Though more and more content with Ogden, she had to admit that talk wasn't his strong suit. He was young and sweet, but he wasn't voluble.

For all her happiness, Dora was not free of all agitation, either. Agitation nagged her like a toothache.

"Is it Blue?" she asked Doosie one morning. "Is that why you're so sour?"

"That's why," Doosie said, a little relieved that Dora had finally figured it out. She didn't like feeling angry at Dora—it spoiled the day.

Dora sighed. It seemed it was always Blue when there was agitation or disturbance. He was there, like a worm in the fruit, to remind one that nothing was really perfect.

"What makes you think I have to be concerned about Mr. Blue?" she asked, annoyed that Doosie seemed to be on Blue's side and not hers.

"Because you married so quick," Doosie said. "You was afraid he would come. He gonna come anyway, though. Then what?"

"Then he'll find I'm a married woman," Dora said, getting angry despite herself. "He's married too, remember? There's nothing either one of us can do about it now."

She found it very annoying that Doosie had deciphered her sharp impatience to marry, when she had only half deciphered it herself. Of course she had feared Blue would come and destroy her future with Ogden.

Ogden might be too young for her, she might be too old for him, he might start giving her orders, he might be killed, she might die, they might come to hate one another; still, she wanted it and she wanted it immediately.

However odd it might seem to others, for now her marriage was something good, and Dora had spent her share of years without very much that was good. Blue and she were beyond good and bad, in any clear sense. They were part of one another's fate, perhaps the heart of one another's fate, but they were never going to be one another's whole. She wanted someone with whom she could have a whole, even if it changed, even if it led to tragedy. Having it and losing it seemed less terrible than never having it.

"What are you going to tell Ogden when he comes?" Doosie asked. The arrival of T. Blue—in her view it was sure to happen—had been preying on her mind of late.

"What are you going to tell Mr. Blue?" she added.

"The same thing he told me one day—that I'm married!" Dora said, her eyes flashing. "And you know something? I can't wait! I wish he'd walk in right now."

"You're crazy!" Doosie said, alarmed at her boss's hot hunger for confrontation. Ogden was just out in the backyard. If Mr. Blue came just then, somebody might end up dead; she had seen several people end up dead, and in cases where far less enduring emotion was involved.

Dora grabbed a book and threw it through the door into the saloon. No one was in the saloon at the time, but the book narrowly missed a spittoon.

"I doubt he'll ever come!" she said. "I doubt he thinks I'm worth this long a ride. And I don't care! He's welcome to spend the rest of his life up on the Musselshell for all I care!"

An hour later Ogden found her sitting on their bed, trying desperately to stop crying. The sight made him weak in the legs. He had a terrible fear that he must have done something wrong. Why else would Dora be crying? It was a pretty day, and he had done all the chores. He racked his brain but could remember no error, or call to mind anything he might have forgotten.

"Are you sick?" he asked, looking at Dora's red, anguished face. It was not the face he was used to seeing every morning. The sight of it alarmed him so much that

251

he felt he might cry himself. Ogden knew what it was to cry—his brother Joe had accidentally cut his foot off with an ax one day, and the shock had killed him. Sometimes Ogden still cried about Joe, but only when alone. At times he felt low, even lower than low, for Joe had been his only friend.

But the fact that he himself cried provided no guide as to how he might help Dora. He felt helpless—perhaps she didn't want to be married anymore. The minute that thought occurred to him, Ogden became convinced it was true. It had always been hard to believe Dora wanted to marry him, and that she wanted it no longer wouldn't surprise him. He turned to leave, hoping to make the barn before he was overcome.

But Dora sprang up and threw herself into his arms. She didn't say a word; she just clung to him, sobbing. Ogden felt it meant she didn't want the marriage to cease, and he was too relieved to speak. He held her and stroked her hair.

The next day T. Blue, feeling merrier the closer he came to town, loped into Belle Fourche and asked a blacksmith to point him to the Hotel Hope.

"You're too late, the girls all quit," the blacksmith said. "You better go back to Deadwood, that's my advice."

"If my horse throws a shoe I might want your advice," Blue said. He thought the blacksmith far too casual with his opinions. "I expect I can still find a girl, if I can locate the hotel," he said.

The blacksmith pointed to a house across the street and about fifty yards east. A youth the size of a tree was whitewashing one wall of the house. By standing on a bucket he could reach well up to the planks of the second story.

"Who's that giant?" Blue asked, rather surprised to see such a large youth working at Dora's house.

"His name is Ogden something," the blacksmith said. "I think he comes from Ohio."

"I don't guess I care where he comes from," Blue said. "He looks like he could dig a mine all by himself. I won-

252

der why he's wasting his time whitewashing Dora's house.''

"Because he's married to her, that's why," the blacksmith said. He didn't care much for cowboys—they were usually arrogant, in his view. Still, he hadn't expected his remark to inflict such a shock on the cowboy with the fine buckskin mare. The man, who had ridden in looking rather ruddy from the brisk weather, had suddenly turned white as a sheet.

"That giant boy's married to Dora?" Blue asked. Since the blacksmith seemed so casual, perhaps he was only making an attempt at humor.

"They're married—it's the talk of the town," the blacksmith said.

"Mister, are you all right?" he asked after a bit. He had seldom seen a man go so abruptly from ruddy to white.

"I guess I don't want the whorehouse—I guess a saloon will do," said T. Blue.

3

THE NEWS THAT BLUE WAS IN TOWN WAS NOT LONG IN reaching the Hotel Hope. One could look out any window and see most of what was happening in Belle Fourche. Doosie looked out the kitchen window and saw a familiar-looking buckskin mare hitched in front of a saloon a little way up the street. The sight depressed her so much she could scarcely go on with her cooking. When the whorehouse closed and business fell off in the saloon, it seemed she might get some rest from her cooking, but then along came Ogden, who ate more at one meal than all the whores and customers in a normal day. The rest Doosie had hoped to get was one of those things that were mainly nice things to think about—in practice they never quite came.

Though Doosie had predicted that Blue would come, she hadn't predicted he'd come immediately; but he had. The fact disturbed her so that she *did* stop cooking; she sat down in a chair with a big tin cup of coffee. She liked drinking coffee from a tin-miner's cup—a few cups of coffee might help her get a grip on her feelings. The virtue of the tin cups was that they kept the coffee at a scalding temperature for quite a while, and Doosie liked it scalding. When she was low—and she was certainly low at the moment—scalding coffee was her comfort.

Doosie thought gloomily of all the years she had attended to Dora and Blue; how careful she had been to nurse them through their many quarrels and disputes, the separations and disappointments; she had also tried to keep them behaving decently during their ecstatic reunions. At times Dora was even more of a problem than Blue; she was so glad to see him that she made little effort to control herself. Doosie had always hoped that someday they would settle down together and stop fighting so much. When T. Blue was around, Dora was happy; so was he. Why people who were only happy in one another's company contrived to stay apart so much was puzzling to Doosie. She herself didn't like men, on the whole, and had usually been content to see the last of the many who pestered her when she was younger.

But Dora, her kind boss, was far less critical of men than she was. Over the years, Doosie had seen Dora take fancies, usually brief, to any number of men, including some Doosie had been reluctant to let in the door. Dora wasn't as hard on men as she should be, Doosie felt— anyone who would compliment her, dance with her, or just make her laugh would be welcomed for a while. Of course, Blue did all those things better than anyone else; little wonder Dora had kept on loving him through the years.

However, he *had* married—it had been a blow to Dora —but then, he was stuck off on a remote ranch most of the time and could not be blamed for wanting company. It was hard for Doosie to imagine Dora living on a ranch; also hard to imagine T. Blue staying any place for very long. Dora didn't even like horses—the only pet she could tolerate was her bossy parrot, Fred.

Now, however, things were really in a fine mess; both old lovers were married, and not to one another. The confusion, the anger, the tears the situation would produce made Doosie wonder if the whole business—romance—could possibly be worth it. She herself had long since reached negative conclusions on the matter of the worth of romance, but the only person she could find who shared her view was Calamity. They had discussed the subject several times and agreed that no pleasure men brought was worth the havoc they wreaked through selfish and contrary behavior.

Doosie drank two scalding cups of coffee, felt a little better, and went upstairs to inform Dora that her old boyfriend was in town. Maybe being a married woman for the first time in her life would have brought her finally to her senses. Maybe she'd refuse to see Blue. On the other hand, it might go the other way; she might run off with him, in which case Doosie would be stuck with Ogden to feed—and Ogden took a lot of feeding.

"I know, I see his horse," Dora said, when Doosie came in. "He must have found out, else he wouldn't have come here. Do you think he found out?"

"I ain't no mind reader, you need Skeedle if you want to know what he found out," Doosie said.

"Anyway, he's across the street getting drunk," Dora said. "What am I going to do?"

"It wasn't two days ago you said you hoped he'd come," Doosie reminded her—she loved to catch Dora in contradictions, and had caught her in thousands over the years. It surprised her to find Dora looking so frantic, though—she looked nervous enough to fall out the window.

"Why do you always remind me when I say something foolish?" Dora said. "I felt that way then, but now I just wish he'd go. What if he shoots Ogden?"

"He better shoot him hard if he shoots him," Doosie remarked. "Ogden's big."

Dora hadn't expected Blue to arrive so quickly, nor did she suppose she would feel so upset when he did. Yet the moment she saw his horse, an anxiety gripped her as powerful as any she had ever felt. Part of her yearned to see him—the same old yearning to see him that had never diminished in all those years—but another and newer part wanted him to go. What if he and Ogden fought? What if Ogden found out how long she had loved Blue, and as a result ceased to want her himself? After all,

Ogden was very young—how could he be expected to understand what she herself scarcely understood: her love for T. Blue, and her need for his love in return?

With a shock Dora realized Doosie had been right to wear a long face: for she *had* acted against her own heart —at least she had divided her own heart. She *did* still want to see Blue; she *did* still love him and want his love. But that need and that feeling didn't cancel Ogden, her young husband. What if both men condemned her—she knew the sex well enough to be fully aware of that possibility. What if they both left her?

"I don't know what to do," Dora admitted, throwing herself on Doosie's mercy. "What should I do?"

Doosie liked it when Dora appealed to her; it confirmed what she had always been convinced of—that she, not Dora, was the one with good sense. She wasn't the one looking distraught and half crazy, with her hair uncombed.

"You bought Ogden that new gun," Doosie said, thinking quickly. "Tell him to go shoot us a deer, or an elk if he can find one. He'd be gone for a while, and we might get some elk meat, too."

Dora adopted the suggestion at once. In twenty minutes a slightly bewildered but willing Ogden, relieved of his paint bucket and armed with his brand-new Winchester, was trotting out of town on a mule named Charley, an animal Dora had taken in settlement of a debt. Dora had seemed a little upset when she sent him off, but she had also given him a nice kiss and squeezed him hard, so he didn't feel that her upset reflected any dissatisfaction with his whitewashing. Although Charley was a tall mule with a rough trot, Ogden felt that was a small price to pay for the opportunity to go elk hunting on a day when he had expected to work. He had been so surprised that he couldn't speak when, a few days earlier, Dora had presented him with a Winchester—it was still a daily wonder to Ogden that Dora liked him. He meant to waste no time in showing her he was worthy of her liking; he meant to kill the first elk he saw. Of course, if it was a fat elk calf, that would be so much the better.

The bartender in the Moosefoot Saloon—the saloon Blue had chosen to drink in while he absorbed the shock he had just received—was an old friend from Texas days. His name was Restless Frank, and he answered to Restless rather than Frank. Blue had first met him in Tascosa, many miles and many years back down the trail.

Restless knew T. Blue was disturbed the moment he saw him. If he had known Blue was in town, he would have known he was disturbed without even seeing him; T. usually strode in like a lord of the prairie, but this morning his carriage was that of a whipped dog.

"If that unfriendly blacksmith has lied to me I'll kill him," Blue said, to open the conversation.

"I don't find Jones unfriendly," Restless remarked, hoping not to have to address any painful subjects before lunch, or after lunch, or any time.

"Friendly or not, I might shoot him," Blue said, thinking what a relief to his feelings it would be to pop a few shots at the blacksmith. He and Calamity had often relieved pent-up distress by shooting at rocks for an hour or two.

"Now, Blue, I hope you won't disturb the peace," Restless counseled. "The jail ain't up to your standards. Besides, we need Jones. He's far more reliable than the other blacksmith we've got."

"Well, you're free to move to a town with better blacksmiths," Blue said irritably. "There's plenty of communities with fine blacksmiths. You've spent most of your time moving anyway, or you'd still be in Tascosa. What's keeping you in Belle Fourche?"

"The pleasant company," Restless said dryly.

As he turned from setting a nicely polished glass on the bar, he happened to see Ogden trot past on Charley; the mule, though large by local standards, looked as if it should have been riding Ogden. Restless stood in the door and watched Ogden ride away; the news that he was leaving might provide just the lift Blue's spirits needed.

"She must still like you," he said. "There goes Ogden. Your old girlfriend must have coaxed him off on a hunt."

Blue jumped to his feet and went outside to watch

Ogden go. He then came back in, feeling slightly better, and finished his whiskey.

"I doubt one whorehouse will keep that youngster in mules," he said.

"That's a new rifle he's carrying," Restless remarked. "Maybe he'll waste up all his ammunition shooting at buzzards or something and not have any left to kill you with when he comes back and finds you with his wife."

"Buzzards could feast a long time on a carcass as big as his," Blue said moodily.

"Oh, can that talk," Restless said. "You're a cowboy, not a killer. You never scared nobody much in your Tascosa days, and you were tougher then."

Blue let that pass—Restless Frank had always been hard to impress. "Anyway, he ain't gonna catch me with his wife," he said. "I just come to Belle Fourche for the ride."

"I'm the one who's named Restless," Restless said. "I doubt you'd ride all the way from the Musselshell just to listen to your horse grunt.

"You always have an excuse when you show up to see Dora," he added. "This has been going on for twenty years, which is as far back as I can remember. Why do you still think you need an excuse?"

"If I were you I'd polish them glasses, and mind your own business while you're doing it," Blue said.

"Anyway, you should have had her roped and branded years ago, if that was your plan," Restless said.

"I guess you consider yourself an expert on marriage, is that right?" Blue said, irked by the man's effrontery— he was even more casual than the blacksmith.

"Personally, I prefer just to bartend," Restless said. "If there wasn't nice saloons to go to, I doubt many marriages would hold. I tried a couple when I was younger. Give me saloons any day."

Blue plunked down his fifty cents and strode off without saying goodbye. He had decided to leave at once— mount up, ride directly out of town, and make an attempt to put the past behind him. If Dora DuFran wanted to communicate with him, she could post a letter.

As he passed the Hotel Hope he happened to glance up. For a second he glimpsed Dora's face in the window. It was only a glimpse, but it stopped him dead: How many times, as the two of them climbed the ladder of years, had he raced up to some rough house in some rough town, and looked up to see that face in a window, waiting for him to race up? He stopped his horse; the window was empty for a bit, then Dora came back and looked down at him. She didn't smile; neither did he. But in a bit he rode around the house and hitched his buckskin mare by the back door.

4

"WE CAN'T DO THIS ANYMORE—I'D BE TOO ASHAMED of myself," Dora said, nervously fastening her dress.

She already felt too ashamed of herself. Blue had merely been sitting in the kitchen, teasing Doosie. It was she who had drawn him upstairs; he had seemed uncharacteristically reluctant; for once he might have preferred to stay in the kitchen and enjoy his chat with the cook.

T. Blue felt a little melancholy, though he was not distraught to the extent that Dora was. They had disappointed themselves—why, he couldn't quite grasp; their long love had not been built on disappointment. Still, it seemed to him that Dora was more upset than the occasion required. Life was a sturdy business; it wouldn't founder because of one mess in the morning.

"What possessed you to marry?" he asked, clinging to her hand. He felt that if she would just settle in his arms for a bit she might calm down and things might go better. But Dora, with the hand he wasn't holding, was brushing her hair desperately, as if well-brushed hair would hold back chaos.

Dora dropped the hairbrush in discouragement: what

was the point? She allowed him to pull her back on the bed, though for a while she remained stiff.

"I don't know, T.," she said. "He carried me out of the mud—I guess that's why."

T. Blue couldn't help grinning. It was the sanest reason for getting married he had yet been presented with. Few of the other explanations he had heard made half as much sense.

"Now why didn't I think of that, in Dodge or somewhere?" he said. "There was plenty of mud around when we first got acquainted. If I'd just spotted you in the slush somewhere, we might have ten grandkids."

"Don't talk about it," Dora said miserably. "Don't talk about things that can't happen. I'll get too sad."

"Oh, hush that!" Blue said. "Stop this moping. The sky ain't fallen that I can see. You've got a strapping youth to help you now—I'm sure he'll serve you far better than a broken-down cowpoke like me."

"That's fine, but I love you most," Dora said. "I can't help it. I love you most."

"Well, I know you do," Blue said. Dora was in such a delicate state, he thought he had best exert himself and be tactful. "You've had sort of a tricky way of showing it, though."

Dora immediately bristled. "Tricky?" she said. "I deny it! When I can get you to show up, I show it fine. Don't I?"

Blue had been referring to her long refusal to marry him, but he felt there was no advantage to be gained by clarifying the matter.

"You show it fine," Blue agreed; in her state, if she had said the moon was green he would have agreed.

After a bit Dora felt a little calmer and became a bit less stiff.

"Things just get away from me," she said. "You live so far away now."

That was a little too exasperating to let pass, Blue felt. "Who moved?" he said. "Who moved to Belle Fourche? Was it me?"

"No, but you married first," Dora said, realizing she had been a trifle illogical in her last statement.

"Let's not argue that," Blue said. "We can argue that till bulls grow teats, and not agree."

They both slowly relaxed; they took a little nap. When Blue woke up Dora had spread a towel under his head and was trimming his hair—it had grown shaggy in the last months. Trimming his hair had always been her special joy.

"Sit up," she commanded. Blue sat up sleepily, and she finished the job.

"Now I'll itch all the way home," he said.

"It will serve you right—you deserve to suffer worse!" Dora informed him, but she was no longer distressed.

"What's that strapping youth like?" Blue inquired. "Is he old enough to talk yet? Has anyone taught him his letters?"

"He reads better than you can, I'll have you know," Dora said. "Don't be mocking my husband. He's a peach of a boy and I'm mighty, mighty fond of him."

"I intend to call him Ox," Blue said. "An ox is a beast that has only one use, and that's to tug you out of the mud. If you'll restrict him to mud duty, you'll hear no complaint from me."

Dora almost laughed, as she had so often laughed at his sallies, but the laugh never came.

"T., he's my husband," she said. "I wanted someone —Ogden's nice."

Then she put her face in her hands and began to cry. Her hands were covered with his hairs—likewise the bedsheet. Quite a few had made it down the back of his shirt.

"Oh, no, now, this is tiresome, it's a pretty day," Blue said. "I was merely joshing—I've joshed you a thousand times. What's the matter?"

"I'm sorry—I'm sorry. I'm not myself," Dora said.

Doosie had fixed a fine meal. They lingered at the table a long while, and Dora repaired her mood a little. Blue, trying hard, persuaded her to play the piano. He insisted on dancing with Doosie, hoping it would make Dora laugh. She did laugh, but mainly at Doosie, who was far too proper a woman to keep up with Blue in a dance.

Still, underneath the effort, the day was a failure. They were able to be their old selves only for a few minutes; the other parts of their lives could not be pushed away as neatly as had once been the case. Dora could not stop worrying that Ogden might make a quick kill and return while Blue was still there. The thought crossed Blue's mind too. At other times, whatever the obstacles, when he really put his mind to wooing Dora he had always succeeded; it was just a matter of persisting until he uncovered the real Dora, the woman who had no need to resist him, and every need not to.

The sky might not have fallen, but that fact didn't preclude let-downs and other disappointments. When they kissed at the back door, Dora thought she saw a tear in T.'s eye. She kept smiling when he mounted the buckskin mare and rode off; when he turned at the edge of town and waved she waved back vigorously. But Blue didn't turn away again and leave briskly and dashingly, as he always had. She could only see the white spot that was his face, still turned toward her—just his face, looking. Finally he did go, but for the rest of her life, in moments of sadness, she would remember that distant white spot —T. Blue's face—hanging there at the edge of Belle Fourche, looking at her.

It was sad; Dora went upstairs and did what she always did when he left—cried for two days.

When Ogden walked into town on the third morning, proud as could be, the mule Charley loaded with most of an elk, he felt fine until he saw Dora, and then lost the shine off his mood. She kissed him and hugged him tightly, but she looked worn, as if she had been mighty upset while he was gone. Doosie was happy with the elk, and Dora happy to see him, but Ogden wondered guiltily if perhaps he had stayed gone too long.

5

DORA FOUND OUT SHE WAS PREGNANT THE DAY CALAMity and Bartle finally returned. She had been married three months; almost two months had passed since Blue's visit. Once such news would have made her joyful; this time she received it with foreboding—a foreboding that had little to do with the question of who the father was. She felt convinced that T. Blue was the father, but was not ready to face the question of whether she would inform him of her conviction once the child was born.

The task that caused her to worry came before any question of choosing a father: before she needed to decide on a father, she had to get a living child. Her first child, a girl, had scarcely lived three hours; her second, a boy, had lived almost two months—she remembered all too well the year of grief that had followed his death. Without Blue, she herself would not have lived, she was convinced.

She had known women who had lost five or six children—it was common on the frontier—but could not imagine that she herself would want to survive such a load of grief.

When she told Doosie her news—she had already told her of her suspicions—Doosie at once tried to order her to bed.

"Get in it and stay in it," Doosie said. "You ain't gonna do a lick of work until you have that baby."

Dora ignored her. Ogden was off hauling some freight to Deadwood—he was due back that evening. Dora felt her first dilemma was whether to be truthful with him—or, rather, to decide how much truth would be good for him. She doubted that Ogden knew much about the technicalities of reproduction; he had begun in complete ignorance of all matters connected with it, but had quickly acquired a lot of enthusiasm for some of them. But certain niceties of timing might be lost on him unless she explained them. Ogden's trust in her was profound; he would believe whatever she told him.

"I've got too much to think about just to get in bed," Dora said, pacing around the kitchen.

"Well, think lying down," Doosie said. "You can't just walk around in circles in my kitchen for six months."

"You seem to be mighty cheerful—you're not the one who has to have it!" Dora said, annoyed that her moody maid had suddenly turned into a sunbeam.

"I hope it's a little girl," Doosie said. "Be nice to have a little girl around here. Wouldn't be so dull if we had a little girl."

"I don't see what's dull about it now," Dora said. "I'm out of business, and I've got a husband who can eat a beef a week."

"This girl might not be too little—it's got a big Daddy," Doosie said, watching Dora closely to see if she would confirm the statement.

Dora didn't confirm it; instead she went upstairs and stayed in her room all day, with only Fred for a companion. She felt that if prizes were to be given for doing everything wrong, she would win them all. The memory of Blue's face—the white spot at the edge of town—was still fresh. How it haunted her. Why had he stopped and looked that way, unless it was a last look? He never meant to return again; he hadn't said it, but she knew it.

Their love had become too awkward, too much a strain on both of them, now that both were married.

So why, after all their years, had she waited to take a child from him until their very moment of parting? Of course, maybe she was wrong; maybe she held Ogden's child—Ogden had vigor enough to make plenty of children. And they *had* been married two months before Blue came. Everything argued for Ogden—except her heart and her instinct. And through the day, in moments when her spirit lifted a little, when she felt some touch of excitement at the thought that after all her disappointments —there had been two miscarriages, also—she might finally have a child, the thought that it was Blue's was part of the gladness. He might never come back, might never know about the child, but she would, and maybe, someday, the child would, too. Even if Blue never came back, there might in time be a way for him to know about the child—to know that at last something more than just the fussing had come of all their times together.

As if the news that a baby would be arriving in six months or so was not enough excitement for one day, Potato Creek Johnny came rushing in with another startling piece of news. Calamity and Bartle had been spotted a few miles north of town; they were said to be taking their time, but would make town by nightfall or sooner unless some accident befell them.

"Calamity and Bartle?" Dora asked. "What'd they do with Jim?"

"The news is Jim is dead!" Johnny said.

"Dead of what? Did he get smallpox?" Dora asked.

"Well, I've heard different stories," Johnny admitted. "I think a stagecoach fell on him. Another story is that it was suicide."

Dora didn't like getting such news—she fretted most of the afternoon, looking out the window a hundred times or more. But the horizons to the north remained empty, and when someone finally showed up it was Ogden, stomping up the stairs to hug his wife. Ogden's hugs were perils in themselves; he had little sense of his own strength. More than once Dora feared her ribs might give way, but in her jangled state she was glad to see Ogden —there was so much of him that after a few minutes beside him on the bed, body heat alone relaxed her and calmed her down. The only nuisance was Fred, who was jealous of Ogden. Fred had already pecked the buttons off all Ogden's shirts—if Ogden forgot him for a moment, to kiss his wife or something, Fred would reach in and crack another button.

Ogden was an impulsive hugger and kisser; it often prompted Dora to impulsive actions too, or, at the very least, impulsive talk. After returning some of his impulsive kisses it was on the tip of Dora's tongue to tell him about the baby, but before she could do so she looked out the window once more and spotted a familiar black horse, with a familiar black dog. Limping beside the horse was Bartle Bone, looking very much the tired, foot-weary mountain man.

"It's Calamity!" Dora said. "Calamity and Bartle!"

Calamity had been keeping a lookout for Dora as she rode through Belle Fourche. Dora often ran to meet her when she'd been away awhile.

"Here she comes," Bartle said. He had spotted Dora and Doosie the minute they stepped outdoors.

"My God, who's that?" he added. A boy so large he had to turn edgewise to get out the door had appeared behind them. He was the largest man Bartle had seen since his last visit with Touches the Sky, the Miniconjou chief. Touches the Sky was taller than the young man on the porch, but not by much, and he was far from being as large in bulk.

Calamity, too, was startled by the size of the youth. Dora looked tiny beside him. Calamity had been fighting back tears all day at the thought of seeing her friend— now she could stop fighting them back: there was Dora!

"Get down, get down, you're here!" Dora said.

"We ain't all back. Jim's dead, we buried him in Dubuque," Bartle said. He felt it best to deliver sad news promptly.

On the long ride up the Missouri and the walk south he had suffered more than he had expected to suffer from the absence of his old *compañero* of the trails. They slid past the banks where he had so often camped with Jim; then, walking south over the gray plains, he was constantly afflicted by memories of Jim Ragg—at times he almost felt he was traveling with a ghost, so strongly did Jim Ragg still haunt the Missouri country.

Calamity had got tired of hearing about it; she had liked Jim too, but enough was enough, and Bartle was as voluble as ever—just ten times as lugubrious. They took to drinking at opposite ends of the boat; once they left the boat, Calamity soon had to insist on a separate camp: she didn't want to spend any more evenings listening to Bartle cough up memories. She concentrated on getting home to Dora. Dora had told her she could have her own room.

The big boy looked shy. He stood well back from the hugging, which went on a considerable time. But he kept his eye on Dora.

"What did happen to old Jim?" Potato Creek Johnny asked, when everyone was hugged out. He was shocked at the appearance of Calamity and Bartle; they looked gaunted by travel, or drink, or both. He himself had walked out of Miles City with them only a few months before; he didn't feel any the worse for having lived a few months, but both Calamity and Bartle looked as if they had aged several years—and neither of them had looked any too young to begin with.

Ogden, too, was a little taken aback by the appearance of the odd-looking woman and the rough old mountain man. He had heard Dora and Doosie talk about them and knew they were old friends of both. He had pictured them in his mind as fine, attractive people—old-timers, adventurers. But these two old people just looked like wrecks; they looked dirty, wobbly, and sad. He wondered if some terrible massacre had occurred of which they were the only survivors.

"What did happen to old Jim?" Johnny repeated. Both Bartle and Calamity had ignored his first inquiry.

Suddenly Bartle slammed him in the face with his fist,

sending him reeling backward, though more from surprise than hurt.

"Damn you, I'll strangle you if you call him old again," Bartle said, fiercely angry for a moment.

Johnny quickly apologized. "It just slipped out. I'm sorry," he said. "But what did happen to him? We heard a stagecoach fell on him."

Neither Bartle nor Calamity really wanted to reveal the unflattering facts, but Calamity finally decided she might as well get it over with.

"A loco in Chicago stabbed him with a pocketknife," she said.

"A pocketknife?" Johnny said in disbelief.

"A pocketknife can kill you if it hits just the right spot," Bartle said, embarrassed for Jim.

Dora, realizing Ogden had been left out, led Calamity over to him.

"Martha, this is Ogden," she said. "He's my husband."

To Calamity the news was as unexpected as a slap, or more so. Ogden looked like a decent boy, but it was still a slap of surprise. After a moment she offered her hand but found she had to struggle to say anything.

"Howdy, I guess for once I'm tongue-tied," she said. "Chalk it up to the long trip."

6

A MONTH OR SO LATER, OGDEN NOTICED THAT HIS wife's shape seemed to be changing. The change surprised him, but he didn't feel he should be asking questions. He knew very little about women—just what he could deduce from being with Dora; in all likelihood their shapes were supposed to change from time to time.

Dora, still mulling over her dilemma, decided to wait until Ogden asked before discussing the baby. But he was so slow to ask that it provoked her. Ogden's deference was beginning to irritate her almost as much as Blue's cheekiness had; with men, if it wasn't one thing it was another. One morning in a fit of irritation she blurted it out.

"Can't you tell I look different?" she exclaimed. "Don't it interest you?"

"Your face looks the same," Ogden said in his own defense.

"It don't, my eyes are puffy," Dora said. "The reason I look this way is because I'm going to have a baby."

Ogden received the news calmly; for a time he didn't connect it with anything he might have done. For some reason Dora got even more provoked with him and flounced off downstairs. She had been provoked with him several times lately; each time he was startled, but seldom said anything. It made him sad that he didn't know how to behave. Usually he would conclude that each new failure meant he would have to go back to the lonely life, but before he could get himself moving, Dora would show up, in an improved mood, acting as if nothing had happened.

Only later in the day, thinking a little more carefully about what he knew or had heard about the genesis of babies, did it come to him that *this* baby could be the result of something he had done.

"Will I be the Pa of the baby?" he asked tentatively that night in bed.

Though in general Dora seemed to be looking forward to the baby, she evidently had not been looking forward to his asking such a question just at that moment.

Sometimes, even when they were in bed together, Dora seemed to live distantly from him. Ogden had no grasp of why that should be—he never wanted to live distantly from Dora, in his mind or anywhere else. One moment they would be holding hands; Dora would be right with him; then, because of some word, she seemed to move herself away, even if physically she didn't stir or flounce out as she did when provoked. On the whole Ogden preferred it when she flounced out. He would be left alone to wonder what he had done wrong; but when Dora went away without actually leaving, he felt even worse.

This time, a long silence grew between them; Ogden wished fervently that he had had the good sense to keep his mouth shut and just wait to be instructed about the baby.

Dora didn't look angry, though—she just sat on the bed and looked out the window. It was a cold winter night, but Dora liked the window open. He heard the creak of a wagon down the street. Ogden realized she might not even be thinking about him, or about the baby, either. She might be thinking about old times. Since Calamity had returned, the two of them often sat together for hours; it was old times they mostly seemed to talk about. Ogden relaxed a little, and yet he couldn't completely banish worry. Dora kept looking out the window into the deep night. Her face seemed fearful; it seemed sad too—and Ogden couldn't stand for his wife to be sad or afraid. It made him feel he wasn't doing his part as a husband. It had been complicated enough even before he knew Dora meant to have a baby, but now that she did mean to have one—and he knew she *did* mean to; he could put his hand on her swelling belly and feel, now and then, a slight movement; Dora called it a kick but Ogden felt as if a very small fish, a mere minnow, had brushed against his hand—it seemed things were even more complicated. He wondered why people bothered to make babies, if babies only complicated their lives so. He meant to try to talk Dora out of making any more, since it made her more easily provoked, or else fearful and sad.

Dora had been prepared for Ogden's questions; she could see his curiosity rising daily. She had discussed it with Calamity. Calamity had no actual experience of babies, but that didn't mean she was free of opinion. Her opinion was that Blue was too unreliable to involve in fatherhood; Calamity liked Ogden, though the way she expressed her liking might have seemed disparaging to some.

"He's a whopping piece of dough," Calamity said. "But he ain't set yet. You can roll him into any kind of biscuit you want—only do it quick. You can never tell when a boy like that will set."

Dora didn't regard it as particularly good advice, but she was grateful to Calamity anyway. Whether she knew what she was talking about or not, she was someone to share confidences with. When Calamity had first returned, her whole face had been bloodshot from drink; she rambled and got vomiting-sick almost every day. But with steady food and no chores and a clean room to stay in, she had improved somewhat, and was beginning to recover some of her ginger. The two of them, with Ogden, went on picnics, and all had fun. Once on a zero day she and Calamity had even tried on ice skates—the new fad in Belle Fourche—but this venture frightened Ogden nearly out of his wits. Neither woman had any caution—they skittered right to the middle of the river, where the ice was crackly. Of course, Ogden being so large himself, it would have been a chancy rescue, had either of them fallen through.

But they hadn't fallen through, and she hadn't decided what to tell Ogden about the baby, either. Doosie, her other oracle of wisdom, was of the opinion that it didn't matter much. Babies came, and then you dealt with them; on the whole, men weren't much help, whether they had happened to father the baby or not.

"Babies got to take what they find," Doosie said. "They can't be worrying about this Pa and that Pa. Let 'em have two Pas, if you can find two. It ain't gonna hurt nothing."

"Oh, blow your nose!" Dora said. "Everybody tells me something different. I should have stayed single. It's how I've lived my life."

Then she burst into tears.

Sitting on the bed with Ogden, she felt no impulse to tears. She just felt stuck in a crack, the crack between past and present. When she looked out the window she might become sad in reverie, remembering all the best parts of the past; she might become fearful that someday the window would close, and with it her passage to that part of her life. But there was no denying that on the other side of the crack a very large boy was waiting in her bed. Ogden was there; she had firmly and immediately made him her own; she might as well answer the question.

"Ogden, you'll be its Pa," Dora said.

7

BARTLE BONE HAD BEEN A CHEERFUL MAN ALL HIS LIFE; he had never really been able to understand Jim Ragg's melancholy. What was there to be so low about? With the rising of the sun in the cool morning, a fresh day presented itself: to Bartle a fresh day was a gift that might produce any manner of wonders. He and Jim could encounter a great animal—an old silvertip, for example. They might run into ten or fifteen young Sioux out looking for sport, in which case there could be a fight to the death, or a race for their lives. They might be challenged by a blizzard or a flood. They might stumble into some town and discover a pretty woman with a tooth for pleasure; they might spot some gold in the bottom of a creek.

Even if no adventure presented itself, they always had their minds. They could just sit around and talk about matters practical or impractical; or at least they could sit around and *he* could talk: Jim had rarely delivered himself of the kind of speculative remarks that Bartle favored. Calamity occasionally liked to speculate, but Jim Ragg just liked to travel. On the whole, even when they had come out on the short end of a fight, Bartle had

seldom found cause to take the dark view of life. Even at
its worst it was something interesting to wake up to.

The melancholy that he had felt since Jim's death was
thus an unfamiliar and a distressing thing. Every day he
felt sure he'd wake up and recover his old lift. But after
a month and a half in Belle Fourche doing nothing, he
knew he might as well face the fact that his old lift was
just gone. He would walk outside, relieve himself in the
snow, and not be able to think of another thing to do.
Belle Fourche was a dull town; there was not a person in
it who excited his curiosity. But as Calamity often
pointed out, he wasn't chained to Belle Fourche. The
whole west lay around him under its great ring of sky. He
could go anywhere, if he could just summon some of his
old interest in going. But a lack of interest in going—or
in staying, either—was at the heart of his problem. In the
meantime, as Calamity plainly let him know, he had become poor company.

"Jim's the one who died," she pointed out one morning. She had persuaded him to load his gun and go hunting with her. A miner who had got drunk in Dora's saloon
the night before claimed to have seen three moose between Deadwood and Belle Fourche. No one gave the
claim much credit except Doosie—she always got excited at the prospect of a different animal to cook.

"Go kill me one!" Doosie commanded. "And don't
forget to take the sweetbreads."

It was a bitter day, the skies like slate. Bartle had even
lost his old indifference to cold; they had marched five
miles before he even stopped shivering. Cold didn't
bother Calamity—she had a bottle in her pocket, but was
not nipping much.

They hunted all day, making a wide semicircle, first
west, then south, then east of Belle Fourche. They saw
no moose—they also saw no elk, no antelope, no deer.
By nightfall they reckoned themselves to be ten miles
southeast of town and too tired to make it back. Calamity
was so tired she even considered throwing away her rifle.

After an hour spent attempting to arrange a decent
camp, they were even more tired, as well as hungry and

discouraged. The camp was a shambles, the arrangements windy, the wood supply low. Jim Ragg had always made the camps, arranged the fires, seen to the wood, and secured windbreaks when possible; he was meticulous about his camps. True, on their walk down from the Missouri, he, Bartle, and Calamity had made several inadequate camps but then it had been fall, and not so cold.

"We'll be lucky not to freeze tonight," Calamity said. "This fire won't last till morning. It's been a year since I slept out in weather this bad."

"Hug your dog," Bartle suggested. Cody had supplied them with a skinny grouse for supper.

They didn't freeze, though Bartle had a crust of ice on his beard when morning came. Calamity had to flounder around for an hour to gather enough firewood to thaw them out. Even the sun was the color of ice; the wind had picked up, meaning worse might come. They had not meant to camp and had brought no coffee.

Once Bartle would have considered such circumstances of no consequence at all; now he found them painful, unrelieved by any element of excitement. He and Calamity struggled upwind for four hours before finally reaching town. Doosie greeted them critically; she had expected them to bring meat, and instead they had arrived shivering and starving.

"It's a good thing we got Ogden to depend on," she said. "Ogden don't never come home without meat."

That stung, but Bartle let it pass. He spent what was left of the day in the saloon, warming himself inside and out. Calamity slept awhile and then came down and joined Bartle and Johnny in a card game. Johnny was fresh, they were tired—he won all the money they had, and some they were never likely to see. What troubled Johnny worse than the difficulty of collecting was the dead look in Bartle's eyes. Calamity was the more rowdy of the two by far.

When Johnny left to see if a whore might be standing around one of the other saloons, Bartle decided the time had come to say his piece. A night in a cold camp had helped him arrive at a conclusion he knew he should have arrived at sooner.

"We should never have come back here," he began.

Calamity didn't appreciate anyone telling her what she should or shouldn't have done; she had never welcomed advice.

"Speak for yourself," she said. "I got no complaints about Belle Fourche."

"I don't mean the town, I mean the west," Bartle said. "There's nothing to do. We walked all day and didn't even see a deer. There's no game. There's no beaver. There's no Indians that are of any account."

"There's gold," Calamity pointed out.

"I ain't a miner," Bartle reminded her.

"You can drive a wagon," she said. She was getting the sad feeling that Bartle wanted to leave.

"Well, but who wants to drive a goddamn wagon?" Bartle asked. "Who wants to be a goddamn cowboy? Or anything else there is left to be, in these parts?"

"I admit it's thin," Calamity said.

"Too thin," Bartle said.

"Thin or not, I'm too young to die," Calamity said. "I can't speak for you, but you will die unless you learn to build a fire better than you did the other night—if you can't beat that, you best give up winter travel."

"I'll give up winter travel in these parts," Bartle said, getting a little aroused by her brash tone. "I'm ready to go back and sign on with Billy. He's the only honest one of us, anyhow."

Calamity stiffened at that. "I like Billy Cody but I consider myself fully as honest," she said.

"Well, maybe I should have said smart, not honest," Bartle admitted. Calamity's temper rose quickly; she looked as if she might suddenly reach the point of pulling her pistol. He had had to disarm her many times over the years; there was always the possibility that he'd move a little slow, one of these times, in which case he might receive a bullet wound.

"Then go ahead and be a showman," Calamity said

hotly. "I ain't ready for it—anyway he wouldn't hire me. He'll remember that I fell off the stage!"

Calamity still felt embarrassed by her fall—many times she wished she could do the stage ride over; if only she could, she'd take more care with her balance this time.

"You ought to come, Martha," Bartle said more gently. "Better to be honest showmen than a couple of old drunks. This west is full of braggart drunkards now. You can go in any saloon between here and Laredo and scratch up five or six. They'll be talking about how they fought at the Alamo or Adobe Walls or the Washita or the Rosebud or the Greasy Grass."

"All the whites died at the Alamo," Calamity said. "All the whites died at the Greasy Grass, and plenty of them died in the other fights—I heard it was just Custer's damned luck that kept him from getting wiped out at the Washita."

"Don't you suppose I know that?" Bartle said. "I know where the graves lie. That wasn't my point."

"Well, I don't know what your goddamn point is, but I'm sure I despise it," Calamity said. She was getting angry.

"Youngsters Ogden's age won't have our information," Bartle said. "They want to see it. Otherwise they'll believe the drunks—of course maybe some of the drunks was in some of those fights. That ain't the point either."

"You're so full of goddamn points today!" Calamity exclaimed—the rush of anger, on top of so much whiskey, left her feeling a little sick to her stomach.

"Your points won't save you in a blizzard—you just need to give some attention to building fires," she added, remembering how bleak she had felt as the cold evening descended on them—shaky as they were, any cold evening like that could well be their last evening.

"I'd rather be a showman," Bartle said. "Why not? It's a job, and it pays."

"I never thought I'd hear you wishing you had a job," Calamity said. "I think you just like them English whores."

Bartle didn't admit it, but Calamity was right: he did miss the English whores. After a lifetime in the uncrowded west, he had discovered there was something to be said for cities. The music halls in London had a hundred times more to offer than any western saloon. He missed the noise and the singing; he missed the clowns and the burlesque; certainly on cold nights he missed his Pansy. Now that they were far away, he began to remember all the girls on the London streets. There were plenty of other girls as nice as his Pansy; there might even be some who would prove less fickle.

"Jim Ragg would have a stomping fit if he heard you turned into a showman!" Calamity said, growing angrier the more she thought about Bartle's plan to desert her.

"Be fair now," Bartle said. "You saw how Jim hated to leave those beaver. If he'd lived I expect he'd have ended up working in a zoo himself. For a man that's run wild all his life, feeding tame animals is about as silly as working in a zoo."

"He didn't stay in London but I guess he'll be staying in Dubuque for a while," Calamity said, feeling morose suddenly; she had an ache for her dead friend. Jim was no talker, but he had been a staunch friend. They had been a kind of gang—a little gang—she and Jim and Bartle. Blue and Dora had joined the gang sometimes, sometimes not. They had seen some sights together over the years. Now she and Bartle were the only ones who could keep the old life going, and Bartle didn't want to. He wanted to leave, to play-act for Billy Cody.

"I ain't going back to England," Calamity said. "You go on, if you want. I'll stick it out in the west."

"We could always come west and summer," Bartle suggested. He hated making Calamity sad; it was happening more and more often.

"There's nothing wrong with a show," Bartle went on, trying to coax her into a better humor. Once he had been able to coax her out of her worst moods, but lately his coaxing hadn't been working so well.

"You could just play yourself in the show," Bartle

said. "Billy's thinking of having me play Kit Carson, since Lewis and Clark didn't work out."

"What a spectacle, you playing old Kit," Calamity said. "I thought you despised him."

She didn't like the way things were getting so mixed now, what was real, or what had been real, mingling more and more confusingly with what was made up. Although she was annoyed with Bartle, she still considered him a better man by far than Kit Carson; it was depressing to think of the one playing the other.

"I think I'll just march down the Platte and see if I can locate No Ears," she said. She found that she missed the old man.

"No, don't do that until it warms up," Bartle said. "You've got a warm room at Dora's. You ought to stay."

Calamity was tired of talking, tired of everyone giving her advice she didn't want. They were always cautioning her—they acted as if she hadn't taken care of herself all the years of her life. She got up suddenly and went out on the cold porch to smoke.

Of course, she had come back from England intending to do just what Bartle suggested: accept her room at Dora's, and stay. All the time in England, and on the long voyage home, she had thought of nothing but how comfortable she would be in her room at Dora's. She had looked forward to being back and having her room as much as she had ever looked forward to anything.

Now she had it; and it only demonstrated how foolish it was to look forward to things. Once you finally got what you were looking forward to getting, something would always have changed so that it didn't seem as nice or as important as it had seemed when you were merely imagining it. Life was too slippery, and people too changeable.

She had always assumed that when her wandering years ended she would live with Dora—and Dora had always encouraged her to assume it. Now she was there, and Dora seemed pleased to have her; Dora would never ask her to leave—there was no question of that.

What changed the whole situation was that Dora had

married. Calamity didn't blame her for it, either. After all, the boat could have sunk or something; Dora had no way of knowing whether she would ever show up again. With Blue farther away than ever, Dora had herself to think about.

Ogden, the big boy she had taken, was a nice enough ox; he had first place with Dora now, that was plain. Soon the child would come, and then the child would have a big claim on Dora's attention. She herself might be perfectly welcome to remain with the household, but it wouldn't be she and Dora together—just them!—as she had hoped. Dora had got herself a family; Calamity could choose to live with it, but she would never be part of it. Ogden was a little scared of her at the moment, but Ogden might change. He might not want her smoking or cussing or getting drunk around his new child.

It struck Calamity that she was probably being prideful to be so stiff about Billy Cody and the Wild West show. Billy might not approve of her falling off the stagecoach, but he liked her and would never refuse her work, even if the work was just tending to the horses or helping the blacksmith or something. She ought to drop her pride and go with Bartle; she might improve her shooting or her riding and end up famous, like Annie Oakley.

Dora found her sitting out on the steps, half frozen. What was wrong with her?

"What are you doing, you'll freeze!" Dora said, a good deal put out. It took nearly constant watchfulness to keep Martha Jane from doing things that might make her sick. She just would not respect liquor, or weather either.

Calamity came in meekly. Her face was chapped from the severe wind. She knew Dora was put out with her, but she didn't respond. She was afraid to, for fear she would break down and reveal how sad it made her that the two of them were no longer going to live together as they had always planned: no Bartle, no Blue, no Ogden, no baby: just them!

It would have been a fine way to get old, Calamity felt: just herself and Dora in a snug house. Of course, visitors might come, Blue or Bartle, Potato Creek Johnny or anyone they liked. But the house would be theirs—just theirs.

The thought that it would never be that way caused her such an ache that she was a long time getting to sleep, even though Dora, fearful that she would catch cold, piled more quilts on her than she needed, and she soon thawed out.

No Ears met with nothing but trouble and vexa-
tion on his journey up the Platte. He located a few of his
people in scattered and not very prosperous villages
along the river; but the troubling thing was that he could
find almost no one from his own time.

It made him feel that his time was over, but that he had
foolishly been too stubborn to die and had lived beyond
it. If you lived beyond your time it was hard to find people with the proper sensibility, people who could evaluate
important facts when they were discovered. Three or
four old women heard his story of the whale fish, but the
old women were only half alive; most of them had outlived their children and they had little interest in hearing
about a great fish. They had little interest in hearing about
anything; they lived in sorrow, and No Ears did not have
the energy to make them listen carefully to his information, important though it was.

He did locate one man even older than himself, a man
he had known all his life, whose name was Many Belts.
It struck No Ears as very unfortunate that Many Belts
was the one survivor from his time, for the old man was
a notorious braggart. and also very selfish. He didn't like

it that No Ears had come back. He wanted to be the only old person in the village; that way he could get all the attention himself. He listened to No Ears for a while but then rudely informed him that he considered his report on the whale fish and other matters to be nothing but a pack of lies. Many Belts didn't believe that such a fish existed; anyway, he wanted No Ears to keep quiet and listen to some things *he* had to say. No Ears listened, but all Many Belts wanted to talk about was how active he was with his two young wives.

At the second village No Ears reached, he made the mistake of trying to make people realize the seriousness of his mission by exhibiting his wax ears. It got their attention, too. A few of the most sensible people were so startled by the sight of the ears that they could talk about nothing else. Still, the exhibition proved to be a mistake. Most of the people were discouraged and had abandoned many essential disciplines. The behavior of the young men was slovenly and ill-mannered; some of them were almost as ill-mannered as young white men—indeed, quite a few of the young men seemed not to know whether they were red or white. Naturally they coveted his English ears and promptly stole all but one of them. That one wasn't in the box Billy had given him; No Ears liked to sleep with it in his hand in case he suddenly needed to wake up and do some close listening. Because of this habit, one ear was saved, but the rest were lost.

The loss made No Ears angry; it occurred just as he was on the point of changing his name to acknowledge the fact that he now possessed ears—twenty-four of them, in fact. He thought he might start calling himself Man Who Gets Ears; but of course the robbery ruined that plan. The robbery, plus the rudeness of the young people and the discouragement of the old people, convinced No Ears of a sad fact: it was not his destiny to live and die with his own people.

Looking back over his long life, he realized that his destiny had been to be separate; most of his life, through one circumstance or another, he had strayed from his people. Long ago he should have changed his name; he should have called himself Man Who Walks Apart—such a name would better describe the life he had actually lived.

When he woke up and saw that he was down to one ear, he decided to leave his people forever—they had become too unruly and undisciplined to provide the kind of calm atmosphere he hoped to enjoy in his last years. He decided to go find Martha and travel with her. She too walked apart; she too slept outside the houses of her own people much of the time.

As No Ears crossed the plains alone—it was the dead of winter, and a sharp winter, too—he had plenty of time to reflect on his adventures, and he decided that he had been foolish to take pride in the ears from England. Because of his great desire to acquire ears before he died, he had made the worst mistake of all; he had allowed himself to be deceived by the look of things. In fact, the objects he had taken such pride in had not been ears at all; they had merely been wax. He himself could find some bees and steal their wax and probably shape ears almost as good as those made by the Englishman with the goiter.

But he himself should have known better: wax was not flesh, and real ears could not simply be taken on and off, like hats. Once real ears had been removed, as his had been, it was better to accept the fact and change one's name accordingly, and then forget about it.

Once he recognized his pride for what it was, No Ears felt better; once again he began to rely on his eyes and his nose, the two senses that had brought him safely through so many years and so many dangers. His nose was as good as ever, his eyes perhaps not quite as good as ever, but still good enough for most purposes. He soon recovered his confidence and began to enjoy his trip, though the weather was bitter and he was three times forced to take shelter from blizzards and wait for them to pass.

That was easy enough. No Ears had long since perfected a method for dealing with blizzards; he merely located a snake den and denned with snakes until the storm passed. It was easy to smell snake dens—snakes smelled like cucumbers—and in many cases the opening of the dens were large enough that he could squeeze through. He had no fear of the snake people; they were harmless when in hibernation and not really very harmful even in summer. With a blizzard howling above them, the snake people were too stiff to pose a threat, and if he found himself growing hungry he had only to kill one or two, peel their skins off, and eat his fill.

In earlier days he had sometimes found it convenient to den with bears when blizzards came. Bears, too, were easy to smell, and in times of extreme cold made warmer bedfellows than snakes. More than once, denned bears had saved his life; on the other hand, denned bears were much less reliable than denned snakes. One had to approach them with caution and respect. A denned bear might not be polite enough to sleep all winter; it might get hungry and eat whatever happened to be denned with it. Snake dens were chilly, but on the whole, because of the unreliability of bears, No Ears preferred them as stopping places in blizzards. Anyway, there were few bears left, and none at all along the lowland rivers, whereas there were still thousands of snake dens everywhere.

No Ears usually preferred to walk so as to make close observations while he traveled, but now and then if he happened to meet some soldiers moving along in the direction he was going he might ride a day or two with them if he received an invitation.

Always it was the older soldiers who asked him to ride with them; it seemed to No Ears that the older soldiers missed Indians. Now that they had killed so many of them they suddenly realized that Indians were valuable people.

The younger soldiers were a different matter, though. They knew little or nothing about Indians; they were so silly about Indians that they were even afraid of him, an old man traveling with only a shotgun and a few shells. He had been given the shotgun by embarrassed elders in the village where his ears had been stolen. It was a very weak gun, its stock held together with some buffalo-tendon wrappings from a long time past, but it was enough to throw a scare into some of the young soldiers No Ears traveled with.

So scared were the young soldiers to have an Indian with them that one night, camping on the Powder River, a ridiculous thing happened. Some of the young white soldiers were so terrified that he might wake up and scalp them that they slept with their guns cocked all night—a very bad practice, as was quickly proven. A young soldier with red hair must have had a bad dream; the dream upset him so that he discharged his gun while asleep. The bullet went through a passing sentry and hit a horse. The sentry lived but the horse died—it had been the favorite horse of a major, too. This showed how hard it was to predict what a bullet would do. The foolish young soldier was immediately put in chains. He was forced to ride in the wagon all day. No Ears rode in the same wagon and observed that the young soldier was so low in spirits that he would probably freeze on the first cold night unless covered up well. The boy's spirit put off no more heat than a candle flame, and that would not be enough to keep him alive the next time a strong blizzard struck.

"You should crawl up by a horse," No Ears told the boy. "Look for a horse that's lying down. Otherwise you might pass away."

"Don't care if I do," the boy said miserably. "I'm ruint now anyway. What will I tell my Ma if I'm court-martialed out? I'm the hope of my family."

An old sergeant named Grisom, with a fat brown mustache, came over and offered No Ears some coffee. He didn't offer the sad boy any. No Ears had known Grisom for years. He had fought at the Washita, the Rosebud, and in many local encounters; there were rumors that he had been among the baby-killers at Sand Creek, but No Ears didn't know about that. So many white people had done terrible things in those years that it was hard to keep straight who had committed disgraceful acts and who hadn't. No Ears rather liked Grisom and hoped he had not killed any Indian babies at Sand Creek or elsewhere.

Grisom had been with Crook the day No Ears came to camp and informed them that Custer was dead. Grisom was not very smart and had not believed the information.

"There's not enough Indians in this world to defeat George Custer," he had said, foolishly.

"Shut your damn trap, Sergeant," Crook had said. Crook was smarter than Grisom, which is why he was the general. He knew perfectly well there were enough Indians in the world to finish Custer; after all, but for luck, the same plentiful Indians might have finished Crook himself on the Rosebud.

"I think this boy was just scared," No Ears said. He had been moved by the boy's distress over having disappointed his family.

"The idiot, he slept with his gun cocked," Grisom said. "It's a good thing the horse died and not the sentry, or we would already have hung this young sprout."

No Ears got down and walked with Grisom for a while. Grisom had a horse but was walking in order to keep his feet warm. It was so cold that the little clouds made by the freezing breath of all the horses made walking tricky. The horses produced such clouds of vapor that no one in the rear of the column could see anything. Grisom seemed in low spirits; indeed, all the soldiers seemed in low spirits. It was apparent that most of the soldiers didn't really enjoy their work, now that there was no fighting. They were almost as demoralized as the people in the poor villages along the Platte. The war might have been pretty bad, with many severe things done and much bloodshed, but at least war kept people alert; it sharpened their spirits.

That night, several of the older soldiers invited No Ears to share their supper. They were all experienced men and knew that he was not going to attack the force with one shotgun or sneak around scalping them during the night. All the men seemed excited to be talking to a Sioux of some age and experience; just having No Ears in camp reminded them of the old days, when life had been more exciting for soldiers. Before they had been talking very long, it became apparent to No Ears why

Cody's idea of a show worked so well. The soldiers going up Powder River—at least the older soldiers—were so excited to be talking about old times and battles of the past that No Ears had no doubt they would have paid money to see Cody's show. At first, when No Ears described the show, some of the men had been skeptical, but when he talked about some of the Indians who were there, particularly Sitting Bull, Cuts the Meat, and Red Shirt, their skepticism diminished.

"Did Sitting Bull kill anybody while he was in England?" Grisom asked. "I always did consider him a dangerous foe."

"He would have liked to kill the warthog," No Ears said. "It was a very ugly hog. But he behaved well with the people, and the Queen gave him a saber."

"I bet he'll cut a throat or two with her dern saber before he's through," a fat old corporal remarked.

"No, he is very well-behaved now, he likes white people's money," No Ears said. It irked him that the soldiers were so in awe of Sitting Bull—not a particularly deserving chief, in his view.

Then a lanky man with only one arm began to question him about Crazy Horse; he said he had heard Crazy Horse was still alive in a secret part of Canada, and would sweep down from the north someday with an army so determined that the war he was planning would make the Custer battle seem like nothing.

No Ears had not actually seen Crazy Horse's body, but he had heard detailed accounts of his death from many reliable sources—it puzzled him that the white soldiers were so poorly informed. Hundreds of people, both red and white, knew exactly what had happened to Crazy Horse; there was really no excuse for these rumors that the man was alive. The notion that he was lurking with thousands of braves somewhere in the north was so ridiculous that No Ears didn't bother to say much about it. He decided later that the reason the soldiers wanted to believe Crazy Horse was alive, or that Sitting Bull would break free again, was that they were just so bored. They were soldiers without a war—and yet the only reason for being a soldier was to make war. Who could blame the soldiers for being bored when all they had to do was haul flour or molasses from one fort to another?

After a while, most of the soldiers became too drunk to talk. Grisom was not quite too drunk to talk, but he said things that were so stupid that No Ears began to wish he would drink a little more and pass out. Grisom could not get Crazy Horse off his mind and kept repeating ridiculous rumors about Crazy Horse's having been seen in cities like Denver—a place Crazy Horse would never go even if he were alive.

"I was with Crook," Grisom said several times, as if No Ears lacked memory rather than ears.

"They don't make 'em like Crook anymore," Grisom added. "Crook knew his business."

Personally No Ears thought Grisom overrated Crook, who, in his view, had just been an ordinary general; he had barely survived the Rosebud and had taken an awfully long time to catch Geronimo—and then had only done so by breaking his word.

Still, No Ears knew that it was in the nature of soldiers to overrate the generals whose skill and knowledge they depended upon. All soldiers liked to believe their generals were smart; it made them feel they had a better chance of living awhile.

His own people did much the same, overrating chiefs whose skills were rather ordinary. If Geronimo had taken the trouble to think, he would have known Crook meant to break his word and would never have walked into the trap. Sitting Bull had gone to Canada and had been starved out, although Canada was known to be a place where game was scarce, and Black Kettle had let the foolish Custer ride into camp and kill him on the Washita, although he had plenty of warning that Custer meant to do just that.

Finally Grisom did pass out; he rolled over on his face, almost in the fire. No Ears had to drag him a foot or two back or sparks from the crackling fire might have set him aflame during the night.

Later, observing that several of the young soldiers still

slept with their guns cocked, No Ears decided to leave, and to travel no more with soldiers. The comfort of a wagon ride was not worth the aggravation of having to sleep around frightened young whites who might have bad dreams and fire off their guns without even waking up to see who they might be shooting. Also, he was tired of having to be polite while the white soldiers were talking nonsense about people who were dead, or over-praising ordinary figures who still happened to be alive.

Later that night, taking care not to walk in front of any young soldier who looked as if he might be having an uneasy dream, No Ears left camp. There was only a little snow on the ground, and he made good time. It pleased him that he was still able to travel so efficiently. Travel with soldiers was never efficient. They took half the morning to get their teams hitched, and then made camp much too early in order to start getting drunk and talking nonsense.

The next day, taking advantage of a shortcut he knew, No Ears crossed Crazy Woman Creek and happened to notice a sage bush that looked familiar. It startled him a little, for it was the very sage bush he had hidden behind to watch the cranes. No cranes were feeding in Crazy Woman Creek that day, and there was nothing to worry about that he could see, but he felt a little uncomfortable anyway. It was not wise policy to keep showing up in places where disquieting or threatening things had occurred. The cranes might not manage to snatch your soul on the first try, but that didn't mean they wouldn't succeed in snatching it if given a second chance.

No Ears resolved to avoid that shortcut in the future. He hurried on toward the Black Hills. One of the soldiers had told him that Martha was living there with her friend Dora. The soldier had been there and had beaten Martha at cards.

Not long before he got to Belle Fourche he encountered three moose grazing on the side of a hill. He had never seen moose in the Black Hills before and found their presence startling. With so many miners and hunters around, it seemed odd that the moose hadn't been killed. They were large moose and represented a lot of meat, but his shotgun was behaving more weakly than ever and he felt it would be unlikely he could bring a moose down with it. After watching the moose for a while he decided they were just lost. Moose were very foolish; these had probably wandered hundreds of miles from home and now had no idea how to get back.

It was after dark when No Ears walked into Belle Fourche. He had no trouble locating Martha Jane because her big black dog was standing on the porch of a house. The dog smelled him and immediately began to bark. No Ears said a few words to the dog before knocking on the door. A giant opened the door, which startled No Ears considerably. He was prepared for Doosie, who often lectured him on habits she didn't like, but he was not prepared for a giant and was about to turn and go when Martha spotted him through the open door.

"Here you are—I've been wishing you'd come!" she said, grabbing him and pulling him into the kitchen. Dora was there—she was heavy with child—and Bartle came in when Martha called him. Bartle did not look well—he seemed drunk, and Martha smelled drunk. No Ears had lived almost entirely outdoors on his walk from the Mississippi, and the hot air in the kitchen made him feel a little faint. Still, there was one important piece of information he felt he should deliver, in case the heat caused him to pass out.

"I saw three moose this morning," he said. "I think they are lost, but they are fat moose. Maybe tomorrow some of us can go kill them."

"I guess that drunk miner knew what he was talking about—what kind of hunters does that make us, Bartle?" Calamity said.

9

As her time came near, Dora began to wish Blue would appear. She began to dream of him almost every night—some of the dreams were so pleasant that she tried to cling to sleep, hoping to stay in them a little longer. Others were less pleasant—either she or Blue seemed to be leaving. In several dreams she was on the steamboat, going downriver, and Blue wasn't with her— no one was with her. After those dreams she woke up feeling dizzy and confused. Often she cried.

In fact, she cried so much in the mornings that everyone began to avoid her. Ogden got up early and started his chores earlier than usual in order not to be caught in the bedroom when Dora began to cry. Doosie brought her coffee and turned and left, unwilling to stay around someone who was so irrationally sad. Calamity often slept through the mornings. Generally, by noon, Dora's mood had improved, so Calamity seldom saw her crying. But she heard about it from Doosie and knew that Dora's mood was not the best.

"Don't you want the baby?" Calamity finally asked. She had encountered Dora looking puffy-eyed once too often.

"I might as well want it—what choice do I have now?" Dora asked. It was not the first time she had been asked the question, and it always annoyed her. The baby would come in less than a month; it was considerably too late to mope about whether she wanted it.

She had wanted all her babies—the two who had died, the three that she lost—and yet she was forty-one and had had nothing but grief and disappointment from her wanting. She *did* want the child inside her—twice she had dreamed that it was a girl—and yet she felt confused and wearied by the vexing circumstances she found herself in. Ogden was as kind as ever, but he was childlike himself; she felt she would soon have two children, one of whom she would be married to. She didn't regret Ogden; he was too sweet and too helpful to be merely regretted, but she slightly regretted her own impetuosity. She now felt she might have been content with a looser arrangement, but of course it was too late for that, too.

To complicate matters further, she had had the surprise offer of a commercial opportunity in Deadwood. A banker came to visit with an attractive proposition. The local hotel had failed, due to mismanagement, it was felt. The owner had disgraced himself over a Chinese woman and had acquired the opium habit to boot. The bank was owed money. Dora's probity and her skill in running tidy establishments were well known in the region. The banker, a Mr. Fortescue, whom Dora had once flirted with briefly in Abilene many years before, came calling one day and asked her if she'd like to take over the Deadwood Hotel and help the bank recover its investment.

Mr. Fortescue was slightly dashed to find Dora both married and pregnant. He had entertained a few fancies of a romantic nature on the ride over from Deadwood; one glimpse of her, eight months pregnant, drove them out of his mind, for the time, at least; also, the sight of her large young husband reminded him that he had, after all, come in pursuit of profit for his bank. As for the rest, once she had the child and recovered her figure, time would have to answer for that.

Dora knew at once that she wanted to buy the hotel.

The mines in Deadwood and Lead were by no means exhausted; the town received a constant stream of speculators, most of them with money to spend—she had no doubt that she could make the enterprise a solid success. Belle Fourche, on the other hand, was not flourishing, and probably never would.

Also, her oldest dream had been to run a proper hotel —maybe even an elegant hotel. She knew she could do it and turn a profit. Of course there would be dining and drinking and cardplaying—but it was a fine hotel she wanted to run, not a fancy whorehouse. The times were changing; the western towns were filling up with churches, getting respectable. There would always be some frolicking done in a mining town like Deadwood— Dora had enjoyed the frolicking times and had no wish to reform the world and render it dull and churchly—but the era of the buffalo girls, as she and Martha had known it, was clearly coming to an end. A fine hotel that showed a nice profit would be the very thing; it would also provide an ideal environment in which to bring up a child.

Before a slightly saddened Mr. Fortescue, his romantic hopes in shreds, left for Deadwood, Dora had signed a paper making her the owner of the hotel. She had put down eight hundred dollars cash, which Mr. Fortescue entrusted to a bank in Belle Fourche. Bandits crawled like ticks along the road to Deadwood, and he could not take the chance of losing money on his way home.

When the proposition first came up, Dora had intended to argue for a reasonable delay—two months perhaps— before she took possession. In that length of time she felt sure she could have the baby and recover sufficiently to set about running her hotel.

The minute she signed the paper and handed Mr. Fortescue his money, that intention fell by the wayside. A tremendous impatience seized her, an impatience even more insistent than the attack which had caused her to marry Ogden two weeks after he carried her out of the mud. She woke up the next morning ready to cry, as usual, only to realize that she didn't feel like crying. She now owned the Miner's Rest, a hotel in Deadwood, Dakota Territory. Besides having a hotel, she was married and about to become a mother. Hopes she had harbored since she walked into Abilene many years before, a starved girl wearing her dead father's shoes, had finally been realized. So why was she moping around Belle Fourche? She had almost a month before the child was due. The thing to do was move and get the Miner's Rest spruced up and working as a fine hotel should work. Why waste a month? Spring was coming, the trails would thaw; mud that could swallow a wagon, its team, and its driver, too, would soon lie between herself and her exciting new property. The thing to do was go now.

Keen to move, Dora flew downstairs and astonished everyone by announcing that they were moving forthwith. She sent Ogden off to lease two extra wagons. Bartle had been about to depart for St. Louis, but Dora collared him and got him to agree to drive one of the teams. Calamity would drive another, and Ogden the third. Doosie began to try to talk her out of such a hasty departure, pointing out that the baby could come at any time. Though an accomplished midwife, Doosie didn't look forward to having to deliver Doosie's baby in a wagon, particularly if the wagon were stuck in the mud somewhere between Belle Fourche and Deadwood.

But Dora didn't stay to hear Doosie's cautions—she was out the door and across the street, where she promptly sold her present house to the shrewd old man who owned the hardware store.

By the end of the day the three wagons had been rented: Ogden, Bartle, Calamity, Doosie, and Potato Creek Johnny were carrying things out of the house and stuffing them hastily in the wagons. They did their best to follow Dora's rapid instructions, but none had been prepared to be converted so rapidly into a moving crew; many mistakes were made, things were put in the wrong boxes or the wrong wagon or else not put in at all, just left to sit where they dropped. Dora was sharp in her corrections; Calamity, a little unnerved by the suddenness of the move, was caught drinking several times and scolded for it. By the day's end everyone's nerves felt as if they had been raked by a blacksmith's hasp, Dora being the blacksmith. She herself felt fine. She lay awake beside a worn-out Ogden most of the night, restless with excitement. The beds were the only things not packed— the beds and a few pans Doosie needed for cooking breakfast.

Down below, in what had been the bar, Calamity, Bartle, and Johnny were passing around a bottle. They had to drink out of a bottle because Dora had already packed all the glasses. Calamity felt like crying, although she had nothing against Deadwood and no fondness for Belle Fourche. The move had just seemed too prompt. Bartle had spent a week working up to leaving, and now Dora had caught him and passed him in one day.

No Ears was stretched out on the top of the bar. He considered that the bar made an excellent bed, and he often napped on it when business was slow. It gave the effect of sleeping on a ridge—but this ridge had a roof over it. He had taken little part in the moving; it surprised him that the whites had taken three wagonsful of possessions out of one small house that hadn't seemed to have much in it. The bulk of white people's possessions amounted to a severe handicap in his view. Among his people whole villages could be disassembled, moved, and reassembled with much less fuss and bother than the whites had expended in getting the wagons packed. Watching them grow nervous and wear themselves out trying to fit bulky objects into the wagons, he began to feel lucky. He himself owned only his blanket, his pipe, his shotgun, and his wax ear. He could travel anywhere at any time and not worry about encumbrances such as glasses and plates—it was hard to understand why whites found such things to be necessary.

"I never thought we'd be leaving Belle Fourche this quick," Calamity said several times.

"I wisht I'd left for St. Louis last week," Bartle said. "Dora's fierce when she gets in a hurry. I'd about as soon step in front of an Indian charge."

"I wouldn't," Johnny said. "I'd rather have a tongue-scalping than a real scalping. You've lived safe for so long you forget what trouble is like."

"Trouble is like having to drive a damn wagon to Deadwood," Bartle said. "It's in the wrong direction."

"Maybe we'll see them moose," Calamity said. She and Bartle had spent another fruitless day hunting the three lost moose; this time, though, they had been careful not to hunt so far from Belle Fourche that they couldn't make it back for the night. No Ears had offered to go along to help them locate the fat animals, but they had pointed out to him that he had just had a long walk and that they were perfectly capable of finding the moose themselves. At this they promptly failed. No Ears was too polite to mock them for their failure, but others were not so kind. Doosie and Johnny, both of whom had been looking forward to some moose sweetbreads, were rather scoffing.

Dora had them up and started for Deadwood an hour before sunup. At that hour Ogden was the only one who seemed very lively—but the trail was good, there was no mud, and the two new wagons followed Ogden's lead while Calamity and Bartle dozed over the reins.

Before she had been in the Miner's Rest three minutes, Dora knew she had made the right choice. The stairway was grand, the banisters beautiful! Even Doosie's spirits picked up when she saw the kitchen, which was far more grand than any she had ever commanded. The hardwood floors needed polish, but otherwise were splendid. There was a huge cash register—it was empty, but Dora meant to remedy that, and promptly.

No Ears had come with them. Some of the better rooms on the second and third floors had little bay windows, and he settled himself in one of the bays to smoke and watch the birds fly. Calamity and Bartle were too exhausted to do much unpacking, and Johnny had jumped out of his wagon and walked off just before they got to town, seduced by the gurgle of a creek he hadn't prospected in a while.

That left Ogden to do all the unloading alone—a task he didn't mind, although Dora's orders were rather confusing. She was in such a state of excitement that she would order him to put a table or a chair in one place and then, a minute later, to pick it up and put it somewhere else.

Ogden willingly did the lifting and relifting—it was clear that Dora was happy, as happy as she had been since they had married. Often she would catch him and give him a kiss, or pull him into a room to show him some pleasing view, or ask his opinion about where a bed should go.

By the time the three wagons were unpacked, the confusion was so great, boxes, chairs, tables, drapes, and kitchenware piled everywhere, that Doosie grew discouraged and had recourse to tobacco, a drug she used only when her nerves were taxed to the limit.

"I ain't never moving no more," she said, installing herself in a big chair in the bare kitchen. Dora was happily unpacking glasses.

"Well, you shouldn't say you'll never do something," Dora told her. "Say it and life will spit it back at you. Look at me. I must have told you five hundred times that I'd never marry—look at me now! Did I marry?"

"You married, but I ain't you, and I ain't moving no more, either," Doosie said. "If you sell this hotel, just sell me with it. I'll go back to slavery before I'll stuff up in a wagon again and move off to a new place.

"It's hard on my digestion, all this moving," she added.

"Blow your nose," Dora said. "Look at how beautiful our hotel is. Pretty soon we'll have customers like you won't believe."

"I'll believe 'em," Doosie assured her. "I don't mind you getting rich—I just ain't moving around this earth no more."

That night in bed—they had put up their bed first, mindful that the baby might come soon—Ogden put his big hand on her belly. It was his new pleasure; he liked to put his hand there and feel the baby. Dora was large, and so warm she was like a stove. Both of them had begun to imagine the baby and to try and decide on names. Dora wanted to call it Mary if it was a girl; her favorite sister, who had died of diphtheria, was named Mary. Ogden wanted to call it Bob if it was a boy. He thought Bob was a simple, useful name, too short for people to forget or mix up with other names.

Looking out her new bay window at the high moon that shed a pale light on the Black Hills, Dora felt, for once, both right and smart. After all the turmoil and torment of her earlier years, she had at last bought the right business; she had also married the right man—the very man whose large hand covered the growing child within her. Ogden might be only a boy, but he was a good boy. In the mixture of calm and excitement she felt spending her first night in her new hotel, she began to recognize a little of what Blue had so often tried to tell her about his marriage. It was not what *they* shared, she and Blue—not so sharp, not so deep, not so keen. But it framed her in a comfortable, restful way. Her hot impatience had not been a whimsy, or a mistake of the passions. She fit with Ogden; she liked him there beside her; his size and his simplicity were a comfort. Blue was too much of a devil —she could not run a hotel successfully and be wasting her energy in tantrums and tear storms that were the inevitable result of dealing with T. Blue.

When Ogden slept, and his hand slipped off her stomach, Dora wished for a moment that T. Blue could be there outside her window. She wished she could walk over and whisper to him for a few minutes—admit that he had been right.

But Blue wasn't there—just the half-moon was there, shining on the new town she had come to, the little town in a crack in the hills. The conversation she wished for might always have to remain only a conversation in her thoughts.

But even to think it was a solace and a resting after the years of quarrels and dashed hopes. Dora couldn't wait for the morning; she felt happy, and so full of energy it seemed a pity to have to waste hours in bed. She meant to be up with the dawn, to start prettifying her new hotel.

10

"SHE MUSTN'T!" CALAMITY SAID, STRICKEN. "WE could pack some snow and bring it to her. That would cool her."

Fred stirred in his corner, disturbed by Calamity's tone.

"I'll go right now, Ogden," she added, wishing Dora would open her eyes.

Almost as she said it, Dora *did* open her eyes—but they were the eyes of a woman wild with fever. Her forehead and upper lip were slick with sweat, though she was pale and shivering.

"Blue," Dora said. "Blue, when are you coming? I want you to hitch the wagon so we can leave."

Ogden sat dumbly on the other side of the bed. He didn't understand why his wife kept calling out for someone named Blue, but he didn't care. He just wanted her to sink out of her fever and get well. Only an hour before, she had calmed enough to feed the baby—a whopping big boy; true to their intention, they had named him Bob—but now she seemed worse than ever. Her feverish eyes looked at him but didn't really see him; even so, she didn't want him to leave. Ogden had never felt so sad or so confused.

"It's a bright moon—dance by the light of the moon," Dora said. "Don't you hear me, Martha?"

"I hear you, but hush and rest," Calamity said, barely able to get the words out. "You need to mind Doosie now. You need to hush and rest."

"No, I don't want to rest, we're going to fix up the hotel!" Dora insisted. "I want pretty glass in the doors." She tried to sit up. Doosie rose for a moment from her seat by the bed, mopped Dora's forehead and lip, and eased her back down. The mopping did little good; beads of sweat reappeared almost at once. Doosie, who had been through many birthings and recoveries, was afraid the sweat would soon give way to chill, and it did. Though warmly covered with quilts, Dora was soon shivering. Calamity went out of the room to cry. Ogden sat dumbly across from the bed, and the baby boy, one of the largest Doosie had ever delivered, waved a small red hand from a box of blankets that had been hastily fixed as his crib.

The day faded; Calamity came and went, more drunken every time she returned; Ogden was allowed to go do his chores, but told to hurry. Dora wanted Ogden there; time and again she would try to find his large hand with her weak one. The baby wailed. Doosie took him in her arms and rocked him a little; he was a healthy boy and soon became quiet. By then, Dora's mumbled talk was only whispers; she had no strength left to turn in the bed. Her fever burned; it burned more fiercely as the night deepened; the half-moon rose and lit one side of the room. Ogden came back and sat dumbly on the dark side of the bed. Doosie felt her boss's forehead; she felt her fluttering pulse. Very late in the night, with Ogden asleep, his head and forearms on the bed, the rest of him in the chair, with Dora's breath weakening with every time she strained to hear it, Doosie knew a woman's life was ending.

Of all lives, it was the one she would have most liked to save—Dora, for all her sharp tongue, had shown her years of kindness—but Doosie had sat by many beds and knew that what one human wanted was not enough to save the dying once they had passed a certain point, had lost the strength it took to live. Neither the doctor's skills, nor hers, nor her love nor anyone's, was going to save Dora now—it was not likely she would see the sunrise.

Wearily Doosie got up and went out for a moment to seek a slop jar. The old Indian without ears sat smoking in one of the bare rooms off the hall. Doosie passed without speaking to him, but having found the slop jar, she stopped on her return and looked at No Ears.

"Do you know anything about this?" she asked. He was an old man; he might have some knowledge she herself lacked. "If you do, come help me," she added, going back to Dora's room.

Since the dying woman had been very polite to him over the years, giving him food and shelter and even tobacco when he needed it, No Ears felt it would be no more than good manners to follow the black woman into the sickroom, though he did not suppose there was anything he could do for Dora. Birth was as dangerous as death and indeed often brought death with it for mother or child or both.

He stood by the bed a moment. The black woman was rocking the large baby. "He's big," he said, meaning the baby, though certainly the husband was large, too.

"Well, she couldn't help that," Doosie said. "The child just grew."

"I don't think she will be able to live," No Ears said.

"You don't know anything do you?" Doosie asked. She was feeling desperate and would have liked to pass the burden of being the one with knowledge onto an older person; she would have liked a wiser person to contradict what she knew, which was what No Ears had just said.

"One of my wives died of this too," No Ears said. "She was too old to be making children, and the child she made was too big."

The old man left; Ogden slept; there were no sounds from downstairs. Calamity had gone somewhere to drink.

Now and then the baby would wave its hand, a small shadow in the moonlight. Doosie slept a little, hunched over her knees. Then she felt Dora's hand moving on the quilt; she straightened up. Dora's eyes were open, shining, watching her. Doosie felt her forehead; there was no sweat, but when she searched for a pulse she was long in finding it, and it was very faint.

"I hope you'll stay and raise Bob," Dora said, her voice scarcely louder than a breath.

Doosie felt too broken to answer; dying women were an old story to her, but she had not expected to sit by while this one died.

"Did you hear me? I want to know if you'll do it," Dora said.

"Hush, miss," Doosie said. "You know I'll be staying. Where would I go?"

Dora reached for Ogden's hand, but could not find it. Not being able to reach him troubled her; she wanted to reach him. Doosie went around the bed and touched Ogden on the shoulder. Ogden didn't really wake up, but he put out his hand and Dora found it.

"Martha can help—where'd she go?" Dora asked.

"I don't know," Doosie said.

"She nursed all those boys with the smallpox," Dora said. "Why won't she stay and nurse me?"

"You, you, though," Doosie said. "She can't stand it when it's you."

"But you're going to stay. You said it!" Dora insisted. "You're gonna stay with Bob."

"Yes, miss. I said it. I'll be staying."

"Bring me Bob," Dora said. She felt that the deep rest was near; she wanted to see her boy again. Doosie brought him—Dora touched him, put her fingers on his cheek, saw him wiggle, make a fist, rub his eyes. She uncurled his fist and put her finger in it. "Put him back to bed, he's sleepy," she whispered.

As Doosie took the baby to his box she looked out the window and saw Calamity standing below in the street. Calamity just stood there, looking up at the window, which was open.

"You better be coming up," Doosie called. "You better come on."

Calamity just stood there; she didn't think her legs would make it up the stairs. She stood there, feeling bad. Finally she made her slow way up, but when she got to the bedroom, Dora's eyes were closed.

"Is she gone?" she asked, shaking—she couldn't see well in the dim room.

Doosie shook her head. "Not yet," she said.

Dora held onto one of Ogden's fingers, as Bob had momentarily held to one of hers. Rest surrounded her, easy rest, and yet there were things nagging at her: she wanted pretty glass in the front door of the hotel—and another thing nagged, too.

"Martha, you better go tell Blue," Dora whispered. "Or if that's asking too much, make Ogden do it."

"Tell Blue what, Dora?" Calamity asked. She sat down in a chair by the bed.

Dora tried to wake up to the question but she couldn't, she wanted to accept her rest.

"Just tell him, I guess," she said.

Later in the night, No Ears felt a difference in the house. He went into the sickroom. All the weary people in it slept—the baby in its box, Martha, the black woman, in chairs. The big youth slept in his chair, too; the parrot was silent on its perch.

But the woman in the bed wasn't sleeping; her spirit had gone where spirits go. No Ears closed her eyes.

11

DORA DUFRAN WAS KNOWN THROUGHOUT THE BLACK Hills; she was known in Montana and Dakota, in Wyoming and down the plains and the cattle country, all the way to Texas. Some who had admired Dora did not hear of her death for months, or even years. On the day of her burial in a grave on Mount Moriah, the hill was crowded with boys and men, miners and cowboys mostly. Mr. Fortescue wept profusely; he had lost a light hope, and also had to grapple once again with the problem of that deuced hotel.

Bartle, who had left Deadwood the day after the move, heard of the death before he reached the Missouri. He gave the news to Billy Cody in Buffalo, New York. The show was in camp and Billy was doing a stage show called *Pawhaska, the White Scout*. The white scout stumbled through his role that evening; he locked himself in his dressing room for two hours, and later was seen dead drunk in a saloon. Because of his stumbling performance, the show closed a week later.

In the days after the funeral, Calamity thought of Blue. Doosie looked at her reproachfully whenever his name came up. Doosie thought Calamity ought to set off at once and do what Dora had asked her to do; but Calamity wavered. She felt too sad to set off alone. In the mornings she felt so poorly that it seemed she might die herself, and she didn't care if she did. She attempted to postpone the question of Blue by helping Doosie with the baby, but that didn't work very well. The baby didn't like her; he squalled every time she picked him up. Also, she was shaky and nearly dropped him once or twice when he wiggled. Doosie didn't really trust her with the baby and kept snatching him from her before she could win his confidence.

Calamity felt out of sorts with Bartle Bone for leaving. She missed him, and she also felt sure that if he had been there to go with her to find Blue, she could have worked up to taking Blue the sad news. But he wasn't there to go with her—which left No Ears or Potato Creek Johnny as the likeliest traveling companions. She sounded out Johnny first and found him not at all enthusiastic about the trip.

"Why go?" he asked. "It'll be the same news, whoever he gets it from. Some cowboy will run into him and let him know, I guess."

"Dora asked me special, though," Calamity said. "It was the last thing she asked. I know I ought to do it. Blue's *my* old friend, too."

That night, she asked Ogden abruptly if he would mind taking Blue the news. She had found Ogden difficult to talk to, more so since Dora's death. He did little but sit on the porch of the hotel, looking sad. Occasionally he would rock his baby. Mr. Fortescue had been to see him about running the hotel, but Ogden didn't want to run it. He didn't want to do anything. All his vast energy had left him; he felt too tired to move.

When Calamity came to him and asked if he would find the man named Blue and tell him Dora had died, Ogden had a hard time figuring out what she was talking about. Dora had babbled about a man named Blue as she was dying, but he had been too stunned by the fact that she was dying to pay any attention. He just wanted her not to die; she had died anyway, and now he felt he had to wait out his life before he could die too. He didn't know why Mr. Blue would need the news of Dora's death, or why Calamity wanted him to take it to the man. He had never heard of the Musselshell River and had no idea how to find it.

"I might get lost," Ogden said. Although very sad, he still tried to be polite, and it didn't seem polite just to give Calamity a flat no.

"It's northwest of Miles City a few days," Calamity said. "Everybody knows T. Blue. If you just ask cowboys, you'll find him easily."

"What if I don't see no cowboys?" Ogden inquired.

"Oh, there's plenty of cowboys around," Calamity assured him. "There's nobody else much in that part of the state—just a few Indians and the cowboys."

No Ears heard the conversation, and to Calamity's surprise volunteered to guide Ogden. Once Ogden heard this, he wondered why No Ears couldn't just take the news himself.

"Well, he could, but Dora asked special that it be one of us," Calamity said. "It was just before she went. You were asleep."

"I'll do it, since she asked," Ogden said. He had no will to refuse.

The morning they left, Calamity felt odd—part of her wanted to go with them, but part of her didn't. Mainly, she didn't want to have to see Blue struggle with the terrible news. She herself had struggled with it alone, and probably he would want to, also.

But she felt wrong, all the same. No Ears looked so dried up it was hard to believe he could walk to the Musselshell and back, though she knew he had just walked from the Mississippi, a distance vastly longer. The old man looked so thin, it made her sad to see him—though almost everything made her sad these days.

"Why do you want to go?" she asked No Ears. "Ogden's a big strong boy. He could just do it himself—it ain't gonna hurt him."

"I want to see the Greasy Grass again," No Ears said. "I might stop there on my way back. There might be some Cheyenne around—I always liked to visit with those Cheyenne."

"Will you come back?" Calamity asked. She had an apprehension that No Ears was going away to die—and he was the one person left she could depend on. Johnny was a fine fellow to drink with, but you couldn't depend on him for much. She didn't want No Ears to go away and die.

"It will depend on the road, and whether I find those Cheyenne," No Ears said. He realized that Martha Jane was very troubled, but he still felt the question to be inappropriate. It was not good to ask a person about such things—particularly an old person who had to keep alert and watch his thoughts in order to continue to keep his soul with him.

Ogden was too tired to walk; he rode one of the wagon horses. No Ears was offered a horse but declined. He considered them unstable animals and preferred to use his own two feet while he could.

12

BLUE WAS OUT WORKING WITH TEAT, TRYING TO PULL
a cow out of a bog, when he saw the large boy and the
tiny old man coming. The boy rode a dusty sorrel; the old
man was walking along spryly, as if he had just started
life's walk that day.

That Blue at first felt no apprehension was probably
due to exhaustion from an hour of struggling with the
bogged cow. It was one of those mornings when grim
circumstances caused him to wonder why he had chosen
the life of a rancher. After all, it meant a lifetime of working with animals who were often as stupid as the present
cow; it was not easy to find a bog in northern Montana in
a dry year, but the old hussy had found one and proceeded to lead her calf into it and then bog herself well
past the flanks. He and Teat had both turned themselves
into mudmen getting the calf out; it was a big yearling,
and it fought their efforts vigorously.

Teat was amused by such doings and grinned at Blue
with white teeth from out of a mud-coated face; but then,
Teat had just been a cowboy for a few months and was
still amused by the many absurdities that ranch life involved one in. Teat still thought that being thrown off a

bronc was amusing; the efforts of cattle to escape being roped amused him so much that he could scarcely ride, much less rope. Swimming in mud to rescue a cow and calf didn't discourage him in the least.

Blue had been at the whole business longer; his livelihood depended upon saving as many cows as possible; on the whole he found being coated in mud to the collarbone less amusing than he had when he was a young sprout trying to impress his bosses with his fervor. He yelled at his horse to pull on the rope attached to the cow's horns, he pulled on it himself, and Teat, the brown mole, twisted the cow's tail and pushed from the rear. The effort gained perhaps three yards before both gave out and had to rest. The mud, disturbed for a moment, flowed back around them.

"I don't want this cow anyway," Teat said. "She should not have come in the mud. Why don't we let the mud have her?"

"Because she's young," Blue said, wondering why Dora's husband was wandering around the Musselshell with old No Ears. "She might have ten more calves that I can sell—she might even have a dozen. It ain't her that we're saving, it's the ten calves."

Ogden saw that the two men were not making much progress with the bogged cow. They were a very muddy pair. He had asked at the ranch house a few miles back and had been told by a pretty young woman that Mr. Blue was working to the north. She had been kind enough to offer them buttermilk. He had drunk a quart, and No Ears a smaller amount.

He had not expected to meet Mr. Blue in such a muddy state—but then he had not really expected to meet Mr. Blue at all. When he got to the bog he dismounted and waded into the mud to help, an act which seemed to surprise the two muddy men.

"Let me have the rear," he said. It was apparent to him that the Indian boy who was handling the cow's tail end didn't have the strength to lift her out of the mud.

Teat didn't argue. He took one horn and Blue the other. Blue yelled at the horse, but with Ogden lifting, they scarcely needed the horse. There was a sucking sound as Ogden lifted the cow's rear from the mud and began to shove her forward. He shoved so hard and the cow made such sudden progress that both Blue and Teat forgot about pulling and just tried to get out of the way. Both tried to scramble aside and ended by falling backward into the mud. Ogden kept walking and propelled the quivering cow up on the bank. He then went back and offered the fallen men a hand.

"We're much obliged to you, sir," Blue said. "I believe I've seen you before, in Belle Fourche. Isn't your name Ogden?"

"Yes, sir, are you Mr. Blue?" Ogden said.

Blue walked over and took the rope off the muddy cow. "Git," he said. "And stay out of the damn mud for a while." Her muddy calf was standing fifty yards to the west, bawling for her, but the cow promptly turned and began to trot off to the east.

"If you're looking for work, Mr. Ogden, you're hired," Blue said. "Teat and me are smart but we ain't stout—it's easier to be smarter than a goddamn cow, but it ain't easy to be stouter."

He meant the offer as a joke, but Ogden looked at him solemnly, as if he were really considering it. Blue's thoughts began to move a little faster—maybe the boy had left Dora, or been thrown out, in which case, why not hire him? He would be a great asset with the haying and barn-building and such. He himself was no carpenter and had made little progress on a barn, though he had ranched on the Musselshell for five seasons. Why not hire the man? If he had left Dora it would only make it all a richer joke. The man didn't shy away from messy work, either—a big advantage in cowboying.

Ogden found that he liked Mr. Blue, who was grinning merrily despite being coated with mud. The Indian boy was also grinning. It would be good to work out in the sun, under the open sky. Deadwood was in a crack, shady or outright dark much of the time; it was hard to rise out of a low mood in a place where the sun rarely shone.

"I'll have to bring Bob, and I'd like to bring Doosie," Ogden said. "Doosie won't want to leave Bob, and neither one of us could get by without her."

"Oh, I know Doosie, she's a splendid cook," Blue said. "I can't imagine Dora would part with her, though, and I don't know this fellow named Bob."

Ogden began to feel shy. Mr. Blue looked so cheerful, and yet such bad news awaited him. He was glad to discover that he liked the man, though. It made Dora's life seem a little happier that she had had such a fine cheerful man for a friend.

"Well, Bob's the baby," Ogden said.

Mr. Blue looked startled by that news.

"Oh," he said. "Bob's the baby. You mean you and Dora had a baby?"

"Yes, sir," Ogden said, feeling his lowness coming— it was even more powerful than his shyness.

"How could I hire you then, mister?" Blue asked, stumbling a little in his thoughts. Surprising information was coming rather quickly, and he wasn't sure it was information he liked.

As if suddenly worried, Teat walked away several yards. He began to try to clean the muddy rope, rubbing it in the grass.

"You can't tell me that Dora would let you and Doosie and a baby go, all at once," Blue said, puzzled. "Dora would have to be dead before she'd hold still for such as that."

Ogden looked numbly down at his hands. Mr. Blue had unexpectedly given himself the bad news; all Ogden needed to do now was confirm it—yet he couldn't speak.

Seeing the sad look spread across the boy's big face, Blue felt a fear seize him—he felt a sudden panic.

"Say, is Dora all right?" he asked. "I'm a friend . . . we met way back down the trail."

Ogden remembered how Dora looked when she whispered to him last; he remembered how she looked lying dead; he couldn't speak. He looked up and saw that Mr. Blue had gone white under his coat of mud.

No Ears saw it too—it was odd that whites never ex-

pected one of their own to die. They were as children
when it came to death; they rarely thought of it, although
it was never farther than a breath away.

Seeing Ogden so unhappy that he had forgotten how to
speak, No Ears thought he had better help.

"Your friend died making the child," he said. "It was
too much for her, but the child is big and strong. When
he cries, he's loud."

Ogden felt ashamed that No Ears had had to complete
his task for him; at the same time, he felt grateful.

"Oh, say!" Blue said, sitting down suddenly. The
news knocked his legs from under him. He took off his
hat and flung it far out in the mud.

"She wanted Martha to come and tell you," Ogden
said, finding that he could talk again. "Martha wouldn't
—she's sick too much."

"From liquor I bet, and I don't blame her!" Blue said.

"Dora asked that one of us come," Ogden said. He
had not really understood his wife's request and could
not explain it—he just said it.

"I think she felt you'd be upset," Ogden said, wishing
he had more skill at talking and could put things better.

"Upset? I guess I'm kilt!" Blue said, getting unsteadily
to his feet. He went straight and mounted his horse. He
started to ride away but checked himself and attempted
to summon his manners. "You men must be tired," he
said, speaking stiffly and carefully. "You're welcome to
rest as long as you like at my ranch house—Teat will
take you back."

He started to turn away again, but checked himself
once more and looked at Ogden. "The offer of work still
stands," he said. "Bring Doosie, and bring . . . Dora's
boy—Bob, I believe. I pay fair wages, and we'll build a
bunkhouse. Will you do it?"

"Yes, sir," Ogden said.

"Good, take 'em home," Blue said to Teat. "Help
Mary look after the stock until I get back."

Teat didn't ask when that would be; he handed Blue
the rope he had been trying to clean.

"Help Mary look after the stock," Blue said again. He

nodded at No Ears to thank him for walking so far to bring him a hard piece of information. No Ears raised a hand in acceptance of his thanks.

Then T. Blue turned his horse south and rode away. It was three days before he stopped, well south of the Yellowstone. In his mind he was traveling south to yesterday, to the distant evening when he had ridden into Abilene all covered with trail dust and danced his first dance with Dora. He was so dusty he sneezed all through the dance, but she swore she didn't mind. Later in the evening he rode his horse into the hotel and tried to spur him up the stairs to Dora's room, but the horse shied and kicked off the banister; the manager got hot, the sheriff came; Blue's foreman, who happened to be drinking in the saloon at the time, was amused by it all and offered to make good the damages, which satisfied everyone.

Often, in later years, he and Dora had laughed about his dustiness and her sneezing and the kicked-down banister—it seemed a fine beginning, and was the talk of Abilene for a day or two.

Oh, the fun they had then—the cowboy and the buffalo girl.

13

NO EARS DECIDED HE HAD TRAVELED FAR ENOUGH with the whites. Blue's wife, the half-Cree woman, fed him several tasty biscuits and some more buttermilk. With the North Star still bright in the heavens, he left to walk down to the Little Bighorn, but when he got there he changed his mind about looking up the Cheyenne. Some of them talked too much—and the Crow talked even more. In No Ears's opinion both the Crow and the Cheyenne ought to move south, far from the Greasy Grass; then perhaps they wouldn't bore their guests with endless talk of Custer.

He himself had no regard for Custer or for any white soldiers; he was happy enough that Gall and the others had killed him and all his men; but it was easily possible to make too much of such a victory. What was one battle to the grass, which had swallowed the men's blood at once and their bones within a few months? The grass forgot the dead it took; probably the ocean, the great plain of water, forgot those it swallowed, too. It was silly of men to suppose they would be remembered long, once the earth or the sea had taken them. The Greasy Grass had swallowed Custer as easily as the gray ocean had swallowed the foolish elk that jumped off the English boat.

No Ears traveled on south, avoiding men. He was not in the mood for silliness, and where men went there was likely to be silliness. Traveling alone, he could devote himself to watching birds fly; lately he had become more interested in plants, though for most of his life he had not been a student of plants. The most interesting question about plants was why some of them chose to grow underground, although most preferred to reach upward toward the sun. What were the ones that grew downward trying to reach? Could there be an underground sun?

It was while he was thinking about plants that No Ears noticed the sage bush for the third time. Once again, without thinking, he had wandered back to Crazy Woman Creek. No Ears knew that this return was bad news; his thoughts were no longer working as they should, or he would not have done such a foolish and dangerous thing.

No cranes were in the creek, but that in itself was not enough to reassure him; their tracks were there in the mud. No Ears decided to pull up the dangerous sage bush at once. He seized it with both hands and did his best, but it would not come up. The sage bush was stronger than he was; he broke off a few branches, but he could not pull it up—it wouldn't leave its place in the ground. No Ears grew angry at himself and at the bush. He had been foolish to return, but the sage bush didn't need to be so stubborn either. He hacked at it a bit with his knife, but his anger had tired him; it left him exhausted and distracted. He began to wish Martha Jane was there, or Bartle, to help him remove the stubborn, offensive sage bush; even if they didn't succeed they could help him watch for the cranes. But he grew more and more tired; his hacking at the bush had seemed to suck away his breath. When he stretched out to sleep, he put on his one wax ear and tried to position himself so he could hear the great wings if they came. It occurred to him too late that he had made another mistake on Crazy Woman Creek: the cranes had only wanted Jim Ragg—it was the sage bush itself that wanted him. It had wanted him badly enough to call him back a third time. He felt very foolish; all his life he had made little effort to understand plants, and now a stubborn one had caused him to use himself up. He crawled away from the bush for many yards until he was too weak to crawl any farther; then he lay on his back looking upward until the dark sky sucked the last of his breath.

IV

Darling Jane—

Forgive me Janey, it has been years since I wrote. I know I am not a good mother, you must be almost grown now and what do I know about my darling? Very little— I don't even know if your Daddy is still alive.

Yesterday I was in a store in Tucson, they had some tablets and pretty papers, I thought I would try and scribble you a letter after all these years.

I came all the way south to the Gila to find Bartle Bone, someone told me he was prospecting in Apache country. I don't think it's true, if it's true he sure managed to dodge me.

The heat here is terrible Janey, I could not live in this desert, I would soon sweat to death. I had not expected to like it, I just came in hopes of finding Bartle. I don't think Bartle likes me anymore, I think he dodges me, still I need to find him—we are old *compañeros*. He is a talker and will give me the news of our friends, if any of our friends are still alive. Not many are now, Janey, the years have taken their toll.

It is unfamiliar to me, this writing, Janey—I got out of

the habit somehow, wandering too much I guess. Drinking too much, others would say.

I am headed for Albuquerque, and then north. I better stop and get some specs if I can find any. I can scarcely see this page I'm writing on—of course the firelight ain't good.

Goodnight darling, forgive my long silence, Dora died —after that I lacked the spirit to take up my pen.

Your mother,
Martha Jane

Darling Jane—

An awful thing happened Janey—Fred flew away. It has been so long since I mentioned him, you probably don't remember, Fred was Dora's parrot. He used to say "General Custer," now he don't, and no one would know what he was talking about if he did—the Custer battle was more than twenty-five years ago.

Dora had her boy, then died, it was the worst pain of all. I still cannot talk about it and will not try to write about it, just say it was grief. Blue hired Ogden—it was me that caused that, I sent Ogden to give Blue the bad news, Blue hired him—of course Doosie and the baby went too. The boy Bob is nearly grown now, Blue says he can either lift an ox or eat one—however, Ogden his Daddy was struck by lightning the summer after Dora died. They were working cattle in one of those bad lightning storms, which was foolish. Blue saw him get struck —he and Teat tried to revive him, I don't know why— you would have to be lucky to survive lightning—at least luckier than Ogden was.

Blue wanted me to have Fred, after all he ended up raising Dora's boy, he thought I ought to have her parrot. I couldn't count all the times I sat and watched Dora play with Fred when she was happy.

Anyway, I took him and he has been with me till last week. He learned to ride on the front of my saddle— Satan didn't like it at first but later he got used to it, he would even let Fred clean out his ears. Cody my dog got used to him too, Fred would sleep with Cody on cold nights—Cody could have eaten him in a second but he never did.

I guess we made a funny-looking team Janey—an old woman, an old horse, an old dog, and an old parrot, though who knows what's old for a parrot? When we come into towns people come out on the street and look at us and it isn't just because I'm Calamity Jane or any of that nonsense.

Once in a while Fred would fly up in a tree but he liked company, he would sit in a tree for a while and try to act like a bird, then he'd come down and settle on the saddle again. He had a cozy life, though not as cozy as with Dora I admit. We spent some pretty cold nights out on the baldies. I'd throw a robe over Fred and pack him in with Cody—he may not have appreciated it but he survived.

The last weeks all I could think of was getting out of that desert heat—I don't know this country like I know the plains. I came up too high and ran into a canyon. An old trader in a place called Ganado told me about it—it's called the Canyon de Chelly, the Navaho consider it holy.

There are plenty of Navaho around, I wouldn't call them friendly but they have not bothered me, they can see I am just a wild old woman. Anyway, the canyon is sheer, there was nothing to do but go around it. Near the south end there is a skinny column of rock sticking straight up from the canyon floor. They call it Spider Rock, it sticks up nearly a mile I guess. This morning Fred began to flap his wings—he does that sometimes. We were camped at the edge of the canyon, before I could think, Fred flew off and tried to make Spider Rock.

He didn't, Janey—Fred was never much of a flyer, anyway he was out of practice. He did his best but he lost altitude and landed about halfway down the rock. He was there all day—I yelled myself hoarse trying to get him to fly back. I was even prepared to ride into the canyon from the north end and try to coax him down. This morning, though, he was gone. There are many eagles here, I expect one got him. Even a hawk could have easily whipped Fred, he wasn't a big parrot.

Janey you may think your mother is a silly woman to write a whole letter about a parrot, of course you have never seen this parrot, why would you care?

Yet it broke my heart to lose him, I keep looking up in trees hoping he's there—parrots play jokes, you know, all this could be some big joke of Fred's. I rode down into the canyon from the north end, the walls were hundreds of feet tall all around me. I thought Fred might be hopping around the bottom of Spider Rock or sitting in some little bush or eating some of the corn the Navaho grow. I didn't want to give up, Janey, but I had to, I never saw a feather or anything to indicate Fred had been there.

Even now if a crow flaps out of a tree I think it might be Fred—I look around to see if he's following us as a trick. I know he can't be following us, he wasn't a strong flyer. I will always wonder why he flew off, do you suppose he just had an urge to be a bird?

Anyway he was all I had from Dora except her silver hairbrush and I pawned that in Cheyenne, I had to.

Your mother,
Martha Jane

Darling Jane—

I will take this opportunity to write you while I am in a place where the light is good—it is pretty good in this saloon, better than it would be by a campfire. Potato

Creek Johnny is here, he has only got one arm now, he fell down in front of an ore car and the ore car pinched off his left arm, fortunately he is right-handed.

Johnny says Bartle is back in Deadwood—we are heading back there tomorrow. It has been a long time since I have seen Bartle, but to my surprise I recently ran into Blue. They have these roping contests now—I guess the cowboys ain't satisfied with showing off for the homefolks, they come to town and rope steers or take turns trying to ride pitching horses. I think it's silly.

I was in Cheyenne and went out to the roping contest to see if any old friends were there, sure enough Blue was. He is as much a devil as ever, only now his mustache is white—it ain't as white as Billy Cody's hair, but it's white.

"Are you so lazy you have to come to town to do your roping?" I asked—he got a kick out of that—then he pointed out Dora's boy, Bob. He is a champion roper and also a fine rider, he won all the prizes, how proud she would be. Of course even a pitching horse would have to work hard to pitch off a boy that big. I cried when I saw him. Blue wanted to introduce us but I hung back. I look a sight, and I wasn't too sober—I thought best just to look.

I guess all these years I thought the child might be Blue's, I thought he and Dora deserved a child for all the love they shared. Things don't work in such a way though Janey—the boy is Ogden all over. I said to Blue I thought he might be yours, T. Blue just smiled. "I got to raise him for her, ain't that what matters?" he said.

Blue wanted to take me home with him to his ranch on the Musselshell, he said I looked as if I could use a rest, and my horse too. I didn't go Janey, perhaps I will later after I've gone to look for Bartle. Blue is still married to his wife, they have five or six children. Johnny says they are nice. I don't think I will go, Janey, I would feel embarrassed. I ain't respectable enough for such a household. Blue might still be a hellion, I expect he is, but his wife might not appreciate a rough specimen like me living under her roof.

Blue and I were both afraid to talk of Dora, I can tell he still misses her, just as I do. We sort of circled her, we didn't talk of her much—it's too upsetting. Blue bought me all the drinks I wanted, of course I accepted too many. He said he heard I had been in jail and what was that all about—who did I kill?

Your mother is not a killer, Janey—I just get rowdy. If people mess with me I want them to know they are messing with a wild one. I don't care if it's women or men. I rarely start the fights though, Janey, I said to Blue I just wish they'd leave me alone to go to hell in my own style and bury me beside Bill Hickok when I die.

I'd choose better than him to be buried by, if I had my choice, Blue said—he did not care for your father, they were both young roosters when they knew one another. I didn't want to argue with Blue after he bought me drinks, I let it pass, but no one else but Blue could get by with speaking ill of your father. Anybody else would get punched, if they didn't get worse.

It was good to see Blue though, he is an old-timer like me, we are among the last of the fieries and snuffies from the cow-town days. I didn't want to quarrel with him, your father is dead, it is of little consequence that I liked him and Blue didn't.

Janey if I don't find Bartle I think I will just stay in Deadwood, I am about through with roaming this west. My eyes are cheating me now, I don't see half what I used to see, I might miss the trail someday and wander off and die like No Ears did—I guess he did anyway, he left the Musselshell in good health and was never seen again. Someone is supposed to have found his wax ear in Wyoming, I didn't see it though, that is probably just a tale. I miss No Ears too, ain't it strange? I miss Jim Ragg —well, I won't write the whole list, I'd rather get drunk than do that.

Your mother,
Martha Jane

Darling Jane—

I finally did catch up with Bartle Bone, I scarcely knew him he is so improved. He is an actor now, he travels with a little troupe. They have two or three plays that they do. I saw them do one in Silver City—Bartle played a villain named Black Bart, I laughed myself sick. Bartle has taken up with a redheaded woman named Kate who bosses him around. I guess she thinks she is Lillie Langtry, I didn't enjoy her, she talks too English. If she was Lillie Langtry she wouldn't be traveling around these old greasy mining towns.

Bartle was kind to me though, when he could escape his evil whore. That was not often—she has a ring in his nose for sure and jerks him around pretty good, of course it serves Bartle right he broke many a heart in his earlier years. Heartbreakers deserve to end up with a ring in their noses. Bartle says it was Billy Cody who got him to try acting. It seems he has a gift for it, he made the miners laugh and then he made them cry. I cried too but it wasn't from the acting, it was just from seeing Bartle Bone after all this gap of years. He says he is going back to join Billy, they are taking the Wild West show to Italy soon. He says I could come—Billy asks about me—but I can't drag myself that far, it is too far. I am getting blind Janey, I would get lost along the way. Worse still I might get lost in Italy, I don't speak the lingo, what would become of your mother?

I am glad though that Bartle went east and made a success of himself. Success was what he was meant for, to see him now you would hardly believe he spent all those years following Jim Ragg around looking for beaver that weren't there. Now he gets barbered every day, dyes his beard and wears a cravat half the time—he says he has to, people won't pay to see you unless you look fine. Bartle was always handsome, he does look fine—I think back to how close to dying we both came that day we went moose hunting and had to make a cold camp, in those days Bartle looked so gaunt it was hard to believe he would last a year.

Bartle will head east soon and meet up with Doc Ramses, it is their job to go to the reservations and hire Indians for Billy's show. They won't get many of the great chiefs, not now, they are all dead. Sitting Bull was massacred years ago at Wounded Knee. I found that regretful, not that I liked Sitting Bull, still he was just an old man with a few boys with him, what could he have done?

Bartle and I have made a pact to meet at the big Cheyenne roping contest next year, he wants to take me to Billy Cody's house. It is called Scout's Rest and it is in Nebraska—they say Billy has bought a place in Sheridan, too. I suppose he is rich. Nobody made as much money off the Wild West stuff as Billy Cody. He was never unkind to me, I wish him well.

Bartle says Billy works hard but he is not too happy, he finally divorced Lulu. I never met Lulu and have no opinion on the matter, though it was clear they were not close—she was never with him. Bartle says Billy still gets tears in his eyes when he speaks of Dora, well, we all do, I told him, I get tears in my eyes if I even hear her name. It is odd what a hold Dora had on her men, they all loved her, even Bartle confessed that he had been her sweetheart for a night.

I guess I am just an odd one, Janey—it was never my good fortune to affect people that way. If I affected anybody it was Dora herself. She would often hold my hand and try to persuade me I was pretty—she would hug me when I was low.

Now I am old and going blind, half the time I wander over the plains and don't even know what town I am looking for. Perhaps I am only looking for the past, Janey —how do you find the past?

I hope I can last till next year Janey, I will go to the big roping contest in Cheyenne and see my old friend Bartle with his dyed beard. I don't know if I'll go to Cody's house though, it sounds too grand for me.

If I can find Blue he will take me to the roping, maybe

this time I'll be sober and let him introduce me to Dora's boy.

Your mother,
Martha Jane

Darling Jane—

There are things I should be writing, Janey—things you ought to know about your mother. Each time I take up my pen I think I will write them, then I don't, I talk about Bartle or Blue or my wanderings instead.

I want to tell the truth but then I don't—it's a reproach to me, or at least it's too sad. I always thought I was truthful, it is only when I start one of these letters that I realize I ain't.

Now all I do is piddle around in my memories. You've seen children make mud pies? That's what I do with my memories, I pat them into the shape I want them to take . . . they're just mudpies, Janey.

Have I informed you that Cody was killed—the dog I mean, not Billy. He was an old dog, the wolves caught him. Cody killed many wolves when he was in his prime, I guess they got their revenge. I didn't find him, Johnny did, he said it looked from the blood on the ground like Cody put up a good fight. He died snarling, Johnny said.

I believe that means the end of my traveling, Janey. I would be afraid to venture far without my old dog. Satan is wearing out too. He has been sorefooted lately and the blacksmith can't figure out why—he shoes him carefully. I know why Janey—he's old. Satan and Cody and me have covered the miles—well, we've covered the west. Now Cody's dead and Satan's worn out. My ankles swell so I can hardly walk myself.

This is not the letter I meant to write, it is just another list, I might as well stop.

Your mother,
Martha Jane

Darling Jane—

I have failed again Janey, I come up here to the Yellowstone only to get another piece of bad news, Doosie has died. Johnny told me—he is like a walking newspaper, my old friend Johnny, he's just got the one arm but he keeps pacing up one trail and down another, looking for the creek of gold.

I was headed for Blue's, I am almost too decrepit now to navigate for myself—Blue always looks me up and buys me drinks when he's down in the Black Hills, he has invited me to live at his ranch many times, I finally decided to take him up on it. I began to have a yearning to see Doosie, she is an old-timer too and was faithful to Dora through all their years.

But I got here to Miles City and found out she had developed a tumor and died. I think I will just turn back Janey, Satan is too sorefooted now to go all the way to the Musselshell. I think I will leave him here in Miles City, he has carried me far enough. Probably there will be a wagon going down toward the Black Hills, maybe the boys will let me ride with them. Blue still travels everywhere, he'll be restless the day he dies I guess. Blue will find me, I'm too tired to find him. The next time he's in the Black Hills we will have a visit.

> Your mother,
> Martha Jane

Darling Jane—

I left my old horse, Janey—for my part it was hard to leave him. I think Satan was too tired to care. I borrowed ten dollars from Johnny and paid for Satan's keep at the livery stable in Miles City—I requested that he be shot when the cold weather comes if he looks poorly. His teeth are gone, I would not want him to have to endure another hard winter.

The boys who drove the wagon were just young sprouts. I made a bad choice to throw in with them. They tried to tease me and insult me, they were very rude, I have seen men treat Indians that way. Finally I pulled my pistol—I am not a child to be played with, boys, I told them, keep it up if you want to be shot. After that they let me be but showed me no respect—it made me feel I had outlived my time, no doubt the Indians feel the same way. We are treated like jokes now—these young men are just braggarts, they think they are great adventurers when all they do is drive wagons along the Bozeman trail. I would have liked to see them take that road when the Sioux and Cheyenne were in their glory, they would have been killed like dogs, they wouldn't be bragging long, they'd have all they could do to keep their hair, not many of them could even do that much.

Your mother will never travel again Janey, not unless Blue or Bartle or somebody, maybe Billy Cody, comes and gets me in a buggy.

Your mother,
Martha Jane

Darling Jane—

There will not be many more letters, Janey, my eyes are fading fast. I wish I would procure a photo of you before my eyes are too far gone to allow me to see my darling.

I have been thinking about Cody a lot lately, Janey—Bill, I mean, not my dog. I had a letter from him, he wants to come and see me—he says he misses his friends from the old days. I would be ashamed to see Bill Cody, Janey—he is the most successful person ever to come out of the west, and I am the worst failure—how could we ever sit at the same table? Billy took an idea and sold it to the whole world—he has supped with kings and queens. They say that he has buffalo and elk on his ranch, and fine cattle and horses.

But I am just an old drunken woman, too poor to keep a horse. Not that Billy would scorn me—he has never scorned anyone.

I mop out a saloon in Deadwood, about all it gets me is drinks and a little shack to bunk in. I'm afraid I will end my days a fallen woman—mopping up a saloon in Deadwood is about as far as you can fall.

> Your mother,
> Martha Jane

Darling Jane—

Your Daddy, Mr. Burke, was kind, Janey. If he is alive I send him my blessings. Wild Bill had married the Lake woman, I hated her, I was at my wit's end. It ended when I met your Daddy. It was not love—not love as Blue and Dora knew it.

It was only kindness Janey—you should always respect your Daddy for that.

> Your mother,
> Martha Jane

Darling Jane—

I feel I will not be here long now Janey, I had better try and tell the truth. Sometimes when I'm drunk I lie, or when people scorn me I exaggerate—I put myself in adventures I didn't have. The battle of the Rosebud, for example—I wasn't there but sometimes I say I was—it is just storytelling Janey. People like to hear stories about the old times, Bill Cody made his fortune on such a fact. Bill Cody only killed one Indian, but look what it got him. If you put yourself in the stories people like them better.

It is not of that that I want to write about now, those tales can die with me, I don't care.

You may hear people say your mother wasn't even a woman, Janey, don't believe it. In my youth when I was always traveling I dressed like a man, it's easier.

Then later I disguised myself as a man to get work—in those days nobody would hire a woman mule skinner, even now they wouldn't think of it, not unless they were desperate and there was not a man within a hundred miles.

I worked with men so much I guess I thought I was one at times—it was partly too that women had such hatred of me, all except Dora and a few others. They didn't like it that I went my own way and cussed and smoked—I had to face off so many old biddies that I got tired of it, I gave up and went off with the men, at least I did when I could get work.

You can't run off from what you are though—you have to make camp with what you are, every night, Janey. I'm glad I met your Daddy Burke, otherwise I might not have believed there was kindness among men, I had collected too much scorn and was about to give up and go off and die.

I was born odd though, Janey—not that I was an idiot or didn't have enough toes or fingers—there are other ways of being odd. When I was young I looked more like a man than plenty of these little soft fellows—I think there are plenty of fellows who would have been happier being a woman—but of course they were not given the choice, no more was I. It's sad to be odd, Janey—I used to envy Dora, to think what a comfort just to be a woman as she was, even though at the time she might be crying her heart out because of some trick of Blue's. Dora wasn't always happy but at least she was never odd—stuck in between, as I was.

I went to several Doctors Janey—even in London I snuck off and went to a Doc, no one knew it, they just thought I got drunk and got lost. It was a disappointment, the Docs didn't really know what to make of me either, they used names that I won't repeat—I can't spell them anyway—to refer to my condition. The old Doc in London was the most interested, he wanted me to stay around so he could study me. You can believe I told him off fast, I was not such a freak as to want to stay around London and be studied. Doc Ramses wasn't a real Doc, but he knew I was odd, he was always sniffing around—it was just business with Doc Ramses though, he wanted to put me in a medicine show. He didn't quite have the nerve to mention it though, and a good thing too, I would have killed him.

Can't write no more. Can't write no more about this now, I remember those doctors' offices and get too sad. It is a discouraging business sitting around those places waiting to be studied.

Your mother,
Martha Jane

Darling Jane—

This may be my last letter Janey, I have the shakes so from drinking I can hardly hold the pen.

I used to have guts, Janey—nobody denied me that. Now I had better muster what I have left of my guts and write the truth.

I remember that first night, when I sat in the evening dews upon the Yellowstone, looking at the tablet in the firelight. I only meant to keep a diary—it was at Buntline's urging, when I first knew him he was always encouraging me to note down a few of my adventures—he planned to put them in a book and make me as famous as Billy. I thought I would just oblige him and keep a diary, plenty of cowboys keep them—even Blue has one. If he put *his* adventures in it and his little wife ever reads it Blue will have to light out for the hills, she will scald him for sure, though who knows if Blue is truthful, even in his diary.

I started to write "Dear Diary" and I wrote "Darling Jane" instead. I wanted you so much I made you up—it was not planned, I had no intent to deceive, the words just came. No sooner had I written them than I could see you, all pretty in your school dress—then I could not give up my own fancy. You are the child I would have chose, Janey, had I been normal—why can't I at least have you in my head? In my hopes I am normal, so was your kind Daddy Burke, we would have had you if it had been possible. It was a disappointment to both of us that it wasn't. I didn't mean to invent you when I sat down with the tablet, I just meant to scribble a few memories to send to Buntline.

I guess you rose out of my hopes, Janey—I had thought I put them out of my heart long ago, when all the doctors told me I couldn't bear a child. None of them were kind about it—I would have thought my hopes would have died then and there, in one of those old dingy offices.

But we don't have the say about our hopes, Janey— truth, if that's what it is, can't stop us from hoping. Or didn't stop me at least—why else did I scratch down your name on that tablet? It was the name your Daddy and I planned to give you before we became discouraged.

So I wrote those letters Janey—you could say they are letters to my heart. I could not resist imagining the sweet girl I would have had if I could.

In my mind I made you alive, Janey—that's better than nothing ain't it?

I understand now how Buntline and them other writers dash off their tales—once I began with the tablet, pictures just came to me. I saw a well brought up little girl living a nice life in Illinois, pretty dresses and school.

I made up the best life I could for you Janey, it is the

opposite of the life I have lived out here in this mess they call the west. Though I love the west, for all its sadness.

I suppose Buntline hoped to be a hero, like Custer or Wild Bill—he wasn't, so he flung all his hopes into stories about Billy Cody, who was only a half-hero himself. Though I will respect Bill Cody till I die, he treated me fair.

Once I started the scribbling I couldn't behave—I guess I wanted to outdo Buntline or something, that's why I wrote of my romance with Hickok.

I am ashamed of that one, Janey—couldn't resist flattering myself, I guess. Wild Bill practically held his nose when I walked by, he would have as soon wallowed with a pig in the mud as to bed down with me—I only saw him three or four times anyway.

Yet I wrote in this great love that never happened. I don't recall that Wild Bill even spoke to me—if he did it was just to borrow a match or something.

Once I wrote it I guess I convinced myself, I started blabbing about it, now everyone believes it, I'm sure they'll bury me beside him when I die. That's a joke not many will appreciate—certainly Wild Bill wouldn't have appreciated it. Well, the man's been dead twenty-seven years, what can he do about it now?

I even believed my own tale to the point of nearly attacking Blue, who spoke ill of Hickok once in Cheyenne. Of course Blue knew well what the man was, and so did I—I improved him in the letters, never expecting it to get stuck in my head the way it did.

I will close now Janey, I am just writing to myself anyway—why take the trouble?

Your mother,
Martha Jane

BUFFALO GIRLS

Darling Jane—

I meant to stop writing these letters—here I am doing it again. What does that say about human beings?

I will not destroy these letters Janey. To do so would be to destroy you—I feel you live now in some way, maybe you will always live—you were the finest of my hopes, may you always live.

I keep these letters in my saddlebags, I don't have a horse now but I still have my saddlebags. If some stranger should find them before the rats chew them up I hope he will take them to Blue. But if a stranger should read them and find them demented let the stranger consider that I was very lonely.

Your mother,
Martha Jane

BARTLE BONE, POTATO CREEK JOHNNY, AND SEVERAL other old-timers chipped in and hired a wagon to bring Calamity's body back to Deadwood from Tinville, where she died. Bartle, whose troupe was not prospering, nonetheless bought her coffin himself.

She was buried on Mount Moriah, just above James Butler Hickok. A crowd in drunken spirits climbed up the hill and then stumbled down again to try and become more drunken still.

Bartle and Johnny filled in the grave themselves—it was a small measure of economy. Johnny meant to be off the next day, to try his luck in Idaho. Bartle had a show planned in Denver in three weeks—if the receipts were favorable he meant to retire to Sheridan, Wyoming, and open a saloon.

"I don't care if I never see these goddamn dreary Black Hills again," Bartle said. He and Johnny sat on a wheelbarrow by Calamity's grave, having a smoke. It was Johnny's new wheelbarrow—he was so proud of it he never went anywhere without it, not even to funerals or wakes.

"Why, you'll be back," Johnny said. "I will too, unless I fall off a hill."

"If you could just learn to roll yourself in your new wheelbarrow your travels would be a lot easier," Bartle said.

Johnny, no humorist, didn't consider that funny. He smoked a cigar he had meant to give the preacher—but the preacher had found so little of a favorable nature to say about Calamity that Johnny didn't consider he was really owed a cigar.

Bartle Bone felt sad. With Calamity dead, who was there left to see in the lands of the west? Billy Cody was always touring, T. Blue was always ranching—if you visited him you were far too likely to be put to work—and Potato Creek Johnny was too single-minded to be much fun.

Since he never expected to encounter Johnny again, Bartle thought he might just see what the man knew about something he had been curious about for a long time—namely, whether Calamity had been a woman or a man.

"I traveled many a mile with Martha Jane," Bartle said. "She was with me in Chicago when Jim was kilt—the memory will sting ever time I think about it. You knew Martha nearly as long as I did. I'd like to ask you one question. Did you ever hear that Martha was a hermaphrodite?"

Doc Ramses had explained the meaning of the term to him.

Johnny twitched a little—big words often made him twitch. He tried to remember if he had ever heard that particular term applied to Calamity, and could not recall that he had.

"No, and you know what? I don't care what religion she was," Johnny said. "I just liked the old girl."

My compliments to the shades of:

Martha Jane Canary
Dora DuFran
Teddy Blue Abbott
William F. Cody
Jack Omohundro
Sitting Bull
Annie Oakley
Daisy, Countess of Warwick
Russell of the *Times*
Potato Creek Johnny
and a few others whose stories outgrew their lives